THE MANOR

By Jessie Keane

JESSIE KEANE

THE MANOR

MACMILLAN

First published 2020 by Macmillan
an imprint of Pan Macmillan
The Smithson, 6 Briset Street, London EC1M 5NR
EU representative: Macmillan Publishers Ireland Limited,
Mallard Lodge, Lansdowne Village, Dublin 4
Associated companies throughout the world
www.panmacmillan.com

ISBN 978-1-5098-5502-5

1 3 5 7 9 8 6 4 2

A CIP catalogue record for this book is available from the British Library.

Typeset in Plantin by Jouve (UK), Milton Keynes
Printed and bound by CPI Group (UK) Ltd, Croydon, CR0 4YY

Visit **www.panmacmillan.com** to read more about all our books
and to buy them. You will also find features, author interviews and
news of any author events, and you can sign up for e-newsletters
so that you're always first to hear about our new releases.

To Cliff, who threatens that one of these days
he's going to write a book called *Living with a Writer* . . .

ACKNOWLEDGEMENTS

To all the people – friends, fans, helpers, all of you – who get me up in the top ten bestseller charts, time after time.

Thanks. It's appreciated.

'Nearly all men can stand adversity, but if you want to test a man's character, give him power.'

Abraham Lincoln

1980s

PROLOGUE

Belle Barton was learning the true meaning of terror. She was learning that it brought cold sour sweat to your body and hot burning bile to your throat, bile you had to choke back because you couldn't, you didn't dare, show how frightened you were. Because he'd love that. He would *feed* on that. He was watching her, that mocking half-smile on his face. She wanted to lunge at him, to *damage* him, to make him pay, but she couldn't. Two big men were holding her still, one on either side of her. She knew them. Had even grown up with one of them. Now, they were her enemies. They were Harlan Stone's boys, his puppets, his creatures, and they would do exactly what he said. She had no power here. None at all.

'I bet you're thinking, round about now, that you wish you'd been nicer to me,' said Harlan.

Belle stared at him with hatred in her eyes. Sweat trickled into them, making them sting. Outside, thunder rolled. Rain battered the roof. Inside, it was a jungle, wet ferns brushing her legs, humidifiers roaring, the heat crushing and damp, the trickle of small waterfalls a constant noise. Charlie Stone's reptile house was kitted out with no expense spared. There was a large pond, black, brackish. Things moved in there, but she wasn't going to think about that.

Water torture.

Yes, that was what this was. Belle's legs were trembling. Her brain was in a panic, like a rat caught in a trap. There had to be a way out of this.

But there was no way.

I'm going to die.

The thought popped into her brain like gas rising out of a bog, bringing a fresh surge of terror with it. She was perched on the edge of the pond, standing on big ornamental rocks, the men holding her there. Water from the domed roof dripped, ran down her face. So wet and hot in here. Hot as hell. Stifling. She thought of her parents then, and pain roared up through her stomach, up into her throat. She was going to be sick.

'Pretty little Belle,' said Harlan, shaking his head. 'Bet you wish you'd played ball now, eh? Been nice? But you never were. Were you.'

Belle glared at him, standing there so elegant; so handsome and calm and in control, with his neatly brushed honey-coloured hair, his pale emotionless grey eyes. While she was barefoot, wearing a tattered rag of a dress, soaked in sweat, her blonde hair plastered to her head. She was scratched and bloody from where they'd dragged her in here. If the men hadn't been holding her up, she would have collapsed to her knees.

'So go on,' he said.

Belle gulped and stared at him. *What?*

'Go on,' he said again. 'Beg me.'

She said nothing.

'Beg me for your life,' he said.

Belle looked down at the water. There were things moving in there. Something long slipping in from the opposite side. Eyes, she could see eyes. Reptilian and cold. The powerful swish of a tail. Her mother's words came back to her then.

'Keeping bloody snakes and lizards and caimans! Only weirdos do that.'

Caimans.

Belle knew that Charlie had fed them on whole dead chickens.

A caiman was like a crocodile, it could take a pig. They were plenty big enough to do that. They could also take a human being. No bother at all. You needed a licence under the Dangerous Wild Animals Act to keep them, which Charlie had acquired without any difficulty.

Friends in high places.

Low places, too.

Oh Christ help me . . .

'Waiting,' said Harlan. 'What do you say, Belle?' He was smiling.

'I know what you did,' said Belle.

'Did?' He frowned. 'About what?'

'You know very bloody well,' she said. 'Beezer. Jake. And the business. The manor. I know what it is.'

The smile dropped from his face, leaving it blank.

'Throw her in,' he said.

1950s

1

'You're nicked, my son,' said the copper, grabbing hold of nine-year-old Charlie Stone's collar with one beefy hand.

Terry, Charlie's best mate, kicked the policeman in the shin and hefted a dead rat at him. It was so ripe, the tail dropped off and its innards spattered the copper's legs. The stench was horrible.

'You dirty little bastard,' said the copper, swiping at Terry while trying to keep a grip on Charlie, who was wriggling like an eel.

Terry darted in and kicked again. The rest of Charlie's gang had scarpered already, headed back to the den. But Terry wouldn't desert Charlie. They were a pair, these two. They skived off school together. Went scrumping together. And together – today – they'd shinned over the back gates of the grocer's and started lobbing apples and pears over the top for their mates to catch.

Everything had been going good, then this filth had come out the back door of the shop. One of the neighbours must have raised the alarm.

Terry kicked again.

'Little fucker,' roared the copper, and let go of Charlie.

Charlie tore off and scrambled back over the gate and was gone, Terry hot on his heels. The copper snatched at Terry's short trouser leg but Terry was up, he was over – he was away. Him and Charlie ran off down the street, gasping and laughing fit to bust.

★

Charlie Stone was leader of the gang. And their den – *his* den – was set deep in scrubby woods where the gang met under Charlie's rule and divvied up their bounty. Bill 'Beezer' and little Col Crowley's father owned a sweet shop where Charlie had spied out a big half-pound box of chocolates set high on a shelf. If Beezer and his little shadow Col wanted to be part of the gang, then that was the price.

Beezer paid it. The chocolates, the fruit from the grocery store, other things. He robbed stuff out of a few cars, teaching little Col how twocking – take without owner's consent – worked. Then everything was taken back to the den and laid at Charlie's feet.

'More,' said Charlie every time. 'We need more.'

They were the Charlie Boys gang, and Charlie was their king. They charged across the old bomb sites on the manor, armed with dustbin lids for shields and wooden swords. Slowly they grew in strength, and purpose, and bulk.

2

At fourteen, Charlie found there were plenty of opportunities for theft and he exploited every one of them. The Charlie Boys were now teenage tearaways, villains in the making while the manor was ruled by *real* gangs, much older and more dangerous. Things were changing. Churchill had resigned and Eden had taken over. Charlie and Terry started boxing a bit, but they had no real talent for it, so Charlie decided crime paid better.

Charlie was leader, so Terry agreed. Why not? All Charlie's mad schemes seemed to pay off. They started doing more cars – only nobs, flash gits and doctors had cars, so the pickings were good – and then a few houses. They nearly got caught when they were clearing out some candlesticks and jewellery from one house, but Terry tripped the furious owner up and took a punch in the back of his head that made it spin, just to let Charlie make a clean getaway.

Afterwards, in the den, when it was only the two of them, Charlie expressed his gratitude.

'He would have caught me,' he said.

'Nah, you were off on your toes, mate,' said Terry.

Charlie's button-like dark brown eyes held Terry's. Charlie was a short, solidly built boy, brown-haired and red-faced, while Terry was thinner, taller. With his red-blond hair and green eyes, he was shaping up to be a good-looking man one day.

'That ain't the truth,' said Charlie. 'The truth is, Tel, you saved my arse, and I'm grateful.'

'It was nothing.' Charlie was Terry's mate, had been ever since the cradle. They were war babies, tough as old boots, the pair of them. He'd fall under a bus for Charlie, gladly. 'My job, innit? I'm number two, so I protect number one, don't I? Simple as that.'

'Yeah, I s'pose.'

Terry eyed his mate. 'Forever, Charlie. I'll always look out for you. You know that.'

'Forever,' echoed Charlie, and held out his hand. 'We're going to run this whole fucking manor, Tel. You and me mate. Together. You see if we don't.'

Terry shook Charlie's hand. 'Forever,' he said.

And that was it.

The pact was sealed, the deal done.

1960s

3

At nineteen, Charlie Stone and his mob were Teddy boys, getting into all sorts, slouching around in the new coffee bars with their duck's-arse hairdos and brothel-creeper shoes, lounging around in the cane furniture surrounded by rubber plants and big-skirted girls while listening to Tommy Steele and Cliff Richard on the juke. Charlie's ideas were getting bigger and better all the time. They were pretty well off now, Charlie and his crew, and they were dangerous enough for Charlie to receive a warning off one of the big boys, Gordie Howard, a Scottish loan shark who'd beaten back fierce competition from the Maltese and who now ruled the manor.

Charlie and Terry came out of the Palais one night and instantly they were set upon. Charlie was taken down an alley by two men and given the thumping of his life while another two blokes held onto Terry.

Finally, humiliatingly, Gordie held a battered Charlie down on his knees and pointed an old WW1 bayonet at his throat.

'You see this, ya cunt?' he asked in his thick Glasgow accent.

Charlie could barely nod his head, he was that beaten. He spat out a tooth. 'What's that then? A fucking butter knife?'

'Clever bastard, aintcha? Well next time I see your fat grinning ugly mug, I'll slice you open with it, you got me, pal?'

Charlie stared up at him.

Gordie pressed the bayonet harder against Charlie's neck.

'I *said*, you got me?' he snarled.

Charlie had to nod or die.

He nodded.

Afterwards, Terry helped Charlie home where his mother Joan threw a fit. Charlie was patched up and put to bed. Next day, Joan was ranting that they should call the police, but Charlie – through a swollen jaw and several broken teeth – insisted it was nothing, a bit of a ruckus, forget it.

When she left his bedside and only Terry was beside him, Charlie said: 'I'm going to kill that cunt Howard.'

'Just rest up, Charlie.'

'I mean it. That arsehole thinks he's the big noise around here? He's joking. He ain't even *English*. I'm a Cockney. Born to the sound of Bow Bells. These streets, this manor, they ought to be *mine*. I got enough foot soldiers to crush that cunt and I'm going to do it.'

Terry felt bad. He'd been right there, on the spot, but unable to help. Helping Charlie was his job in life, he'd given his word on that. And he'd failed.

'I'll do it,' he said, feeling uneasy. Around Charlie, things moved fast. *Too* fast, he thought. He wasn't sure, as Charlie was, of their capabilities when it came to mixing it with the big gangs.

'We'll do it together,' said Charlie.

'Yeah. But rest up first, OK?'

'Yeah. I'll do that.'

4

When she was seventeen, Nula Perkins fell in love with nineteen-year-old Terry Barton, Charlie Stone's handsome number two. How it happened was like this: she went ballroom dancing with her brother, who got off with the girls while she sat there alone at the edge of the dance floor listening to song after endless song and being thoroughly ignored. Finally Jim Reeves was crooning out the last number of the night – the smoochy one where couples always got together. Couples, but not her. She sat there, red-faced, a failure. Somehow she wrenched herself out of her seat midway through the song and went into the bogs and cried. When she came out, teary-eyed and blotchy, Terry Barton was standing there.

'Want to dance?' he asked.

She was so grateful. And she fell for him, right then and there, because with her mousy hair and her big nose she was no looker – and she knew it. Terry was being kind; he'd rescued her from an embarrassing situation.

Of course, he didn't linger. Once the dance was over he was out the door like a shot, with not a single glance back in her direction. She watched him peel out of there with a group of young men, at the head of which was short, bulky, hard-eyed Charlie Stone. Charlie Stone was always in the lead and, wherever Charlie went, it seemed Terry Barton was never far behind.

Still, Terry had turned her disaster of an evening – and oh yes, she'd seen her big brother laughing at her with his mates and their girlfriends as she sat there, her face burning with shame – into a good one.

'You want to watch him,' said her brother Jimmy on the drive home in his cream Ford Anglia, which shuddered as it went round corners. Its heater was clattering and throwing out no real heat at all.

'Who?' Nula asked.

'Come on!' Jimmy shot her a laughing glance. 'Terry fucking Barton. He's in with a bad lot.'

'What, you talking about Charlie Stone?'

'Course I bloody am. You don't want to fuck around with that crowd, believe me.'

'He's a good dancer,' said Nula. 'Terry.'

'Don't get no ideas, our Nula. I *asked* him to ask you to dance. He did it as a favour.'

Nula shrank into her seat. So Terry hadn't actually *wanted* to dance with her at all. And why would he? She was fat, plain and short-sighted – although she refused to wear the NHS specs she was supposed to. She sighed over her dismal life. Their parents'd had both her and Jimmy late. Mum and Dad were Victorian in their attitudes, elderly in their ways. They were plain people; worthy, church-going, spectacled, cheaply clothed. Thick in their heads and around the middle. Jimmy was the same. None of them seemed to have an ounce of drive, none whatsoever. They were in the gutter and were content to stay there. Ambition was a dirty word to them.

But not to Nula.

Nula Perkins might be *in* the gutter, but by Christ she was looking at the stars. Her life had to amount to more than it did; she'd had a piss-poor education and was now in a sorry excuse for a job on the cake and biscuit counter in Woolies. Her big weekly treat was window-shopping in town with her mates around the market in Carnaby Street and looking longingly in

Biba, because she could only look; she could never afford to buy anything and anyway nothing would ever fit over her fat arse.

'Terry Barton's sweet on Jill Patterson,' said Jimmy. He'd plunged the knife in and now he was twisting it. Nula wanted to hit him because she knew it was probably true; she'd seen Terry and Jill in town together recently, holding hands.

'I could get him off her,' said Nula, stung; she knew she couldn't.

'What?' Jimmy was laughing at her. Nothing new there. Nula was used to being laughed at. She'd been laughed at her entire fucking life, by everyone but particularly by Jimmy. Four years older than her and wearing an air of smug superiority, he loved nothing so much as taking the mick out of his little sister.

Like on one of their rare family holidays, when she'd been dancing the hokey-cokey with new-found friends: 'You looked a prat doing that,' said Jimmy when she came off the dance floor, making her glowing smile instantly wilt to nothing.

Or the time she'd been singing in the church choir, performing a solo for the first time ever; she'd been so proud – and then he'd grinned at her afterwards and said: 'You were off bloody key, you should have heard yourself. You sounded like a cat caught in a mangle.'

'You know her? Jill Patterson? Wasn't she in your class at school? She's a stunner,' he was saying now.

Nula felt her cheeks glow hot in the darkness. Yes, she knew Jill. Her of the silky straight blonde hair and lovely blue eyes and fabulous figure. *Fucking* Jill Patterson. At that moment, as they racketed along in the tinny noisy little car – nothing cool or sporty for Jimmy, he was boring as fuck, they were *all*, her entire family, as boring as fuck – with her breath pluming out in the cold night air, Nula came to a momentous decision.

Somehow, she was going to *change*.

5

Gordie Howard always drank at the Pig's Head with his crew all around him. Everyone knew that Gordie was tooled up as a matter of routine because of the bayonet thing when he'd pasted Charlie. No one ever *mentioned* the bayonet thing, not in Charlie's hearing and certainly not in Terry's. But Charlie's boys all knew, and approached the problem accordingly, arming themselves with knives, machetes, spiked knuckledusters and a few leftover service revolvers.

When Charlie was better and his scars healed, he made a plan. He had to take Gordie out, he knew that. And he didn't want to leave any other members of Gordie's gang loose about the place to take over where Gordie left off. Charlie made this plain to his boys, and they all nodded their agreement and set off on the evening's entertainment.

'I'm going to enjoy this,' said Charlie as they trooped out into the night, mob-handed.

'Too right,' said Terry. 'Arsehole's got it coming.' But he wasn't sure. He feared Gordie Howard's crew and thought Charlie a fool not to.

As soon as Gordie and his heavies emerged from the pub, Charlie's boys dived in. Soon the bodies were piling up on the pavement, but Charlie wasn't letting anyone else have Gordie Howard but himself. Some of Gordie's boys ran off when it looked like things were going against them, leaving a hardcore few grouped around Gordie like guards around an emperor.

Blood flew and before long there was no one left but Gordie, on the ground, dazed and reeling from tens of punches, cut to ribbons. Then whistles started blowing.

'Get him up,' said Charlie, gasping and blood-covered. 'Let's go.'

They hefted Gordie into the back of Beezer's old Ford van and had it away before the coppers could arrive on the scene and start making trouble. They drove him down to the docks and hustled him, barely conscious, into an empty warehouse.

At Charlie's instruction, Terry slapped Gordie around until he came out of his stupor. Then they tied him to a chair and Charlie stood in front of his enemy in triumph, staring down at him where he sat beaten, all the colour draining out of his face because he knew this was going to be bad.

One of the boys handed Charlie an iron bar.

'Christ,' panted Gordie, and seeing the man's terror, Terry stepped forward.

'I'll put him out of his misery, eh, Charlie?'

Charlie stepped back a pace. Glared at his fallen enemy. Then he nodded, once.

Terry hit Gordie hard in the jaw. They all heard the snap as it broke. Gordie's head flew back, and then he was out of it, unconscious. Terry gave Charlie a nod and got out of the way. Charlie stepped in and swung the bar back and crashed it into both Gordie's legs and then his arms, pulverizing his limbs. Finally, satisfied, he threw the bar aside. It hit the dirty cement floor with a clatter. Charlie was breathing hard with the effort.

'He won't give us no more trouble,' said Charlie. 'Get him out. Dump him back by the pub when it's clear.'

After the Pig's Head incident, no one heard of Gordie Howard around town any more. He was – literally – a broken man. For a full month after the event, Charlie's boys cruised the manor in their cars, herding up any stragglers from Gordie's gang and seeing them out of town, until there was no one left and there was a change in the air. Now everyone knew Charlie had taken control.

The manor was his.

6

There were some things Mum saw as a treat, and having Nula accompany her to the hairdresser's once a fortnight was one of them. There the same female hairdresser – Candy – would poodle-perm Mum's hair into submission, leaving it frizzed out, lifeless and ready for a shampoo and tight set. Soon, Candy was doing the same for Nula. But now, having come to a decision about the direction her life was taking, Nula spoke up.

'I don't want her doing my hair any more,' she said.

'What?' Mum looked poleaxed.

'I don't, OK? I'm growing this perm out.'

'Well, if you want,' said Mum.

'Yeah. I do.' Nula chewed her lip. 'And I hate my bloody name. Nula the Loser they call me at school. What'd you call me that for?'

Mum's myopic eyes were full of hurt. 'It was my mother's name,' she said.

'Well I hate the bloody thing.'

That little fracas caused a chill to descend that lasted for days. Nula hated to cause her mum pain, but she steeled herself to do it. Things had to change. Things *had* to be different. And then Nula had to find another hairdresser. She saved up and went to a new trendy one in town that everyone was talking about, Mr Fox, where inside everything was black and gleaming. As she entered, Elvis was singing 'It's Now or Never' on the sound system.

Nerves cramping her stomach, sweat dripping from her

armpits and her overtight new bra digging in under her non-existent tits, Nula tried to look together but she was feeling out of her depth. The stylists were scary. Cool, young, brimming with confidence. Beautiful. Everything was about beauty these days. Like Jean Shrimpton, who she'd read about in *Marie Claire* – Jean was having a hot affair with the photographer David Bailey. Oh, to be part of that world, that *life*.

Nula felt about two inches high the minute she stepped through the door of the salon. The pretty mini-skirted girl who took her coat and hung it up looked at it like it was a rag – which, to be fair, it was – and then she looked at Nula, barely stifling a mocking smile.

So what? thought Nula. *I'm used to that. People laughing at me, sneering, making fun.*

She'd had it at school, in the new awful communal changing rooms after the hell of games or gym or – the worst – cross-country running. She'd lumbered around, unable to keep up, red-faced and breathless. Then, after the ritual humiliation of the showers, there was dressing. Her old-fashioned Mum'd still had Nula wearing a vest at fifteen, which had been the cause of much hilarity in the changing room. Also, Nula was flat-chested, while most of the other girls were blossoming into young women, wearing pretty starter brassieres and beginning to take an interest in boys.

Not Nula. She knew her chance of attracting boys was zero. Her mirror confirmed it.

But now, having had her hair washed in an excruciatingly painful back-basin, she was draped in a black towel, plonked in front of yet another mirror, and was confronted with her reflection. Pale. Fat. Frizzy-haired. As Michael Holliday sang 'Starry Eyed', the apprentice wrenched a comb through it, pulling at the knots. It hurt.

Then the stylist came over, a stunning young man in hipster jeans, black shirt and a big TEXAS brass belt buckle. He pawed over her wet hair with a frown and said: 'I'm Simon. So what can we do for madam today?'

'I want you to cut it, please. In this style.' Nula produced a hairdressing magazine and pointed to a picture of a ravishing girl with a long casual bob. 'And I want to be blonde. Like that.'

'Blonde? You sure?' He was staring at her like she was demented.

'Absolutely.'

He shrugged, disinterested. The customer was always right. Nula wondered if perhaps he might do a small test on her hair, to see how it would take the colour. He didn't. Instead he went off to a back room and returned with a dish of lilac-coloured gunge, which he proceeded to slap onto her head. After fifteen minutes, it was stinging. Then he wrapped her head in foil, put her in a chair with a pile of last year's magazines, set a timer and left her there.

Now her head was actually hurting, but she was too intimidated to cry out. When the alarm went off and Simon returned, she nearly sobbed with relief. The stuff was washed off, and Nula was once again placed before the mirror while Simon clipped away at her now reddish hair.

'Um,' said Nula.

He looked at her expectantly.

'It's not blonde,' she said. So with barely concealed impatience he put some more gunk on her head, and slapped the timer back on.

7

The Charlie Boys had got used to pilfering from cars and then nicking the cars themselves and selling them on. Charlie and his gang also became expert housebreakers. Summers were particularly good for this. People hot in bed upstairs, windows left open downstairs. Perfect.

They were earning very nicely now by criminal means and were starting to think bigger. Charlie had the manor all set up in his favour and they were raking in cash around the restaurants and clubs. Charlie had his boys on the doors, and before long they had the club owners *out* the door and were taking over. Added to that, they were screwing three or four big houses every week and getting away with it. But soon the word spread, the Old Bill were after them, and they had to go further and further out on the rob, or invite trouble. Charlie was growing bulkier by the day and Terry and Beezer were too big to get in small windows, so they trained up Beezer's little brother, baby-face Col, for that job.

It was like a holiday jaunt, a return to the old days, the housebreaking. They drove out into the countryside in Terry's Cortina, where the pickings were a lot better and where their chances of detection were halved thanks to country plod's relaxed attitude to law enforcement.

Once at their target area, they found a nice big house and sent Col in to knock on the door. The deal was this: if nobody answered, the job was on and Col would be shovelled through a small open window – or they would break one – and then Col would open the front door to let the rest of the troops inside. If someone *did* answer, then Col would innocently ask for directions and leave the householder in peace.

It was a system that seemed foolproof, and one that they used again and again. They would get in, dump empty boxes out of the boot of the car and into the hallway. Then they would put all the stuff they were robbing into the boxes and exit by the front door.

Then one night they were doing a big place, bigger than usual. Col rapped at the door, nobody answered. All was fine. They moved round the side of the building in the moonlight, laughing because they looked like they should have a bag marked 'swag' on their shoulders as they tiptoed along. They found an open window. Beezer wasn't with them tonight, but they had enough backup should they need it. Terry clasped his hands together and boosted Col up there. Col grabbed the window frame and wriggled through without any trouble at all. He dropped down onto the floor inside.

Outside, Charlie and Terry were still laughing, waiting for Col to open the front door. Then there was a noise.

Terry stopped laughing.

'What the fuck was that?' asked Charlie in a loud whisper.

All of a sudden, Col screamed. It was the most godawful spine-tingling, bowel-loosening scream either of them had ever heard.

Charlie was fumbling for his torch, unable to find it. Terry was leaning into the window, but he couldn't see a fucking thing inside. But the screaming. He could hear the screaming, loud and clear.

Charlie found the torch. With shaking fingers he flicked it on and aimed it at the window and for a second all he could see was the reflection of his own bleached-out face. Then he angled it down.

'Oh *shit!*' he muttered, feeling hot stinging sick rise in his throat, threatening to choke him.

He staggered back a step and Terry grabbed the torch off him.

'What?' Terry was demanding, over and over. 'What is it . . . ?'

Then Terry looked along the torch's beam and he saw.

Little Col was being dragged around the room inside there, and he wasn't screaming any more. A Rottweiler as big as a tank was gripping Col by the neck and yanking him this way and that. A liquid pool of dark red was spreading out, staining the floor-boards. Col's eyes were closed.

'Shit,' said Terry, flicking off the torch, his face frozen in horror.

'We got to clear off,' said Charlie flatly. 'He's dead.'

'What? No! We got to get him out of there,' said Terry, wondering how the hell they were going to break this to Beezer.

'You bloody serious? That bastard's finished him, and he'll finish us too. Come on. We're going.'

It was the talk of the streets for weeks after.

'You knew that little scrote Colin, didn't you? Didn't you used to hang around together at school?' Mum asked Charlie. 'Bloody thieving off people. Still, what a way to end up. Nobody should finish like that.'

'I knew him. Not very well,' said Charlie, wishing the old girl would shut her mouth.

'Robbing off people's houses. It's disgusting.'

And then there was the funeral. Baby-face Col's mum and dad were in bits as they followed, stumbling and crying behind the hearse bearing their youngest son up the road and into the church. COLIN was spelled out in red chrysanthemums beside the coffin. Col's older brother Beezer trailed along beside his parents, his face blank with grief.

All the time the funeral went on, Charlie wouldn't meet Terry's gaze. The Bill had questioned them. The coppers knew they were dodgy and that Col and Beezer always hung around with Charlie and Tel. But they both denied all knowledge, and soon it blew over. Charlie, Terry, Beezer and the rest of the Charlie Boys didn't go housebreaking any more though. They concentrated on bigger and better stuff around the manor. There was no more arsing around fencing gear or giggling in the backs of vans. Somehow, they'd lost their taste for petty thievery.

8

With housebreaking behind them, Charlie was looking for new avenues of interest and mugging was an easy deal for his mob of heavy-set lads. Him and Terry and three others started queer-bashing; they hung around the toilets and robbed the cottagers, knowing they wouldn't ever report the incident to the police.

Then they tried football grounds and racecourses, confident of rolling over plenty of drunken punters with cash on the hip. Word of their activities was starting to spread, and soon Charlie and his mob were offered five hundred pounds to play minder to a rich bookie who'd had a few threats made against him.

This was great – easy money. They were still doing the club doors, Charlie being very careful to have some of his lesser-known lads start a hell of fight so that, when he turned up offering protection, the club owners nearly bit his arm off in their haste to take him up on his offer. Then, of course, Charlie would shove the owners out and take over.

So Charlie and Terry and the boys were doing all right. Dressing like film stars and dining out with lots of cash in their pockets. Beezer got morose sometimes and spoke about little Col, but Charlie reasoned that he had paid for the fucking headstone, what more could he be expected to do?

Life was sweet.

And soon, it was going to get even sweeter.

'We got the clubs now, and the snooker halls, but what about the *real* meat?' said Charlie.

'Like what?' asked Terry. Charlie was like a runaway train. His ambitions really did know no bounds.

'All sorts,' said Charlie. 'Factories. Banks. Loan-sharking, even. Coin it on the interest. All right?'

'All right,' said Terry.

9

Two weeks after her visit to Mr Fox, Nula was admiring her now blonde and restyled hair in the mirror in her bedroom when she noticed that a chunk of it was missing from the side. Two days after that, more was coming out. As she combed it, it snapped off an inch from the root. And no matter how gently she tried to wash it and style it, more hair was coming off day by day.

She could have cried.

Everyone was noticing. Her parents – although her mum was sweet about it, saying not to worry, it would grow back in no time – and Jimmy, who thought it was hilarious. Her mates at work. *Everyone*. Once again she was a laughing stock. She *couldn't* go back into that posh place and face up to Simon. She went to another salon, where the middle-aged female stylist took one look at the damage and said: 'Who the hell did this?'

'Simon at Mr Fox,' said Nula.

'You ought to go back. Complain to the management.' The woman lifted a few brittle strands and looked at Nula with compassion. 'There's only one thing to be done with this, I'm afraid.'

'What?'

'Cut it short to the head, recondition heavily and let what's left of the colour grow out.'

Christ!

'All right then. Do it.'

So an hour later Nula had patchy half-coloured hair cropped short to her round dumpling face. She looked *worse*, not better.

She held the tears in until she got home and was safely penned in her bedroom with chocolate bars and crisps. Then she ate – and cried.

10

Nula's hair was growing out. Getting longer, getting – thanks to her latest stylist – stronger, too. When the last of the blonde was chopped off, there she was again: mouse-coloured Nula Perkins with her hair cropped close to her fat head.

Well, the hair would grow. And she'd try again with the colour, that could be solvable. But . . . her *fat head*.

The truth was, Nula loved food. It was her consolation for all that the uncaring world threw at her. Comforting Sunday dinners, sausages and mash, Sunday teatime treats of cream and tinned peaches. Salty crisps and big chocolate bars and ice cream. Her parents were fat. Her brother was fat. Even her grandparents had been fat. But she kept reading things like *Vogue* and *Harpers*, wherein beautiful young things with glossy rich-girl hair and skinny figures pranced and danced and lunched out on steak and salad. No roast potatoes. No treats.

She still went up Carnaby Street with her mates, who had been – like her – the school losers, the quiet unpopular ones; she was Nula the fat arse, then came Stella with the stutter, Hilda with the limp, Joanie with the cleft palate that made her talk funny, and Sylvia with the ears that stuck straight out from underneath her thin brown hair like radar scanners.

In misery, they'd banded together. They weren't like the popular girls, the pretty hair-tossing ones the boys all lusted after like Jill Patterson and her mates, or the tough ones, the tomboys who'd bloody your nose if you dared talk about them. But there was strength in numbers.

Now they trawled around Carnaby Street and tried on dresses – Nula hated trying on dresses, but the others were doing it and so she had to join in. And there it was, the awful, undeniable truth. Staring back at Nula from the dreaded changing-room mirror was the confirmation of all her fears. She was fat, and fat she would stay, because she ate too much.

One or the other, you could have. But not both. A good figure . . . or all that lovely food.

It was crucifying. Nula knew two things. One: food was her only real pleasure in life. Whenever she was laughed at, mocked, depressed, she would take refuge inside the larder, would stand there covertly eating seedy cake or apple pie, one eye on the door, her ears alert for footfall. And two: Mum wanted her to eat and moaned and fretted and threatened visits to doctors if she didn't.

So she was fighting her mother *and* herself. But Nula was obstinate. Once committed to a path, she wasn't one to deviate.

Skipping family dinners became an art form to her. She said she was playing hockey (she wasn't) or down the chess club (not there, either) or at the youth club (all lies). She skipped breakfast, ignored her rumbling stomach and the temptation of the biscuit counter, lunched on fruit, crawled home starving and pushed the food around her plate, much to Mum's displeasure.

It was all such an *effort*.

But after a few months of this – she didn't dare weigh herself on those big high-street machines in public and face yet more scorn and humiliation, and her family had never possessed any bathroom scales – she thought that something was happening to her.

She was getting *thinner*.

She would stand naked in front of her bedroom mirror and

force herself to look. There was a suggestion of ribs now, where before there had just been a spare tyre. Her belly didn't bulge out the way it had. Her thighs didn't rub together quite so painfully any more.

Nula started to feel something almost like happiness. It was hell, it was horrible, but – for fuck's sake! – it was actually *working*.

So stuff Mum and her treacle sponges and massive portions. Nula stuck to her guns, kept avoiding mealtimes, and stared and stared at her new emerging body.

Her clothes started to hang on her. Which was OK, she *hated* her clothes. Then came the glorious day when she went and bought something. It was in a size she'd never even attempted before so she hadn't dared try it on for fear it would be so tight on her she'd look like an overstuffed sausage.

She came back home with the minidress in a bright red bag. It was a multi-striped (vertical, not horizontal, she wasn't *that* full of herself yet) simply cut mini with no sleeves and a zipper on the front.

It was a size fourteen.

Nervously she took it out of the bag, stroked a hand over the velvety material. Before, she'd squeezed into an eighteen, really *squeezed*. She unzipped it, slipped it over her head, refastened the long zipper, ruffled up her hair then dared to look in the mirror.

A stranger was looking back at her. A stranger with a good figure, wearing a mini dress, with a fuzz of soft head-hugging mouse-coloured hair making a frame around her features.

Nula turned back and forth, examining her reflection. She'd had hardly any tits before and now she had none. But she was *thin*. She looked at her face. Her eyes were well-shaped and hazel coloured. Her mouth was fine. But her nose was a monster. It reminded her of Schnozzle Durante. It was the Perkins family nose, they all had it. But as for the rest of it . . .

She looked OK. Her legs were nice. Long and shapely. Her arms were fine. She had cheekbones now, that was new. She stared again at her face and she frowned. She felt tears prick her eyes but she blinked, gulped, forced them back. She *wouldn't* cry.

Now, she had to save up some more.

She had to save up a *lot*.

11

Nula went into the bank where she had a small savings account, and they laughed her right out of the place – turned her down flat because, the manager said pompously, he 'didn't want to encourage her to overstretch herself, financially'.

Nula went home in a low mood that day. She stood inside the larder and eyed up the chocolate cake Mum had made for Sunday tea. God, she wanted it. But she stepped back out of the larder, closed the door.

'You all right, our Nula?' asked Mum, coming into the kitchen and making her give a guilty start.

'Yeah. I'm fine.'

Her mum patted her on the shoulder. 'Can I get you anything, lovey?'

'No. Thanks.' Again Nula had to blink back tears. Her mother loved her and meant only the best for her, so it hurt Nula to have to go against her, to refuse the cupboard-love Mum so frequently offered.

There had to be a way to get what she needed. Next day at work she spoke to Sylvia, her old mate with the radar-scanner ears, the poor cow.

'Where would I get a loan from?' she asked.

'What do you want that for?' asked Freda, whose life was small, limited to this fuck-all work in Woolies, to home, to telly, to nothing very much at all. Sylvia had no ambition. She was a sweetheart, but she was thick as two planks covered in pig shit, there was no getting away from that fact.

'Never you mind. No matter. Forget I said anything,' said Nula.

But Sylvia didn't forget it. She came in next day and said: 'There's a bloke does loans. My dad said. Here's his address.' She handed her mate a scrap of paper.

'Thanks.' Nula eyed it with suspicion before slipping it into her overall pocket. She'd try another bank, see what she could come up with. She didn't like the idea of some bloke off the street, it didn't seem official, or business-like.

The next bank laughed at her, too. She was a shop girl with no savings, and she was asking for a sizeable loan.

Nula slunk home again and stood inside the larder door and actually *ate* a large slice of the cake, before going out into the yard and sticking her fingers down her throat to bring it all back up again. Crying, choking, she sat on the cobbles beside the tin bath hanging from its nail on the wall.

Then she dragged herself to her feet, went back into the scullery and pulled her dirty overall out from the washing pile. The note from Sylvia was still in the pocket and she got it out, spread it, stared at it.

She straightened, took a breath.

All right then.

Charlie Stone.

12

What Nula hadn't expected when she pitched up at the address on the note was that Terry Barton would open the door. It threw her completely. She felt her jaw actually drop as she stared at his handsome features. He'd always been tall, but now he'd bulked up, gained a lot of muscle. He looked fearsome. More of a man than he'd ever looked before. And worse – humiliatingly, awfully worse – he had *her* there with him, giggling and twining around him like bindweed. Slim pretty Jill Patterson who'd been in Nula's class at school, her of the blonde hair and sparkling blue eyes. Nula *hated* Jill. Jill had been one of those capable *winning* girls, first a milk monitor and then a prefect, bossing the other kids around while Nula had skulked in the background, envious and silent, with all the other no-hopers.

'Yeah, what is it?' Terry asked.

As he stood there staring at her, half-laughing because Jill was in his arms and she was tickling him, it struck Nula: he didn't recognize her. Didn't know that the fat pitiful ball of lard he'd once danced with out of sympathy was *her*.

Well, that was good. She'd had humiliations enough to last a lifetime.

'Can I see Charlie Stone?' she asked. 'Is he in?'

'What d'you want to see him about?' asked Terry, pushing Jill away from him with a smile. She pouted, smiling back. Then her eyes went to Nula.

Nula gulped hard, avoiding meeting Jill's gaze. 'I want to talk to him about a loan,' she said to Terry.

'Right. OK then. Come in.'

Nula went in, looking around curiously. Charlie Stone's house was much like her own parents' place – a plain little two-up-two-down. Nothing fancy. Not what she'd expected, at all. Someone with money to dole out to other people should have a better place to live in than this, surely?

Terry went to a door at the end of the hall, knocked once, then opened it. Nula, growing doubtful, wondered what the hell she was getting into. She stepped into a room and the door closed behind her. It was shabby in here. The sofa looked like something left over from the war. There was a desk in the corner, and behind it sat a man.

She recognized him, of course. The one that poor little Colin Crowley, who'd died doing that housebreaking job, used to hang about with. That had been tragic, really. Her God-bothering parents had taken the view that the little bastard had broken into someone's drum, and when you did that, you got exactly what you deserved – and Col had. Torn to ribbons by a Rottweiler, apparently.

Nula shuddered. Christ, what a horrible way to go.

He was looking at her now, Charlie who had never so much as given her a second glance. She had always been far beneath his attention.

And him?

Well, she'd been always been aware of him, obviously she had. But he was on another level to her, she'd understood that for a long time. Charlie Stone was going places. Today he looked the part in a suit that was clearly bespoke and not off-the-peg. He had the air of a successful businessman already. And he wasn't exactly *bad* looking.

Charlie Stone was *squat*, that was the word. He was about five eight, and solid. In twenty years, Nula reckoned he would run to fat. But for now he was heavy-set, compact, with Brylcreemed dark hair. His hard, dark button eyes were skimming over her without any real interest at all – the way they always had.

'I hear you do loans,' said Nula, going up to the desk and sitting down with every appearance of calm, while inside she was scared shitless and she could feel her knees knocking together like castanets. If her parents or Jimmy could see her here, doing this, they'd hit the roof. They didn't believe in Hire Purchase or in loans of any kind. 'If I can't afford it, I don't bloody have it,' Dad always said primly.

Charlie eased back in his seat, king of all he surveyed. He stared at her. 'Don't I know you?'

That threw her. She knew *him*, everybody did; but she had never supposed that he had noticed her.

Nula shrugged. 'Probably from the dance hall. I'm Nula . . .'

Charlie's face split in a grin. He slapped the desk hard and pointed a finger bristling with gold rings straight at her. Nula jumped. 'The little fat bird!' he burst out. 'Jimmy Perkins's sister.'

Nula cringed. That was her. The little grey fat bird. Unnoticeable. Forever fading into the background. Not worthy of anyone's attention.

'Yeah,' she said, feeling a hot blush of shame colouring her cheeks. 'That's me.'

'So you want to borrow?'

'Yeah. I do.' But now it all seemed like madness.

'OK.' Charlie whipped a notebook and pencil out of the drawer, put it down on the desk and looked at her expectantly. 'How much?'

Just like that?

Nula couldn't believe it. After the bank, this seemed like child's play. But this bloke, who could grin at her and look friendly one moment, then look downright threatening the next, this bloke she knew from schooldays – him and Terry had been two years above her – squat little Charlie Stone, was a *loan shark*.

'Um . . . a thousand?' she ventured.

Charlie's mouth dropped open. *'How* much?'

'A thousand,' mumbled Nula. 'If I can pay it back over – say – two years? Would that be OK?'

'Yeah, but the interest,' said Charlie, staring at her. 'What you want a sum like that for then, girl? That's a lot of brass.'

'It's for something personal,' said Nula, her lips in a thin line. She wasn't going to tell him about *that*. What, give them all something more to laugh at her about? At Nula, the little fat girl with the big conk?

Charlie was still watching her face. Then he nodded. 'All right then,' he said, and started to explain about the interest rates while Nula sat there, amazed, not listening to a word.

As easy as that!

She was going to get the money she needed.

It was going to be *done*.

She nearly floated out of the door when their business was concluded. Then Jill, still out in the hall with Terry, said: 'Hey – you're Nula, aintcha?'

And her balloon was popped. 'Yeah,' she said, deflated.

'Gawd, you've dropped a bit of timber aintcha, girl?'

Nula didn't answer, she just shoved past her to the front door, and out.

13

Charlie was ambitious, wanting to make the next move, wanting to be *respected*.

'You got that,' Terry told him. 'Everyone around here respects you.'

People stepped carefully around the Charlie Boys on the manor now. Nodded. Smiled. Charlie liked that. Terry didn't mind it. He didn't *crave* it, not like Charlie did. He was happy that they had cash, and that Jill loved him. He didn't want more. But Charlie always did.

They started watching security vans. Whenever Charlie saw one, he'd make a note of the date, the time, the location and the registration number of the van. Then he'd be back a week later to see if this was a regular thing. Then a week after that, seeing how the people involved operated, which route they took in and out of the premises. Then again, checking the fine detail.

When Charlie was happy that everything was covered, him and the gang did the job, tooled up with one shotgun, two toy hand pistols. They targeted a clothing manufacturer's place, where Charlie believed the pickings would be rich.

The boys crashed into the factory in hoods and boiler suits and went straight to the small glassed-in office where an inside operator had told them the wages were kept. Machinists started screaming as they kicked at the door. It was locked. Inside, through the bulletproof glass partition, they could see the female cashier.

'Open the bloody door!' yelled Charlie.

She backed away, shaking her head.

'Fuck it!' Charlie booted the door but it wouldn't give. He motioned to big heavy-set Terry, who came up and rammed it with his shoulder. No good.

Then Terry kicked it hard, splintering the lock.

Another kick, and the door juddered open, the partition beside it caving in, glass and all, with a monumental crash.

'On the floor!' Charlie shouted at the cashier, and she got down straight away. He looked around for the safe. Couldn't see one.

'Where's the safe?' he asked her, prodding her back with the shotgun. 'Where's the money?'

She pointed a shaking finger at the desk. 'In the drawer,' she said.

Charlie almost laughed. A proper business, and some silly bastard had been too mean to fork out for a safe! He went over and wrenched open drawer after drawer – each one was *stuffed* with money and small half-filled brown envelopes. The cashier had been in the middle of doing up the wages.

They emptied the loot into their bags and scarpered. Then they went back to one of their safe houses on the manor and counted the takings. They'd expected a hundred grand – and ended up with sixty.

Charlie was fuming.

Terry, who was in charge of cleaning up after jobs, took their boiler suits and hoods plus the gear they were wearing underneath and stuffed everything into a bag. Later, he'd burn it. Beezer, who had been little Col's adoring brother until little Col topped himself off by getting on the wrong side of that Rottweiler, refused to let Terry burn his designer jacket.

'Come on,' said Terry.

'No way,' said Beezer, who prided himself on his togs, the

45

flashier the better. And he'd bought the jacket on a trip to honour Col's memory. It had sentimental value, he said.

Terry shrugged. They divvied up the money and departed.

Ten days later, the Bill were round asking questions – everyone knew where the villains were on the manor, and Charlie had a reputation as a real heavy face now. They got hold of Beezer's jacket and matched up fibres from that with some near the smashed office door.

Beezer got handed down two years and the rest of them got off with nothing.

Beezer's sentence was unfortunate in one way.

But in another?

It was a cast-iron miracle.

14

With the loan she'd got from Charlie, Nula paid to have the operation on her nose done at a private clinic. It was two weeks of unbelievable pain, during which there was Mum forever at her bedside asking what had she done a thing like that to herself for? Nula was a pretty young girl with everything in front of her.

Yeah, including a monstrous conk, thought Nula, enduring her mother, patiently waiting for her to be gone. Hating herself for feeling like that, too: she knew how much her mother loved her, but she *also* knew that she wanted out from this suffocating little world that her sweet, placid, old-fashioned mum inhabited.

'Our mum's right,' said Jimmy, eating the grapes he'd bought her as she lay in the nice private room in the swish hospital. 'You must be off your head, our Nula, bothering about your fucking nose.'

So there was pain, and there was discomfort, and there was her mum fussing around and her brother who *always* had a go at her, he couldn't resist it, and Dad who stayed away because he never could stand hospitals.

In between, there was the very nice plastic surgeon, and nurses who actually took trouble over you, not like in the NHS place she'd been in as a kid to have her tonsils out, where some of the nurses couldn't be arsed to fetch you an extra blanket if you were cold, or even a pot to piss in when you were dying for the loo.

Then came the day when the gauze and tape was to be removed. She feared that when the big reveal was effected, her nose would be exactly as it always was. Huge. Lumpen. Yeah, shaped like a potato. *Awful.*

She held her breath as the nurse lifted the gauze free of her face. The air felt chilly, strange on the newly exposed skin. She'd already seen her reflection in the bathroom mirror, the big patch of gauze and above it two spectacular black eyes. Now, she would see *everything.*

The nurse was smiling. She was handing Nula a mirror. Nula lifted it nervously, and looked.

'Oh my God!' she burst out.

'What do you think?' asked the nurse.

Nula couldn't speak.

There was bruising. There was blood, a little. But also . . .

She had a *normal nose.*

It was dainty. A little turned up. Extremely cute.

'It's beautiful,' she said, in a state of shock.

'Yes,' said the nurse, smiling. 'It is.'

15

Charlie Stone was surprised when Nula turned up to his gaff again.

'You look different,' he said, trying to place exactly what was changed about her.

Before, she'd worn plain clothes, cheap stuff that made her vanish into the background, and her unstyled hair had been pure mouse, thin and horrible. Today, she was in a short pale blue dress, her hair was styled in an urchin cut. Charlie thought she looked tasty, actually. Surprisingly so.

'My nose,' she said.

Charlie stared. *That* was it. But she was thinner too. Quite *fanciable*. 'Ah. That was the loan, yeah?'

'It was. Yes.'

'You're a week behind, incidentally,' he said sourly. He was in a bad mood. Beezer getting banged up had shaken him. He *still* couldn't believe it. What a cunting arse the bloke was, with his fancy designer gear. And look what it had cost him. It had been close for the rest of them as well. *Too* bloody close.

'I've been in the hospital. Having my nose done. Then getting better.'

'Have you. Well good for you. But lateness incurs extra interest.'

'What?' Nula eyed him in disbelief.

'It's all part of the deal, as I explained to you when I made you the loan,' he said. 'Fifty per cent interest now, and if another single late payment occurs, that doubles to a hundred for six months.'

'A hundred per *cent*?'

'That's correct.' Charlie was staring at her face. She looked *terrified,* and he rather liked that. Made him feel powerful. Which, of course, he was. His mood lightened a bit.

'You . . . you're joking.' Nula was stretched to the limit as it was. She couldn't afford a single penny above what she was already paying. And he was talking about doubling her debt.

'Does this face say joking?' asked Charlie.

'I can't afford that,' said Nula.

'Well, you had *better* afford it, because that is the price and it's non-negotiable,' said Charlie, picking up his pen and nodding toward the door. 'See yourself out.'

Terry and Jill were loitering out by the front door again, Jill all over big handsome Terry like a rash, as always. Nula barged past the pair of them, her mind in turmoil.

'Oi! Manners!' she heard Jill say as she shoved off down the path.

16

Nula's life became one huge round of debt. Bing Crosby crooned 'White Christmas' all over the city as Christmas came and slowly went. She was working like stink to raise cash, taking all the overtime she could, but it still wasn't enough. So she took another job in the evenings, working the bar down the Dog and Duck, and then when even that didn't cut it she took *another* job on Sundays, polishing tables and cleaning out the disgusting bogs in the local working men's club.

Finally she broke down in tears and told Jimmy. It was humiliating to have to confide anything to that smug bastard, but she couldn't tell her friends because she was too ashamed of her own stupidity, wandering into this deal with her eyes shut, and she couldn't tell her parents because she never told them anything, not ever, and she wasn't about to start now.

'Right,' said Jimmy, puffing himself up while Nula sobbed at the kitchen table. 'I'm going to have a *word* with that fucker.'

'That won't do any good,' she gasped out.

'Oh won't it? We'll see about that.'

And Jimmy belted off out of the kitchen and down the hall, slamming the front door behind him.

Jimmy didn't come back for his tea. Mum was fretting as they waited and Nula was fretting even worse because she *knew* where Jimmy had gone and she didn't dare say a word about it.

Mum set Jimmy's dinner on a covered plate over a simmering

pan of water to keep it warm. It sat there for over two hours, until it was turned to mush. Then Mum scraped the lot into the bin and started pacing around while Dad took to standing at the front door, gazing out into the night, letting in gusts of cold air. Nula sat at the table, fearful of where this was all going to end, nervous that Jimmy's meddling was going to bring her secret out into the daylight.

Then there was the sound of a motor revving out in the street, a shout went up and there was heavy footfall by the front door. Presently, Dad staggered into the kitchen holding Jimmy up. He was bleeding from cuts to his face. His skin was grey and he was clutching his guts.

'What happened?' asked Mum, as she helped her husband ease their son into a chair. 'Oh Gawd son, what they done to you?'

Through one half-closed eye, Jimmy stared at his sister. His expression said it all. *You daft cow, this is all* your *fault.*

'Charlie Stone beat me up,' he mumbled.

'Why? What for?' asked Dad.

'Just for the hell of it, I s'pose,' said Jimmy, as Mum started mopping away the blood from his face.

Dad started swearing and saying that bastard needed taking down a peg, he thought he was king of the bloody manor now Gordie Howard and his crew had been chased out of it.

Nula said nothing. She was thinking that she'd better not let the laugh that was building up in her escape to the wild. Yes, for certain Charlie Stone was a bastard of the first order; but he'd beaten the shit out of Jimmy, who had spent the better part of her life making it a misery – bullying her, mocking her, generally being a complete pain in the arse.

Charlie Stone had delivered Nula's revenge for her. All right, he was also caning her for a lot of cash and she was in the shit for sure, but . . . *he'd beaten the crap out of Jimmy.*

She could only admire *anyone* who did that.

17

It looked like Charlie had in fact gone easy on Jimmy, because save for a few spectacular bruises he was back at work in the car showroom within a week, and he didn't mention Nula's debt or Charlie Stone again.

But the debt remained, and she had to pay it. Stretched to the limit, too worried to sleep at night, Nula gathered together what cash she could and went to pay Charlie Stone back his stinking money. Well, some of it. Now she wished she hadn't bothered with the nose job. All right, her vanity was appeased. An average slim young girl looked back at her from the mirror now, with no huge unsightly bastard of a nose marring her features.

But . . . oh God, the price she'd paid for it. Was *still* paying for it.

Terry let her in and her heart did its usual backflip at the sight of him. But – also as usual – he barely seemed to notice her. At least there was no Jill here today, thank God for small mercies. Terry ushered Nula along the hall, into what passed for Charlie Stone's office.

And there was Charlie, squat and powerful, sitting behind his desk looking a question at her as she came in and closed the door behind her. And . . . her eyes fixed on his hands. Big blunt-fingered hands, loaded with gold rings. The knuckles of his right hand were scabbed, the skin there only newly healed.

'You got some front, girl, sending your brother round here to mug me off,' he said.

Nula drew in a breath, wrenched her eyes away from the evidence of Jimmy's beating. 'I didn't *send* him,' she said.

'Well whether you did or whether you didn't, that means the debt's gone up, OK?'

'You *what?*'

'You heard.'

'I'm struggling to pay it now.'

'Struggling? You're failing. The payment's late. I trust you've come here today to settle up?'

'I've come here today to pay a bit towards it.' Nula looked in her handbag, extracted three fivers, and put them down on the desk. Then she looked him in the eye. 'And to say I can't pay the rest.'

Charlie sat back in his seat and eyed her beadily. She was a pretty little thing really. And she had backbone, fronting it out like this. Way back, he could remember her as podgy and plain, with her hair a mess and her nose dominating her whole face. Now, there was a big improvement. In fact – yeah – he fancied her.

'You probably got the hump over me giving your brother a pasting,' said Charlie.

'No,' said Nula. 'I was glad you did.'

'You what?'

Nula shrugged. 'I don't like my brother.'

'Right.' Charlie was eyeing her up. 'So what if I was to say, come out to dinner with me one evening? Pay off your debt in kind, as it were?'

Nula returned his stare in surprise. She hadn't expected that. No man had *ever* come on to her before. She was plain little Nula. Deep down she still felt like that, despite the evidence that looked back at her from her bedroom mirror these days. Outside, she was different. Inside, reality had yet to sink in. If it ever would, which sometimes she doubted.

Charlie had given Jimmy a thumping, and she liked that. Also
. . . if she got close to Charlie, then she was getting close to Terry
too, and it was Terry she was interested in. Maybe if Charlie
noticed her, then somehow, by some miracle, Terry would too?

'What would that involve?' she asked bluntly.

Charlie frowned at her. 'Having dinner. Talking. That sort of
thing. You know. Normal boy-girl things.'

Nula thought of Terry, out there in the hall.

'OK,' she said.

18

Charlie took Nula out to dinner at the Ritz; it was posher than anything Nula had ever experienced in her entire life. Of course, her parents and Jimmy ganged up on her before she went out on their date.

'Charlie Stone's a villain,' said Jimmy, face black with temper. He liked to control Nula. With Charlie sniffing around, he wouldn't be able to do that any more. 'You ought to be ashamed, our Nula, going out with the likes of him. One minute he's chasing you for money, now he's treating you to dinners? You want to go careful.'

'What money?' said Mum.

'Nula got a loan off the bastard,' said Jimmy, landing her right in it. *Deliberately.*

'Our Nula!' Mum's eyes were wide with shock behind her glasses. 'You didn't.'

Nula didn't answer.

'He comes round here, I'm going to tell him to piss off,' said Dad, disgusted.

So for Nula the evening didn't get off to a flying start. She got dressed up and wondered why she was bothering. Charlie was going to be seen off at the door, and not by big blustering Jimmy but by Dad. She cringed when she heard the doorbell go at five to seven and stood in her room upstairs waiting to hear raised voices.

She waited.

Nothing happened.

Cautiously she went down the stairs and into the hall. There was laughter coming from the kitchen, where the family always gathered in the evenings. She walked along the hall, pushed open the kitchen door.

There was her mother, sitting at the table blushing like a girl and smiling up at Charlie Stone. Jimmy was loitering over by the fireplace, not quite scowling but arms crossed over his middle in a defensive posture while Charlie held Mum and even Dad in thrall.

'I wondered where Nula got her looks from, and now I know. You have a lovely daughter, Mrs Perkins, you should be very proud.'

Nula watched Charlie in fascination. She hadn't known he could be like this: charming, smiling, exuding this magnetic bon-homie that even seemed to be sucking her po-faced father into its orbit. All she had seen so far was the threat, the big-noise gangster. Here was another side to his character, and it amazed her.

He turned his head, still smiling, as she came into the room. 'Nula!' he exclaimed, eyeing her up and down. 'Don't you look the business.'

For once, Nula was almost prepared to believe him. She'd chosen a dusky-blue dress for the evening, and it suited her skin and hair to perfection. She'd applied make-up and even she knew that she looked pretty good. It wasn't that artless, natural looking good that Jill always seemed to manage without even trying – no, Nula had to *work* at it. But she'd pass for OK.

She thought that Charlie looked good too, wearing a suit, a crisp white shirt and a tobacco-brown tie that matched his eyes. He looked . . . *expensive,* that was the word. He wasn't a working-class loser like her father and her brother. Charlie Stone looked like a man on the way up.

He came over to where Nula was standing in the open door-way and then he did the most amazing thing: he took her hand, brought it to his lips and kissed it.

'Doll, you look a million dollars,' said Charlie, his eyes never once leaving hers. 'Come on. Let's go.'

19

That night was the start of something big.

It surprised them both, but within a few months they were going steady, and it was pretty much agreed that soon Nula was going to stop being plain Nula Perkins and start being Mrs Charlie Stone.

So *this* was what the world was like, the world beyond the stifling borderline poverty she'd lived in for much of her life. Charlie introduced Nula to luxury and she lapped it up. He seemed to be known in all sorts of places, was greeted like an old friend in most of them. He took her to fabulously posh events, kitted her out at one of the swish Bond Street boutiques with a dress and matching hat, then took her to Ascot for the flat races on Thursday, which was Ladies Day. It turned out he actually *owned* a racehorse.

'I keep it in training in a place near Newbury,' he told her.

He wasn't lying, either. The trainer came and shook his hand and said Cordon Off had a chance today. The horse came third, but still. They stayed for the Gold Cup and she saw the Queen. She couldn't believe it.

Charlie took her to Henley for the Regatta, had the best tickets for Wimbledon, flew her out first class with him to see Graham Hill win the Monaco Grand Prix. This was such a different world from the plain, dull one she'd been born into. The job at Woolies was a thing of the past now, and she spent most of her time – scandalously – staying over at Charlie's place or roaring around the country with him in his new Rolls-Royce, staying at five-star hotels. She barely ever went home and she didn't give a single shit about that, either. And all the while – much to her surprise – Charlie was the perfect gentleman. It was separate rooms, every time.

This was bliss.

It was *fabulous*.

This was her life now, and she loved it.

20

Beezer was out of jail, released a month early for good behaviour. Charlie, Terry and the rest of the crew assembled down the Pig's Head to welcome him back. He looked thinner, paler, less elegant than he used to; generally, he looked fucked. They bought him beer and toasted him.

'Nah, nah, boys. Never mind all that. There's something I got to tell you,' he said, his voice hoarse from all the reefers he'd smoked inside.

'Relax,' said Charlie, patting Beezer on the back so hard he nearly lost his pint over the table. 'You're out, mate. And you've learned a lesson, yeah? All the togs you wear on a job, you burn. *All* of them.'

'Charlie,' said Beezer. 'Forget about that. What I am going to tell you now is going to change your life.' He glanced around the group. His eyes were feverish. '*All* our lives.'

'Yeah?' Charlie was grinning. Beezer was always one for the big idea. Flogging one thing or another that would net them a fortune, according to him. Sadly, it never happened that way. You had to graft in this world. Put in the hours. Rob the warehouses and the banks and the racecourses, take over the nightclubs, do the loan-sharking – like Charlie had been doing over the past few years – and you had to do it *carefully*.

'When I was in stir . . .' said Beezer, glancing around as the barmaid Vera passed by with a tray of glasses. He fell silent. Then

Vera was gone, back behind the bar, and he gestured for them to lean in.

'Blimey, what is it, mate? You joined the secret service?' laughed Terry.

'There's a gold rush on,' said Beezer, looking wild-eyed at Charlie.

'What the fuck?' Charlie blew out cigarette smoke, watching Beezer curiously.

'I shared a cell with a bloke. Finnan Marks.'

'I know Finnan,' said Charlie. 'He's done some jobs. Big bloke, yeah? Into all the body-building malarkey like Terry here. He got caught, the silly fucker.'

'Well he won't be doing bank jobs no more,' said Beezer.

'What, he's retiring?'

Beezer shook his head.

'Nah, listen, Charlie, this is *serious*. I was in the cell with Finnan one day, there we was, just shooting the breeze, talking about this and that, the door wide open and people passing by. Finnan had a gallery of pics on his wall. It was an artists' paradise in there. Big-titted women and motorbikes and sports cars. We were saying which car we liked best, and Finnan slapped a hand on this red job hanging on the wall and said that this was his dream car, the car he was going to own one day. It was a Ferrari 250 GT Spyder California. Then this weedy little bastard – wet behind the ears, he looked – he stops outside the door and looks in and says, "I've got one of those."'

'Go on,' said Charlie, beckoning Vera to bring another round over.

'Well, Finnan says to him, fuck off, what you talking about? The bloke was smiling at Finnan and, mate, I was fearful for the kid. Finnan's like that. You look at him the wrong way, he'll take your head off, and he thought this student type was taking the piss.'

They all nodded. *Everyone* knew this about Finnan.

'But the kid said he'd been bringing weed in on a big scale from abroad and was graduating to coke soon as he got back outside. He told us all about it. I'm telling you – that boy had a lifestyle like a film star. I'm not fucking around here.'

'Yeah, really? What about Customs?' asked Charlie.

Beezer snorted. Vera brought the drinks, smiled, departed. Beezer took a long pull of his beer, gave a belch and then said: 'Customs is crap. You go over to France or Spain or Holland or wherever, send your granny with a couple of kids so no one will ever suspect she's a mule. She carts it back in, you sell it on the streets.'

Everyone was silent, digesting this.

Beezer stared around at Charlie's crew. 'Now you tell me,' he said. 'Which is easier? Robbing bloody banks or buying a tonne of coke off the Colombians.'

Charlie was looking thoughtful. 'That would cost though,' he said. 'A tonne? That would cost a *lot*.'

'But you've done the banks, aintcha. You've *done* all that. So you've got your start-up cash. You buy the stuff for three grand a kilo, and sell it on in the UK for *thirty to forty thousand*. Once it's bought, that's clear profit.'

They were all silent.

'Minimal risk,' said Beezer, looking around at them. 'And a fucking great payout at the end of it.'

None of them said a word. It was true that bank security – hell, security *everywhere* – was getting tighter all the time; Beezer's jail term had given them all a chilly feeling. Maybe it really *was* time to let the hard game go.

'What do you reckon on that?' said Beezer. He put his hand over his heart. 'On my dead brother's grave, I swear to you, Charlie – this is a fucking *revolution*.'

21

'You know what? I'm getting involved in a new line of business. It's exciting,' said Charlie.

They were lingering over coffee and brandy after the best slap-up meal Nula had ever eaten. This was not food like her mum cooked – plum duff, plain roasts, shepherd's pie on a Monday, heavy fare that stuck you to the floor.

This food was light, exquisite. Lobster bisque that tasted of the sea, lemon soufflés, steak so tender it melted in the mouth. She was getting used to all this now, she loved it. The brandy was making her head swim pleasantly. A whole new world had opened up before her, a world of luxury, of being treated with *respect*, because she was Charlie Stone's girl.

'Oh?' she said.

His business didn't interest her much, but she *loved* his life-style. Her only concern now was that he hadn't tried to sleep with her yet. She was wondering what it would feel like if Charlie went all the way with her. He was so self-confident that you couldn't help but be impressed by him. Everything was excess with Charlie. He ate hugely. He was loud, he was tough. He'd grab your arm or nudge you to make a point, and you'd have a bruise there for a week. When he was in a room, he filled it; he seemed to suck out all the available air.

Of course Charlie wasn't *Terry*, but still. She was quite sweet on him, really. But he'd been the gentleman with her for so long, doing little more than kissing. Oh, she let him fumble with her tits, and touch her downstairs sometimes. But Charlie never went any further. Now she was starting to get anxious. Didn't he *want* to sleep with her?

'Getting tired of the loan-sharking then?' asked Nula.

Charlie looked at her, long and hard. Then he smiled. It was a standing joke between them. The loan he'd given her had never yet been repaid – in cash *or* in kind.

'You're a cheeky mare. But I like that in a woman, you know. And in answer to your question, no, I'm not tired of loan-sharking – and incidentally I haven't forgotten you still owe me. Trust me, you *will* repay.'

'Right.' Nula didn't feel in the least alarmed by that now. It was flirtation, the way they were staring into each other's eyes, tossing words back and forth. 'But as I told you, I can't afford it. Not with the interest you keep piling on top.'

'Yeah, it's a problem, innit?' Charlie's eyes were dancing with suppressed laughter.

'So what's this new business then?'

Charlie tapped the side of his nose, took another pull of his brandy. 'Secret,' he said.

'What, is it bad?'

'Very.'

'Right.' Actually Nula found that quite a turn-on. She was having dinner in a swish restaurant with a very dodgy hot man, and though it was a crying shame it wasn't Terry, it was *Charlie Stone*. Charlie was a boss to his boots, and she liked that.

'How *are* you going to pay me then?' he asked. 'And when?'

'In kind, I suppose, like you said,' said Nula, and daringly she put her foot up under the table and touched it firmly to his crotch.

Charlie sat up sharply and Nula smiled straight into his eyes.

'If that's what you want? If you're sure?' he asked.

Nula gulped in a breath and ploughed on. *Was* she? 'Yeah. Of course.'

Charlie was staring at her face. 'I didn't want to push it,' he said. 'I know your family's religious, so I didn't want to offend you. I thought maybe you were saving yourself for the wedding night.'

Nula stared at him. 'Is there going to be one then? A wedding night?'

'Yeah. Sure there is.'

'Then we don't have to wait. If you don't want to.'

And then – when they were about to get down – at last! – to the *real* business of the evening – in comes Terry, with Jill all wrapped around him like always.

Terry and Jill hustled up to their table.

'Terry,' said Charlie in greeting.

'We got some news,' said Terry, beaming at Jill. He gave Nula a glance. 'Sorry to interrupt.'

'That's—' said Nula.

'Yeah? What?' Charlie asked.

'We're getting married,' said Terry, and despite herself Nula felt the world all around her freeze into immobility. Her heart literally sank. But this was reality and she had to take it on the chin. All her dreams of Terry were fruitless, stupid. The fantasy of her ever getting with him was done. Instead, she had Charlie Stone.

It was Charlie for her now, or nothing.

That night, they had sex, *proper* sex, for the very first time. But while Charlie was doing her, kissing her, caressing her, Nula couldn't help it: she wanted to, but she couldn't. She thought of Terry, and her climax nearly sent her crashing through the ceiling.

22

Charlie discovered that there were other things besides *dealing* drugs; for instance, you could tax the people who did it. Rob them of their stash. After all, what could they do about it? They couldn't go to the police. Charlie was mob-handed, he owned the manor and he was expanding at speed; he had the toughest crew for miles around. The victim's only recourse was to tap on some other underworld mobster's door and hope he'd help – which was unlikely, once he heard that Charlie Stone was involved.

And Charlie had other things taking up his time now. Nula, for one. Nula had come as a shock. He'd never had a lot of time for women, but he actually *liked* her. Now she'd lost that gigantic phizog of hers she was a pretty girl. She fucked like a weasel and sometimes she had a tongue on her sharp as a whip; he liked that very much. She answered him back and no one did that. No one except Nula.

On the morning of Terry and Jill's wedding, Charlie was sitting on a chair with his trousers round his ankles and Nula was straddling him, bouncing up and down on his cock with enthusiasm. It had come as quite a surprise to Nula that she enjoyed sex. She thought it surprised Charlie, too.

Nowadays Nula barely went home at all; mostly she stayed with Charlie right here in his house. They had been together all yesterday evening and overnight. Then they'd got up, cleaned up, and Nula had put on the peach gown and the matching ostrich feather hat and the high silver heels she had selected to wear for the wedding.

She was still wearing the hat and the silver heels: nothing else. Charlie had come back into the bedroom saying how fantastic she looked in the dress, and next thing he had it off her, and her underwear, and then they were on the chair and Nula was shimmying up and down on Charlie's prick.

Charlie was quiet this morning. Usually he was very vocal during sex, shouting 'Yes! Yes! Yes!' as she attended to him, but today he was clearly not himself.

'Something up?' asked Nula, panting, stopping mid-bounce.

Charlie pulled a face. 'Terry getting wed. Things changing. I dunno.'

Nula had long suspected that Charlie was going to be put out by his friend's nuptials. Maybe even as put out as *she* secretly was. Maybe Charlie thought Terry would go soft on him. Charlie liked to be in charge of matters, and this was something that was beyond him.

'It'll be OK,' said Nula, placing both Charlie's hands on her breasts. She gave him a laughing glance. 'Keep your mind on the business in hand, OK, mister?'

Charlie half-smiled at that and squeezed a very small double handful as Nula got back to the job. She could feel the pleasure building now, accelerating her movements.

'You know what we got to get you, doll?' he asked her, leaning back, enjoying himself. He was staring past her and he could see them reflected in the dressing table mirror, could appreciate the back view of her.

Another thing that had surprised Nula was Charlie's rampant sensuality. He seemed to have no sexual borders. *Nothing* was off the table when it came to sex, not with Charlie. Swinging parties? He loved them. Nula was nervous about the whole thing. Strange men, pawing at her? But this was part of the deal, she understood that; part of being Charlie Stone's girl, so she did it.

'You ask someone if they "partake",' he'd told her. 'If they say yes, there's your answer. They like to swing too.'

To Nula, it opened up a whole new world – one she wasn't entirely sure she liked. But really – what did it matter who she had sex with? The only man she had ever *truly* wanted was lost to her. So, what the hell.

'You've got a fantastic arse,' Charlie said. He slid his hands around and grabbed her buttocks. 'A real woman's arse, ain't it?'

'It's the only one I've got,' said Nula, amused. 'So what have you got to get me? I could do with a car.'

'Nah, something much better than that.'

'What then? You going to offer me drugs, Charlie?' He'd told her a long while ago about the business he was in these days. Not that she cared. She wasn't interested in *any* business, straight or otherwise; that was Charlie's domain.

'Hey!' Charlie gave her a stern look. 'What's the golden rule, doll? What do I always tell you?'

'You never, ever, touch the product,' said Nula. 'Cool it, Charlie. I was joking, that's all.'

Charlie was staring at her chest now; it was the one thing that Nula was still self-conscious about, her lack of bounty in that area. The rest of her she was pretty pleased with. *Especially* her arse.

'What you need is a decent-sized pair of tits,' said Charlie. 'Double D or something. I like to see a nice pair bobbing up and down in this position. Your nipples are fine, look at 'em standing up there – ain't they cute? You'd be up for that, wouldn't you, Doll?'

Nula looked at him. What was she, a bloody plastic Barbie doll that he could adjust for his own personal requirements?

'I had a girl once, she had tits down to here,' Charlie went on, holding his hands against her waist. 'Fucking great things they were. Course, she'd been feeding kids so they'd dropped a bit, but jeez they were such a turn-on. You'd like a bigger pair, am I right?'

Nula nodded. Why not?

Charlie smiled happily. 'When we've done *that,* you'll be bloody nigh perfect.'

Nula laughed at that. A stupendous pair of tits to go with the rest of it? Why the hell not. She didn't care if he was a drug dealer or a bank robber or Jack the Ripper. She'd had a shitty poor-girl childhood and life with Charlie was just one treat after another.

'But you're paying,' she said, and bounced harder.

23

Terry found it new and strange, the drugs taxing business. A bit worrying. He knew that sometimes Charlie would get a call from a dealer saying someone had robbed his stash and he'd like Charlie's help getting it back. That was just fine with Charlie. All he had to do was corner the perpetrator and do a bit of intimidation. But what these small-time dealers didn't realize at first was that Charlie Stone had absolutely no intention of giving them their stash back. Once he had it in his hand, it was *his*. He was, after all, lord of the manor. No argument.

'You're gonna make a lot of people very angry,' Terry warned him.

'So?' Charlie asked. 'What'll they do?'

'Kill you seems favourite.'

Charlie was moving upward very fast in this brave new world they'd found themselves in, and it was making Terry uneasy. He had responsibilities now. All this money was fine, but he was a married man. There was Jill, and she was already up the duff with his kid. He was pleased as punch about it, but fearful too, and fear was a thing he'd never really known before Charlie started on the drugs business.

Of course, Charlie was putting down roots as well. After a series of low-rent slappers, he seemed to have settled on the most unlikely one of all. Suddenly he'd married Nula Perkins and whisked her off to the Costas on honeymoon, shocking them all.

Nula gave Terry a mild case of the creeps and Jill actively disliked her.

'She said something really weird to me,' Jill told him one night in bed. 'She said, "Do you partake?" I didn't know what the hell she meant, but I'm guessing it was either sex or drugs or both.'

'Ah, it was probably nothing,' Terry told his wife, but he was thinking of the way Nula was always eyeballing him – even though she was now officially Charlie's girl.

Charlie had told him how hot Nula was, up for anything.

'Hot as fucking *mustard*,' he'd told his mate with a wink.

Terry was thinking about that 'partake' comment. All right, he knew Charlie was wild, but a woman, well, you expected her to have some standards. He counted himself lucky that his Jill was a one-man woman. He was proud of that fact. And she hadn't protested when he'd told her about the business they were involved in.

'We all got to be friends,' he'd told Jill. 'We work together.'

'Yeah, and soon we'll practically *live* together an' all, won't we?' said Jill acidly.

Terry sighed.

Jill had kicked off when she'd been told of Charlie's new plan. A two-up two-down on the manor was no longer good enough for Charlie and Nula Stone. They were looking at big gaffs out Essex way, talking about having one house for the Stones and another nearby for Terry and his tribe. What, live in Charlie's pocket and in close proximity to Nula, who was *already* lording it over her because she was Mrs Charlie Stone? Jill's shrieks of protest could be heard in the next county.

'It won't be attached, doll,' Terry promised, to calm her down. 'It'll be separate, our own little place. No mortgage to bother about, no rent.'

'And all paid for by Charlie Stone.'

'So what? I work for Charlie. You know that. He wants me close.'

Terry knew that Charlie had decided, when the money had really started to roll in, that he needed space and country air. Charlie and Nula had scouted out a huge grand house with a pool. Him and Nula would live in the main house, which was practically a mansion, Terry and Jill in the much older – but still very grand – gatehouse down at the end of the drive. Jill didn't like old buildings and protested about the idea, but she didn't have a leg to stand on. Charlie wanted this, and he wanted Terry right there as his wingman, just like always; so the deal was done.

Since boyhood, that was the way it had always been with them. Charlie forging ahead, Terry following on. But now Terry was full of doubt. The world Charlie was plunging headlong into was darker and more dangerous than anything they'd ever been involved in before. Charlie was self-confident as always, but how much of that confidence was misplaced? Terry thought that Charlie was getting drunk on his own power. Terry missed the old manor. Life had been simple then. Now, Charlie had bought up a cover company, a failing furnishings manufacturer with several factory sites and offices. He'd got it for a song. Then he introduced Terry to a group of shady accountants, bent solicitors, oily bankers – people who'd shake your hand and rob your wallet, all at the same time.

Over dinner at the Dorchester the group explained how Charlie's increasingly complex business finances could be managed, running one entirely legitimate front business – Stone Furnishings Ltd – alongside 'the product'. They made it sound simple, like everyone did it. With port authorities in Charlie's pay, the suits were going to set up a 'special purpose vehicle' in one of the low-intervention jurisdictions.

'Like Switzerland?' asked Charlie.

'Like the Caymans,' said one of the suits. 'The SPV lends money through the Bahamas and Panama in a series of transactions that are impossible to trace until the cash comes into your account, but of course your name doesn't appear on the shares register.'

'Once the money's rolling in,' said another, 'you start to donate to charity, right? I mean, *hugely*. Makes you look squeaky-clean. Then who knows? One day you get the gong.'

Charlie stared. 'The what?'

'The gong. The knighthood. You'll be *Sir* Charlie Stone. And lovely Nula'll be Lady Stone. How'd she like *that?*'

So this was their life now. They dealt with a network of iffy accountants, questionable fund managers and clever lawyers, all of them with expensive habits to feed – women, drugs, gambling. And Terry was caught between the devil and the deep blue sea, with a wife he loved to distraction and a mate he'd had all his life, closer than a brother, but who seemed to be heading in a direction that could spell disaster for the lot of them.

Finally Charlie snapped when Terry kept moaning on about it all.

'Look,' he said to Terry, 'maybe it's best we have a parting of the ways, what about that?'

'No,' said Terry, shocked that Charlie would even think it. 'I don't want that. It's just . . .'

'You don't want it? Good. Then pipe down, all right? All this is doing my fucking head in.'

Terry was silent. Brooding.

'And you don't like the taxing business?' Charlie went on. 'All right then. We'll stop it dead. Stick with the importing. How'd that suit?'

'Yeah. Fine,' said Terry, and felt a bit happier.

But not much.

24

Nula was made up with her new house. She had a whale of a time decorating the place – not that she ever lifted a finger herself, of course. There were kitchen designers and architects and painters and decorators and plumbers all swarming around for months on end, refurbing the place to her exact specifications.

Nula no longer saw her drab parents or her overbearing brother, and in a way that suited her. She'd never been close to her dad and brother, but she did miss Mum. However, she realized that her poorly raised but very sweet mother was a bad fit for this progressive new life of hers. Painful as it was, she was going to have to cut the cord, slice through the ties binding her to that unsatisfactory past, so that she could fully enjoy the new. Yes, they'd all three come to her and Charlie's wedding – Nula had invited them because it would have looked odd if she hadn't – but there the association had ended.

These days Nula was in a different league. She'd found her Mr Right, or Mr Almost Right, anyway. Charlie was a bombastic noisy bastard, and he was plain exasperating most of the time, but he sure knew how to treat a girl.

Now it was party time! Nula became the go-to hostess for all the crims and their ladies. Terry and Jill, down there in the gatehouse at the bottom of the drive, never came to these shindigs.

Nula loved the fact that Jill's place was so old compared to hers. They even had bats up in the loft of the gatehouse, which caused Nula no end of amusement. Jill might have the prize in the shape of Terry, but she *didn't* have the grand house to live in, only a bat-infested ruin. Oh, Terry had summoned the decorators to pretty the place up, and he'd complained to the council about the vermin, but the council weren't interested.

'Up in the loft it stinks to high heaven. Like ammonia, you know?' Terry told Charlie. 'The droppings.'

'Clear 'em out then,' said Charlie.

'I been told they're pipistrelles.'

'Fuck that. They're vermin,' said Charlie. 'Just get rid.'

But Terry didn't. Actually, he didn't mind the bats like Jill did. He liked to stand out in the garden at night, watching them ducking and diving against the starlit sky.

Meanwhile, up at Charlie's it was party central, and the parties were every bit as wild as Jill and Terry suspected they would be. Keys in the dish? It was such a laugh. And spin the bottle. Charlie told Terry that they had two-way mirrored walls in several of the rooms, so people could stand behind it and watch the gymnastics going on. It was *fun*. You never knew who you were going to wind up with, but it was agreed between Charlie and his wife that condoms would *always* be used at these events.

'I don't want some cheap tart showing up at the door claiming to be carrying your kid,' said Nula.

'And I don't want you up the duff to another man,' said Charlie.

'You'd think Terry and Jill would enjoy this,' said Nula, feeling an edge of irritation at what he'd said. Christ, this had all been Charlie's idea anyway. She only took part because he wanted her to.

'What, the parties?'

'Yeah. It might spice things up a bit for them. Put some sparkle back in the bedroom.' Despite all her best intentions, Nula was picturing herself having sex with Terry. She felt herself grow damp at the thought of it.

'Nah,' said Charlie. 'Terry's not the type for it. And neither's Jill. She's a lady, that one.'

Nula felt a deeper stab of annoyance at that. So Jill was a *lady*, was she? And what did that make her?

Not that it mattered. She calmed herself, looked around at all that she had, with Jill down at the bottom of the drive playing poor relation. It wasn't perfect, but it was good enough. Nula was content.

Money wasn't a problem for Charlie, so now they had this party-central house, swish motors in the four-car garage, a brand-new set of double-D tits that she showed off in plunging empire-line gowns whenever they had a party – oh, and they had *lots* of those – and now she'd been to the doc and he'd confirmed that she was pregnant. When she broke the news to Charlie, he was so pleased he nearly cried.

'You little beauty!' he burst out, picking her up and twirling her round.

Nula had to laugh. His child-like enthusiasm was infectious.

'We'll need to get the nursery done up ready,' she told him as he set her back down on her feet.

'No problem, baby doll. You hum it, I'll play it. Get the designers in. Whatever you want, no expense spared.'

Nula nearly purred with satisfaction. No longer was she Nula the loser, shunned at school with the other wannabees, a dull ugly girl from a dull ugly background. Now – at last – she was sought after. Tradespeople kowtowed to her, wanting her money. All Charlie's mob and their wives and girlfriends stepped around her very, very carefully, because she was Charlie's, and if you upset Charlie, you were going to be in the shit.

She understood that Charlie was in a dangerous game. But

Charlie was smart; he had a strong sense of self-preservation. And of course Terry was always there, watching over him.

Nula had to sigh over that. *Yeah, Terry was always there.* Having Terry hovering in the background was like having a beautiful red fox fur or a huge box of Belgian chocolates right where you could see it, but always out of reach. She'd fallen in love or lust or *some* damned thing with Terry on that long-ago night when he'd – out of pity – asked her to dance. Now she had Charlie. Charlie was the bigger prize, she knew that, but . . . she still had that yen for Terry.

Maybe she could make him have a yen for her?

Unlikely. Terry wasn't a player, and Jill was in the way. There was Charlie to consider, too, and Charlie wasn't a man you wanted to upset, not ever. She knew his pride would be hurt if she managed to get Terry into bed. He'd lose it. Kill Terry, possibly kill *her*, too. She'd sounded Jill out, asking her if she 'partook', but Jill had just looked at her with blank dislike. The silly cow hadn't even understood what Nula meant. Now Nula supposed all their fun evenings were going to have to be stopped, anyway. It was a relief, to be honest. She'd only ever done the parties to please Charlie. No way could she, pregnant with Charlie's child, get up to those sort of tricks any more.

Yeah, Charlie was OK and she *loved* being Mrs Charlie Stone. He was over the moon at the baby news. But irritatingly she still had that *itch* for Terry.

Much as she wanted it to, it never seemed to go away.

25

It was a total bloody bore, being pregnant. Nula didn't like it. She was massively sick for the first three months, then feeling sore and bloated and just plain damned *ugly* for the remainder. It reminded her of how she had been, back in the day – the little fat bird. Her mood was foul and Charlie took to staying out much more than he usually did, scarpering into town on business or down to the gatehouse to sit in the saintly Jill's kitchen – Nula had lumbered her huge ungainly form down the drive and found him in there, twice, chattering away to Jill. That had *seriously* annoyed her.

Why couldn't he talk to *her*? She was his wife. All right, she was having a rough time with the baby, but for fuck's sake! *He* was the one who'd made her pregnant, all her discomfort was down to him, didn't he see that?

They had a monumental row about the kitchen gatehouse visits. It was hard on Nula, seeing Jill so pretty, so appealing. Jill's trouble-free pregnancy was way behind her and now she had a beautiful golden-haired little girl called Belle in the crib in the nursery under the gatehouse eaves.

'If you don't like me going down there, doll – and it's stupid, old girl, I'm telling you, there's nothing in it – then I won't do it. OK?' he'd said.

'OK,' agreed Nula, but when she was being driven back to the manor later one night, much later than expected because the car had been held up in traffic, she *saw* Charlie through the gatehouse window, in the kitchen with Jill. And where was Terry? Oh yes. He was out in Turkey, conducting some business or other on Charlie's behalf.

They weren't having their 'parties' now, and she and Charlie weren't having sex much any more.

He was too scared for the baby.

'My boy's in there,' he kept saying, patting her bump. 'Last thing he wants is my old man poking him.'

Charlie had always been very sexual. She was weary of that, truth be told; life with Charlie was stressful. She was always having to jump through hoops, trying to monitor his moods, and she was never sure how high those hoops would be – or if they were ringed with fire. Once, he'd encouraged her to take part in the parties – well they were *orgies* – but really? She knew that deep down he hadn't actually *liked* the fact that she'd joined in. Nula fretted over where Charlie might be getting his jollies these days. Where was his outlet for all that now? Maybe he had a mistress, tucked away out of sight. How would she know? She fretted, right up until the moment when her waters burst, and then she had much bigger and more important things to worry about.

After the hideous pregnancy came the marathon session of the birth. She struggled and sweated and screamed for hours, and where the fuck was Charlie? *Well* out of the way. He had a habit of doing that whenever she needed him, sloping off and vanishing 'on business'. The *fucker*.

Of course the midwife kept telling her it was all fine, baby's heartbeat was fine, everything was just fucking dandy, so why the fuck didn't the kid *come out?* Suddenly, she wanted her mum. But she'd shunned her, ignored her for so long, that she knew that wasn't going to happen.

After eight hours, the baby's heartbeat was faltering. *Then* came the alarming news, as yet another midwife came and prodded at Nula, that the baby had twisted, it was breech, it was *in trouble*.

By that time, Nula was almost too weak to scream any more. Everything hurt. She was drenched in sweat. When they finally called on someone who knew what the fuck they were talking about and she was wheeled down to the operating theatre to have the baby delivered by caesarean, she was so grateful that she didn't even care if she died in the attempt. The mask came down over her face, and she was gone.

Nula awoke to a thin wail. For a moment, she thought it was her, still shrieking and crying and telling those idiots that something was wrong.

But no. She was back on the ward, and a *new* nurse, smiling, was placing the baby in her arms.

'You've got a little girl,' she said.

Nula looked down at the kid, who was squirming lightly. The baby blinked and yawned. Nula touched a hand to the baby's cheek, and one of the little starfish hands grabbed onto her finger and held it. A wave of true love hit Nula then, and she felt emotional tears slide down her face.

'What are you going to call her?' asked the nurse.

'Millicent,' said Nula. It was the name she and Charlie had agreed on. 'Milly,' she amended.

Nula looked around. There were five other mothers in this small maternity ward. At every other bed but hers, there were flowers, big handsome bouquets of roses and lilies. And there were men standing or sitting by each bed – the fathers, all proud and smiling. And where the *fuck* was Charlie?

Away somewhere. On business. Nula sank back onto the pillows, weak and worn out.

She had a daughter.

But . . . she knew Charlie would be put out. She knew how much he'd wanted a son.

Next time, she would have a boy and he would be happy.

It would all work out.

Then her consultant called round at ten the following morning and reeled off lots of medical terms that she didn't even understand.

'Meaning what?' she said when he'd droned on for what felt like hours.

'Nula – this is it, for you. You're not suited to childbirth and it would be too dangerous for you to go through it again,' he said.

More kids? A son to delight her husband?

No.

That wasn't going to happen.

Not any more.

26

When Charlie finally came home and Nula broke the news about no more kids to him, he seemed to take it well. Although he petted his daughter and cooed at her, Nula could sense his disappointment. But more and more he piled his time into the business. Charlie was busy spreading his net wider. Leaving Nula at home with little Milly and with Terry in place to watch over them, Charlie took off again. Ketama this time, high in the Rif mountains of Morocco, to shake hands with a fresh supplier. He didn't listen to Terry's objections about him needing his wingman alongside him.

'You got family too,' Charlie told him, slapping him on the back before he left for the airport. 'So you know. You watch things here. You watch Nula and the kid, I don't trust no one else to do that. Beezer's going to come with me on this trip.'

Terry said: 'I'm sorry as fuck about Nula not being able to have any more, mate.' He was thinking that Beezer would be as much use as a chocolate teapot if things got lairy. Poor idiot didn't know his arse from a hole in the ground.

Charlie shrugged. Only Terry could have mentioned personal matters to him and not got a bunch of fives for his trouble. 'These things happen. It would have been so much better if it'd been a boy. How can a bloody *girl* take over in the business we're in? But what the hell. It is what it is.'

'I'll keep a tight eye on things here,' Terry promised him.

'Stay up at the house, will you? Nula gets nervous at night. It's a big place.'

'Sure. If you want,' said Terry. He didn't think Jill was going to be too delighted with this plan, and he wasn't either, but if that was how Charlie wanted it, then that's how it would be.

Charlie didn't like Morocco, but this was good business, he sussed that straight away. Cannabis crops supported more than a million families up in the mountains. They called it *kif* and it was their saviour in a land far too harsh for growing olives or wheat.

'Two thousand tonnes of good *kif* brings the country two billion a year on the black market,' Saddam, his contact, told him.

Charlie was stunned by the sheer scale of it. Everywhere you looked, as far as the eye could see, were cannabis plantations. He haggled with Saddam over a good price, and wrangled over the difficulties of exporting their product while at lunch in a five-star Tangiers hotel.

Saddam said transport would be no problem. 'We can stash the *kif* in the lorries coming out of some of our friendly warehouses.'

'Ain't that risky?'

'Look,' said Saddam with a broad, gold-toothed grin. 'It is safe, my friend, I promise you. We load the trucks with perishables. Fresh flowers. Oranges. Lemons. Then they are sealed shut with Transport Internationale Routiere bonds so they get through Customs checkpoints easily.'

'Yeah?' Charlie still wasn't sure. He was thinking that it couldn't be *that* easy, could it? And he was beginning to mistrust this smiling little bastard.

'OK,' said Saddam patiently. 'Another route? We fly the product straight from the Rif to the Spanish provinces. Quiet places, small airfields. Easy.'

Although it all sounded tempting, Charlie was still not

convinced. Morocco gave him a bad feeling. He thought the souks and medinas were full of thieves and cutthroats and he couldn't go into raptures about the beauty of the mountains. He was there to do business, that was all, not to go on the ruddy camel rides that dopey Beezer suggested. *Fuck* the camels. It wasn't very long before he was regretting his rash plan to leave Terry at home and take Beezer out into the Moroccan wilds with him. Fucking place this was. It was hot and dry and somehow *alien*. But Saddam taught Charlie a lot about *kif*. He witnessed the whole process from the reaping, the pressing, the crushing and the oil-making.

After the luxury of the Tangiers hotel, their trip out to Saddam's home village was a shock. Him and his family of nervous, cowering women made Charlie and Beezer welcome. The food was foul. Sheep's heads and stuff like that, *revolting* things. After they'd finally agreed a deal for a couple of tonnes, Charlie fell into a troubled sleep in Saddam's fly-ridden, charmless little hut of a house, which was set in the middle of a slum area outside Ketama. Charlie couldn't believe that people really lived like this, pissing in the gutters, dodging swarms of flesh-eating bugs and eating crap. He was uneasy about his poor surroundings. Worried about the way these people looked at him. He was carrying a large amount of money to seal the deal, and Saddam was looking less and less like the civilized, trustworthy acquaintance Charlie'd first met in London's Mayfair, and more like a lowlife robbing bastard who would happily turn him over and keep the product for himself.

At ten o'clock in the evening, Charlie gave in to his jittery feelings. He roused Beezer, who could sleep on a damned clothesline, the idiot, and was already snoring away peacefully while Charlie's nerves were jangling at every slight sound he heard. Together they legged it out of the village and to a hotel up the road that refused locals entry. Then Charlie felt safe. He started chatting to the staff in the hotel about his contact, and the word was that Saddam was a bad lot and had probably been planning to rob Charlie and his companion and murder them in the night, so keeping both Charlie's money and peddling the hashish on to the next unwary traveller.

'Oh really?' said Charlie, fuming.

At four next morning, Charlie and Beezer returned to Saddam's place and grabbed the thieving bastard. He cried and pleaded his innocence as Charlie told him all he'd heard.

'No! I swear it's not true!'

'Fucking *liar.*'

Together Charlie and Beezer dragged him out from the village, into the dunes. Beezer knocked Saddam down and then Charlie fell on him and grabbed his throat. Inch by inch, the light vanished from Saddam's eyes as Charlie throttled him. Finally, he was still.

Charlie stood up, still quivering with fury.

'Cunt!' he swore and kicked the corpse.

They hid the body away, burying it deep in the sands. At nine o'clock that same morning, Charlie contacted one of the tribal elders Saddam had introduced him to, and he got his deal made. He paid up, and a taster pack of two hundred and fifty kilogrammes of prime *kif* was on its way back to England. Feeling glad to be still in one piece, Charlie gave Beezer the nod and they both headed home.

27

Nula was getting used to Charlie jetting off all over the world. She actually rather enjoyed his absence, it was peaceful. Charlie was like a whirlwind around the house; so noisy, so full of himself. While he was out in Morocco, Terry was in the big house with her, having stayed overnight at Charlie's request.

She came down to breakfast while the au pair – of *course* she had an au pair – saw to baby Milly, and there he was in white shirt and well-worn jeans, his sleeves rolled up to the elbow showing his muscular forearms fuzzed so fetchingly with blond hair.

'Morning, Nula,' he said. 'You sleep well?'

'Yeah. Fine, thanks.' She always slept well when Charlie was away, and she never had to get up in the night with the baby, she let the au pair do that. Milly's birth had kicked the crap out of her, but she was feeling much better now. It was going to be her last experience of all that and she *knew* Charlie was devastated. He did care for his daughter Milly but he *craved* a son. Terry would probably have a son one of these days. Jill – the sainted beautiful Jill – would give him one, without any effort at all. But it was beyond Nula, she couldn't deliver more children, she was a rotten failure as a woman, and that ate at her, dug deep into her insecurities.

'Coffee?' Terry asked.

'Thanks.'

Terry poured her out a mug. 'Sugar? Milk?'

Nula shook her head. She was working herself up to something bold, something *major,* and now was the time to do it. Charlie was due back tomorrow. She was over the birth now, she felt fine. Fully functioning. Figure back to normal. Tits still looking good.

She'd prepared for this, but now she felt nervous.

Fortune favours the brave, she thought. Didn't they say that?

But now the moment had come, she wondered if she could go through with it. Yes, she'd planned this. She was wearing her sky-blue silk robe and she'd done her make-up, styled her hair. She'd checked herself out in the dressing room mirror before she'd come downstairs. She'd opened up the gap over her now quite spectacular breasts – she hadn't breastfed Milly for an instant longer than completely necessary, no bloody way – then she'd fluffed up her hair, smiled at herself in the mirror. She looked good. Didn't she?

'Terry,' she said, taking a sip of coffee.

'Hm?' He glanced up from the paper and his gorgeous green eyes met hers.

'I'm going to say something to you. Just once. And if you don't like the sound of it, that's fine. If you do like it, that's fine too and we'll go ahead. But we won't talk about it, ever again. It'll be forgotten.'

He was frowning at her. God, he was handsome. Charlie was not bad looking, but he was dark and short. Terry by contrast was tall as a Greek god. For years Nula had been fantasizing about him. Oh, her and Charlie had messed about with some of their other 'friends'. But Terry was Charlie's closest buddy, in a separate league to all those others.

She remembered her arsehole of a brother saying that Terry had only taken pity on her that long-ago night in the dance hall. Maybe he had; but she was so changed now.

'What I have to say is this,' said Nula briskly. 'Look. I've fancied you just about forever. So tonight, let's sleep together. No strings, no commitment, it need never happen again. Just this once, OK? What do you say?'

Terry said nothing. The silence was thick in the kitchen all of a sudden, stifling. Nula could feel her face burning, could hear her heart racing in her chest. Why didn't he speak?

Then Terry pushed his chair back and stood up, yanking his jacket from the back of it and slipping it on. He was breathing hard and when he looked at her his face was twisted with disgust.

'What the fuck are you talking about?' he said tightly. 'Charlie's my best mate. You're supposed to be his *wife*. I can't believe you'd say something like that.'

Nula stood up too, bile prickling in her gullet as anxiety tore at her. She'd misjudged things. Terry being polite to her as Mrs Charlie Stone didn't translate into Terry fucking her. She could see that now. Terry, usually so even-tempered, looked *furious*. She tried a smile, a shrug, although inside she felt sick with humiliation.

'As I said,' she told him, 'no problem. I've asked, you've said no. That's good enough for me.'

But it *wasn't* good enough. Once again she felt like the awkward one, the fat big-nosed flat-chested cow in the communal changing rooms at school.

Nula the loser.

She could still hear the girls chanting that, laughing at her in her vest when they were all in starter bras. All the good-looking boys at school had been beyond her, *way* out of her league. Now, with Terry, nothing had changed. She was *still* the same girl. The same *loser*.

'I'm going to check the grounds,' he said, then went to the kitchen door.

Everything was in lockdown these days. With the drugs game

came the need for ever-increasing security. There were gates. Alarms. Heavy-looking blokes everywhere. Thinking of all that, Nula realized that she hadn't felt truly *safe* in a long, long time. Sometimes she really wished they could step the whole thing back a gear. Expand the legit cover business, the furniture factories, and ditch the drug stuff. But this was Charlie. There was no chance of that ever happening, not while he drew breath.

Suddenly Terry turned back and stabbed a finger in her direction. 'We won't talk about this again.'

Then a horrible thought occurred to Nula. 'You won't tell Charlie?' she said faintly. Now she *really* felt sick. Charlie would go ballistic, and that was a terrifying thought. Charlie in a rage was not a pretty sight.

Oh Christ, I got this wrong . . .

'Tell him what? That he's married to a cheating cow? I don't know, Nula. I really don't know.'

Then he was out of the door and gone.

28

Charlie realized he'd been lucky to get out of Morocco with his life. But now – thankfully – he had a new link made out there, with a more trustworthy connection, and shipments were coming into docks and airports with no trouble and the money was flowing freely from that direction at last.

Now, with the Moroccan link set up, Charlie was looking to expand his manor even further. A Turkish deal soon followed; his manor was building up nicely. But he wasn't done yet. He felt ready to go on and conquer the world. Colombia next. The big cartels. Maybe the Matias crew, the biggest of all. They were already sniffing around, looking for established firms to handle the British end of their operations.

'Sky's the limit,' he told Nula when he eventually came home. Then he looked at her. She was pale, her mouth set in a grim line. 'You OK, babe?'

'I'm fine,' said Nula, but she wasn't.

The truth was, Terry's rejection had scorched her soul and she had been on tenterhooks ever since, waiting for him to tell Charlie, waiting for the whole thing to blow up in her face. Up to that point, she hadn't realized how desperately she'd wanted him. Now, she knew. And now *he* knew, too. It was humiliating, being knocked back hard like that. It had rekindled all those feelings of failure and embarrassment she thought she'd left far behind her in her former life on the old manor. Now she was finding it nearly impossible to be civil to Terry, or Jill. She'd felt so bad that she'd gone to the doctor's and he had given her some nerve pills when she broke down on him in the surgery.

'Ah, you missed me, did you, doll?' asked Charlie, grinning, pulling her in for a hug.

'I told you,' said Nula, shrugging him off. 'I'm fine.'

'Bloody hell! Time of the month, is it?' He rolled his eyes.

Nula was about to say something cutting when the au pair came in with little Milly. Charlie was instantly all smiles, embracing his daughter.

'Come to Dada,' he said, scooping her up, throwing her into the air. He produced a small stuffed camel from inside his coat and Milly grabbed at it, smiling. 'Dad's been away on business. Mummy missed me, did you miss me?'

Nula watched them together. Poor plain little Milly was the spit of her when *she'd* been a little girl. The kid was delighted with her father's return and with the gift. Charlie always brought Milly back little treasures like this; flamenco dolls from Spain, even a voodoo doll from Haiti, which gave Nula the creeps: she'd burned that. She didn't like the thought of the sinister thing sitting on a shelf in her daughter's room. After half an hour, the au pair took the little girl away upstairs and Nula and Charlie were alone again.

'You know what I reckon?' he said.

Nula shook her head. Maybe one of these days Terry would tell him what she'd proposed during his Morocco trip. And on that day, she was going to be in a shitload of trouble. Again, there was that feeling of sickness, of things spiralling out of her control, of the previously solid earth moving, swaying under her feet. The doctor had told her to join a club, do something *physical*. She hated the idea of that. She wasn't sporty, or particularly sociable. He'd suggested she keep a journal, to express her feelings. She'd started doing that, pencilling in how she felt day by day, all that was happening around her.

'I reckon you're broody. All that stuff after you had Milly, realizing you couldn't have any more kids, I think it hit you hard,' said Charlie.

'It hit you, too,' Nula pointed out.

'Yeah. I can't lie, it did. But you know what? I've had an idea.'

'Oh?'

'I think we should adopt. What do you reckon?'

Nula looked at him. Christ, he was such a piece of work! Charlie Stone thought that *anything* could be overcome. Even a wife who couldn't pop out sprogs any more.

Adoption? It wasn't something she'd considered. But if Charlie wanted more and this was the way to further secure her position – just in case Terry ever did spill the beans – then maybe it wasn't a bad idea.

'We'll do it proper. A government adoption agency. It'll all be kosher, I promise you,' Charlie told her.

'Yeah,' she said. 'Why not?'

And Charlie hugged her and kissed her, beaming with pleasure.

'A little boy this time, yeah?' he said.

'OK,' said Nula.

29

That same day, after Charlie had driven off to town, Nula went looking for Terry out by the garages. He was often there, tinkering with the cars. He loved engines; should have been a mechanic. Her hunch proved right: he was under the bonnet of an old Alfa Romeo. When Nula approached he straightened up, his face setting in stern lines as he wiped his oily hands on a rag.

'All right?' he said.

'You didn't tell him then,' said Nula, moving closer.

Terry stared at her. 'No. I didn't.'

'Why?' Maybe he was protecting her; she liked the idea of that.

'Because it would hurt him. And I don't want that,' said Terry.

Nula felt deflated. Hurt. So he'd been thinking of protecting *Charlie;* not her. She took another step closer. They were alone under cover in the garage; no one was about around here today.

'Neither of us want that,' said Nula, watching him. She moved closer still. She was standing right beside him now. She could feel the heat coming off his body. She could smell the scent of his aftershave and the oil on his hands. The thought of those hands on her . . . !

Without even thinking of what she was doing, Nula reached up and kissed him. She couldn't help it. Her tongue licked his lips and nudged them open. Her hand went first to his muscular chest and then slipped down, down, until she found the length of his cock under the worn denim of his jeans. Her fingers groped lower, cupping his balls. Nula moaned, feeling heat rush through her, knowing – oh *shit* – that this for her was serious. That she actually *loved* him, that she always had. It wasn't just the pull of sex. Terry was the better of the two men. Unlike Charlie, he did have some finer feelings.

But as quickly as she had kissed him, touched him, Terry stepped back, shoving her away.

'What the *fuck*?' he burst out, wiping his mouth.

'Sorry, sorry, I . . .' Nula was holding her hands up, trying to apologize. In the heat of the moment, she'd done what she'd always wanted to do.

Terry looked disgusted. 'What the hell d'you think you're doing?'

Nula dragged her hands through her hair. She was blushing with shame. He'd knocked her back last time, but this time was worse.

'You won't tell him?' she asked urgently. 'I'm sorry, OK? I didn't mean to do that.'

Terry's face was red with rage. 'Piss off, Nula,' he spat out. 'Just piss off out of it before I do something I bloody well shouldn't, all right?'

Nula didn't argue. Trembling with embarrassment and hurt, she left the garage and went back up to the house.

30

'What's up with you, honey?' Jill asked Terry while they sat in the kitchen over breakfast. He'd been quiet the last few days, not himself. He'd changed somehow. That worried her, set her on edge. Their lovely little daughter, five-year-old Belle, was zooming up and down the hallway in the toy pedal car she had nearly outgrown now, blonde hair flying, making honking noises, giving them grinning flashes as she zipped past the open door.

Jill watched her daughter with proud exasperation. Belle was a spectacular child in every way. Super-bright and pretty. Milly, who had quickly become Belle's little playmate, was running right there alongside her, laughing and yelling encouragement. Milly – and this was surprising, given that she had come from the loins of Charlie Stone – was a sweet little thing, much quieter than Belle, no trouble at all. Jill watched as Belle screeched to a halt and let Milly clamber into the driver's seat; then she pushed her little friend along to pick up speed.

Terry took a sip of coffee. 'Nothing's wrong,' he said to his wife.

'Look, Daddy, look!' shouted Belle as both girls went shooting past their eyeline once again.

'That's great, darlin',' said Terry absently to his daughter.

Jill looked at him, her big handsome husband. So solid, so dependable. Their rise through poverty to comfort to luxury had been almost too fast for any proper adjustment to be made. For quite a while she had felt that Terry was growing uneasy. Well, damn it. She was too. She was still a poor kid at heart, just like

Terry was. They had risen on the tail of Charlie Stone's bright comet, shooting heavenwards in his wake. It made Jill nervous.

For a long while, she'd been ignoring the hidden business that Charlie Stone had dragged them all into. But when Terry had started talking about security measures – passwords, codes for hide and codes for run – her nerves had turned to real fear. She knew that under the cover of importing parts and manufacturing furniture for big retailers, Charlie Stone was feeding a nation's appetite for drugs and making a fat profit doing it. But now they were in the thick of it all, she found it worrying. Shocking. And she'd had another shock, a terrible one, that she had never even told Terry about.

She *couldn't* tell him.

God, what had they all come to?

They were profiting from a sick, horrible trade that caused misery and poverty and death. She doubted she'd ever get used to it. Come what may, she was determined that Belle was never, ever going to know about it, never going to be touched by it. *Never.* And Terry agreed with that. Their innocent daughter would stay that way: innocent. Untouched by all this filth. She knew that Nula and Charlie felt the same way about Milly. The girls would be kept out of it all; they would be protected.

'What's up with you?' Jill asked him. 'Come on, babes, talk to me.'

Terry's eyes flickered upward and met his wife's enquiring gaze.

'It's nothing,' he said.

'Well it's *something*. You're not right.'

'Nula,' he said with a shrug. 'She came on to me when I was in the garage. It's been playing on my mind.'

Jill's mouth dropped open. 'She did what?'

'It isn't the first time. You know when Charlie was over in

Morocco on business with Beezer? He left me there in charge of the big house. *That* was the first time.'

Jill remembered, all too well. They'd had a row about it. *Jill* was here on her own in the gatehouse, but Queen Nula up there in that fucking mansion needed Terry close up and personal to protect her.

Don't I need protecting too? Jill had raged at him.

She knew she did. Why couldn't Terry see that? Why had he *never* seen it, and left her exposed to danger?

Now, this. Didn't that bitch up there have enough? She had the better house, she didn't have this older place, nice as it was, with a fucking loft still full of bats. She had Charlie Stone, who said to Terry jump and Terry just asked how high. That irritated Jill to death.

'And . . . what did she say? The first time?' she asked, shocked.

'She said we could sleep together that night, and it'd be never mentioned again. No strings, no nothing. Charlie would never know. *You* would never know. And this time? She was a bit more direct.'

Jill was stunned. Bloody Nula, making a move on *her* husband. The sheer fucking *nerve* of the woman. God curse those bloody Stones, they wanted it *all*.

'It was nothing. I'm only telling you now because I didn't want you hearing about it from anyone else. From Nula herself, maybe, claiming that something happened when it didn't.'

Jill picked up her mug and drained it. She rose, walked over to the dishwasher, put the mug inside, then she stayed at the sink and stood there, leaning both hands on it.

'And didn't it?' she said faintly. Once, Nula had been a plain, unattractive girl, but she'd had the work done to turn her into a good-looking woman. Jill knew that Nula had always hated her and Jill had always sensed the reason why. It was because of

Terry. Jill had him; Nula didn't. And now the bitch had come right out with it. She wanted Terry for herself.

Those fucking *Stones*.

'What?' Terry stood up, came over to the sink and wrapped his arms around his wife's waist from behind, pressing the whole length of his body against the back of hers.

'Did nothing happen, Terry? Really?' said Jill in a choked voice. Knowing what she knew about the Stones and their sexual habits, she was ready to take a hammer blow when he told her the truth, confessed that he'd done it with that loose-living *cow*.

'No! Come on. Why d'you think I'm telling you this? I didn't have to, did I, you daft mare. I wanted you to hear it from me. Nothing happened. Nothing ever could. You're my wife.' He planted a kiss on her neck. 'I've never wanted anyone else. You know that.'

Jill leaned back against Terry's hard body. She loved him so much. But Nula worried her. Nula had influence with Charlie. And Charlie frightened Jill, very much.

31

Charlie was learning that his promise to Nula about the adoption would be a difficult one to keep. They seemed to have been sitting in offices, answering questions about his business and their social life for bloody years, and he came out of every meeting in a thunderous mood. His business was *his* business. He didn't like these government types, these official prats, taking out a microscope and looking in. It was dodgy, bearing in mind the business he was *really* in. But he'd promised Nula, so he forged on with it even though he was unhappy with the deal and increasingly thinking he should never have mentioned the possibility of adoption.

'It'll be worth it, honey,' Nula always told him after the meetings, patting his arm, knowing how much he hated this sort of thing.

'Yeah,' said Charlie, and it would, he *knew* it would, if it got him a son to carry on his name. He tried not to resent poor Nula over her failure to bear another child, because it wasn't the poor bitch's fault, she couldn't help it.

He knew Nula got depressed sometimes and he found that hard to deal with. He was strictly of the 'pull yourself together' school of thought. He had no patience with Nula when she was in one of her low moods, crying over nothing. He'd seen her scratching away in those damned notebooks that were supposed to be therapy for her and he'd hit the roof.

'You ain't mentioning my business in there are you?' he'd yelled.

She'd sworn she wasn't.

'It's just how I feel about things. Day-to-day things. That's all,' she'd told him.

Meanwhile, there was trade to attend to. The London-based Stones and a dozen other 'families' based in London, Liverpool, Newcastle and Glasgow had met and formed an alliance as powerful as the Mafia's; inch by inch they'd seized control of the whole country's drug trade. Charlie was going from strength to strength, getting increasingly distant from the street life he'd once known. He was a top man, bringing in the gear, then it was broken up and sold on to the ten-kilo men. They then sold it on to the one-kilo men, who distributed it to their network of dealers. The Matias crew had come over from Colombia. Charlie and his associates met with them at the Dorchester, wined and dined them; it was going good.

All in all, Charlie was pleased with progress. But . . . what did it all mean, if he was married to a miserable depressed cow who couldn't have any more kids, if he had no *son* to pass the whole thing on to?

He'd got in the habit of intercepting the post so that Nula couldn't see what was coming in. One, because anything and everything upset her. Two, because he was sure the adoption agency was going to give them the thumbs down, and of course then she'd be gutted and would plunge into more gloomy crying if he didn't get there first and somehow soften the blow. The sparky, light-hearted sexed-up party girl of yesteryear was long gone, it seemed.

As time passed, Charlie felt that he would be almost relieved if the adoption idea didn't work out. No more ups and downs, no more tiptoeing around his moody mare of a wife. No more government toadies nosying around in his furniture-manufacturing business. It made him sweat, operating this close to the wire, he had a lot to lose.

Finally he became convinced that the whole idea was a bad one. He didn't tell Nula. Didn't know *how* to, really. Then he got a letter from the agency asking more questions about his firm, asking to arrange a visit to his premises. Sure, he *had* legitimate business premises, damned sure he did, six factories churning out three-piece suites for the big retailers, but the *real* gravy went on at the separate offices that serviced the paperwork for the furniture business. There was the background business where the drugs were cut and packaged and shipped out. He couldn't have government types sniffing around. It was no good.

At last his overstretched patience snapped and he phoned them.

'Look, we've decided not to go ahead. It's too stressful for my wife. Too upsetting. Call it off.'

'Well, if you're sure . . .'

'Yeah, I'm sure. Forget it. We don't want to go on with it. Cancel our application, OK?'

'If you could put it in writing to us . . .'

'I will,' he said, and slapped the phone down.

He scribbled the note then and there, and went straight out and posted it. So it was done. But how to tell Nula? Well, he'd have to. Somehow. Or . . . maybe make up something, get one of their boys to forge an official-looking letter saying their application had been turned down. That was favourite. He'd get something cobbled together, and that would shut her up. There'd be no son, and he was sick about that, sad and sorry, but he couldn't take any more of this delving into his business dealings. It was too dangerous.

'We haven't heard from the adoption place recently,' said Nula over breakfast one morning.

'Ah, you know how it is with these official things. They're quick enough with the tax bills, but when *you* want anything? You can fucking well stew,' said Charlie, pushing his empty plate to one side, then draining his coffee cup and slipping on his coat. 'I'm off, doll. See you later.'

32

Charlie had arranged to pick Terry up at one of the houses he kept as boltholes in the old manor, take him along for a meet with one of the ten-kilo guys. As Charlie drove, he told Terry about the adopting dilemma, just as he told Terry about everything. Well, *nearly* everything. Some things were a bit too near the knuckle for open discussion.

Like – for instance, and he felt really bad about it – the fact that he'd once fucked Terry's old lady Jill, years back. He wished he *could* talk to Terry about that, apologize, say that it had been a one-off, which it had, but Terry was his mate and he . . . nah, he wouldn't understand. No way, no chance. Now Charlie regretted that he had been weak, that he'd given in to the impulse.

He'd been down in the gatehouse kitchen with Jill and Terry had been away somewhere, on drugs business. Jill had made him a cup of tea and they'd talked. Jesus, she was pretty. And she was uncomplicated, *steady* – unlike Nula. Jill had always seemed wary of him, a bit nervous. He sort of liked that. He liked her clear blue eyes and her blonde hair and he had often wondered how she'd look naked.

Charlie was annoyed that Terry had always been such a cunt over their sex parties. If Terry and Jill had joined in, they would have enjoyed it, he knew they would. He'd invited Terry time and again, but Terry had always refused.

Standing there in Jill's kitchen when *it* happened, Charlie knew damned well that his invites to Terry had not so much been to include his mate in the fun, but to have a crack at his mate's missus.

And why not?

After all, Charlie reasoned to himself, he *kept* her, didn't he? Her and her husband? It was *him* who paid for the roof over their heads, *he* was the boss here, wasn't he?

Yes. He fucking well was.

He remembered it so well. Felt bad about it. Of course he did. But turned on by it too. He'd put his cup down, crossed the kitchen. Her eyes had flared with fear as he moved, and he liked that, he *loved* it when people when scared of him. Then he'd pulled her into his arms. She'd put her fists against his chest, but he was far too strong for her.

'Please,' she said, turning her head away.

'Come on,' he'd said, and kissed her.

'No.'

'Come on,' he said against her mouth. Then he put the boot *right* in. 'Or I'll tell Terry you started it.'

Her eyes widened. 'He wouldn't . . .'

'Don't kid yourself. He'd believe me. Me, his mate since we first started crawling, or some woman who's come late on the scene? No contest. I could tell him the sun was pulled up on a fucking rope and he'd believe me.'

'No . . .' It was a plea.

'Yes. Now come on.'

She'd been *delicious*. She'd cried a bit, but what choice did she have? She let him do the deed.

And what the hell, what was her problem? All cats were grey in the dark and a cock was a cock. It wasn't as if she was a virgin or anything.

He had to keep it to himself. He knew Jill would, too. Neither of them would want to distress Terry or cause him pain, upset the bloody applecart.

'So you've cancelled the adoption plans,' said Terry.

'Yeah,' said Charlie, snapping back to the here and now.

'Probably for the best.'

'I know that.'

'But Nula don't know.'

'Nah.'

'She'll be pissed when she finds out,' warned Terry.

'I know that too.'

33

They parked up outside the pub where they were meeting their contact, and went in through a dark, seedy little bar and from there to the back room.

'Charlie!' Landon Bloom greeted him with a hug. He was a big man, fat around the middle, florid of face but sharp of eye. 'Good to see you.'

Then he shook Terry's hand. They sat down. Landon was one of the ten-kilo blokes, a local gang boss, and he was doing well out of the drugs trade. He also ran door contracts and protection rackets on the side, and although he lived in this dingy little hole and was sitting there in a dog-eared shirt, torn cardigan, shiny trousers and worn brogues, he was worth millions.

'So what's the problem then, Landon?' asked Charlie, when they had addressed the civilities, asked about each other's wives and kids. He felt they'd skirted the issue long enough. 'Trouble?'

'Druggie bastard shot one of my boys,' said Landon.

'I'm sorry to hear that. You sorting it?'

'It's done. Last seen floating down the river, if you get my meaning. His girlfriend's still squatting in the house, shouting the odds, but I thought it could be a good place for a stash once we've booted the cow out the door. However, Mr Stone, I wanted your approval before I made the final decision on it.'

Charlie nodded. He appreciated the respect Landon was paying him. Landon was all right.

'Well, let's get over there and take a look,' said Charlie.

Landon drove them over to Barking and pulled up outside a beaten-down row of Victorian terrace houses. The front gardens were thick with grass and weeds. Stray roses poked through the undergrowth, long neglected. Old chairs and mattresses were slung out on the pavement. To Charlie it was home; his manor. You could smell piss on every corner, and hot oil from the chip shops. Suddenly, he missed it. Wanted to be back here day-to-day, not out in the sticks. He was bored and he was actually wondering if he could pep things up by revisiting the Jill thing, maybe go and give her another good stiff talking to. He'd love that. He got hard even thinking about it. But . . . shit, he couldn't do that to Terry again, could he? And anyway – Jill had young Belle under her feet now, and you couldn't get a good, satisfying poke at the mother over the kitchen sink with a kid wandering about the place, now could you?

Landon pushed open the unlocked door and shouted out: 'Hello?'

There was no answer. Inside, the walls were black with mould, the lino under their feet was sticky with muck. They walked along the hallway to a kitchen where the sink was brown with tea stains and . . .

'Christ!' said Terry, slapping a hand over his nose.

Meat flies buzzed around a small object in the middle of the kitchen floor. The smell hit Charlie and Landon too, and they covered their faces. The woman was curled up as if asleep, but they could see she wasn't going to wake up this side of eternity. She was wearing a mint-green T-shirt and black shorts. Her skin was mottled purple and white where the blood had settled after death. Her arms were criss-crossed with needle tracks. Beside her on the floor was a used syringe.

'Shit,' said Landon.

'Fuck,' said Terry.

'Well she won't be giving anybody trouble any more,' said Charlie.

'We'll get her moved out tonight,' said Landon.

Charlie was looking around. As a place to store a haul, it might do. He went to the kitchen door, then back out into the hallway. There was a sound, right by his ear. He stopped. Tensed. Opened the door under the stairs. Then he stepped back in surprise. There was a small boy in there, looking out at him with wide pale grey eyes.

The boy didn't move, didn't blink. He must have heard the commotion and hidden himself away. That whore in there, that disgusting junkie who'd topped herself, was probably the kid's mother. Charlie stooped down, putting himself on the boy's eye level.

'Hello,' said Charlie.

'Who are you talking—' asked Terry, coming out into the hall at the sound of Charlie's voice. 'God Almighty,' said Terry, seeing the kid crouched in there.

Now Landon came out too. The kid backed away further. Charlie was staring at the boy, his mind whirling. He was thinking that this was one of those moments when the good angels came and changed your life for you. It had happened to him once before, after Beezer's fortuitous spell in jail. And here it was, happening again. Was he a lucky bastard, or what? Well of course he was. He was Charlie Stone. King of the world!

'It's all right, mate,' Charlie said gently to the boy.

He was running it all through his head. He'd had to bin the legal adoption, but here was another, easier route for him to take, and he was going to grab it. Nula need never, ever know a thing.

'Don't be afraid,' he said.

He held out his hand and the boy hesitated for only a second. Then he took it.

'What's your name, kid?' asked Charlie.

The boy blinked. 'Harlan,' he said.

34

When the woman from the adoption agency rang and said they'd found a child who might be suitable for the Stones, Nula was relieved. No more hassle, no more *pressure,* but a son – at last! – to please Charlie. Along with Milly, it would make their family complete.

'There are a few more questions I have to ask,' said the woman on the phone. 'I've just taken over from Mrs Mulville, she's left the agency now, so I'm familiarizing myself with her casework at present.'

'Anything,' said Nula, knowing that this whole thing was giving Charlie a bad case of the shits, but he was doing it for them both, and she was touched by that.

'Well, Mrs Stone, Harlan's a delightful boy. Quiet, pleasant. I'll bring him for a visit, if we could finalize a time next week . . . ?'

'Yeah, sure,' said Nula. She'd been feeling so down, so deep in depression that the doc had given her some stronger pills, but this cheered her. Charlie would be home soon, she couldn't wait to tell him. She put the phone down and went to fetch her journal, to write up the good news.

'She buy it?' asked Charlie as Candice put the phone down.

'Yeah,' said Candice, whose boyfriend was one of Landon's one-kilo boys. She was rough as arseholes but she could put on this very nice Home Counties telephone voice, so Charlie had selected her to play agency lady on the phone to Nula, and Nula had swallowed it whole.

'Good,' said Charlie, and bunged her a twenty. 'No one ever hears about this, though, OK?'

'Of course not, Mr Stone,' said Candice, grabbing the cash and dreaming of her next hit. She looked at the boy, sitting quietly at the table in her kitchen. 'He'll need cleaning up. He's fucking filthy.'

'You can see to that, right?' Charlie peeled off more notes. 'I'll get some paperwork done, make it look good and official, you'll clean him up, get him some new togs, and then next week you'll visit with the kid, Nula will fall in love with him, and we're sorted. Bit more chat on the blower, couple more forms to fill in, then couple of weeks after that, the kid arrives at the house – with you – and he stays for good. Yeah?'

Candice looked dubious for a moment, so Charlie peeled off yet more notes. Personally, Candice thought the kid was a bit, well, *odd*, but this was Charlie Stone, and he was paying, and whatever Charlie Stone wanted, he got. You didn't question it. If you did, you'd be sorry.

'Yeah, that'll work,' agreed Candice, looking at the money.

'It better.' Charlie's button-bright brown eyes went from friendly to threatening in an instant. 'This will work. And you'll keep shtum.'

'Yeah, Mr Stone. I will.'

'Or I could get angry.'

'I won't breathe a word.'

35

The boy Nula and Charlie adopted was a handsome seven-year-old with honey-coloured hair, a long pale face, an unsmiling mouth and serious light grey eyes. Charlie was delighted with him. Little Milly was affronted; her dad was suddenly lavishing nearly all his attention on this interloper. But Milly had a consolation prize: of a similar age and living in such close proximity to Belle Barton, the two girls had become firm friends, so Milly wasn't too badly put out about Harlan's arrival in the Stone household.

Talk about the odd couple, Nula thought whenever she saw Milly and Belle playing in the grounds together. Milly, plain as a pikestaff, always shy and too eager to please, and pretty little Belle who could afford to be cool. Nula knew it was unkind to think that way, but she'd had her own struggles with her looks and she could see that poor Milly was going the same way. Belle wouldn't, though. She noticed that although Harlan might ignore his new 'sister' most of the time, little Belle fascinated him. Nula remembered him coming into the house for the first time, looking around, taking it all in, absorbing it almost greedily. Then picking out a tiny room to be his alone. Private. Keep out. He had that same faintly obsessive attitude around Belle. Whenever she was near, Harlan watched her with total attention, like a cat might watch a bird. If she spoke to anyone else, to Milly, or little Nige Pope from school, with his shock of red hair, who clearly adored her, Harlan always elbowed his way into the conversation. He was sort of *possessive* about her.

Nula felt bitter about Belle. Trust bloody Jill to have such a little charmer. Already Belle was showing signs of easy sociability. She had a wide circle of friends. She spent hours down the riding stables, hacking out on the ponies, helping with mucking out. Although Belle always encouraged Milly to join in, Milly preferred to sit at home, reading books; she was scared of horses. And she hated meeting new people. She was scared of every bloody thing, it seemed to Nula. In that, Nula realized – painfully – Milly was very much her mother's daughter.

'We ought to have a party for the kids,' said Charlie.

They'd settled Harlan into the nearest school, the same one Belle and Milly went to, and he seemed to be doing OK. He wasn't chatty, or popular, but he was doing fine.

Nula thought about it. Charlie was cock-a-hoop over his new son. He'd set up what he laughingly called a 'petting' zoo down on the far side of the orchard and was busy stocking it with reptiles, frogs, all the stuff that he and Harlan took a keen interest in, all the stuff that turned Nula's stomach. What the fuck was the point of having a 'petting zoo' full of things you were scared to pet? All through the summer there was hammering, cranes in the garden, men in hard hats working on the newly erected building, men digging in cables to connect the house phone to the cubbyhole in the feed room down there so that Charlie never missed a call. Then – at last – it was finished.

'We've got the zoo up and running now, we can get Harlan to cut the ribbon on the day, the kids'll love it,' said Charlie.

So it was arranged. Overwhelmed by the idea of organizing it herself, Nula hired in a party planner and caterers. They made a cake in the shape of a yellow-and-green boa constrictor, laid on sandwiches, jellies, all the crap kids love.

Then it was everyone down to the zoo for Harlan to declare it open. Cheers and applause from all the mums and dads, then the children filed inside with their parents yelling and screaming at each exhibit: a Mexican rose-toed tarantula. Electric-blue poisonous frogs, safely tucked away behind glass. A chameleon, its eyes swivelling to look at them all. The boa constrictor, already five foot of tensile strength, lying still in its big heated tank. Then the caimans, in the pièce de résistance – the huge central pool.

'They're not that big yet,' said Charlie to the assembly. 'But they'll grow.'

After that there were games and goody bags back at the house. Nula felt a flash of irritation when she found Milly sitting on the back stairs reading a book instead of joining in the fun like Belle was. She hustled her daughter into the sitting room where the others were running riot. 'Son of My Father' by Chicory Tip was crashing out of the sound system, all the kids singing along. Belle was there in the thick of it, with an adoring crowd around her – Gillian and Amanda, who she'd met at the stables, and friends from school too, among them Boris Paddick, Angie Cruise, Nigel 'Einstein' Pope, who was off-the-scale intelligent and destined, like his brainy parents, for great things.

Everyone was about to go home when Nula realized that Harlan and one of the other boys – Nipper Warren, one of the rough poor boys from the nearby village – had gone missing and Charlie was getting annoyed.

'That boy should be here to say goodbye to his guests,' he grumbled.

Nula went off and searched the house for the two of them. Not finding them upstairs, she came back down to where the parents and kids were waiting in the hall and she heard one of the mums say: 'Yeah, but he's a queer little thing, ain't he? Weird as nine-pence. He don't *say* anything, just stares at you with those spooky pale eyes and you wonder what the fuck he's—'

The woman saw Nula approaching and stopped speaking.

They're talking about Harlan, she thought.

'I expect they're outside,' she said to Nipper's dad, who was thick-looking, just like his mountainous lump of a son.

Nula went out to the garages and there they were, down the side of the building.

'Har—' she started, then she saw a flash of white, heard the screech of the cat as it wriggled out of Nipper's grip. A match flared. As the cat raced past her, she smelled scorched fur.

Both boys turned to her. Harlan dropped the match and it fizzled out on the ground.

'What the fuck?' burst out Nula. She glared at them, Harlan so slim and elegant, Nipper huge, straw-blond and muddy-eyed.

They'd been *torturing* the damned thing.

She felt shaken. 'Get inside, the pair of you,' she snapped.

Harlan stared back at her, not moving.

Nipper fidgeted, eyes downcast.

'Go!' shouted Nula, and finally they went.

36

For a while, everything was fine in the Stone world. Charlie was making big bucks, Nula started to feel easier about what had happened on the day of the zoo party. It was just boys being boys. Cruel little fuckers, sometimes. It was all forgotten, and that was for the best. Belle continued to be a source of fascination for Harlan while big oafish Nipper followed Harlan everywhere, hanging on his every word. They were always huddling in corners, whispering, laughing, shoving each other. Life was OK. She kept up her journals, kept taking the pills. Some days, life was almost sweet.

Then suddenly, Nula got sick. She'd wake up and rush to the loo and vomit. Her body felt puffy. She had vile headaches when she wasn't even hung-over.

'Maybe it's one of those thyroid things. Underactive or something? You ought to get checked out,' suggested one of her old girlfriends from the Smoke.

God, Nula hated doctors. She'd been reading something about bad breast implants, maybe it was something like that, the things were leaking and poisoning her system? She'd always craved big tits but not at the cost of her life. No *way*. Now she was frightened. She might be really, seriously ill. She might have something *fatal*. She couldn't check out yet – she had this fabulous lifestyle, she had Milly, and now she had the boy as well, Harlan. He might creep her out sometimes, but Charlie was so pleased with him, so delighted to have a son at last, eager to get him started in the business. She *couldn't* die of anything. Not yet.

Finally, Charlie nagging at her had the desired effect and she went to the doctors and broke down in tears that she had been suppressing for weeks. She'd been so anxious, so scared. She'd never been seriously ill before. And she thought now this was going to be *it*. The end. And it was too *soon*.

Oh Christ . . .

Charlie was no help. He was away again. He was often away. It was Turkey this time, where heroin production was kept in line by the Turkish Maffya. From there he was off to Peru where, he'd told her, a thousand pounds' worth of coca leaves from a Peruvian hill farmer would convert to cocaine and fetch a million pounds on the London streets.

Like she cared. They had their high-end life. There was everything here. The house overlooked one of the most exclusive golf clubs in the country. There were ten bedrooms, all en suite. Three drawing rooms. Massive staircases, a downstairs hallway you could hold a dance in. A gym. An indoor and an outdoor heated pool. Outside, the house was skirted by a huge terrace, then a massive lawned garden with an integral sprinkler system. There was a deep pond full of koi carp, a boating lake, a tennis court, a walled vegetable garden and orchard, tended by four gardeners. There was now also the 'petting' zoo, which Charlie added to on a regular basis with the creepy reptiles and crocodile-type things he seemed to like so much. It was a bit of a hike down there, so he kept a buggy parked up in the workshop beside the garages.

On this trip Charlie had taken Terry with him, and feeling so ill, so low, Nula was glad about that. Charlie had left a couple of his other men on the door of their house.

Nula often wondered if one of these days her bumptious risk-taker of a husband was going to be returned home to her in a box. Maybe they could have a joint funeral, the pair of them. Leave it all to little Milly, and to their adopted son Harlan.

So she had to endure her ill health on her own and although she was scared shitless, she was glad of Charlie's absence. He'd be fidgeting, shouting, thumping the table, demanding answers. She just wanted to be told, quietly and calmly, what the fuck was wrong with her. That was all.

The doctors ran a raft of tests. They prodded her, poked her, weighed her, and a week later the consultant called her back in. By this point she was screaming inside, scribbling wildly in her journals, wondering if taking up drink would be a good idea. Or cigarettes. Fuck it, if she was dying *anyway,* what would it matter?

Then it was off to see the consultant, all on her own. She sat there in his office, waiting for the axe to fall. He came in, smiled and sat down.

'Congratulations,' he said. 'You're pregnant.'

37

Reeling, Nula went home. Gary on the door told her that Jill Barton was in the living room, wanting to see her.

'Oh for fuck's sake,' said Nula.

Her brain literally spun. *Pregnant?* A visit from sickly-sweet Jill was the last thing she wanted right now. When she'd had Milly, *that* consultant had told her she could have no more kids, it was too risky. *This* one said, with the proper care, there should be no problem.

Now she had Jill pitching up at the door. It would be to do some committee thing for the parish council. Jill was always doing some daft cake-baking thing, or ferrying oldies to hospital, trying to get in tight with the locals. Christ, didn't she know what they were, what they *all* were, Charlie's mob? Of course none of the locals had the faintest clue about it, but it was drug money that gave Charlie Stone and his entourage this swish country lifestyle. How would the vicar and his coven of WI harpies react if they knew *that*?

Sighing, Nula went into the sitting room. Jill was there, standing by the window, sunlight streaming in on her silky blonde hair. It made Nula sick to think how she had to work at looking good, while this *cow* threw on a baggy old jumper and jeans, dragged a comb through her hair, and somehow always managed to look stunning.

'What can I do for you, Jill?' asked Nula, tossing her bag onto the couch. 'Only I'm pretty busy.'

'Busy doing what? Filing your nails? Having your hair done? You cow! I *know* about you trying it on with my Terry!'

Oh Christ.

That knocked Nula back. So Terry had told her! And what if he told Charlie? Oh, he'd been OK with the parties back in the day, with her doing it with all and sundry. But this was *Terry*, his mate since the cradle, his best pal. Nula knew damned well that Charlie would kill her if he heard about this.

She felt her heartbeat quicken. Shit! She was going to have to front this out, there was nothing else she could do. She swallowed. Her mouth was dry, a pulse beating hard in her temples.

'Oh, he told you,' she said, as casually as she could.

Jill crossed the room fast. She came and stood right in front of Nula, glaring into her eyes.

'For Christ's sake,' said Jill in a low angry voice. 'Haven't you got enough, Nula? Here you are, sitting on top of the pile with Charlie bloody Stone, and you're still not satisfied! You want *my husband* too?'

Nula felt a lurch of sickness but she forced a mocking smile onto her face.

'Only on loan, dearie,' she said. 'I didn't want him for keeps.'

Jill's hand connected with Nula's face in a resounding slap. *Crack!*

Nula raised a hand to her throbbing cheek as Jill bore down on her, wagging a finger right in her face.

'You *cow*,' spat Jill. 'You keep your thieving hands to yourself. Terry's *mine*. You got that? *Mine.*'

'Look,' said Nula, holding up her hands in a 'peace' gesture. 'It's old news, I promise you. I was a bit drunk at the time and it clashed with my medication. There was nothing to it. Nothing at all.'

Jill stepped back. Her eyes were still flinty with rage. 'What, both times? You think I'm stupid? You fucking Stones! You want it *all,* don't you? You want everything.'

'Meaning?' asked Nula, getting sick of this.

'You got the morals of alley cats, the pair of you,' said Jill.

'Yeah, yeah.' Nula was turning away.

Jill grabbed her arm, turned her back to face her. 'There's something you ought to know about. Then maybe you wouldn't be Lady Muck any more, so *up* yourself. Maybe you'd remember what you're married to. What he *is.*'

'Really? So what is he then?'

'He's a fucking *rapist.*'

38

Nula's world was crumbling into dust. Distantly, she heard the front door close behind Jill after she'd dropped her bombshell. Christ, had Gary on the door heard any of that? She hoped not. But someone was moving about out there. She went into the hall. Harlan was fiddling with one of his games down by the skirting board right outside the door. Had the kid heard?

No, Nula decided. Harlan was always in a world of his own. Harlan loved gadgets and was obsessive about them, collecting them and playing with them for hours. Once absorbed, he was totally unaware of anything going on around him. And the boy was scrupulously neat, always putting his toys away every day in their allotted box in his bedroom when he had finished with them.

Nula went back into the sitting room and closed the door. That *bitch* Jill. She'd be sorry, she was going to be very sorry indeed, making up stories about Charlie, lying through her teeth like that. He wouldn't do that – would he? *Rape* someone? Nula's face still stung from that slap. She was thinking of the few times she'd seen Charlie with Jill, through the gatehouse window. Just talking, he'd said. Not according to Jill, though. Jill said Charlie had forced her into sex, that he was an animal and that him and Nula deserved each other.

She felt the nausea rise again and clamped both hands to her belly. She was *pregnant*. The consultant at the hospital had smiled and said it was strange how these things happened; you relaxed because you thought your child-bearing days were over and then bam! You got up the duff the natural way, no problem at all. The human body was an amazing thing, he'd said. Nula was remembering the agony she'd been in when she gave birth to Milly. Afterwards, the consultant had told her it would be too dangerous for her to go through it all again. Maybe fatal. He'd also said it was *extremely* unlikely that she would ever conceive again. So she'd trusted his professional judgement. She hadn't bothered with contraception.

Bloody doctors.

But this new doctor thought it would be OK. He'd been so *positive* of that.

'Oh Christ,' she muttered. Then she thought of Charlie, *her husband,* forcing himself on Jill, and headed for the cloakroom to be sick.

39

Jill hurried down the driveway to the gatehouse, wishing she was a hundred miles away from the Stones and all the crap they brought with them. Even Terry was getting jumpy lately as they rose higher and higher in this dangerous world.

Just a week ago, he'd taken her to one side and said he had something to show her.

'Yeah? What?' she had asked, expecting a gift, a surprise, something light-hearted and fun.

But Terry looked grim. He'd taken her upstairs to the master suite and pointed out the cupboard set into the eaves.

'You know I was talking to you about hide codes? Run codes? Because of the business we're in, with Charlie,' he said.

'What?' she asked again, puzzled.

'I've fitted a bolt inside.' He went to the cupboard and opened it. Inside, Jill could see the silvery gleam of the bolt. She looked a question at Terry. 'Look,' he said. 'If anything kicks off, anything that frightens you, then you and Belle hide in here, OK?'

Jill had gone pale as he spoke. 'You're scaring me,' she said.

'I don't mean to. I just want you to know it's here, that's all. In case.' Terry closed the cupboard door and turned to his wife, kissing her lips.

'Yeah. Got it.'

'You remember the passwords? Well, more of a pass*phrase*. One for run, one for hide.'

'I remember.'

'What's the "run" one then?' he asked.

'Oh for Christ's sake Terry . . .' Jill was busy today, she didn't want to be wasting time with this. And it spooked her, even talking about it.

'What is it?' Terry persisted.

'Chipboard.'

'Right. And the hide one?'

'If you want us to hide, you'll ask if your pen is in the bag in the hall,' said Jill.

'Never forget that. OK?'

'OK.'

Now, hurrying back down the drive, Jill remembered all that and thought that she'd felt so much safer when they'd all been young and Charlie Stone had been into the hard game, not the drugs.

Safer, and happier too.

1970s

40

Charlie was one of the big criminal *capos* now, pushing the boundaries in every direction. He had forged a close connection not only with families up and down the country but also with the Matias crew who fronted a cartel in Colombia, so that Charlie's gang could take care of things at the London end. For the last few years he'd been doing a brisk, steady trade in hashish through Morocco and Turkey, but he always wanted to push further.

'I'm like a shark,' he said. 'Stand still and I die.'

He'd started importing Thai cannabis through Gatwick airport, paying baggage handlers to remove cases of drugs.

Now he used that same system – and others – to import his cocaine through his cartel associates in Bogota. Eighty kilos was worth about twenty mill on the streets, which was a big deal to the English gangs but chickenshit to the mega-wealthy Colombians.

When even bigger loads were being imported, Charlie turned his attention to the docks in Southampton where he already had people set up on the take and knew he could get containers coming through unchecked.

'The Matias bunch keep flapping over security, but it's sewn up tight,' Charlie told Terry. 'I own the ports. I own the police. I'm in charge. There's no problem.'

Everything was working out nicely. These days, Charlie could only wonder at the modest beginnings of his life of crime. Now here he was – king of the entire fucking world, just like he'd always planned. Living a grand life in a grand mansion out in the sticks, but – he had to admit this was true – his heart was still back there on the old East End manor he'd been born into, wrapped up in the lifestyle he'd once known.

He didn't mix much with the locals out here, and Nula didn't either. Their old mates from the manor came out sometimes, but they never stayed long.

Their cash was welcome here, though. There was always somebody banging at the door asking for handouts. For the church spire. For the community centre's new bogs. For the replacement of the village hall's decaying porch. Charlie stumped up plenty at first, thinking that this was a route in and that it might please Nula to be part of it all.

But gradually the penny dropped. They were seen as dodgy newcomers, unwanted outsiders, and were asked repeatedly what line of business they were in. Charlie gave his stock answer to this one – he was importing wood for sofa frames, textiles for armchair covers, padding, springs from China, all that shit, and manufacturing and assembling furniture in his English factories. But the people around here never seemed convinced. The community withdrew from the Stones, and frankly Charlie was relieved.

In fact, after having been in love with the idea of a grand country manor, of literally 'lording' it among the yokels, he now felt that the whole 'moving out' business had been a big mistake. Yes, he'd fallen for the *idea* of living it large in the country, but the reality was, he didn't care for it. He caught himself longing for the dirty streets of the city with that exciting air of seedy danger. He missed the rough sleepers, the even rougher old spit-and-sawdust pubs, the place that he truly, in his heart, still called home.

Now he was living a different life. He regularly attended charity events, kept up the pretence of being a legitimate businessman. In evening dress, him and Nula went everywhere in high society, to the royal enclosure at Ascot, the masked ball at Versailles, where once the Sun King Louis had reigned. Now Charlie Stone held court there, drinking Cristal champagne and eating beluga caviar. He attended the carnival in Venice, his costume – and Nula's – extravagant in the extreme, their masks trimmed with gold thread.

They took luxurious breaks in Cap d'Antibes at the summer home of their Colombian associate, Javier. He had an exclusive and breathtakingly beautiful seafront villa there and treated them as his honoured guests to lavish lunches and trips over to Monte Carlo, where his superyacht was moored up in the bay.

'This is a bit of me, all this,' Charlie said when he was laid out on the sun deck of Javier's yacht. But inside, he was starting to wonder if it really was.

Charlie was over the moon that Nula was pregnant again. Lady Luck was smiling down on him. He could have his longed-for son. Oh, he had Harlan, but Harlan was *adopted*. This boy would be his own flesh and blood, and a carefree life in the country was what every kid should have, he really believed that.

So for now? He was staying put.

41

It was another hellish pregnancy. Low already, shocked to the core by what Jill had told her about Charlie, Nula plunged into carrying the baby and her moods were unfailingly dark. Only her journals gave some relief while she carried the child; she wrote in them almost manically, jotting everything down. She had to come off the tranquillizers she routinely took because of the baby.

Her moods sank lower, and lower. This time, she was convinced, whatever the consultant said, she was going to die. She was sick, horribly sick, for most of this pregnancy; it was far worse than it had been with Milly and travelling around with Charlie was no help because every day she longed to say to him, *I know what you did, you bastard.* But she couldn't say it. Didn't dare.

She felt like a bloated Zeppelin, engorged while this alien *thing* grew inside her, robbing her of vitality, cheating her of life.

She was going to die.

She knew it.

But then, when her waters broke and finally the day came and she was transported to the hospital to give birth – and Charlie wasn't there, *again,* as per fucking usual – it all went like clockwork. Four hours after she hit the maternity ward, their son was born. Her precious baby boy, her beloved baby Jake.

42

'That's it then, yeah? No more after this,' said Charlie. Finally he'd pitched up at her bedside and now he held his newborn son in his arms.

'Yeah. No more,' agreed Nula, lying back dishevelled, exhausted and cut to ribbons. She had more stitches up her fanny than a fucking tapestry. But she was happy and in a private hospital bed, not out on the main ward with the rest of the oiks. She looked around. Harlan was there, staring at her with that flat emotionless gaze of his. 'You didn't bring Milly.'

'No, I left her with Jill, I didn't want you getting overtired. You been through enough. You can get out of here and catch up with Milly then. Won't be long. Or I can bring her in tonight, if you want.'

'Yeah,' said Nula. 'That would be nice.' Poor little Mills, she thought, watching Charlie – that *arsehole* – as he cuddled their son. Milly wasn't going to get a look in, not now Charlie had his boy.

Charlie was so happy he felt he could burst with it. He couldn't believe it. His *own son*. Milly was great, but she was a girl. It wasn't the same. You couldn't have girls involved in the business; it was too rough. Then he looked down and saw Harlan staring up at him with that cold questioning expression he always wore.

'Look, Harlan. Your baby brother!' he said, grinning. Well, sort of, thought Charlie. Not even a half-brother really, because Harlan wasn't blood, not like this little fella.

He knew it was mean, what he was feeling. Wrong. But

shit – would they even have bothered to adopt at all, if this tiny miracle had occurred *before* all that adoption bull crap happened?

Now Charlie was wondering vaguely how difficult it would be to give a kid to the care system. Bloody nigh impossible, he reckoned, given all the twists and turns he'd gone through with those official bastards. Or maybe he could palm Harlan off on one of the girls on the manor? Well, it was a fact that Harlan was a funny little fish, cold as a fucking haddock really. He'd never exactly *warmed* to the kid at all.

Yeah, because you thought that was it for you. No son, only this thing *to fill in the gap. You'd accepted that.*

Oh, he'd treated Harlan well enough. Bought him the best gifts at Christmas and on his birthdays, gifts that matched Milly's in expense. He was careful to do that, to try and play fair, treat the kids as equals. But Harlan's reactions were always muted. Fucking kid always seemed to be *watching* you, somehow. As if he didn't understand normal reactions but was sort of copying yours in the hope that his own would look right.

'Can I hold him?' Harlan asked, his eyes on the baby.

'Nah,' said Charlie. 'Not yet, he's too little. You might drop him.'

Harlan nodded and looked at Nula. Nula held out her hand. She wasn't mother of the year, not by any means, but she could see how Harlan must be feeling right now. Yes, he might be a bit strange, maybe even sadistic – she could never forget him and Nipper burning the cat's fur on the day they'd opened the petting zoo – but of course he was going to feel cast aside. Charlie was in raptures over the new baby. He had *never* been like this with Harlan, not even when he'd been a novelty, freshly adopted.

Nula forced a smile and said: 'You're going to help us get the nursery furnishings finished, aintcha, Harlan? Now that we've got it all decorated nicely.'

In fact Nula had felt so insecure, so uncertain about the baby's arrival that she'd left all of this until the last minute. It wasn't that she didn't want to jinx it. It was that she didn't believe that she and the kid would pull through. But here they were – to her shock – safe and well.

Harlan said nothing, and Nula felt a twinge of irritation. If the kid was just a bit livelier, a bit *bubblier,* then she felt that her arse-hole of a husband would respond to him better. There would be similarities then, at least. But there were none. Harlan's attitude niggled her more than she cared to admit, so God alone knew what it did to Charlie.

'Can I hold him when we get home?' asked Harlan.

Nula shot Charlie a look. To Harlan, she said: 'We'll see.'

43

When Charlie left the hospital with Harlan, Terry was waiting back at the house with Beezer. They both looked grim.

'We got trouble,' said Beezer.

'Oh?'

There was a container coming into Southampton Docks from Ecuador, full of balsa wood. The wood had been hollowed out to accommodate the true payload: one metric tonne of cannabis and nearly two hundred kilos of cocaine. The cocaine alone had a street value of fifty million pounds sterling.

'Customs and Excise been watching for months, our boys down there reckon,' said Beezer. 'Now they've seized it.'

'And?' demanded Charlie.

He felt sick with anxiety. This was bad. But he was bewildered. There was *no way* this shit could touch him or anyone near him, they were all rigorously careful. *He* was careful beyond measure. He told his crew – not Terry of course, Terry was different – only what they needed to know; nothing more. Then even under duress they couldn't blab. He didn't make calls from his house and neither did any of his men, he was meticulous about that. They all used public phone boxes in obscure places, they were *all* cautious to the point of obsession.

And yet *this* had happened.

'But they can't tie any of the shit to us,' said Charlie, looking to Terry for confirmation.

136

'They can't. That's true. But . . . it means we got a leak some-where. We need to tighten up.'

'I'd better get down there,' said Charlie.

But there was nothing to find. All the dock workers and Customs men in his pay pleaded their innocence. He kicked a few about just to make sure, applied pressure – but there was nothing. No clue as to how this had happened. It pissed Charlie off.

While he was down on the south coast, trying to find out what the *fuck* was going wrong, Charlie decided to cheer himself up by chasing a long-held dream of his. The Southampton Boat Show was on and he was walking up and down the pontoons – which moved a little as the tide lapped them – not eyeing up the ordin-ary yachts, the ones any fucker could afford, oh no – he wanted a *superyacht*. A huge beast of a thing with every modern conveni-ence on board. He wanted it *all*.

Terry, who was accompanying him, was sceptical of the idea of Charlie on the open waves. Charlie, bobbing around on the water in a dinghy, tugging at sails, wearing a lifejacket over his beer belly and a sailor's hat? Unlikely.

'Yeah, yack it up, arsehole,' said Charlie, when Terry laughed at the idea.

You wouldn't laugh so much if you knew I'd shafted your missus, would you? thought Charlie, grinning back at his mate.

But this wasn't an actual *yacht* – these things were massive floating palaces.

They walked around the deck of one. There was a swimming pool on board, and a jacuzzi. Thirteen crew were needed just to sail the thing. There was a helicopter perched on the upper deck.

'I'm going to learn to fly, too,' said Charlie. 'One of them things. Always fancied it.'

Terry said nothing. He'd heard an old, old saying: there are old pilots, and there are bold pilots. But there are no old bold pilots. Charlie came into the bold category. He'd be lethal to himself and others, flying a helicopter. 'Sure, Charlie,' he said.

An hour later, Charlie was shaking hands with the salesman and the deal on the yacht was done.

'I'm gonna call her *Lady of the Manor*,' said Charlie.

'After Nula?'

'Yeah,' said Charlie, feeling a stab of guilty disappointment at mention of his wife's name.

Nula was a bit, well, *mental* these days, and he had no patience with it. He didn't like it. Then he thought of Terry's old lady and wondered if he might one of these days take another bite out of *that* apple. It was tempting. Really was.

Forbidden fruit.

All right, the leak had troubled him. But nevertheless everything was pretty rosy. Here he was, Charlie Stone, backstreet boy, and now he owned a superyacht just like Javier's. The manor was expanding, day by day. Soon, it would cover the entire world. And he would be its king. So who the hell was ever going to dare to tell him no?

44

Within days, Nula was out of hospital and resting up in bed. She wasn't breastfeeding the baby – Christ, she'd gone to enough trouble to get a good set on her, without causing even more problems in that department. So after expressing some milk for him for the first couple of weeks, the kid went on the bottle and Nula set about getting rid of the baby weight.

Young Milly adored the new baby, constantly cooing over him and bringing Belle up from the gatehouse to admire him.

'He's so tiny and sweet,' said Belle, chucking the baby under his chubby chin.

The girls took turns holding and feeding and even changing Jake, then they were pushing him around the grounds in his pram. Harlan kept his distance. The same au pair who'd looked after Harlan now had the newborn to cope with too. She complained and kept taking time off. Finally Nula sacked her.

'Where's Janine?' Harlan kept asking. He'd liked Janine – Nula thought he'd liked the au pair a lot more than he liked *her*, in fact.

'Never mind her,' said Nula. 'We got a new one coming, a better one. Chrissy from the village. She's a nice girl, you'll like her.'

Chrissy, it turned out, was a peach. She settled Harlan down, read books with Milly, and she made sure that Nula was never troubled with nappy changes or night feeds. Everything, suddenly, was running smoothly.

'To think we put up with that other one for so long,' said Nula, getting back into the gym for stomach crunches and methodically watching her diet. Within months of the baby's birth, her figure was back to normal and she could once again bear to look at herself in the mirror.

'That was the last one,' she told herself firmly, and she went on the pill to be absolutely sure. She went back on her *other* pills too, because she was still dogged by awful black moods. But she tried to cheer herself. Kept up her journal, which ought to help. It didn't, but it was sort of satisfying, writing down all her gripes, all her anguish over her growing hatred of her husband.

Now there was the christening to get through. She wanted to look A1 again for that and she was right on target for it.

'By the way,' said Charlie. 'Did I tell you? I bought a yacht. Thought it'd be nice for the holidays. Take us all off down to the Med. The kids and me and you.'

'Sounds nice,' said Nula. No, he hadn't told her. Another of Charlie's mad schemes. She was so used to them, she barely blinked when he said it. She was cold with him now, withdrawn. He'd shagged Jill. Raped the poor bint. All right, Nula had no time for Jill, but for Chrissakes! She was a woman, and as a woman Nula understood very well that an outrage had been committed and that it was awful – despicable. She couldn't forgive it. The *bastard*.

'And I'm taking flying lessons. Whirlybirds. Helicopters. You know.'

'Yeah sure,' said Nula. 'Why not?'

She wrote that down in her journal under the heading *More of Charlie's crazy shit*.

45

Nula got a new christening gown for Jake from Harvey Nicks, a beautiful long creation in cream lace with pearls sewn into the bib and all around the hem. She treated herself to a lilac outfit complete with hat and after the church ceremony the christening party went ahead. It was a bright sunny day. They had a marquee in the grounds and all their mates and their wives came and had a fantastic time that went on until two in the morning, when Plod showed up at the door with complaints from the neighbours over the field.

Nula and Charlie turned off David Essex promising he was going to make someone a star, fished a few over-partied revellers out of the heated pool at the back of the big house, and the whole lot of them turned in for what remained of the night.

'Now *that*,' said Charlie at breakfast, 'was a proper party. A real old-fashioned East End knees-up like the old folks used to have, you remember, Nules?'

'Yeah,' she said, thinking of her old home back in the Smoke, thinking regretfully of her sweet old-fashioned mum and dad. She felt a pang of sadness. They'd done their best for her, she knew that. Her parents, who could be dead by now for all she knew. And her brother Jimmy, who she *hoped* was dead, the arse-hole. No happy memories there.

People were scared of her on the old manor now. No one reacted to her *normally*, no one passed the time of day with her when she went back there. She could see the difference, straight away. Even in the corner shop, everyone would fall silent when she stepped inside. She was ushered to the front of every queue. At first, she had enjoyed that. Now, she just wished that it didn't happen, that life could be as simple as it once had been.

Charlie Stone's manor covered a lot more than a few mean streets now; it covered the world, and he was its absolute ruler. She was *Mrs Charlie Stone,* and Charlie was such a big noise that even his wife made people nervous. She didn't actually belong *anywhere,* not any more. She was shunned in the country as a common and rather dodgy interloper – and she was feared in London, on what had once been her own patch. She wrote about it, in her journal. About her deep feelings of disconnection, about her unhappiness and about what had happened to Jill at the hands of that *fucker* Charlie, about being trapped out here, caged in. But what could you do?

The morning after the christening party, she was picking her way through the lower floor of the house, hung-over and stumbling over bodies, people still spark out on the floor. Jesus, what a night they'd had. She looked at the enormous pile of christening presents on the end table. Everyone had brought gifts for little Jake. Of course they had. Everyone wanted to get in good with Charlie Stone.

She walked over to the half-unwrapped goodies and rummaged among the stuff there. A coral teething ring. A tiny silver bracelet. A huge snow-white stuffed polar bear wearing a purple velvet saddle trimmed with gold. Jesus, so much *stuff.*

Then at a tiny sound she looked around. Harlan was standing right there. Silent as a wraith, he'd often do that: pitch up and startle the shit out of you. Every time he did it, Nula jumped. Despite her banging head, she forced a smile onto her lips. The kids must have had a pretty rough night, with all the noise going on, even if they did sleep up on the top floor.

'All right then, Harlan?' she asked.

'Chrissy said to fetch you,' he said flatly.

'Why, what is it?' she asked him.

'There's something wrong with Jake.'

46

Nula wasn't aware of anything until she crashed through the door of the nursery and saw Chrissy standing there by the cot beneath the window. The girl was white-faced and staring.

'What's happened?' said Nula, coming to the cot and reaching for her baby.

Chrissy stretched out a restraining hand. 'You shouldn't,' she said.

'What? Get out of the way, I'll have a look at him, what's the . . . ?' Nula's voice seemed to run out of air then. Her eyes were on the child in the cradle, and . . . *oh Christ!* . . . he looked blue. He didn't seem to be breathing.

'I fed him at three, put him back down, he was fine. And then when I came in at seven – he's usually awake then – I found him like this . . .' Chrissy's voice tailed away.

Nula reached down a trembling hand to touch Jake's tiny hand. It was *cold*.

'Oh no. No. No,' she heard herself saying, over and over. She couldn't seem to stop. She was staggering as if someone had hit her. Her legs turned to water and she fell sideways into a chair. She sat there, staring, her eyes wide with shock and terror.

Chrissy was still standing there, wringing her hands, saying words, but all Nula could think was: *No. This can't be happening.*

Harlan stood beside Nula, watching her, silent.

Chrissy was still speaking, but all Nula could hear was white noise.

'What?' she said at last. *'What?'*

'We have to call someone,' said Chrissy, her voice trembling. 'The doctor. Someone.'

Nula stumbled to her feet, approached the cradle once again. 'No,' she said, and her voice had a manic edge to it now. 'No.' She picked up the baby and he flopped horribly, lifeless, in her arms. 'No, he's just . . . he's tired that's all. All that noise last night, that would be it. The party. He's just tired.'

Chrissy was shaking her head, holding out a hand to Nula. 'Mrs Stone, we have to tell someone about this. It . . . I'm so sorry. It's ghastly but it happens.'

'What does?' Nula was cuddling Jake, but he seemed so still and so *cold*. In a moment he would wake up. Or maybe this was all a dream. She was still asleep and she was dreaming. That was it.

'Mrs Stone,' said Chrissy gently. 'I should fetch Mr Stone, shall I do that?'

'No, don't,' said Nula. She was bouncing the dead baby in her arms. 'He's tired – aintcha, Jakey? That's all. It's nothing. Don't bother Charlie. Not yet.'

Nula sank down onto the chair, still cuddling the lifeless baby. At any minute she knew that Jake would be OK and everything would be fine again. Fuck's sake, they'd only had him christened yesterday!

'Mrs Stone,' said Chrissy.

Nula's face twisted in a snarl. 'I said no!' she shouted. 'Go on, leave us alone, we'll be fine, we'll be absolutely fine . . .'

Chrissy recoiled at Nula's tone. She nodded and held out a hand to Harlan and together they left the room. To find Charlie, Nula supposed. To tell him . . .

No!

She couldn't even think it. Nula started to sob, her tears falling onto her baby.

47

Charlie couldn't believe it. The daft mare surely had it wrong. And Harlan was just standing there beside the pale and shaking girl. The kid was blank-eyed like always, not reacting to what the girl was saying, and she was saying his little Jake was dead?

No. That couldn't be right.

'Nah, you got that wrong,' said Charlie, standing up. He'd drunk a lot last night, but he could hold his drink. Nula might be hung-over; he wasn't. But he swayed with shock.

'It's true, Mr Stone, I swear,' said Chrissy.

'No, I gotta . . .' And Charlie was gone, out the door, up the staircase, brushing past Beezer and his other mates who were coming down for breakfast, not seeing them, not hearing what they said. He ran on, and burst into the second-floor nursery beside the master bedroom and there was Nula, cradling Jake, everything was fine, only . . .

Somehow, in his gut, Charlie knew that nothing was going to be fine, ever again. He dashed forward and stared into Nula's ashen, tear-streaked face.

'What the fuck, Nules?' he said, and then he was reaching for the baby and she was clinging on to Jake, and it was almost funny, like they were doing a tug-of-war with the little kid in between them, and Charlie found himself remembering something from years ago, something he'd heard in Sunday school when his mum had with high hopes once sent him there. He'd stuck it out for a few weeks, but then he'd knocked it on the head. Refused to go back. Now he recalled the vicar's words: 'and Solomon said, cut the child in half, and each of the women claiming to be his mother will take a piece.' At which the real mother had come forward and said, no! Let *her* take him.

At the time, Charlie had thought it was funny. Farcical, even. Who'd cut a baby in half anyway?

Now? Not funny at all.

Nula gave up the struggle and let the baby go. Charlie held the body gently against his chest, stared at the blue tone of the skin, and raised a trembling hand to the child's soft cheek, feeling the stony coldness of it.

'We should . . .' he started, then his voice faltered and he tried again. 'We should get him to the hospital, Nules. Right now.'

Nula stared up at him as if he was mad. Then she said: 'Charlie . . . he's gone.'

'No, he's just . . .' Charlie stopped again, heaved in a breath, aware of the girl and Harlan watching from the doorway, aware that tears were falling down his own cheeks, and what the fuck? He never cried. *Never.* Now he was blubbing like a kid.

Charlie half-turned, stared at Chrissy. '*What the fuck you done?*' he burst out.

'Mr Stone . . .' Chrissy flinched. She looked terrified.

'Charlie . . . it's not her fault,' said Nula in a flat, emotionless voice. She was thinking of that first consultant, warning her about trying to have more children. Now she understood. This was her fault. 'It happens. Sometimes. We've . . . we've been unlucky. That's all.'

'*Unlucky?*' Charlie roared, clutching his son to him. His *dead* son. While Harlan stood there, breathing. Alive and well. 'No. This don't happen. I won't *let* it happen.'

And he sank to his knees, still clutching the dead baby in his arms, and began to sob bitter, angry tears.

48

It was Chrissy who phoned the doctor; then in quick succession several things happened. The police arrived and strung tape up across the nursery door and then there were people in there taking photographs, examining the room like it was a crime scene. The coppers asked question after question. Who found the child? At what time, precisely? There was a party last night, was there anyone in the house who might want to harm a child?

'What you saying?' Charlie roared. 'You think I got some stinking pervert among my friends? These people, I'd trust them with my life and with my son's life too.'

'Charlie,' said Nula warningly, clutching at his arm as they sat side by side, shocked, in the sitting room, and answered these questions that were nothing more than an annoyance.

Then most horrible of all, the ambulance arrived and they took the baby away. It was Charlie, not Nula, who clung on to little Jake, who said no, they couldn't take him. It was Nula who calmed him, who said, it was OK, this was what they had to do. That it wasn't their fault.

'Then whose fucking fault is it?' Charlie demanded, crashing about the place like a fury, smashing glasses, turning over chairs, needing something, somebody, *anything,* to hurt.

Then he turned on Nula. 'You never did care about the kid, did you?'

'That isn't fair, Charlie,' she said, while watching their friends, the people they were closest to in all the world, vanish out the door, taking themselves away from this tragedy, out of reach of Charlie's catastrophic temper.

Nula felt numb. She'd been so ill during Jake's pregnancy, so tortured, so afraid, that when the baby had finally arrived, she'd seen Jake as a miracle. A gift from God. But now she knew she'd been wrong to think that. The Stones were cursed because of the evil trade they dealt in. Nothing good could ever come to them. Of course not. She'd been mad to ever think it would. They'd sold their souls to the devil years ago. All they had was Milly, poor plain little thing, who never seemed to be a part of their world, and Harlan, who had never been more than a substitute for the child they *should* have had.

So Jake had been taken from them. It was no more than they deserved. Certainly no more than her raping bastard of a husband deserved, doing that to Jill Barton. Now Charlie was hurting and in a dark secret corner of her heart Nula was *glad*.

The police with all their questions somehow made it even worse. It was already like knives were being dug into her, and those words, those suspicious eyes watching her, turned it into a waking nightmare.

'Just keep out Charlie's way,' she told Chrissy. The girl nodded and left to tend to Harlan.

49

Time passed. It dragged by – minutes, hours, days. Horror upon horror hit the Stone household. The police came back, asked more questions. People in white plastic suits examined the nursery again. Then one of the plainclothes policemen told them grimly that there would be an autopsy.

'This is a three thousand to one shot, cot death,' he told them.

They were going to cut Jake open, abuse his innocent little body. Tormented by the images that were crowding into his brain, Charlie shouted at the copper to get the fuck out of his house. But the autopsy found nothing suspicious.

Days lost all meaning. Now there were things to organize. A funeral. Nula broached the subject to Charlie and was roared at. He was still pinwheeling around the house, snarling, smashing things. He was unshaven and almost unhinged, mad at the world that had robbed him of his son.

Finally it was Terry, coming over because Nula had tearfully phoned the gatehouse and asked him to, who told Charlie that he had to get a grip. Charlie grabbed hold of his oldest, dearest friend, his brother-in-arms, and smashed him back against the living room wall.

'Get a *grip*?' Charlie screamed in Terry's face, spittle flying. 'You tosser, I'll grip you! I'll grip you by your *throat*, then you'll be fucking sorry!'

Terry offered no resistance. 'All right. Go on then. Do it. Or smack me one, right on the chops, if it makes you feel better.'

Charlie drew back his fist. He stood there, quivering, sweating with stress, his eyes filling with tears. Then as suddenly as he'd raised it, he let his arm fall to his side and he shoved himself away from Terry and dragged his hands through his thinning hair, over and over, bending almost double, moaning: 'Oh Christ, oh Christ, why'd this have to happen?'

Terry didn't know what to do. He'd never seen Charlie in such a state. The loss of the baby was affecting Charlie in a way that Terry was sure nothing else ever had. He thought of his own kid. Lovely little Belle. Thought of losing her. It was a pain like no other, losing a child. One he hoped never to experience.

Terry stepped forward and caught hold of Charlie. For a moment Charlie resisted, trying to push free of Terry's grip, but suddenly, as if all the strength was gone from him, all the rage, all the useless, pointless aggression, Charlie was still, held in his friend's arms, unresisting at last. And then he cried.

Quietly Nula came and stood in the open doorway, watching the pair of them. Over Charlie's head, Terry's eyes met hers. Ever since he knocked her back, she'd been trying to avoid being close to Terry. The memory of it still scalded her like a burn. She was Nula Stone. She was important. She *was*. But Terry had refused her and she found herself hating him for that now, hating him and his perfect little life with the lovely Jill and their gorgeous girl Belle. Now she'd lost one of her children, the *best* of her children, and what did she have left?

Milly.

And Harlan. Cold, detached little Harlan, who wasn't really their child at all.

Nula drew back, away from the door, and left the two men alone. She knew that Terry could help Charlie with this, and she couldn't. Didn't want to.

Let the arsehole *suffer*.

151

50

The funeral was the worst thing Nula had ever lived through. Throughout the whole ceremony she tried not to look at the tiny white coffin on the dais in the church, tried not to take any of this in; it was too painful. She didn't think she would ever wipe from her memory the sight of Charlie single-handedly carrying the coffin from the hearse and up the aisle to place it so carefully, so *lovingly*, on the dais.

Since that day with Terry when Charlie had cried his heart out, he seemed to have released his demons and regained some composure. Dry-eyed, he carried his dead son to be laid to rest. Dry-eyed, he listened to the prayers, the hymns, the solemn reassuring words of the vicar who said there was life beyond the grave. Charlie didn't believe it. He clutched onto Milly's hand while Nula, all in black, held on to Harlan. The Bartons sat beside them, Terry at Charlie's right hand, then Belle, then Jill.

Soon it was over. They laid Charlie Stone's son in the ground, and everyone went back to the big house.

Nula was dazed with grief. *Her beloved boy.* She wouldn't see him off on his first day at school, wouldn't fret over him learning to drive, would never see him become a man, get married, give her grandchildren. All of that, she was going to miss. All of it, she'd mourn forever.

'It was fucking tragic,' said Beezer to Nula as he happened to be standing beside her at the buffet table.

He had a paper plate of sausage rolls and Scotch eggs stacked high in one hand, a large Scotch in the other. Flashy, trendy Beezer. He was great with the kids, well with the *girls,* anyway, he didn't seem to care for Harlan much. And as for women? He had all the gear and no idea. He never had a clue what to say to them, they were like an alien species to him.

'Yeah,' said Nula, who felt as if she was floating through a very bad dream.

'Poor little kid,' he said. 'After that party too. At the christening. Christ, what a night we all had. Drunk as fuck, weren't we? Even the kids were up half the night. Felt bad about that. Noisy music and all us lot dossing down everywhere and wandering the halls.'

Nula didn't want to think about the christening party. After little Jake died, she'd sacked Chrissy. Raged at her. Told her to piss off and be glad she wasn't being prosecuted. That she should be grateful Charlie didn't throttle her with his bare hands. Jake had been in *her care.* And Jake had died.

'Poor bloody Harlan, must have been a shock, finding his little brother like that,' said Beezer, scoffing down half a Scotch egg.

Nula's sore eyes focused properly on Beezer for the first time. 'What do you mean? Milly and Harlan were asleep. They were up in the top nursery suite with Chrissy. Harlan didn't find Jake, *Chrissy* did.'

'Well no, I saw him down on the second floor. About four o'clock in the morning, it was, when I got up to have a piss. Stepped out of my bedroom and there he was.'

'He?'

'Harlan. In his pyjamas.'

'What, he was in the hallway?' asked Nula.

'He was just coming out of the room beside yours, the one right on the end.'

Something that felt clammy and fearful was crawling up Nula's spine. She could feel the room starting to sway. Beezer was talking about the nursery adjoining the master bedroom, the one in which baby Jake had been sleeping. Harlan had been coming out of there? Nula thought of Harlan, and of baby Jake who he was always asking to hold. But he wasn't allowed to. He *knew* that. Not unless he was supervised.

He'd gone there in the night.

And next morning – *oh Christ!* – they'd found Jake dead in his cot.

51

For days Nula didn't know what to do. Speak to Harlan, say *What did you do?* Accuse the boy when there might be nothing to accuse him of? Shake the living daylights out of him, demand the truth?

But what truth?

It could have been nothing. An innocent child, restless in the night, wanting to see his baby brother? But somehow Harlan never seemed innocent, did he. *Or* restless. Harlan was neat, precise, calm-eyed. And he was strictly forbidden to pick Jake up unless either Nula or Charlie or Chrissy was there.

Chrissy.

Chrissy was a local girl, the daughter of one of the village worthies; her folks, the Foster family, always attended church on Sunday. Thinking of the whole terrible thing now, Nula knew they should have got a proper trained woman, a Norland nanny maybe. For fuck's sake, they could afford it! But no. They had still been trying to 'fit in' out in the sticks when they had hired Chrissy to watch over Milly, Harlan and newborn Jake.

At that point they had still been trying to be one of the 'country set'. Joining in shooting parties and wearing the wrong gear and feeling like a couple of pricks. What a total waste of time all *that* had been. But Chrissy had seemed a nice sort of girl: conscientious, never flashy. And so they'd hired her to live in and look after the kids, and the worst imaginable thing had happened.

But how was that Chrissy's fault, really?

155

Cot death. It was a horrible thing to even imagine. When it happened to you, you were hit by a steamroller of grief. Of course she and Charlie had kicked off, blamed the girl for it. They'd both been wrecked by the loss of their only real son.

Harlan had been in the nursery at four in the morning. Doing what?

Nula thought that maybe she was *still* out of her mind with the horror of it all. The baby's death, the police investigation, the autopsy . . . ah Christ, the sheer torturous hell of that, of seeing the Y-shaped incision on her tiny little boy's pale body when she had clothed him in his christening gown once more to prepare him for burial.

Now she was thinking terrible thoughts, thinking . . . oh God yes, how could she deny it? She was thinking that Harlan – the boy they had invited into their home, cared for, clothed and fed – had done something awful to Jake.

Day after day Nula sat and mulled it over. Charlie didn't come near. He was out, about, drowning his grief by keeping busy or messing about down in his ever-expanding 'menagerie' beyond the orchard, which still gave Nula the creeps but seemed somehow to soothe him.

It couldn't be right, what she was thinking. She watched him, cool grey-eyed little Harlan with his neatly brushed straight honey-coloured hair, playing with his games out in the hallway, absorbed in his own little private world or giggling in corners with that oik Nipper.

It *couldn't* be right.

But then . . . how much did they really know about Harlan? About his background, about the sort of family he originally came from? Nothing, really. At the time, they had just been delighted to have a son. Nula because it meant she wouldn't have to endure any more pregnancies – which turned out to be not the case, anyway – and Charlie because it somehow seemed to prove him as a man, the stupid prick. And for a while, they *had* been happy. Maybe Harlan was not the sort of boy Charlie would have wished for – he wasn't a rough-and-tumble type, after all – but he was a *son*, to train up in the businesses, both legitimate and otherwise, to carry on after Charlie was gone.

But then had come Jake. Their *real* son. Nula thought about it all for a long time. And then, finally, sick at heart but sure of purpose, she knew what she had to do.

52

'What the hell do you want?' snapped Chrissy's father when Nula rapped at the Foster family door.

The Fosters were pillars of the village's tight-knit community, the very definition of respectability. When Chrissy had got sacked from her job as au pair to these brash newcomers with their sudden disastrous news, the whole village had rallied around the Fosters for support. *Them,* not the Stones, not the ones who were really suffering.

Of course Charlie's reaction had upset everyone. He was going to sue, he was going to see Chrissy in jail, she'd murdered his son in the night . . . Christ, how he'd ranted and raved. Told everyone in earshot that she was a bitch, a cow, and she was going to *pay* for this.

And now Ben Foster, his long, tanned farmer's face twisted with temper, was about to shut the door of his eighteenth-century cottage in Nula's face.

'Wait!' Nula surged forward. 'I just want to talk to Chrissy, that's all.'

'Well she doesn't want to talk to you,' he said.

The door was closing.

'Please, I need your help!' said Nula desperately.

Ben Foster hesitated.

'Look – I need to speak to her. Not to accuse her of anything, don't think that. I want to hear her version of what happened that night. That's all.'

'The police already questioned her. She was terribly upset by it all.'

'I know. I'm sorry. But . . . can't I speak to her? For five minutes? Please?'

Now the door opened a fraction more. Foster's face was stern, his eyes unfriendly. 'I don't want her upset. And she has been. She's blamed herself, and that's not the case. This sort of thing can happen. It's awful, but it does.'

'I'm not looking to lay blame on anyone,' said Nula. 'We've all been so gutted by this. It makes a person half-crazy. I'm sure you can understand that?'

Now his eyes softened, just a bit. 'I can understand. Yes.'

'So can I talk to Chrissy? Please?'

'All right then. Come in.'

53

Chrissy Foster was in her room, curled up on her bed reading a magazine. When her dad knocked at the door and she saw Nula coming in, her expression froze. She scrunched up on the bed, looking much younger than her nineteen years, pulling the sleeves of her frayed orange pullover down over her hands and crossing her arms defensively over her body.

'I haven't come to make trouble,' said Nula quickly, seeing the alarm in the girl's eyes.

Chrissy's father stood there, unmoving. Nula glanced at him. 'If we could have a few minutes alone? Just to talk?'

Ben Foster looked at his daughter. 'Chrissy?' he asked.

The girl stared at Nula's face. Then she nodded, very slowly.

'I'll be right outside,' said Ben. 'If you need me.'

He went out and shut the door behind him. Nula took a step into the room and Chrissy shrank back further on the bed.

'Look,' said Nula. 'Both Charlie and me, we were very upset about Jake. If we took it out on you, I apologize. I mean it. I'm sorry. But we were out of our minds. Don't you understand?'

Chrissy cleared her throat and nodded. 'Yes. Of course.'

'We really don't blame you, Chrissy. Not any more. I promise you. Only . . . somebody has said something to me, and I wondered if you could shed some light on it. That's all.' Nula edged toward a hardback chair loaded with discarded clothing. 'Can I . . . ?'

Chrissy nodded. Nula shoved the garments off the chair and sat down.

Chrissy tucked strands of pale blonde hair behind her ears and eyed Nula intensely. She had big stick-out ears, Nula realized for the first time, and it gave her a vulnerable look.

'What's this thing they've told you?' Chrissy asked.

'Maybe they got it wrong,' said Nula. Now that it was coming to the crunch, she found that she really didn't want to hear about it. She had to force herself to stay here, sitting with her hands on her lap, instead of running from the room. Aware of her chewed, ragged fingernails digging into the palms of her sweating hands, she fought for calm.

'It's just a silly thing someone said,' said Nula, feeling her throat closing, her mouth drying to dust and ashes.

'Oh? What?'

'It's wrong, probably. Only someone said they saw Harlan coming out of Jake's room at four on the morning he . . .' Nula swallowed hard.

But Chrissy was shaking her head, frowning. 'That can't be right. Harlan was asleep in the top nursery. Milly too. I got up at seven to go down and see to Jake and they were both still sleeping.'

'Yes, but . . .' Nula was finding it hard to breathe now. 'Harlan could have got up without you knowing, couldn't he? And gone down to Jake's room?'

'Well . . . yes. He *could* have.' Now Chrissy looked uncomfortable.

'You didn't find Harlan difficult to look after, did you?' asked Nula.

Chrissy shook her head.

'Or Milly?'

'Milly's fine,' said Chrissy.

'Harlan was fine too? Easy to look after?'

Chrissy shrugged. Alarm bells started ringing in Nula's head.

'What does that mean?' she asked.

'Well, he's not exactly an easy child, is he?'

'Meaning?'

Chrissy looked uncomfortable. 'Did you know he hides food under his bed?'

'What?'

Chrissy nodded. 'He does. I've found a few things under there. Boiled eggs. Stuff like that. An old sandwich, it was going mouldy. I picked it up to put in the bin and he threw a fit. I mean, he *really* hit the roof. He said it was his and I wasn't to touch it.'

'Why would he do that?' wondered Nula aloud. She hadn't had a clue about this. Chrissy hadn't told her.

'Have you heard of RAD?' asked Chrissy.

'What the hell's that?'

'I researched it after a few months of looking after Harlan. It's reactive attachment disorder. It means they have no conscience and they don't appreciate the consequences of their behaviour. I think Harlan's got that.'

It was warm in the sunny little room, but despite that Nula felt a chill.

'You looked it up? Why? Did he do something you thought was strange?'

Chrissy hesitated. Then she said: 'He seems very detached, don't you think?'

'Well, I . . .' Nula did think that. She'd thought it for a long time.

'If I were you, I would go to where you got him from, and I would ask some questions. Because honestly, Mrs Stone, he doesn't seem entirely "there". And that would worry me. A lot.'

Nula looked straight at Chrissy. 'Has he ever done anything around you that makes you think he could be . . . not "there"?'

'This is difficult . . .' said Chrissy, shifting awkwardly on the bed.

'Tell me.'

'He's a good boy, mostly. I think he tries. He really does.'

But he shouldn't have to try. Should he? thought Nula. But she said nothing. She wanted Chrissy to keep talking.

'It was about a month ago,' said Chrissy. 'It was . . . I dunno. Spooky, I think is the word. Frightening.'

'What did he do, Chrissy?' Nula was staring at the girl's face.

'Milly and Harlan went to bed as normal. Then I settled little Jake down for the night and went back up to go to bed next door to the top nursery. I have the monitor, as you know, so if Jake cried I'd hear it straight away and go down.'

'Yeah. I know that.' It saved Nula herself the bother of night-time feeds, changes, anything. Now Nula wished to Christ that she'd been more hands-on, more involved. More . . . ah but Jesus, what was the use? She felt the awful depression stealing over her again, blackening her mood. Jake was dead.

'So I went back up to the top nursery and got into bed and went to sleep. And then . . .' Chrissy's voice faltered.

'Go on.'

'Then something woke me. I don't know what. It was bright moonlight. The room seemed full of shadows. So I reached out, switched on the bedside light and . . .'

'What? Go on for God's sake.'

'He was there. Harlan. He was standing right there, leaning over me.'

Good Christ.

'Did he want something? A drink of water . . . ?'

'No.' Now Chrissy's face hardened even though her voice shook. 'He didn't want anything, Mrs Stone. He was leaning over me, and he had a knife in his hand.'

54

Belle was doing everything she possibly could to console Milly over the loss of her baby brother. Jill was touched to see them out on the lawn together, Belle putting her arm around a crying Milly, hugging her. Sometimes, she listened in to what they were chattering about.

'We're the can-do girls,' she heard Belle say to Milly. 'All right? We can be very sad about Jake, but we have to remember, he's safe in the arms of the angels now, and he's happy. The best thing we can do for him is to go on with our lives and be happy too.'

Jill felt choked up to hear it. She drove the girls over to the grave; Harlan didn't want to go, he stayed home.

'There's nothing there, anyway,' he told Belle and Milly callously. 'Dead's dead, that's all.'

'Shut up, Harlan,' said Belle.

'Make me,' he snapped back with a grin.

Belle didn't bother. They took flowers to the graveside, and filled urns carefully, arranging the blooms just so. They looked beautiful.

'I don't like to think of him down there, alone,' said Milly, starting to howl again as they stood beside the grave, preparing to go.

Jill patted her shoulder. Belle gave her a hard hug. 'He's not there any more, Mills,' she said gently. 'He's in heaven. Smiling down on us.'

Jill looked at Belle with pride and had to brush away a tear. Belle was going to help Milly through this. And everything – sooner or later – would maybe turn out all right.

55

Chrissy had suggested Nula get some answers, but *how?* Charlie was away on business. He was *always* away, since it had happened with little Jake. It was like he couldn't face the reality of their situation, that their child had died. He wouldn't even visit the grave with Nula. He got furious if she so much as mentioned it, so she had to go there alone and stand there looking at the tiny prayer book headstone and wondering *why?*

But then she knew why, didn't she? It was because they were *wicked.*

She thought back to those wild parties they'd once had. The unbridled sex, the swinging they'd once indulged in, before the babies, before her depression set in and gripped her so tightly in its merciless iron jaws. And the drugs business. That, more than anything, meant they were damned to hell. Didn't it? Maybe they *deserved* to lose Jake. But her mind kept going back to Chrissy. *He's not 'there'.*

Christ! What did *that* mean?

But Nula knew. Of course she did. She hadn't ever allowed herself to fully acknowledge it before, but she let the thoughts stream through her head now and they made her dizzy with dread. Harlan wasn't normal. He didn't interact properly with other children. Not even Milly, really. There was that one village boy who trailed around after him, that surly bullish creature Nipper, but could you really say that he was Harlan's friend? No. You could not. He was more of a *follower,* she always thought.

Mostly Harlan played alone, out there in the hall, and when he finished playing he would take his toys back upstairs and put them in the box marked HARLAN in the top nursery. He was meticulously tidy; in fact, he hated anyone touching his toys. If any went astray, he threw a spectacular strop that verged on hysteria.

He's not right.

Chrissy's wild, frightened eyes.

He was leaning over me with a knife in his hand.

Of course the kid had only been mucking about. Chrissy had gone on to say that he'd laughed and then she'd taken the damned thing off him, told him he should *never* play with knives. It was only a joke, he'd explained. He didn't mean any harm, he was just *joking*, couldn't she take a joke? It was an old bone-handled knife from the kitchen anyway, nothing really *dangerous*. But Chrissy hadn't found it at all amusing. If it really had been a joke then it had been a pretty damned poor one, and she'd been shaken by it.

Nula couldn't talk to Charlie about this. But there was the woman from the adoption agency, didn't they still have her number? Nula went into Charlie's study and rummaged through the only filing cabinet he kept unlocked, the one that contained household paperwork. It was a faint hope, and she spent a good hour sorting through the mounds of crap that every household accumulates. It was no good. There was nothing there.

Nula paused, looking around the study. Charlie's desk was clear; nothing on it except a dog-eared pink blotter and a silver paper knife. She went around the desk and sat in the studded ruby-red leather chair and yanked at the drawer handles. All locked.

Damn.

She looked again at the blotter, the paper knife. Oh fuck it. She snatched the knife up and jammed the blade into the top drawer, above the lock, and heaved. The drawer snapped open with a *crunch,* and Nula gulped as she saw the damage. She'd broken the damned thing now. Charlie would be livid. But for fuck's sake! If the bastard wasn't so damned shifty, she wouldn't be driven to do things like this, would she?

She opened the first drawer and checked through the contents. Nothing. The next – and it was sort of satisfying now, levering the drawer open, hearing the wood give way – nothing. Some brass knuckledusters. A pile of invoices. Goods Inwards notes. The next drawer? Nothing again. She was getting fed up with this. And nervous. She was wrecking Charlie's desk, and he was *not* going to be happy. She'd do one more, and then she'd get the stupid thing repaired, get a cabinet maker in, before Charlie got home; he'd be none the wiser.

Nula tried the next drawer and there it was.

She pulled out the copies of the official forms both she and Charlie had signed, and there was the letter from the woman who'd delivered Harlan to them, and *there* was her office phone number. Nula was sweating lightly with nerves. She wiped her hands on her skirt, then pulled the phone toward her and dialled, aware of her heart thwacking hard against her ribs. She knew Charlie wouldn't like this, her going over his head this way. But she *had* to do it.

'H'lo?' asked a female voice.

That threw her. The woman sounded half asleep.

'Hello?' said Nula. 'Is that Mrs Bushell?'

'What?'

Nula was starting to get impatient. 'Mrs Bushell, it's Nula Stone. We got a little boy from the adoption agency, you remember? Harlan?'

'Oh!' There was movement on the other end of the line, what sounded like more voices, and when the woman spoke again she sounded sharper. 'Yes. Mrs Stone. How can I help you?'

'Well . . .' Now Nula was actually talking to the woman, she found she didn't know what to say. *Did you send us a psycho?* No. That sounded wrong. 'Look, Mrs Bushell, we've got some concerns about Harlan and what we're wondering is, do you have any information about the kind of background he had before he went into care? That sort of thing?'

'Oh.' Silence again.

'If we could have information like that . . . ?' said Nula.

'Well, I would have to look into my records. If I can take your number, Mrs Stone, and call you back tomorrow?'

'You've probably got it on file,' said Nula.

'Let me take it again anyway.'

Nula reeled off the number.

'I'll get those details for you, Mrs Stone,' said Mrs Bushell, and put the phone down.

Nula went over to the photostat machine and quickly took a copy of the form containing the agency's contact details. Charlie had said it was a *government* agency, completely above board. Then she went out into the hall to head for the kitchen and make herself a cup of coffee. Later, she would phone up and get the desk repaired. And she would phone the agency number again, maybe check it in the Yellow Pages, make sure she had that right.

Now, she needed caffeine. She felt unsettled by the conversation she'd just had with the Bushell woman. As she was crossing the hall, she nearly tripped over Harlan, crouched near the doorway to the sitting room.

'Shit!' she exclaimed, startled.

Harlan looked up at her and smiled that thin smile of his.

Had he heard any of that?

Now she really *was* getting paranoid. Of course he hadn't. He was absorbed in his own little world, as always.

56

Terry didn't like this. That consignment falling prey to Customs down in Southampton? All right, if one was stopped there were still a hundred more that would get through. He knew it wasn't a big deal. But it gave him an uneasy feeling because he had never traced it back to anyone. *Someone* had blown the whistle on them, and if they'd done it once, and gone undiscovered, then they could certainly do it again and possibly with greater consequences to the whole Stone operation.

No shit had stuck to them that time. They'd been lucky. But he didn't want to risk the same thing ever happening again.

Then it did.

It ate at him, his failure to track down the culprit. Charlie had already poked around, seen what was going on, but drawn a blank so he'd asked Terry to go over the whole thing again. But still – nothing. Terry arrived home at the gatehouse day after day, wrung out, frustrated, to tell Jill that he'd questioned dockers, talked to their insiders in the port authorities, done everything he damned well could, and still come up with a big fat zero. This was his job, covering Charlie Stone's back. He'd sworn to do it, right from when they were kids, and he was going to go on doing it while he still had breath left in his body. So to fail in this task was monumental for him. It *killed* him.

They were sitting at the kitchen table. Dusk was coming down and the lights were on. They were eating stew. Nothing fancy. Terry had never developed a taste for posh food like Charlie. He was telling Jill, not for the first time, how frustrating he found it, that he wanted to track the *bastard* down who'd done it, shopped them once again, caused them such trouble.

Suddenly Jill put down her knife and fork and looked him dead in the eye.

'It was me,' she said.

Terry's fork was halfway to his mouth. His hand froze, mid-air. He stared at his wife.

'You what?' he said, thinking he must have misheard her.

'I did it from a phone box in town. I told the police that the consignment was coming in and that there would be drugs in it. I did it the first time, too.'

Terry put the fork down. His eyes were fixed on her face. He couldn't believe what he was hearing. He felt like he'd been gut-punched.

'For God's sake, why?' he managed to get out at last.

Jill picked up her glass and took a long pull of wine. Then she said: 'Come on, Terry. This business. You don't like it any more than I do.'

That much was true. He'd known and understood the heavy game on the rob. *This* was something very different. But for fuck's sake!

'You grassed Charlie up?' he gasped out. 'You mad, girl?'

'People die on this stuff he brings in. You know that, don't you. And we live well on the back of that. We're dealing in death. It's wicked. There's no other word for it. It was playing on my mind. So I . . . I did it.'

That wasn't the full story – not by a long shot – but it was as much as she could bear to tell him.

'We could have gone down. The whole fucking lot of us, did you think of *that*?' Terry burst out. 'If they'd traced it back to us, the shit would have hit the fan big time. What the hell's been coming over you?'

Jill looked at her half-eaten meal and abruptly stood up. 'Look, keep your voice down. Belle will hear.'

Belle was up in her room, doing homework. It was the unwritten rule between them; Belle must never know the true nature of the trade they were all wrapped up in. She was an innocent child, and – like Milly up at the big house – she would stay that way. None of Charlie Stone's dirt would ever be allowed to touch the girls. They'd all agreed on that, long ago.

'I'm not talking about this any more,' said Jill, and left the room.

Him and his *fucking* mate Charlie. It hurt her, how strong the bond was between the two men. She knew that, for both of them, friends came first; wives, second. It devastated her, every day, that Terry was so up Charlie's arse, but she had no choice but to soak it up – when Charlie had done such a dreadful thing to her, right here in Terry's home.

Later, in bed, Terry held her. In the darkness he squeezed her tight and whispered: 'Why'd you do it?'

'I told you,' she murmured.

'There's nothing else?' he asked.

'Like what?'

'It wasn't because of what I told you about that daft cow Nula? Not to spite her, to spite both of them?'

'No. It wasn't that.'

'There was nothing in it. Truly.'

'I know that,' said Jill, and for a moment she was on the point of saying it, out loud: *Charlie Stone raped me. So what the hell else does that rotten bastard deserve but treachery? Why do I have to spend every day here, seeing him, living in fear, wondering if he'll do it again when he sends you away on 'business' to Christ knows where?*

She couldn't say it. Terry's whole world would collapse if she did.

'There's nothing else,' she whispered, and kissed his cheek.

'You'll never do it again?' he asked. 'Swear to me.'

'Never,' said Jill.

She wouldn't. Minutes after making the calls, she'd been shaking with fear. She knew Terry was right. It could be the end of everything, what she'd done. Years in jail for Charlie and Nula, Terry and her. Belle and Milly and Harlan left, taken into care, their lives ruined.

'I swear on Belle's life,' said Jill. 'I will never do it again.'

'Good,' said Terry, and finally he turned away from her and slept.

57

Charlie got a call from Candice, one of the working girls on his manor, when he was at one of his London houses.

'Your wife phoned me,' she said.

'What?'

'Nula. Your frigging wife. She called and she's asking about the kid. About Harlan. About what sort of background he had, before he was with the agency.'

Charlie stared at the phone. 'What'd you say?' he asked.

'I said I'd get back to her, but I didn't. I said I'd have to check the files.'

Charlie gazed across at Terry, sitting there looking a question at him. What in the fuck, he wondered, was Nula asking about *that* for? And where did she get 'Mrs Bushell's' number, which was Candice's number, the same one she had answered as 'the agency' all throughout the process of Harlan's adoption? He thought he'd had that all locked safely away, out of sight.

'Change your number with BT, OK?' he said.

'Christ, Charlie, do I have to? All my clients . . .'

'Do it,' said Charlie, and slammed down the phone.

'What's up?' asked Terry.

'Nothing,' said Charlie, thinking of Harlan as they'd first seen him, crouching pale-eyed and filthy in the cupboard under the stairs in that shit-hole of a squat.

He thought of Harlan's 'background' with his junkie mother. Of course, Charlie had told the kid he must never talk about that.

Never. No way did he want Nula ever finding out about it. And the kid never had. Actually, Harlan never talked much about *anything*. Charlie had been worried that he might speak out, at first. Now, he didn't worry any more. It wasn't in the kid's nature to make conversation, and that was a relief.

58

The cabinet repair man had come and mended the desk. After he was gone, there was a strong smell of fresh varnish in the air, so next day Nula opened all the office windows and hoped for the best. Any luck, Charlie wouldn't be home for a few days and that would give it time to clear. He wasn't the most observant man, anyway. The day-to-day running of the household never seemed to concern him at all. And since the tragedy with Jake . . . well, he'd lost interest in a lot of things. Including sex, which she was glad about because she had never felt less like sex in her life. If the bastard had laid a single finger on her, she would have bitten the thing right off anyway. Any time he tried to so much as *hug* her, all she could see in front of her eyes was *Jill*. All she could think was *rapist*.

She laid out by the pool until mid-afternoon, wondering what the hell had happened to them. She was deep in mourning over baby Jake, and where was her husband? Here comforting her? Not on your life. He was off, burying his pain in business. Nula thought of her mother and wondered whether she ought to try to get in touch, tell her what had happened. Suddenly, stupidly, she really missed her. They hadn't spoken in years. But she didn't think she could bear to talk about it anyway. Any conversation that headed in that direction usually ended with a monumental crying jag that could go on for days. Sometimes she felt that her grip on sanity was hanging by a thin thread; any additional strain was likely to break it.

Even Milly wasn't much of a comfort to her, as a daughter should be. Nula thought with guilty envy of Jill and Terry's girl Belle, who was self-confident and pretty as a new spring day. Then she thought of poor Milly, who'd inherited all the Perkins genes. Milly wasn't a girly girl, not at all. She had no interest in clothes shopping. She was shy, studious, uninterested in make-up. She avoided boys. Didn't bother with pretty clothes. Meanwhile, Jill got a pretty, outgoing, self-confident little princess called Belle. It wasn't fair.

At three Nula showered and had coffee. Then she took the photocopy of the adoption form and went back into Charlie's office – the sickening varnish smell was gone now. She closed the windows and took down the Yellow Pages, sat at the desk and checked out the government agency's address and phone number.

It was a different address. A different phone number.

That was odd.

She sat staring at the Yellow Pages entry for a long moment, then she pulled the phone toward her, tapped in 141 and then dialled the number from the Yellow Pages. It was picked up straight away.

'Good afternoon, who can I connect you with?' asked a brisk receptionist.

'Oh!' Nula was taken off-guard. 'Well, I . . .'

'Which department?' snapped the woman.

'I want to talk to a Mrs Candice Bushell,' Nula glanced at the photostat form. 'She's Chief Adoption Officer.'

The receptionist was silent for a beat.

'I'm sorry, we don't have any Candice Bushell here,' she said.

Nula looked at the phone in bewilderment. 'But you must do. Unless she's left . . . ? She came to our house. Over *five years ago*. I spoke to her on the phone only yesterday . . .'

'I've worked in this office for over twenty years. Trust me, no Candice Bushell has ever worked here.'

Nula found that she was gasping. Her chest felt tight. She couldn't draw air down into her lungs.

'But . . . you must have us on record. Mr and Mrs Stone. We adopted a little boy. Harlan. Maybe there's someone else there I could talk to about this . . . ?' And then another name sprang into her tired brain. 'Wait! There was another woman, this Bushell person said she'd taken over from her, a Mrs Mulville. You must remember her, Mrs Bushell said Mrs Mulville had been with the agency a long time.'

'You must be mistaken.'

'*What?*'

'As I told you, I've been here for twenty years. And there has never, to my knowledge, been a Mrs Mulville working here.'

'No. No! *You're* mistaken.'

'Mrs Stone, please leave me your telephone number and your address, and I will have someone contact you.'

Nula didn't bother. She put the phone down in a daze.

'Mrs Stone?'

Nula was so startled by the voice that she almost shrieked. She looked up and there was the new au pair, Chrissy's replacement.

'Sorry, did I make you jump?' Fern was a meaty, motherly girl, dark-haired and broad-hipped. 'I was about to take the kids up, if you want to come . . . ?'

'No.' Nula levered herself to her feet. Her legs felt like rubber. 'You go ahead.'

The au pair went off upstairs. Nula walked through to the sitting room and slumped onto the couch, gazing out of the window at the flat open fields. It was pretty here and now she hated it. She wanted to be back in London, in the thick of the action, where things always seemed to make much more sense. Where she had once *belonged*.

She sat there until the light started to fade from the sky. The sun set in a burning blaze of apricot and gold on the far horizon, and then the evening star winked on and night started to fall. She supposed she ought to go to bed. She never slept well, not any more. Her marriage was a joke, her life a disaster. Tiredly she pushed herself to her feet. Not bothering to switch on the lights, she walked the familiar path across the big hallway and up the rounded sweep of the stairs.

For once she slept deeply, but it was a bad sleep, wracked with nightmares. She dreamed of dead babies and cool, oily black pools that she fell into and drowned in. But Jake was in there, and he was alive, he was OK. She held him and stroked his face, and felt a breathtaking happiness, such a huge sense of relief. He was alive! And then it was morning and she woke up and realized all over again that her baby was dead, gone forever.

Tiredly, she slipped on her dressing gown and her fluffy pink mules and, not bothering to shower, went downstairs in search of coffee. Then she heard it.

A baby, crying.

Jake?

She could hear Jake, crying. She *could*.

As she hesitated on the third step down from the top, her foot slipped from under her and she felt herself falling, tumbling, until she was at the bottom. She knew she was hurt badly, she couldn't move and soon she started to feel herself slipping away from the world and felt grateful for it because baby Jake was dead, she *knew* he was dead, he was calling to her, and now she was going to join him.

59

When Nula came back to full consciousness she found herself lying in a hospital bed, machines beeping around her. Charlie was sitting there at her bedside, his eyes dark with worry, and there in the doorway of the private room she could see Terry loitering.

Shit, I must look a mess, thought Nula, seeing Terry standing there gazing at her. And then there was another thought: *I'm not dead. Jake's dead and I'm not.*

But she'd heard him.

She hadn't been imagining that; it was Jake's cry, she knew it was, and she'd heard it just before she'd slipped and fallen on the stairs.

Worse thoughts were crowding in now. She was floaty with some sort of painkiller, but still the thoughts wouldn't keep away. The woman on the phone, denying all knowledge of Mrs Bushell and of the Mulville woman too. And then falling, slipping on something. *On what?*

'You're back,' said Charlie, leaning forward, taking her hand. 'Christ, you've been out of it for days.'

Nula tried to speak. Her voice emerged a dry croak. Charlie picked up a tumbler of water and, holding her head, helped her drink. She spluttered. Coughed. Then drank again.

'I . . . I fell,' she said finally.

'You did. The au pair heard it. It was her who called the ambulance.'

Nula nodded. 'Am I . . . ?' she started.

'Bumps and bruises, that's all, the docs said. Nasty crack on the head, though. Concussion. They were worried about that, had to make sure you didn't have a bleed on the brain or some damned thing. But here you are! You're back with us.'

Nula carefully raised her hand and touched her head. Bandages there. Her arm felt heavy, so she let it fall back down onto the bed.

Charlie was standing up. 'I'll get the nurse . . .' he said.

'I stepped on something and I fell,' said Nula.

'That's right, babes. You did.'

'What did I step on?'

'Ah shit, I know, what a bloody thing, eh?' Charlie's face darkened with anger. 'Harlan left his fucking skateboard there. I've *told* him, you got to put your stuff away, boy. Accidents happen that way. Well, an accident *did* happen. You poor mare. But thank God, you're all right.'

Nula sank back onto the pillows. Her eyes drifted to Terry, in the doorway. And there was Harlan, right there beside him, looking blankly back at her. Nula felt a chill sweep over her skin, felt fear claw deep into her.

But Harlan always *put his things away. Even the skateboard. He* never *left them out.*

Not unless he meant *to, anyway.*

She thought of him crouching outside the study when she'd been on the phone to the woman at the adoption agency. Had he been listening? Did he realize how much he creeped her out? Had he heard those comments she'd made about him not being 'there', not being 'right'? And hearing Jake's cry . . . oh shit. The fear gnawed deeper now. Was she going completely bloody insane? Was that it? She'd been depressed for a long time, popping endless pills, having counselling, keeping journals, but nothing seemed to work. Was she losing her mind as well?

'You rest there, I'll get the nurse,' said Charlie, and hurried from the room, leaving Terry standing in the doorway looking awkward.

Harlan moved forward until he stood beside her bed. Nula felt herself cringe. She knew the truth now. And . . . Christ, she was never going to be able to prove it. She knew in her bones that somehow Harlan had killed Jake. Killed off the favoured son, the competition. Killed her baby.

'I'll . . .' said Terry, moving back as if he too would leave the room.

'No!' said Nula, louder than she'd meant to. 'Stay, Terry. Stay here.'

A red-haired nurse came in with Charlie close behind her. She said: 'Well! Mrs Stone, you gave us all a bit of a fright, didn't you. How are you feeling?'

Harlan was hustled away from the bed. Charlie and Terry left the room, taking him with them. Nula relaxed while the nurse fussed around her. When she was better, when she felt *strong* enough, she was going to talk to Charlie about Harlan. And she was going to tell him all about what had happened when she'd phoned the agency. She was going to get to the bottom of whatever weirdness was currently happening in their home. She knew she was in mourning and had been a bit demented with it, maybe she still was.

Jake, crying . . .

However, she was sure of only one thing: Harlan, her adopted son, who she'd nurtured and tried to be a decent mother to, had tried to kill her. And when he'd come close to her just seconds ago? She'd been on the verge of screaming the whole fucking place down.

60

Belle was out by the garages up by the big house, dressed ready for a trip to the stables and waiting for Milly and Beezer, who was driving them, to show up. What she *wasn't* expecting – or hoping for – was that Harlan should pitch up instead.

She'd been standing by the big Merc in the garage and the instant she saw Harlan coming into the garage she pushed away from the car and watched him nervously. There was only a small corridor's width between the car and the end wall, and Harlan was walking toward her, cutting off her exit.

God, she was sick of this.

Ever since she was little, Harlan had been a pest to her. Now they were getting older, growing up, it was getting worse, taking on distinct sexual overtones. She avoided him whenever she could. But when their paths did happen to cross, he never seemed to miss a chance to brush up against her or corral her in a corner like he was doing now.

'Hi, Belle,' he said, stopping in front of her, his eyes crawling over her lower half, which was clad in tight jodhpurs. 'Off riding then?'

'No, taking dancing lessons,' snapped back Belle.

'Funny,' he said.

'I'm waiting for Milly and Beezer.' She flicked a look at her watch. 'They'll be right here, any minute.'

'Right.' Harlan moved in closer. Belle took a hasty step back, very aware that she was trapped here. She couldn't go around the car at the front, it was tight up to the garage wall. Her only possible exit was through Harlan. And he knew it. 'Time for us to have a cosy little chat then,' he said.

'I don't think so,' said Belle coolly.

'Oh come on, Belle. You know you want to.'

'Fuck off, Harlan,' she said.

Harlan stepped closer still. He was so close now that she could feel his breath on her face.

Creep, she thought.

'You should be nicer to me, you know,' he said, coming closer still.

Belle stepped back again. She was nearly up against the end wall of the garage. Nowhere to go.

'Why's that?'

'Because one day all this is going to be mine. You do realize that, don't you. Not dopey little Milly's. *Mine.* And that means it could be yours, too. If you play your cards right.'

'I don't want any part of it, Harlan. *Or* of you.'

'You're just fighting it,' he said, as if she hadn't spoken. 'I know we got something special going on, you and me.'

To her horror, he put a hand on her left breast, over her heart. She gave a start and pulled back, but her back hit the garage wall and Harlan was on her in an instant, fumbling at her tit again, pinching her nipple, hurting her.

Belle didn't even think about it. She shot out a knee, catching him square in the groin. Harlan doubled over, falling against her, nearly pulling her over.

'What's going on?' said a male voice at the front of the garage. It was Dad.

Belle shoved past the bent-double Harlan and ran to where her father stood. Her heart was nearly exploding out of her chest, she was so panicked. Harlan turned toward the pair of them, seeing

Terry there holding Belle, who was white-faced with fear. Still clutching his balls, Harlan gave a teary-eyed smirk.

'Nothing,' he said. 'Nothing at all.'

Terry looked at Belle. 'What happened, honey?' he asked.

Belle shook her head, wondering what the hell would have occurred had her dad *not* come along. All she wanted was to get out, away from Harlan.

Then Harlan said it; the words that Terry would never forget.

'What you gonna do about anything? I'm Harlan Stone, and what are you, Terry bloody Barton? You're just the *help.*'

Terry disengaged Belle's clinging arms and gave her a push toward the door.

'Go down and wait for Beezer by the gate. I'll tell him you're there, OK?' Then he turned back to Harlan. His eyes were flinty with rage. 'We're going to have a talk.'

61

When Nula was out of hospital, she bided her time until Milly and Harlan were out of the way before cornering her husband. 'So what's the truth then, Charlie?' she demanded.

The woman from the government agency had never phoned her back. Probably thought she was a crank. Probably, she was right. Nula felt like her grip on things was loose, at best. She was shaky. Full of anxiety. Her chest was tight every day and her head ached. She hardly slept for fear of waking up one night with Harlan looming over her, knife in hand. Something wasn't adding up about Harlan, something was *off* about the kid, and she was going to find out why.

'About what?' He looked startled.

Yeah, of course he did. *Does he think I've found out about him fucking Jill Barton against her will?* She hoped he was sweating over it, the arsehole. She hated him, but she was stuck; frightened. She didn't want to lose the lifestyle she'd craved and was now so used to. And she couldn't divorce Charlie Stone, not knowing all that she knew. She'd been inside the tent pissing out, and it was too late to think of doing the reverse. He'd kill her. Christ, if he knew all the stuff she'd been putting in her journals, about him and all his crooked goings-on, he'd wring her neck *right now.*

'About Harlan. I contacted the adoption agency.'

'You what?'

'I contacted them and I asked to speak to that Mrs Bushell

woman who sorted out all the paperwork, the one who came here with Harlan a couple of times when he was a kid. You remember her?'

'Where'd you get the details from?' he asked. Suddenly he looked mad.

'In your bloody *desk*, Charlie,' snapped Nula.

'But I keep that locked.'

'I levered the damned drawers open. Broke the locks, then had the thing repaired. You didn't notice anything, did you. Didn't even smell the fresh varnish in there. If you're never going to be straight with me about *anything*, what else am I supposed to do but take things into my own hands?'

Charlie jumped to his feet and paced about. Then he rounded on her.

'I've been straight with you. I've done fucking *everything* for you.'

'Those two things ain't the same, Charlie. You're so used to doing hooky deals that you probably think they are, but they're not. I'm not a child. I don't need shielding from the world. So tell me – did you *really* get Harlan from the agency? That Mrs Bushell, was she *really* an official, or just one of the people on your payroll? Christ knows you've got plenty. And you got print men coming out of your arse, aintcha? Forging a few official-looking documents would be a piece of shit to them.'

'Look . . .' started Charlie.

'Don't bullshit me. I mean it: *don't*.' Nula was trembling with the force of her rage. He really was the lowest of the low. Egging her on so that she 'partook' in those wild parties, the dirty bastard. And then raping another woman – his best friend's wife! There was *nothing* he wouldn't sink to. Whenever Charlie tried to initiate sex with her these days – and thank God it wasn't often – all she could think about was him forcing himself on Jill. 'That weird little fucker tried to *kill* me. And now I want an explanation. I want the truth.'

Charlie was running his hands over his balding pate, over and over. He'd aged, she thought. But then – so had she. 'Christ Almighty,' he muttered.

'There's worse, Charlie,' said Nula quietly.

'Worse?' He spun around, stared at her. 'Jesus, Nules, ain't we had enough shit to last a lifetime?' He blinked and for a moment Nula could see that he was on the verge of tears. 'Losing our boy that way? Little Jakey? And now you've got this *rubbish* in your head about Harlan . . .'

'It ain't rubbish. I spoke to Chrissy Foster . . .'

'*That* bitch? We should never have left her in charge of our boy. *Never.*'

'She woke up one night and Harlan was standing over her bed. He had a knife in his hand.'

That stopped Charlie in his tracks. He stared at her, dumbfounded.

'You're fucking kidding me.'

'I wish I was. I'm not. She said she thought there was something wrong with him. That he had . . .' Nula frowned, groping in her memory. 'She reckoned he had a thing called reactive attachment disorder.'

'This is bollocks,' said Charlie.

'No! She was serious. And if you don't believe *her* . . .' Now Nula hesitated. The next part was *terrifying.*

'What?' prompted Charlie when Nula fell silent.

'Ask Beezer. Ask him what he saw at four o'clock on the morning that . . .' Her voice broke. '. . . That little Jake died.'

Charlie was staring at her, open-mouthed. *'Beezer?'* he echoed faintly. 'What the fuck's he got to do with anything?'

Nula stood up on shaking legs. 'Ask him,' she said, and walked over to the door and opened it. Harlan was there, hanging his coat on the hook that was a mere five feet from the sitting room door. Had he heard? Milly and Belle were upstairs, thumping about. Then Milly's sound system was cranked up to full volume and the bass started pounding faintly through the floor. The Bay City Rollers, 'Bye Bye Baby'. You always knew when Milly was in the building. She wasn't exactly dainty. Now Nula could hear her daughter and Jill's singing along up there. Harlan was different. He was quiet as a mouse. No, not a mouse. A *cat*, maybe, stalking about silently, in pursuit of a kill.

'Hi, Mum,' he said.

Nula went past him, into the kitchen. And then she heard it. Not just Milly's music. She could hear Jake, crying. It was *real*.

Harlan had followed her into the kitchen.

'Can you . . .' she started to say, then her voice died on her and she had to gulp and start again. 'Do you hear that, Harlan? That noise?' she asked him.

'What noise?' Harlan was staring at her blank-eyed. 'What, Milly's row, d'you mean?'

Nula didn't reply. Instead she hurried out into the hallway and up the stairs and along the landing and up more stairs. Then she was running, she was *sprinting* along the second-floor hallway and then she reached the door. The *nursery* door, next to her and Charlie's bedroom.

Her hand reached out to the doorknob and then she drew it back, fearful. She could still hear Jake crying, and it was a sound that wrenched at her. She didn't believe in spirits, in ghosts, but what if she was wrong, what if Jake was crying for his mother somewhere, in torment?

She opened the door and stepped into the room.

'Jake?' she whispered.

Her voice echoed back at her from the walls. The room was

completely empty. After Jake's funeral, Charlie had insisted all the nursery stuff be disposed of, he'd said it was too upsetting for them both to have the room left like some sort of shrine. Nula had resisted, cried, pleaded, but deep down she knew Charlie was right. There was no point holding onto the past. It was gone. It was dead.

She stood there in the empty nursery, shivering with dread. There was nothing now, nothing but the noise of Milly's music and the frantic beating of her heart.

The crying had stopped.

I'm going mad.

'Mum?'

She whirled around with a shriek. Harlan was standing there, staring at her.

'What's the matter?' he asked her.

Nula was shaking her head. 'Nothing, nothing,' she muttered. She was going insane. Completely *crazy*. The baby wasn't crying. The baby was *dead*.

62

'You know what? I think she's going off her fucking head, my girl,' said Charlie. He was in the gatehouse kitchen, talking to Terry.

'What d'you mean?' asked Terry. He'd had his own thoughts about Nula's grip on sanity too, but he'd never voiced them. He stood there, leaning against the sink, arms folded, staring at the top of Charlie's head. Charlie was losing his hair. He was getting older. Well, they all were. Older and sadder, it seemed.

Belle would be home from her secondary school soon, with Jill. Since Jill had told the authorities about those shipments and spoken to Terry about it, he'd been on pins whenever Charlie came down here. What if Charlie found out? What if Jill acted odd around him, somehow gave herself away?

'D'you know what she keeps saying to me? You know that time she fell down the stairs? She said Harlan left that skateboard on the stairs deliberately, that he *wanted* her to fall.'

'That's crap,' said Terry after a beat.

Actually, though? It wouldn't have surprised him. He didn't like Harlan. Harlan was quiet – the exact reverse of Charlie. But you always felt he was *scheming*. Harlan was getting tall now, and handsome. But . . . sort of *wrong*, somehow. For quite a while Terry'd disliked the boy's attitude around Belle, and then to find her in a state of panic after Harlan had clearly been groping her in the garage, intimidating her . . . well, he'd flipped. Given the boy a slap. Warned him, *Stay away*.

Terry didn't like Nipper, either, that local thug Harlan hung around with. He'd heard that the pair of them had been up to all sorts down in the village but got off with a warning from the local police. Stupid things. Robbing washing lines. Pushing dog shit through letterboxes. Leaving a dead fox on a hunt protester's doorstep. *Nasty* things.

'I know it's crap.' Charlie frowned and let out a huff of breath. 'Of course it is. Come on. Let's go and get busy. Bloody women, they're all crazy when it comes right down to it.'

1980s

63

Time was passing and it was healing the pain, just a little. Nula started to live for when Harlan was out of the house. Charlie was still away most of the time. Milly, who was now a teenager and seemed embarrassed by her own mother, spent all her time at Belle's. Leaving her all by herself, with only the cleaner, or the gardener for company. And the men on the door – these days there were always men on the door.

Nula had no friends now. None of her old mates from the manor were interested in keeping in touch. They thought she was happy here, living among the country nobs and thinking herself better than the Londoners she'd once happily mixed with. Which wasn't the truth, not at all. She thought of those old grey grimy streets and longed for them, longed for the old safe, settled life in her parents' modest two-up two-down. But it was too late to even think of building bridges with them now.

So mostly she was stuck here, and then Harlan would come home and say nothing, but he would smile that secret smile of his and her flesh would literally *crawl*. Everything she suspected about Harlan haunted her, filled her every waking moment. She went to the local library and read books on reactive attachment disorder, sat there for hours poring over them, and it was as if it was Harlan they were talking about.

Without a primary caretaker, the books said, a baby passes through several phases: from protest to crying to a sad stage and then to a deep, desolate state of resignation. Thinking of Harlan's dead-eyed stare, Nula wondered about his mother. Everyone *had* a mother, after all. A birth mother, anyway. So where was Harlan's? Had she voluntarily put him into care, or – Nula thought of Charlie's irritation, his rage when she'd questioned him about this – had he never been cared for at all, and was *that* why he never seemed to respond appropriately to anything or anybody?

On the way home from the library, Nula always went to Jake's grave to tend it. She went there every week, pulled out weeds, refreshed the flowers. The girls came here too, Milly and Belle – they brought little posies of buttercups, daisies, cow parsley, which was sweet of them. Harlan never bothered. She thought of her baby, her precious child, lying cold and long-dead in the soil. And she cried. Oh, how she cried. Then she had to go home. Although she detested Charlie, she didn't like him being away, because of the crying.

She'd heard it again, and again. So many times. But maybe it wasn't real. Maybe it was only in her head. She'd caught Charlie looking at her oddly more than once. And then . . . ah Christ, what a fool she'd been. She'd told him about the crying. She shouldn't have done that. Well, she'd better just get a grip. That's what Mum had always told her: get a grip. Pull yourself together. Worse things happen at sea. That was the only useful thing her mum ever did teach her. Dear old Mum. She missed her so much now, missed her like a limb.

Nula didn't think there could be anything worse than losing her baby. She wondered when it would stop hurting, when all the madness would go away. When the crying would stop. Maybe it never would.

When she got home, there was an unknown car on the drive. Paul, her driver, parked up beside it and she let herself into the house. Young Sammy was on the door today. So many people they had to have around them now. To her surprise, when she walked into the sitting room, there was Charlie. And there was her doctor, a tall bespectacled man with thick black hair, and there was a woman with him, petite, blonde, with harshly indented cheekbones and dark circles under her big cornflower-blue eyes.

'Here she is,' said Charlie, jumping to his feet.

Doctor Benson stood up. 'Nula,' he said in greeting. 'This is Sophia Burnett, one of the clinical psychologists attached to the surgery, I believe you've met before . . . ?'

They *had* met. Lots of times. Sophia came forward and shook Nula's hand. The last time they'd spoken had been well over a year ago, when Nula had told her for the hundredth time about her dead baby crying, and the fact that Harlan had tried to kill her.

'Hello, Nula,' said Sophia.

'We've come out to see you because your husband asked us to,' said Dr Benson.

'Oh? Why?' Nula looked a question at Charlie.

'I've been concerned about you, doll,' said Charlie, looking sheepish. 'Worried, you know? When you started on about still hearing the crying . . .'

'I *did* hear it,' said Nula. *I still do.*

'I know. I know that. And when you started ripping my desk apart trying to get information about Harlan, and saying he'd tried to kill you, nonsense like that . . .'

'It's not nonsense.'

'Babes, it *is*. It's . . .' Charlie hesitated, groping for the right words. 'It's not your fault. You've had a tough time and it's all been playing on your mind. The stress of losing the baby, it's upset you, I understand that, and what I think . . .' He glanced at Dr Benson, at Sophia Burnett. 'What we *all* think is that you need some time away. Someplace where you can rest up and recover. You know?'

'What, a holiday?' Nula asked, agog. Charlie *hated* holidays.

'No, more like a retreat. You know the sort of thing. Like that place where the film stars go when they need a . . . a rest?'

Charlie stood there looking awkward.

Nula gazed at her husband, at the two others standing there, and the penny dropped at last. They wanted her committed. They thought she was losing her mind.

'What?' she said, dry-mouthed. Then she thought, oh God – to get away from this place. From the echoing empty halls, the eerie sighing of the wind around the eaves, the sobbing from the empty nursery. From *Harlan*.

'If you would just agree to taking some time out, babes. To getting a rest. We all think you need it. We really do.'

Nula stared at them. You had to agree to be committed. She knew that.

Charlie shuffled his feet. He wouldn't meet her eyes. He was *embarrassed* by her. And she was so tired, so sick and so *tired* of it all. Him. And this place. This awful *fucking* place.

'All right,' she said at last. 'I agree.'

64

You had to feel sorry for the charmless little bastard, really. Jill often *did* feel sorry for Harlan, very sorry indeed, because she didn't think Nula had ever been any great shakes as a mother, not even when she was right in the head, which she most certainly wasn't, not any more. The stress of losing Jake had unhinged her and she'd been in and out of the funny farm half a dozen times since, getting treatment. And Harlan had Charlie for a dad, the poor kid. She guessed that Charlie would be OK with a loud kid such as himself, but Harlan? No way would they ever get on.

Jill often wondered why Charlie and Nula had adopted a boy like Harlan in the first place. Surely there would have been others more suitable? They'd got him as a boy, but surely a small baby would have been a better choice?

Now she was watching all the teenagers as they played by the pool at the back of Charlie and Nula's place. Milly was sitting apart from the others, reading a book, her glasses slipping down her big nose. And Harlan . . . well, if Milly would never win a popularity contest, neither would he. Harlan was a misfit. And as for Belle . . . her lovely daughter was growing up fast. Jill thought that Belle was going to break a lot of hearts. Maybe she would be a model, or an actress. She was good-looking enough to do anything she damned well liked. Jill herself was pretty – but she knew that Belle was one step on from that.

Jill didn't like Harlan at all. He gazed at Belle all the time, like she was an ornament, a trophy, something fascinating and priceless that he would like to own. Jill had been aware of Harlan's fixation with Belle, right from the very first moment they met. But now Belle was blossoming into young adulthood and the problem was more acute. She spoke to Terry about it.

'Don't worry,' Terry told her. 'I had a word with him. He'll keep clear now.'

But having had bitter experience with the Stone men, Jill was doubtful. Milly sometimes asked for Belle to come over to the main house for sleepovers, but Jill would never allow that. Truth was, she felt that the house where Nula and Charlie lived was cursed, tainted by the awful memory of baby Jake's death and then by Nula's depressive illness. And maybe a curse was all they, all *any* of them, deserved. Oh, Belle and Milly still knew nothing about the business. Nor would they ever. Everyone was agreed on that. But Harlan was of an age now where Charlie would want to include him, to train him up to one day take over both the legitimate business and the illegal one. It was a sick, evil trade. They dealt in death. They imported it, made it at the crack factories all around the East End, then they supplied it, sold it to deadbeats on the streets who sold it on again, to kids, to drifters, to bored businessmen and aristos, to people who could one day find themselves hooked and with no chance of ever getting free from the hell Charlie and his crew had introduced them to.

Sometimes Jill wept, full of disgust and fear over the path they'd all come down. How had they come so far from the life where they had grown up hopeful, feeling that the future was full of promise? Jill didn't feel that way any more. She hadn't felt like that ever since that time Charlie Stone had decided it was his right to rape her. She lived her life in constant fear for all of her family, and these days, whenever Charlie showed up, she made sure she kept out of his way. Because it was *him*, wasn't it. That loud repulsive *bastard*. *He* had led them all into this life. Like the devil tempting Jesus he had said, Look, all this could be yours . . . just do this.

And Terry had done it; everything and anything Charlie asked, Terry did. Terry was – even now – Charlie's man, one hundred per cent. That male bond was strong, far stronger even than the one Terry had with his own wife. Jill and Nula had followed on behind their menfolk, not questioning anything. Seduced by living the high life. Living it large. They'd never, ever asked any questions. But bad things had happened. Horrible things. And she just knew there was worse to come.

A yell went up, startling Jill from her thoughts. Harlan was standing by the deep end of the pool and Nipper was thrashing about in the water. Milly looked up from her sunbed, gave a smirk and then returned to her book. Jill hurried over.

'He fell in,' said Harlan with a shrug.

'He bloody didn't,' said Belle, running up in her tiny pink bikini.

Jill felt uneasy, looking at her. Belle had budding breasts and hips that were beginning to curve into the shape of a woman. Jill realized she was going to have to have a talk with her daughter about covering up more when it wasn't just family. Soon. But then – even fully clothed in her plain grey school uniform or in riding jodhpurs, Belle *still* looked like jailbait.

'You pushed him,' said Belle.

'Snitch,' said Harlan, his smile widening to a grin as he saw Belle's temper.

'You did. I saw you,' insisted Belle.

'Oh for God's—' started Jill, then she jumped into the pool and caught hold of Nipper, who was panicking and out of his depth. 'It's OK, I've got you,' she said, and hauled him to the edge.

'I'm OK,' he said, scrambling out, snatching up a towel and starting to rub himself dry.

'Course he is. Aintcha, mate?' Harlan slapped his follower on the shoulder.

'You're such a dick,' said Belle.

Harlan just kept smiling.

65

Milly watched the little drama unfold in the pool and then, hiding behind her sunglasses, got back to her book. She wasn't wearing a swimsuit, although she was uncomfortably hot in her T-shirt and jeans and would have loved nothing better than to plunge into the cool water. And she *would* have, if she'd been alone. But with Harlan there? No way. He called her fat arse all the time, while ogling Belle as she romped about in her too-revealing bikini.

God, it's obscene, thought Milly as she lay there casting covert glances at her adopted brother. Harlan was growing up fast, his shoulders widening, a slender muscularity emerging on his torso. In figure-hugging swimming trunks, the bulge of his cock was all too evident. Not that Belle ever seemed to return Harlan's interest. He was beautiful, she supposed – but cold as alabaster. Milly watched as he went over to where Belle was sitting by the edge of the pool, dangling her feet in the water, and sat down beside her.

She really is pretty as a picture, thought Milly. And Belle was fearless, too; she'd tackle anything, go anywhere, confident of a good outcome whatever she was faced with. Milly envied her that.

'Can I sit here?' said a voice from above her.

Startled, Milly realized that Nipper was standing over her, indicating the sunbed beside her own.

'Sure,' said Milly, and he sat down and stretched out. 'Don't take any notice of Harlan,' she told him, laying her book aside. 'He's just a bastard, he can't help it. It's in his nature.'

Nipper turned and looked at her. 'What's the book?' he asked.

Milly showed him the cover. 'It's boring.'

'He's nothing like you, is he?' he said, his eyes fixed on Harlan. Milly thought that Nipper was Harlan's puppy. Harlan could kick his arse, and he'd still roll over and let Harlan tickle his tummy, even after that.

'Harlan? Christ no.'

Milly turned her attention to Belle. She let out a sigh. 'She's so good-looking.'

'Fancies herself, don't she?' sneered Nipper.

'Must be great, looking like that.'

Milly thought that it would be easy to hate Belle for being so perfect, but somehow you couldn't: Belle was so kind, always will-ing to pitch in and help with anything. And she always tried to include Milly, always making sure she was OK. Belle called them the 'can-do' girls. Milly thought that *Belle* had a can-do attitude, for sure. But her? She was never going to set the world on fire and she knew it. Belle was like the sister Milly had never had; she loved her.

'You're nice looking too,' he said.

He was only being polite, she knew that.

'I mean it,' he said. 'You've got nice eyes. And great legs.'

'And a fat arse.'

'I like your arse,' said Nipper.

'Well you're the only one that does,' said Milly, colouring up.

'It's like a peach,' said Nipper. 'A big . . . what's the word? Yeah a big, sweet peach.'

It occurred to Milly then that something was going on here. For the first time ever, she was being chatted up by a boy. Granted, Nipper wasn't the brain of Britain, but he had nice thick straw-coloured hair. She glanced at him, reassessing. He was big, bulky and tanned from the summer sun. And he was tall. So what if he was Harlan's lapdog? He thought her enormous arse was *nice*.

'Milly!' It was her mother, waving from the French doors leading into the big house, the *better* house, where the Stones resided. Belle might be the golden one, the outgoing and lovely one, but it was Milly's father, Charlie Stone, who had all the power and the dosh around here. 'Come give me a hand with the drinks?' said Nula, who was currently at home and not for once locked up in what Harlan laughingly and unkindly called 'the bug hutch'.

Milly got off her sunbed, aware of her hot flesh sticking to the chair, aware of her own ungainly movements, *hotly* aware of Nipper watching her.

'See you tomorrow?' he said.

Milly paused and stared at him. 'OK,' she said.

66

That summer turned unexpectedly into a haze of gold. Milly spent the long hot days basking under the sun, swimming in the pool, eating *al fresco* and revelling in the attention that Nipper was paying her. She had never been flirted with before, never made to feel in any way special. To her mother – who seemed crazy these days, a woman with wild eyes and jerky movements, trapped in a world of her own – she was an inconvenience; to her father, she was a useless girl, not a boy, not *worth* something, like Harlan. But to Nipper, she was obviously far from the bore she had always believed herself to be, with her nose always stuck in some romantic blockbuster by Danielle Steel or Sidney Sheldon.

To be kissed by him was wonderful. And slowly over the course of the summer he went further, slipping his hand inside her blouse and touching her breasts. Then further still, making her breathless with desire so that her only focus was him, Nipper. Harlan was still there making up to Belle, and Belle's mother was always there too, standing guard over her daughter. Everything else – Jill and Belle included – became an unwanted distraction from the games they played together, her and Nipper.

One hot, humid day they were in the pool house. Nipper had beckoned her over, then, laughing, pulled her inside and shut the half-glassed door behind her. He yanked down the blinds at the windows. Laughing too, Milly looked through the door's top section, back at the pool. Jill and Belle had gone off into the kitchen, and only Harlan was out there right now, sprawled on a sunbed, eyes closed.

Nipper lusting after her had given her confidence; now she wore a one-piece swimsuit, and didn't care if it showed off the size of her arse. He said she was a beauty and suddenly, as if by a miracle, she was.

He pulled her into his arms and kissed her. Their hot skins stuck together; he was only wearing bathing trunks. Jesus, she thought, with a sizzle of alarm and arousal, they were almost naked.

'I can't,' she said, drawing back, breathless.

'You know I want to,' said Nipper.

It was the same old refrain. All through the summer, they'd wrangled about this. He wanted sex with her. She wasn't sure. Now Nipper snaked his fingers inside her swimsuit and squeezed her breast. Her nipple hardened under his touch and Milly groaned.

'It'll be OK,' said Nipper. He dug in the tiny pocket at the side of his trunks and came up with a small square packet. 'Look. I'll wear this. I'll take care of you, don't worry. Feel it, Milly. Feel how much I want you.'

He was pushing her hand down between their bodies. Milly's hand closed over a long column of hot flesh. It was startling.

'God, that feels good,' he sighed.

'We can't,' said Milly weakly. 'Someone could come.'

'God, *I'm* going to come if you keep your hand there,' he said, stepping back a little and looking down the front of his body. 'Nobody's about,' he said, tearing the Durex open with his teeth. 'Come on Mills. Slip your swimsuit off, we'll be quick.'

But I don't want it to be quick, thought Milly. She wanted it to be slow, magical. She couldn't say it. Instead, she nervously pushed the unflattering black swimsuit down, exposing her soft pale body.

Nipper was snapping the Durex onto his cock as if he'd done

this a hundred times before. That made Milly pause. But then he was pushing her eagerly toward the bench.

'Just lean over and rest your hands on there,' he said, pushing her down. 'Oh yeah, Mills. Your beautiful arse, I love it . . .'

And then he was behind her, pushing into her. There was a moment's resistance, and then . . . Milly screwed her eyes tight shut and held her breath . . . it was OK. He was in. And it wasn't magical or slow or any of the things she'd expected. It was quick and it was just like the animals in the field; it was no different at all. Nipper panted and swore and slid in and out of her at ever-increasing speed. He grabbed at her breasts and squeezed them hard, hurting her. Milly wondered if this was how it was for all women. Because that's what she was now: a woman. This was what men and women did.

She turned her head and opened her eyes, wanting to tell him to stop, that she wasn't sure about this, that this was all wrong, not how it should be at all. Then she froze.

Through the half-glassed door, she was looking straight into the mocking gaze of Harlan.

Milly let out a shriek. Harlan was standing right there outside the door, watching them.

Nipper didn't stop; he probably thought her cry was one of pleasure. He kept thrusting at her and then suddenly he let out a yell and it was over. He gave her breasts one last hurtful squeeze and then drew back, laughing, triumphant. Milly was shivering despite the tropical heat inside the pool house. She was embarrassed, humiliated.

'Christ, that was good,' Nipper was saying, pulling off the Durex and snatching up a towel to dry himself.

She thought of the news on the TV, saying Princess Diana had given birth to William, a future king. It was a fairy tale, the royal marriage. Milly wanted that sort of romance in her own life. But instead, she had *this*.

'Harlan was out there. He was watching us,' Milly managed to say.

She struggled back into her swimsuit, feeling sore. This wasn't how it was meant to be. In her dreams, her and Nipper having sex was something that happened on their honeymoon, after they were married, because he couldn't live without her and he told her so, all the time. *You're the love of my life, Milly. I adore you.* Only in reality Nipper had never said that to her, not once, and she knew he never would. And now they'd had sex and she felt cheap and used and dirty.

'Harlan?' Nipper was laughing, like it was a joke. 'Was he? That dirty bastard! Well, maybe he learned something.'

Milly surged past Nipper and opened the door and stepped out into the fresh air. Harlan was back on his sunbed, but when she came out he looked across, grinning, and said: 'Having fun, Milly?'

Milly didn't answer. She was aware of Nipper coming out behind her and she didn't want to stay here a minute longer. She tore off indoors, and went upstairs.

67

Outside Harlan's room, Milly paused.

That rotten shit.

She remembered all too well when he'd come into the house for the first time, looking all around him like he would *eat* the damned place if he could. He'd had a choice of rooms, but weirdly he'd chosen the smallest, the most enclosed – with no view. Harlan had a taste for small spaces, whereas Milly hated them. He loved nothing better than being in that little cubby-hole down in the reptile house where the various feeds were kept, reading his books about all the weird and frankly *creepy* things him and Dad kept down there.

Self-pity swamped her then. She'd been humiliated and hadn't received a single bit of sympathy from Nipper. She was sore, uncomfortable. God, what did she have in her life, really? That arsehole for a brother. Well he wasn't even a brother, not really. He was *adopted*. And she hated him. Mum was always sitting in a corner crying, scribbling in her journals and she still swore that sometimes she could hear baby Jake crying. That was just spooky, bloody *awful*. Then Mum would be carted off to the clinic again to be given heavy-duty pills to calm her down, and she'd be like a zombie.

Milly was busy cataloguing all her woes. She had no affection from Dad, it was obvious she was a disappointment to him, a *girl*. No affection either from Nipper, he'd screwed her like she was a tart or something, there didn't seem to be any actual love involved. She was rotten, academically. Thick as shit. She knew it. Which would have been *fine,* if only she'd been good-looking, like Belle. Belle was her friend, but unlike Milly she had other friends, other interests. She was always off doing stuff. Most of the time, Milly felt so damned *lonely.* So she took refuge in books, in food, and then her arse just got bigger and bigger, she was swelling up like a balloon, she *hated* her whole damned life.

She stood there, looking at Harlan's closed bedroom door. When he was younger, there'd always been a sign on it: KEEP OUT!

Now the sign was gone, but she knew damned well that Harlan didn't like anyone in there. Then she thought of him grinning through the pool house window at her, the bastard. She bit her lip and opened the door and went in, closing it quickly behind her. She looked around. It was a normal boy's room, but scrupulously tidy. That was Harlan, wasn't it. His brain might be a sewer, but outwardly everything was order and calm. He kept a blue-lit tank on one wall, and it held a lizard, standing still as a statue. Crickets jumped around in the cage, unaware of their danger.

Milly went over to the window. She could just about glimpse the pool from here, and she could see Harlan, still laid out on his sunbed. Nipper was in the pool's shallow end. Belle was sitting on the edge of it, shouting instructions, which Nipper was ignoring. Jill was standing beside her daughter as if on guard, with her hands on hips.

Milly started looking around. She'd never been in Harlan's room before. She was curious. It would be useful, having an insight into Harlan, even if she *did* hate the perverted twat. She thumbed through his CDs. Heavy metal, all of them. He had box files stacked on his shelves, royal blue in colour, and she pulled one out, opened it. Just boring bloody leaflets about keeping exotic pets. She snapped the file closed and went on to the next.

More about keeping tarantulas and snakes, pages about caring for gerbils, which apparently were territorial and ate each other at the drop of a hat.

Oh yuck.

The lizard moved, its tongue shooting out. One cricket down, three to go. Milly shuddered. She detested lizards and always avoided going down to the zoo that Dad and Harlan loved so much, where the bigger ones were. The snakes there revolted her. There were boas down there big enough to swallow you whole. The caimans in the big central pool had grown and now they were large as adult crocodiles, and there were warning notices up all over the place. DON'T FEED THE CAIMANS. IF YOU HAVE TO HANDLE A YOUNG CAIMAN, WEAR STEEL-REINFORCED GLOVES.

Well, she was never going to handle one of those damned things. They might look cute when they were tiny, but they were nothing but fucking predators, weren't they? There was something ancient and intensely cold about them that made her stay well away.

She pulled out the third box file: it would be more of the same, she knew it. Harlan had an obsessive streak. She flipped the lid open and stopped dead, staring in surprise. It wasn't about the pets. There were no files inside. There was just an old cassette tape machine, a cheap ALBA one, complete with a plug-in lead. Why the hell would Harlan have an old thing like this, when Charlie bought him nothing but the best and the latest gear?

Milly pressed the OPEN button; there was a tape inside.

'Well that's odd,' she said out loud. She crossed the room and took another peek out of the window. No change down there. She removed the tape deck from the file and found the nearest socket and plugged it in. Then she pressed PLAY but it wouldn't, it was obviously at the end of the tape. She pressed REWIND and it spun back. Clicked when it reached the beginning. Again, she pressed PLAY. There was silence for a while, and then . . .

Oh fuck . . .

All the hairs on the nape of her neck stood up.

It was a baby, crying. A baby she *knew*.

Milly slumped down onto Harlan's bed in disbelief.

God, what the hell was this?

She was listening to *baby Jake,* crying.

68

Summer began to fade into autumn. The thing between Milly and Nipper drifted on.

'I'm so pleased I've got him,' Milly was always saying of her hulking great boyfriend, as if trying to convince herself. If Milly was pleased, that was fine with Belle, even though she personally thought that Nipper was a knuckle-dragging moron.

Meanwhile, Harlan *wanted* to be Belle's boyfriend, but that door remained firmly closed.

'He's a creep,' said Belle to anyone who would listen, including Milly.

The two girls were often sitting out on the lawn behind the gatehouse together, Sony Walkmans on, whispering, giggling, listening to Irene Cara singing 'Fame' and Survivor doing 'Eye of the Tiger'. Their lovely 'Uncle' Beezer drove them into town, bought them sweets, made them laugh at his dumb jokes. They both adored him.

'Yeah, Harlan *is* a creep,' agreed Milly, arranging her legs so that the fat between her thighs didn't stick together quite so painfully. The two of them were eating Twisters and discussing everything.

Milly frowned, as she always did when their chat turned toward Harlan. She hadn't mentioned it to anyone, but she couldn't forget what she'd found in Harlan's bedroom. That had triggered other things in her brain – like the crazy things Mum had said to her, before yet another admission to the mental institution. That Uncle Beezer had seen Harlan going into Jake's nursery on the morning he'd died, and Harlan had always hated little Jake because he'd taken Harlan's place in Charlie's affections. Then Mum, falling down the stairs, her feet slipping on Harlan's skateboard.

She could have been killed.

And ever after, Nula had reacted to Harlan with fear – whenever she was at home, which wasn't often. The death of her baby and the weirdness of her adopted son had screwed with her brain big time. Poor Mum, no wonder she was *crazy*.

'You really like Nipper,' said Belle. 'Don't you.'

Milly thought that maybe 'like' was too strong a word. She knew she wasn't aiming high, having him for a boyfriend, and she wasn't keen on all the sex stuff, but it seemed to make him happy, so she did it. She was pleased to be a 'normal' girl, like any other. She lived in terror of missing her bleeds, but he was careful, and – well – that was a woman's life for you, she'd figured that much out.

She wished she had a proper mother to talk to, but there was no way that any of this shit could be discussed with Nula. The slightest stress, and she went totally off her tree. But Milly was literally dying to share her secrets with *somebody*. She didn't want to even think about the dinner she'd sat through last night, with Dad and that oily little Colombian Javier Matias with his greased-back hair and his paunchy stomach. The guy was her dad's age, and yet he'd – *ugh, disgusting or what?* – seemed to be flirting with her through most of the meal. And Dad had sat there smiling throughout, as if this was perfectly OK with him.

Milly wasn't happy about all this; she liked things the way they were. Dad was comfortably loaded because of his furniture business, and up to now that had meant that nothing was ever expected of her. She didn't have to get involved in the outside world, and she liked that fine. She didn't want to be pushed toward this business contact of her dad's; Javier repulsed her.

Belle was closer to her than anyone else right now. Her best friend in all the world. Belle had always been good to her, tried to include her in things, even coming to her defence when Amanda and Gillian, that snobby pair from the stables, had bullied her, grabbing her school bag and emptying it into a ditch, and then nicking the hard hat Nula'd bought her in the hope she'd get into riding like Belle, which of course she hadn't.

Milly would never forget Belle giving those two the walloping they deserved and *ordering* them to hand back the hat. Faced with an infuriated Belle instead of soft quiet Milly, they'd backed off and never bothered either of them again.

'It must be nice,' said Milly, sprawling out lazily on the grass and staring at Belle's face, turned up to the sun, 'to be pretty.'

Belle looked at Milly. 'You're pretty,' she objected.

Milly gave a small sad smile. 'No I'm not. I'm a dog.'

'That's not true,' said Belle, turning toward her, hitting Milly with the full wattage of that beautiful face of hers. 'You've got lovely eyes.'

Damned with faint praise, thought Milly.

'Oh don't bullshit me. They're like piss-holes in the snow. I don't actually know what Nipper sees in me.' But really she *did* know. Nipper liked sex; and Milly put out.

'He sees a lovely person,' said Belle. She was staring off into the distance, licking the last of her lolly from the stick, then tossing it aside and sighing. 'None of the boys I fancy will approach me, whereas the ones I can't stand seem determined to have a go, if only to prove that they're not the losers everyone thinks they are.'

Milly had to smile at that. 'You're so full of crap,' she said, flopping back onto the grass and staring up at the clouds scudding across the sky. 'I thought you and Nige Pope were getting it on these days?'

Nige Pope was tall, gangly, red-haired and sweet. He was the brainiest boy in the school and destined, everyone thought, for great things.

Belle frowned. 'What, Einstein? We were. He's lovely. But most of the time he's too busy with his textbooks to bother about me.'

'You'll meet someone nice, one of these days,' said Milly, rubbing Belle's arm consolingly.

Belle gave a smile. 'Yeah, maybe.' But she wondered where? Who did she ever meet, out here in the sticks? Sometimes, she felt so restless. So *confined*.

'So who comes on to you that you don't want to, then?' asked Milly after a pause.

'Oh, you know.' Belle frowned. 'People.'

'Who, though? Come on.'

Belle flopped back too. For a while she lay there, looking at the sky in silence. Milly didn't push, she just waited.

'Harlan,' said Belle at last.

Milly sent her a sideways look, holding one arm up over her eyes to shield them from the sun. She'd suspected this. She'd seen how Harlan was too touchy-feely with Belle, how Belle always flinched away from him. 'Is he a pest?'

'He's a pain in the arse,' said Belle. 'Never seems to take no for an answer, the prat.'

Milly was silent for a moment. Wondered whether she should say anything. Then she said it anyway. 'I found something, you know. In Harlan's room.'

Belle propped herself up on one elbow. 'Oh? What?'

'Something weird,' said Milly.

'Well come on. Tell me. Something to do with those things he keeps down in that reptile house of his, I suppose.'

'No, nothing like that. I shouldn't have looked in his room, I do know that.'

'What's in there that's so shocking? I know he keeps lizards up there in a tank. He asked me to go up there once and see them. Which I did not. They're cold-blooded, aren't they. Like him. I can see why he likes them so much. So come on, what was it? What did you see in there?'

'It was a tape recorder. And . . .' Milly hesitated. Would Belle blab about this to anyone? She wasn't sure. But she had to say it now, or choke on it. 'I played a cassette tape that was on it.'

'And?' prompted Belle.

'It was a tape recording of the baby. Of Jake. Crying.'

Belle was very still.

'Do you remember how my mum used to say she could hear the baby, crying? And they thought she was imagining it, didn't they? Before she was committed that first time.'

Belle sat up sharply. 'You're fucking joking.'

'I wish I was. Mum told me that Uncle Beezer saw Harlan at four in the morning after Jake's christening party, going into Jake's nursery.'

Belle was suddenly pale. 'Then they found Jake dead.'

Milly nodded.

Belle dragged her hands through her hair. 'Hold on. Wait. Maybe it wasn't Jake crying. Maybe it was some other kid, and Harlan recorded it to freak your mum out. He'd think that was funny.'

Milly shuddered and hugged her knees. 'No. It was Jake. I'd know Jake's cry anywhere. I could never forget it. *Never.*'

'Yeah, but . . . they didn't find anything *wrong* with Jake's death, did they. They said it was cot death. Awful, but it does happen.'

'Belle – what if Harlan smothered him?' shot out of Milly's mouth. She'd been thinking it for weeks, and it made sense. She

218

thought of the agony of sitting through Jake's funeral, the pitifully small coffin up there at the front of the church. It haunted her. Her little brother, gone, never to return. 'What if Harlan *killed* the baby? And what if he left that skateboard on the stairs deliberately, knowing Mum was always first down in the mornings? What if he's been playing that tape to make her go crazy?'

Belle turned her head and looked at Milly.

'We got to tell someone about this,' she said.

'Yeah, but who? Dad would go *mental* if I said any of this to him. Mum was always on at him about Harlan. It upset him. He couldn't take it, not after losing Jake like that. You know what boys are like. Well, *men*. He'd flip if I started doing the same as she did, saying these things. He'd think I was going crazy too.'

'She's not crazy. Is she? Just sort of depressed.'

'Yeah. I shouldn't say that. It's rotten.' Milly picked irritably at a hangnail. 'But I keep hoping, you know?' She gave Belle a desperate, trembling smile that didn't reach her eyes. 'Sometimes she's all right for months, then something hits her, some stress or worry or *something* – anything will do it, it seems to me – and then she goes into this nosedive, and then it's off to the clinic to get treatment, and then she's OK for a while. Until the next time. And *every time* I hope it's the last, and . . .' Milly bit her lip and stopped talking. There were tears in her eyes. She shook her head. 'But it never is. And . . . in the end . . . I start to feel sort of depressed too. Like there *is* no hope. That it's just wishful thinking that one day she'll be well, be the person she used to be. They're not even a couple any more, you know. I think it's worn Dad out, all the worry of her being like she is. They sleep in separate rooms. They live separate lives.'

Belle reached out and rubbed Milly's soft rounded shoulder.

'I'm sorry, Mills. I didn't know it was so bad. You know – maybe that's it.'

'What?' Milly swiped at her eyes.

'Maybe the person we should be talking to about all this is your mother.'

'We can't talk to her. She's too fragile.'

'I think we have to.'

Milly pondered this, frowning. 'She's coming home in time for Christmas,' said Milly. 'They say she's a bit better now. That's what they *say*.'

'Then we'll speak to her,' said Belle, and they lay back down on the grass and soaked up the last of the sun. 'Gently, mind. When you think she's strong enough.'

69

It was a frosty December day when Nula came home in the Bentley. Terry was in the front passenger seat, and Peter – one of Charlie's old boys who had advanced training in mobile protection work – was at the wheel. Charlie sat beside her in the back, chatting to her, making out everything was fine. Nula had felt like it was, back at the clinic. The doctors had said they were pleased with her progress.

Now, doubts were creeping in again. What they were riding along in was a mobile fortress; the car was armour-plated. They had someone at the wheel who could thwart an attack if one happened. And Terry was armed. When he'd picked up her bag at the clinic, she'd seen the bulge of the gun in its shoulder holster under his suit jacket.

'All right then, babes?' Charlie was asking her, while she was thinking about all this security that Charlie had to have around him now. Because people wanted to kill him. He was a wealthy man with a dangerous secret life, and there were those who would want to take all that away from him and have it for themselves.

'Yeah.' She forced a shaky smile. 'Fine.' She looked at her husband. He was growing older, chunkier. His brown hair had receded until now his head looked like a monk's, with a smooth bald section in the middle. Only his brown eyes were the same as always. He looked tanned. He looked *rich*. Every inch the successful owner of Stone Furnishings Ltd.

The car swung sharply left as they turned into the driveway, passing the gatehouse. Then they were roaring up to the main house and Peter was parking up. The engine died and they all got out, Charlie moving ahead of her, leading the way indoors. Indoors, to the place where her baby had died. And where – she didn't doubt this, not for a minute – their adopted child had tried to kill her.

She hesitated inside the open doorway, looking in at the massive gold-decorated Christmas tree, the loops of ivy and bright baubles bedecking the big staircase in the hall. She could hear David Bowie and Bing Crosby dueting on 'Peace on Earth/Little Drummer Boy'.

'Like it?' asked Charlie. 'We had it all done special, just for you.'

'Where's Milly?' she asked, not answering his question.

'Upstairs,' said Charlie. 'She'll be down in a minute. Can't wait to see you.'

'And is he here . . . ?'

She could see Charlie making an effort to be reasonable. To be patient. Neither of which were Charlie's strong suit. 'Who, babes?'

'Harlan.'

'Mum!' It was *him*, coming across the hall, smiling. Harlan. He'd passed his seventeenth birthday and was growing into a smoothly handsome young man, one of those individuals who were always immaculate. He was wearing a white silk shirt, Harris tweed jacket, stylishly cut jeans and well-polished tan brogues. His honey-brown hair was brushed and gleaming, his face clean-shaven, his cool grey eyes alight with what seemed to be pleasure at seeing her. *Or he's faking it,* she thought.

Nula felt a moment's total panic. She repeated the mantra the psychologist had taught her at the clinic. What happened to your baby upset you, made you see and hear things that weren't there. But you're better now, and everything's OK. Of course Harlan isn't a threat to you. Not at all.

Somehow she got an answering smile plastered onto her face. 'Harlan,' she said, and didn't shudder or shove him away when he came in close and hugged her. Then he hugged Charlie too.

Nula watched the two of them together and thought: *Charlie's committed to Harlan now. He's completely invested in the devious little shit; he's blanked Jake, his real son, his* dead *son, from his mind and locked him away in a box marked* too painful to think about.

Terry put the bag down on the hall floor and said: 'OK, Charlie, I'll leave you to it,' and he left, closing the front door behind him.

Charlie turned to his wife. He thought that she'd aged, the poor bitch. Worry had etched deep lines in her face. Her eyes were anxious.

'Come on babes, let's get you upstairs, get your stuff unpacked,' he said.

'I'll bring the bag,' said Harlan, reaching down to snatch it up.

'No,' said Charlie a shade too sharply. 'I'll take it.'

Despite her efforts, Charlie could see that Nula was rattled by the sight of her adopted son. Right then and there, he made a decision. Harlan was done with schooling now. He'd sort him out a place in town, get him started properly in the business, get him out of Nula's way.

Beezer could keep an eye on him.

It would work out fine.

70

The days turned into months and things seemed just about normal for Nula. Well, as normal as they ever got, living with Charlie. As a treat, he took her out in the Bentley with Sammy, one of the new younger guys, at the wheel.

'For a little surprise,' he said.

Nula felt nervous as soon as she stood out on the drive. Sammy was there, sliding a mirrored stick under the car, moving it back and forth.

'What's he looking for?' she asked Charlie, who was standing beside her, chatting to Terry.

'Explosives,' said Charlie, and resumed his conversation as if this was a normal thing for a person's driver to do.

Then they all piled in the motor and Sammy set off down the driveway. Halfway down, he braked sharply. Nula jerked against her seat belt and looked at Charlie, who didn't even seem to have noticed. He was thumbing through a magazine about light aeroplanes. Christ, he already had a big Sunseeker moored down at Crableck Quay on the Solent, a Maserati and a couple of top-of-the-range Ferraris parked up in the garages at home, a superyacht called *Lady of the Manor* down in Palma marina. He was particularly delighted about the superyacht because it was six feet longer than Javier Matias's. Not a bloody plane now, surely?

'What did Sammy stop like that for?' she asked, feeling her nerves start to jangle.

'Checking the brakes are sound, that's all,' he said.

He means not tampered with, thought Nula. *Oh Christ.*

'Where are we going then?' she asked him. She hated surprises of any sort.

'You'll see.'

They ended up at the heliport in London and Charlie started milling about the place, shaking hands with people, slapping them on the back, cracking jokes, doing his 'everyone's mate' act with Terry right there, sober, sensible and watchful at his side. Charlie pulled Nula forward and introduced her to the guy who seemed to be in charge of operations.

'My wife,' he said. 'Nula.'

'Pleasure,' said the man, and turned back to Charlie. 'I thought the Robinson R22 two-seater.'

'Fine,' said Charlie. He turned to Nula. 'You wait here, babes, with Terry. You just wait and see, OK?'

Charlie walked off toward the smaller of three helicopters.

'He's not . . . ?' Nula asked Terry.

Terry heaved a sigh. 'He's been up here six or seven times, having lessons.'

'Christ, really?' She couldn't imagine Charlie as a pilot. He was nowhere near steady enough to be in charge of an aircraft.

'I bet you any money you like,' said Terry, watching his old mate bouncing off over the tarmac, 'that he'll want to get in the big one today, the blue one. He won't go in the little one, that's not showy enough for Charlie, not with you standing here watching.'

'How about the middle one?'

'The Bell 206 Jet Ranger? Nah. You watch.'

Charlie and the instructor had paused near the smallest helicopter.

'Shit, there he goes,' said Nula with a bitter smile, because this was so typically Charlie. He was heading for the biggest aircraft and the instructor was following.

'That's a beast, that one, the bigger Jet Ranger. Twin engines,' said Terry.

Charlie got in the pilot's seat and the instructor sat in the co-pilot's position.

'Christ, is he sure . . . ?' Nula asked.

'Well he's been having the lessons.' Terry, arms folded, was watching Charlie put on headphones. Then the engines began to roar and Terry ushered Nula back inside the building out of the downdraught.

The helicopter's rotors became a blur and then the thing started to lift up into the pale blue sky before skimming off over the buildings and away. She watched as the Jet Ranger became a darker blue dot in the hazy distance.

'He's ordered one just like it. One point one million,' said Terry.

Nula had to laugh. That was Charlie all right. The tosser.

'Do you ever think . . . ?' she started, then hesitated.

'What?' Terry looked at her.

'That it's all too much? That it's gone too far and something's got to stop it.'

'What, the trade, you mean?'

Nula nodded. 'Yeah. The trade. The product. When we all started out, we never dreamed, did we? That it would turn out like this. That we'd have so much. Or be so . . . so fucking at risk. Armed guards. I've seen the gun you carry, Terry. I *saw* it. And Sammy looking under the car for explosives, and checking the brakes, and . . . I dunno. Sometimes it feels like we're sitting on top of a volcano, and one day soon it's gonna blow us all to fuck. Don't you ever feel like that?'

Terry looked at Nula's face. She'd said exactly what he'd been thinking for a good few years. He'd said as much to Charlie. Warned him. Said maybe it was time to cut their losses and get out of the business once and for all. But Charlie? He'd laughed and slapped Terry on the back. *Getting cold feet there, bud? Don't fret yourself. Everything's under control.*

'No,' Terry lied to Nula. 'I don't feel like that.'

'Must be just me then,' said Nula with a sad little laugh. She could see the blue dot in the sky coming back into focus, could hear the twin-engine roar start to get louder as Charlie turned the craft back toward the landing point.

Terry let out a sigh. 'There's nothing to worry about. Charlie's got things in hand. And as for him getting his pilot's licence? It's never gonna happen. There's a lot of reading to be got through and six written exams to take before you can get a pilot's licence. Charlie hates to read *anything,* even the back of a cereal packet. He'll never stick it out.'

'Yeah. You're probably right,' said Nula. This was the longest conversation she and Terry had had for years. Nula thought that while middle age had stolen Charlie's youthful good looks, it had only enhanced Terry's. Ah, she was a stupid old cow. She had her fair share of wrinkles herself, now. But she still had a soft spot for Terry Barton. Even now, after all this time.

'Did you know that Harlan has a bit of a crush on Belle? I saw him talking to her earlier,' said Nula.

Terry turned his head toward her and Nula was shocked by the vicious expression in his eyes. When he spoke, his voice was harsh.

'You make sure Charlie keeps that little arsehole away from my girl. You got that?' he spat out.

'Well, I . . .' Nula floundered.

'I told him. I'm not mucking about. I catch him anywhere near her again and I'll cut his fucking throat.'

Nula nodded dumbly. *Again?*

'I mean it,' said Terry.

'I can see you do,' said Nula, wishing she'd said nothing.

'Has something happened then? Something I ought to know about?'

Terry shook his head in irritation. 'Nah, it was a while ago. Caught him trying it on with her in the garage. Gave him a slap.'

To their mutual surprise, Charlie did keep going with the lessons. Months later, Charlie got his licence and took delivery of his very own Jet Ranger. Meanwhile, Harlan was busy in town. He was starting to make a few alterations on the manor. And that slap Terry had given him over Belle? He'd never forgotten it. And he never would.

71

Harlan had spent months quietly simmering over being sent away from the family home. So his parents didn't want him there with them. Fair enough. They weren't his parents anyway. Actually, he didn't remember ever having a father. He remembered his mother, just about. A pitiful junkie, always crying and heating up dope on little squares of tinfoil on a kitchen floor covered in dirt and burn marks from past hits. He couldn't remember her ever feeding him properly or acting as a real mother should. He remembered blokes coming in and the noises of screwing from the next bedroom, then she'd have some money and peel off a couple of quid and send him down the fish and chip shop. By the time he got home – if you could call that filthy, rat-infested squat a home – she'd be spark out of it on the kitchen floor again.

But maybe this banishment had compensations. Harlan liked the city. He got bored in the country, even though he could wind Nula up and eye up Belle, both of which activities he enjoyed to the max. But this was where the action was. He moved out of the flophouse Charlie sent him to in double-quick time and moved into Charlie's favourite five-star hotel, the grand one near the BBC building, charging the room – well, the *suite* – to Charlie's account, knowing that Charlie would rage about it but would cough up anyway.

'Your dad won't like this,' said Beezer, one of Charlie's old mates who had been, Harlan guessed, instructed to keep an eye on him while he was in the city.

'So?' said Harlan uncaringly. 'What's going down at the moment, Beezer?'

Beezer shrugged. He didn't like Harlan any more than Nula did. Cold-eyed little bastard. He didn't like the blokes Harlan kept around him either. That Nipper, who looked like he would happily rip your guts out and laugh while he did it. And the other one who seemed to have paired up with Nipper these days, Ludo, the black one who was all polished and elegant, decked out in gold chains, always grinning like a shark.

'Come on,' persisted Harlan. 'Dad wants me to learn the business and that's what I intend to do, OK?'

So they sat in the suite of the hotel and Beezer started explaining first the furniture business and then – more importantly – the drugs trade to Harlan. After all, this was what Charlie had *told* him to do.

'We cover a big area,' said Beezer. 'We cook the crack in the offices—'

'How many?'

'Six. So far. Then the rocks go out to up to fifty dealers, kids and such, from each of the sites.'

'Kids?'

'Schoolkids.'

'Right.'

'The junkies know to go to them to score. In a week, we can do up to four hundred transactions from each site. That's . . .'

Harlan squinted, working it out. 'That's two thousand four hundred hits,' he said. 'What, they don't work weekends?'

'Yeah they do.' Beezer sat back in the couch and knocked back a half tumbler of whisky. 'Seven days a week they work, in balaclavas so they don't show their faces, and they wear bulletproof vests in case of attack from rival gangs. You do get a bit of that. Then we have to step in, sort it out.'

'So what's the take?'

'About twenty grand a week per site. Over a cool million a year per office, anyway.'

'Six mill per annum then. Not bad.'

'Trouble is, some of the little scrotes think they can get away with doing a bit on the side for other gangs, and we don't like that. We deter it, strongly. In fact,' Beezer drained his glass and stood up, 'I was about to pay one a visit.'

'Lead on,' said Harlan.

'Nah, you don't want to see this, do you,' said Beezer.

'I said lead on,' said Harlan, putting steel in his voice.

Beezer looked at him. Charlie was his boss, had been for the whole of his life, and Harlan was Charlie's son. You couldn't say no to the son of Charlie Stone, any more than you would say no to Charlie himself.

'All right then,' said Beezer. 'On we go.'

72

Nula was beginning to relax. Charlie did seem to be taking a bit of a back seat these days; Harlan was busy on the manor, and that was good in Nula's eyes because it meant Harlan was away from her. Charlie'd had him installed in one of his many London houses, until Beezer reported that Harlan had checked out of there and booked himself into the Langham instead – at Charlie's expense.

Charlie's shouts of rage could be heard all over the house.

'What the hell . . . ?' Milly crossed the hall with Belle at her side. 'What's going on?' she asked her mother, hearing the yells coming from behind the closed study door.

'Just your dad, kicking off as usual,' said Nula, who was used to hearing Charlie bawling the place down.

Now she'd had another long spell away, had time to *think*, she realized that her mind *had* been playing tricks on her, that the psychiatrists were right; it had been her imagination, and really she had been cruel to Harlan, *unintentionally* cruel, and he must have seen her wariness around him as a rejection.

She made up her mind that in future she would make an effort to be nicer to Harlan. Now she was better, things would be easier. She had a clear mind. That horrible black dog of depression had let her go. She was still on the meds, of course – just to keep her steady. And still keeping her journal, writing everything up, tucking photos inside the pages, *explaining* her life. But that was all right.

Charlie emerged from the study, red-faced with rage.

'That little bastard wants to watch his fucking step,' he told Nula, and filled her in about the Langham business. 'I'm off down to see to the animals,' he said.

A visit to his 'menagerie' always seemed to soothe Charlie. He said he'd set it up for the kids – but Nula reckoned he'd done it for himself. There were no fluffy bunnies down there, no cute pygmy goats or Shetland ponies. Spiders and reptiles were Charlie's thing. Coincidentally they were Harlan's too. But they were not Milly's, or hers. 'Got some new baby caimans. You want to see them, babes. They're cute.'

Nula didn't think baby caimans were cute. They were creepy, emitting those weird cries and watching you with blank staring eyes that said: *When I'm older, I will eat you.*

Charlie went out. Then Milly came and stood in the doorway, trailing Belle behind her.

One of the new younger guys on the staff called Sammy was sitting beside the front door, reading the newspaper. The headlines shouted about Dickie Attenborough and Ben Kingsley winning Oscars for *Gandhi*. He looked up when the two young women crossed the hall and nodded at Milly. 'All right?' he said.

Milly didn't answer but Belle was suppressing a grin.

'He likes you,' she whispered to Milly. 'Say the word, he'd be yours.'

'Shut up,' said Milly, but she did like Sammy. He was OK. She'd chatted to him once or twice. He worked for Dad, here at the house or on the cars or on the doors at Dad's clubs or snooker halls, or at the furnishing factories. He'd told her about his own dad, who'd been an army man, ballistics or bomb disposal or something like that, and how Sammy had been a disappointment to him when he didn't join the army too, preferring PPO work like this.

'Mum? Can we have a word?' she asked, opening the door to Nula's sitting room.

'What's the problem?' asked Nula.

'I'm not sure about this,' said Milly to Belle.

'About what?' asked Nula. 'Come on in, don't stand in the doorway.'

The two of them stepped inside. Belle glanced back into the hall, and carefully closed the door. Then she followed Milly over and sat down beside her.

'Well?' said Nula, not liking the troubled expression on her daughter's face.

'We don't want to upset you,' said Milly.

Nula smiled. 'Come on. Spit it out.'

Milly glanced at Belle again, then took a deep breath and told her mother about what she'd found back in the summer, in Harlan's room.

73

'What you got to understand is, you work for us, not some pissing pitiful lowlife, all right?' said Beezer.

They were in a flat in Shoreditch. Two of Charlie Stone's soldiers had a kid who didn't look any older than eighteen pressed down on a piss-stinking mattress in the bedroom. There had been a girlfriend in the flat when they arrived, but Beezer had quickly ushered her out the front door and told her to fuck off and not to even think about telling anyone about this or next time he wouldn't be so gentlemanly, did she understand what he meant?

She understood. She went. And that left just her boyfriend, a spotty little oik with spiky blond hair, dressed up in a hat and eyeliner, like Boy George. Ten minutes into the visit, Charlie's boys had his fancy pants off him and were holding him down on the bed while applying his girlfriend's steam iron to his ball sack. His screams were echoing around the room, nearly deafening the lot of them.

'I said, do you understand?' asked Beezer.

'Don't think he did,' said Harlan, grabbing the iron off one of Beezer's cohorts and sending a long jet of steam billowing over the boy's private parts. The screams were dying away to little more than tired choking barks. Tears of anguish were running down the boy's thin cheeks, ruining his prettied-up hairstyle and smearing his make-up.

'He's had enough,' said one of the men.

Beezer nodded. The boy had got the message. He'd be careful

about staying true to the cause, the *Charlie Stone* cause, in future. He wouldn't want to risk this happening again.

'Nah, he hasn't,' said Harlan, and again the steam billowed out with a loud, hungry hiss.

The boy's eyes rolled in his head. He was passing out with the pain.

'Want some more, pretty boy?' said Harlan, leaning over him, grinning.

'I said that's enough,' said Beezer, and snatched the iron away. He moved over to the socket and yanked the plug out and stood the thing on the dressing table among the pots of rouge, an inch of dust and half-opened packets of coke. 'We don't want him out of work too long.'

Harlan drew back, scowling. For a minute, Beezer thought that he was going to get a right-hander off his boss's son. *He's enjoying this. Really getting off on it,* thought Beezer with a cold shudder.

All right, sometimes you had things to do. Unpleasant things. You didn't have to bloody well enjoy it though. You didn't have to be a fucking *monster.*

Then Harlan composed himself.

'OK,' he said with a shrug, and went and lounged in the doorway, hands in pockets.

Beezer went to the bathroom, dipped a towel in cold water and took it back out and dropped it onto the boy's shrivelled, scarlet manhood. The boy's eyes flickered open and he groaned.

Beezer pointed a finger at him. 'You remember this, all right? You work for Ch—'

'*Harlan* Stone,' said Harlan from the doorway.

All the men standing around the bed froze.

'Dad said I was in charge up here and I am, right?' Harlan said, looking first at Beezer and then at the two others. 'If any of you disagree with that, there's still plenty of water left in that steam iron,' he added with a smile that chilled them all.

Beezer didn't think he'd ever once heard Charlie say that Harlan should be in charge. Personally, he wouldn't leave Harlan in charge of a *dog,* much less an outfit of the size and scale of Charlie's. But what could you do? Cross Harlan and you were crossing Charlie too, and if Charlie got upset, blood was spilled. Nobody would be dishing out medals if anyone opened their stupid gobs and spoke out.

'Fine by me,' said Beezer.

'That's good,' said Harlan, and they left the building.

Later, Harlan and Beezer were in Charlie's luxe apartment with a Tower Bridge view. Harlan had ditched the Langham because he was sick of hearing Charlie carping on about the expense of it, but he wasn't going to rough it just to please that tight old cunt. This place would do him nicely, for now. As they sat there, Beezer said he was going to tell Harlan the facts of life.

'You *what?*' Harlan almost laughed. He knew all that shit. He'd had his first girl, a nobody, in the art cupboard at school, dreaming of Belle whilst he was doing it. And he would have Belle too, one day. Properly. He knew it. Her fucking father could say and do what he liked. Who did Terry Barton think he was, laying down the law to *him,* to Harlan Stone?

Terry Barton could go *fuck* himself.

'Not those facts,' said Beezer. 'I mean the real ones. The ones that apply to the trade.'

'OK. Go on then.'

Beezer told him.

'There's basuco, they get that as a by-product in the jungle labs of South America. Looks and tastes like shit. Nobody'll touch that except the street kids in Colombia. Turns 'em into zombies.

The Medellin cartel were looking for something as strong as basuco but nicer for smell and taste, you see? Then a chemist who worked for the Cali cartel got it. Dissolved cocaine powder in ammonia, added water and bicarbonate of soda, heated it until the liquid boiled off. And there it was. Crack cocaine.'

'OK. Go on,' said Harlan.

'Crack is quick. You're on the ceiling, like, instantly,' Beezer enthused. 'And the best thing? It lasts forty, maybe fifty seconds. That's all. Heroin will give you three or four hours' worth of high. Straight cocaine will give you half an hour. Crack takes you higher, faster. It's a high like no other and you come down from it always wanting more. You can get cocaine users hooked – maybe ten per cent of them – within two years. With crack? Eighty per cent of them are hooked within a *fortnight*. A fortnight! Can you believe that, boy?'

Harlan believed it. He could see the years stretching ahead of him, all the money those poor stupid bastards out there on the streets or at their fancy dining tables would fetch him, because he was the sole heir to Charlie Stone's manor.

He was going to rule the whole fucking *world*.

74

Nula always avoided Charlie's so-called 'petting' zoo. Lizards, geckos, tarantulas, snakes, caimans – they were like aliens, she often said. Not like a cat or a dog, something you could stroke and relate to. So Charlie was amazed to see her coming in there.

He was feeding the caimans, tossing chicken carcasses into the water, when the door opened into the superheated interior jungle with its endless running waterfalls, wet moss-greened walls and tropical greenery. Seeing Nula there, he paused, chicken in hand. One of the caimans, the biggest one, George, eased closer, waiting.

'What you doing down here, babe?' he asked, distracted. There was only one buggy and he'd driven it down here. Nula must have walked, all this way. And she wasn't much of a walker.

Nula was out of breath. She hadn't walked. She'd *run* all the way down here, through the grounds and then through the orchard. She had to talk to Charlie. She had to tell him what Milly and Belle had just told her. And that would prove it, once and for all. That she wasn't mad. That she hadn't been imagining things. Then she looked at what was moving near Charlie, hauling itself out of the black brackish water and up onto the stones . . .

'Charlie!' she shouted.

The caiman he'd been tossing chicken to had lumbered further out, over the stones and on to the big ornamental rocks. Distracted by her arrival, Charlie had missed it. He looked down and the thing was *there*, right there. His heart was suddenly in his mouth. He stumbled back as his 'pet' approached, quicker than he would ever have expected. It was near his leg. Near enough to bite. Christ, the things could move. Thirty miles an hour, all the manuals said. He could be dragged in and drowned in an instant.

Panicking, he tossed the chicken into the water, and the caiman instantly turned, plunging back in, its jaws gaping and then snapping shut on the thing, ripping it in half. Pieces of pallid flesh floated and then the caiman turned again, gulping down what was left. Charlie's heart was thundering like a drum. His face was slick with sweat.

Christ! It nearly had him.

Charlie stepped back, out of the caiman enclosure, pushing Nula ahead of him. He shut the big thick plastic door, then rounded on his wife.

'You fucking idiot! You don't come in here when I'm feeding the caimans. You damned near got my leg chewed off, you daft mare.'

Nula had been so shaken by what she'd been told that she hadn't given it a second thought. She'd just blundered in.

'Sorry, sorry, but I had to talk to you, it's important, it's . . .' She ran out of breath and leaned a hand against his chest. 'Oh God. I feel like I'm going to faint.'

Charlie took her arm. 'It's the heat in here. Come on, let's get outside.'

Out in the fresh air, Nula began to feel better. There was a bench set out near to where the buggy was parked. She went to that and sat quickly down, breathing deeply, steadying herself. Charlie sat too, feeling weak with the aftermath of fear, and began rubbing her back.

'You OK now?' he said.

'Yeah.' Nula turned her head and stared at him. 'I've just heard something, that's all.'

Charlie was frowning. 'What have you heard?'

'Milly found something in Harlan's room in the summer.'

'Dirty mags, was it? Come on. We've *all* done that at one time or another.'

Nula gave him a look of pure disgust. *Yeah, you dirty bastard – I bet you have.*

'It wasn't anything like that. It was a tape recorder. She played the tape on it. And . . . he'd recorded Jake crying. He had it right there, recorded. And I think he was playing it sometimes when I was alone in the house, to frighten me. To make me think I was crazy.'

'Babe . . .' Charlie was shaking his head. He looked sad. Like he was going to say any minute now, *Oh babe, I thought we'd covered all this . . .*

'Charlie, listen to me! Beezer saw Harlan going into Jake's room after the christening, on the morning he died. I think . . . Charlie, this is awful but I think it's the truth and I can't get it out of my mind. I think Harlan killed Jake. That he was jealous of him. That he wanted to be number one son. He couldn't stand the thought that Jake was always going to be your favourite.'

Charlie stopped rubbing her back. He stood up sharply, walked away from the bench.

Then he turned back and pointed a trembling finger at her.

'You know what?' he said.

Nula dumbly shook her head.

'You are fucking *crazy*,' said Charlie, and he got in the buggy and drove away, back up to the house, leaving her sitting there, aghast.

75

The parents weren't talking. Milly had sweated over whether to tell Mum about what she'd discovered, and now she wished she hadn't. But it had tormented her for so long. It *had* to be said. And now Dad and Mum were ice-cool with each other, barely polite.

The best thing to do was keep out of their way. She did a few laps of the indoor pool, happy that Harlan wasn't here. She didn't know what he got up to in the city, and she didn't want to know, either. Dull business stuff, she guessed. Learning all about brocades and sofa stuffing. *Really* riveting. After she got bored with the pool, she decided to go down to the gatehouse and find Belle, have a chat.

She dried off, combed out her hair, dressed and set off down the drive. Maybe she'd stay for lunch, escape the parents and the frosty atmosphere; Jill always made her welcome. Felt sorry for her, she supposed, with Nula half off her head most of the time, Charlie always raging.

When she got close to the gatehouse, she let herself in the little gate in the picket fence and was approaching the front door up the path when she heard voices coming from the back garden. She could hear Belle's voice, and Nipper's. Something Nipper was saying brought her up short against the house wall.

'. . . why would you get your knickers in a twist about that? It's just *sex*. Just fun. That's all. I told you.'

'Yeah, well. I'm not sure that's all it is for Milly.'

'Christ, I hope it is.' Nipper gave a harsh laugh, and it was an ugly sound, gloating, unkind. 'Grow up, for Christ's sake. Look, Milly's glad *someone's* shagging her, and I'm getting some relief whenever I'm stuck down here – which, thank Christ, isn't too often any more – without any complications.'

Milly listened and felt like she was going to throw up. His voice was horrible. Cold. Dismissive. They'd been going out for quite a while now and *this* was what he truly thought about her. They'd last slept together only days ago. She felt tears of humiliation start in her eyes and run down her cheeks.

'Milly?'

It was Jill, coming up the path toward her.

Milly started guiltily, shoved herself away from the wall, swiped wetness from her eyes. She didn't answer. Then Belle appeared from the back garden; she'd been riding this morning and she was wearing jodhpurs. Nipper appeared too.

Oh Christ!

Milly shoved her way past Jill and lumbered off down the path, flinging open the gate. Behind her she could hear them all talking, Jill's voice mingling with Belle's and Nipper's. She had to get away, back to the main house, she couldn't face any of them right now, she couldn't bear them to know she'd heard that.

'Milly!'

Someone was tugging at her arm, halting her. It was Belle, her face a picture of concern.

'Milly, stop! We . . . what are you—'

Milly felt swamped with rage then. Perfect, pretty Belle. No one would ever shag *her* as an act of charity, would they?

'You knew,' she gasped out.

'What—' Belle looked pale all of a sudden.

'You knew he was making use of me. I *heard* you, the pair of

243

you, having a laugh at my expense. You knew what he was doing, and you let it carry on, you didn't tell me, Christ I *hate* you.' Milly wrenched her arm from Belle's grasp and ran on, up the drive. A long black car swept past, going up to the house, but she barely even noticed.

'Milly, I didn't . . .' Belle was saying, but Milly didn't stop.

Nipper would have to look elsewhere for his charity shags in future, because *she* didn't want to know. Not any more. Anyway, didn't she have other avenues open to her? That new guy of her dad's, Sammy, liked her. And creepy old Javier Matias had been sending her flowers, asking her to dine alone with him.

Milly knew that Dad was encouraging Javier in his pursuit of his daughter; she wasn't a fool. Charlie was thinking of strengthening his ties with his business associate, who apparently supplied him with cut-price cotton and stuffing from somewhere in Brazil, and if he could nudge his daughter toward Javier, she knew that he'd be chuffed to bits. She was nothing more than a pawn, being used by every bastard that passed by – even by her own family!

'Milly!' Belle was trying to keep up with her. Her face was pleading. 'Oh come on. You're my *friend*, Mills. I warned you about him, you know I did. But you were dead set on carrying on with it. What could I do?'

Milly ground to a halt. Her face was twisted with rage and exertion.

'Oh poor you! Poor bloody Belle, what a tragedy for you all this has turned out to be. But no, not really, is it? Because you're still perfect and pretty with your lovely family, and I'm just a fat convenient nobody that *imbecile* screws when there's nothing better on offer. I've got a loony for a mother and a father who's always losing it and kicking the fucking furniture.' Milly heaved in a breath. 'You can fucking well *stay away* from me in future. You got that? You just stay away.'

And she turned on her heel and fled, leaving Belle staring after her.

Back up at the house, the long black car that had passed her on the drive was parked up. To her dismay she found Javier waiting for her on the porch. He was nearly dwarfed by the huge bouquet of pale shell-pink roses he was carrying.

'For you,' he said with his greasy gold-toothed smile.

'Thanks,' said Milly, awkwardly aware of Sammy sitting there by the open front door, watching this exchange.

'You are so welcome,' he said in his excellent English. 'Where is your pretty little friend? Belle, isn't that her name? I saw you down at the gatehouse, talking to her.'

'She's busy,' said Milly. Every man from nine to ninety wanted to know about Belle.

'Dinner, perhaps? Tonight?' he offered.

'No. I don't think so. I've got a headache,' said Milly. 'Sorry, I've got to lie down.'

She could see he wasn't pleased. But fuck it, she thought as she hared off up the stairs clutching the huge bouquet, fuck the lot of them. She didn't give a stuff.

76

Beezer knew *everything* about the product, and soon, under Beezer's tutelage, so did Harlan. The pathetic old sod had been hanging out of Charlie's arse for years. Harlan recalled the story that was told and retold at family parties, about Billy 'Beezer' Crowley doing a job years back but refusing to burn his designer togs afterwards for sentimental reasons – and costing himself two years inside. Fucking pineapple. Harlan watched Beezer now as he moved around town carrying out Charlie's orders, Beezer with his snappy suits and his Rolex watch and his worn old face, age-spotted from too many holidays down on the Costas.

Harlan watched Beezer whenever he was at home – which wasn't often. Watched the stupid old sod giving Milly and Belle presents, telling them funny stories, making them howl with laughter.

Silly bastard.

Harlan was getting his own comrades around him. A younger mob, the cream of Charlie's up-and-coming crew, like Nipper and Ludo and Sammy and lots of others; not the *old* crew that Charlie loved the best and shoved all the goodies towards. Harlan was busy cultivating the new boys; he liked their fresh approach to old problems. Kept them in money and whores and anything else they desired. Treated them like they were his high-flying executives and he was their CEO, had fun with them on breaks away and in massage parlours.

Him and his men were in one of the parlours on Friday night.

It had been a good week, profitable. Everything running smooth. No worries. Now it was time to relax.

The madam was used to them, looked after them. Gave them high-end booze, stocked the place with only the best girls. Chinese, African, Swedish, each one like a model. And all expensive. Not that expense worried Harlan. Never had, never would. Dad could moan, but Harlan was Number One Son, *only* son, he'd do whatever the fuck he wanted and screw Charlie Stone.

They were lined up in the parlour, all the girls, in skimpy underwear. The men were spoilt for choice.

'Her,' said Nipper. He'd selected a statuesque brunette; they wandered off together, hand in hand, to one of the many luxurious bedrooms in the place.

'That one,' said Ludo, ebony-skinned, lean and supremely elegant in his designer gear.

He'd chosen a milky-skinned redhead. She smiled and they sauntered off.

'And for you, Mr Stone?' asked the madam, smiling.

There was a small blonde at the end of the line. She had big sparkly wide-awake blue eyes, which was a bit of a problem because Belle's were a dark liquid brown, smoky with sensuality, but in other ways this girl did look a bit like Belle, and he liked that. He could fantasize about Belle while he had her. Belle was going to be his one of these days, there was no doubt about that, try as she might to resist. But this one would do – for now.

'This one here,' he said, and walked over to her. She smiled up at him, all teeth, eyes and tits, really working it, and he smiled back and took her hand. 'What's your name, then?' he asked.

'Sugar,' she said, improbably.

'Not for tonight,' he said.

'Oh?' She was still smiling.

'For tonight it's going to be Belle. OK?'

She nodded. Her smile slipped, just a notch, and then was back in place. 'Belle. OK. Yes.'

'Lead on then, Belle,' he said.

77

'That's not on,' said Beezer to Harlan days later. They were in Charlie's Tower Bridge apartment and Beezer had something on his mind. He was pacing up and down between the two big white leather couches, while Harlan lounged on one in his dressing gown, yawning.

'What?' asked Harlan, wondering what the old fool was talking about.

Beezer stopped pacing and looked down at his boss's son. 'You kicking off at Peg's place like you did. Hurting Sugar. It's not on.'

'Hurting her? I didn't,' said Harlan.

'That's not what Peg said. She said Sugar was hysterical. She was covered in bruises. You beat her up. And that's not on.'

'Says who?' asked Harlan, and got lithely to his feet. He crossed to the patio doors and slid them back, admitting a gust of sharp river air. Down below a barge sailed by, leaving barely a ripple behind in the dark olive-green waters. From here, he could hear the traffic passing over the bridge. The sky overhead was full of black roiling clouds, promising rain.

Harlan crossed to the railings and leaned on them, grinning as Beezer joined him out there on the balcony.

Beezer was looking mad, the wind ruffling his thinning hair. 'You know your problem, pal?' he said.

'No I don't. What is it?' asked Harlan.

'You're a sick little pervert,' said Beezer. 'You fuck a girl, fair enough. You didn't have to play rough with the poor bint.'

'I'll send her some flowers,' shrugged Harlan, admiring the view from here, which Charlie had told him was one of the most expensive in the whole of London. He watched the barge float on by.

'Too fucking late for that. Peg's seriously pissed off. She says Sugar left next morning. She's gone back on the streets, she said it was safer. She thought you were going to pissing well murder her, you moron.' Beezer was still pacing, casting irritated looks at Harlan. 'What the hell were you thinking?'

Harlan shrugged and spread his hands. 'I don't think when I'm fucking,' he said.

Beezer stopped pacing the balcony and stared at the younger man, his face twisted with fury. 'No, you don't think at *all*. That's your trouble.'

'You know what? You could be right,' said Harlan.

He reached out and grabbed Beezer's snazzy jacket by its lapels. Then he heaved sideways. The much lighter Beezer, caught off-guard, staggered and had no time to snatch at the railings or even see what was coming.

Harlan lifted Beezer out and over.

With an ear-splitting shriek, he fell.

Then Harlan leaned over the railing. He looked down at the wreckage of Beezer, stretched out dead on the pavement far below, blood starting to ooze in a crimson tide from his shattered body.

'Certainly didn't think about *that*,' he said to himself with a smile. Then he drew back and went into the apartment to get dressed. 'But I'm glad I did it.'

78

Charlie Stone was in shock. Harlan broke the bad news to him in the sitting room of the Essex house, with Nula there beside him. Harlan was visibly upset.

'I was there. I *saw* it,' said Harlan in a choked voice. His eyes were wet with emotion. 'I'd just got out of the shower and he was talking, not making much sense. He was saying sometimes he didn't know how to go on. Said he'd never really got over his brother dying like he did, all those years ago. That he felt over-whelmed. That he didn't like the business any more but he didn't know how he could tell you.'

Charlie, who had been standing, now sank down beside Nula on the couch. He was shaking his head, over and over.

'Why didn't he *tell* me, the silly bastard?'

'You know Beezer. He would have felt he was letting you down. He was *devoted* to you. And I suppose no man wants to show weakness,' said Harlan. 'Not in our game, anyway.'

'Go on with what you were saying,' said Charlie with a deep, shuddering sigh.

'Yeah. Well.' Harlan sat down and looked at Charlie. 'He just kept saying there was nothing to go on for. He'd never married, never had kids, he had nothing except the business, the manor, and he thought it all stank and he couldn't stand living with it for another day.'

'And what did *you* say?' asked Charlie, gulping back a tear. His old mate! He'd had no clue Beezer felt this way. Sure, Beezer had black moods sometimes. Didn't they all? And Col's death! Charlie could still remember it, in all its awful detail. So had Beezer, obviously. But Charlie had never guessed that Col's death had stayed with Beezer like that, tormented him, driven him finally to do something like this.

Harlan shrugged. His face looked pained; his voice was sombre. 'I told him not to be stupid. To take a break somewhere, have a change. You wouldn't mind. I'd explain to you for him, I told him that, there was no need for him even to face you with it.'

'And . . .' prompted Charlie.

'He wouldn't listen. He stood up and went over to the balcony doors and before I could even realize what he was about to do, he did it. He just . . . jumped.'

'Christ!' Charlie put a hand to his eyes. His shoulders shook.

Nula, her eyes fastened on Harlan the way you'd keep your eyes fastened on a cobra, said: 'Nobody else saw it happen?'

Harlan shook his head. He looked like he too was ready to shed genuine tears over this. But Nula knew her 'son'. She knew he was cold right to his heart but he could make all the right noises, appear to care when he didn't give a single shit. So far as she knew, Harlan had always disliked Beezer intensely, always mocking him for being 'behind the times'.

'So only you saw it,' she said.

Harlan nodded again. 'Yes,' he said.

Nula's eyes were still fastened on him. She'd never once known Beezer to be cursed with what she herself suffered from: clinical depression. He wasn't the type. But of course Harlan was being clever, claiming that Beezer had concealed his condition, as many men did. She thought this was pure bullshit. She thought, in fact, that if Harlan was the only witness to this event then he was lying through his teeth about what really happened.

What Nula thought was more likely was that Harlan had

pushed Beezer to his death. And why would he do that? She knew why. It was because Beezer was Charlie's man, not his. She'd seen the young thugs Harlan was starting to surround himself with – Ludo, Nipper and all the others. They were a different breed to Charlie's old gang. They laughed over the pain of others, drove flashy motors, enjoyed a level of wealth and ease that very few of their age could even dream of. What she thought was that Harlan was busily getting rid of the old and supplanting it with the new. She knew how dangerous he was. She wondered if Charlie knew it too, or if he thought her warnings were just the demented ramblings of a madwoman.

'I'm so bloody sorry,' Harlan was saying.

Charlie was still sitting there with his head in his hands. Nula was still watching Harlan.

He was having a clear-out of the old guard. But she knew that if she warned Charlie about it, Charlie would laugh in her face, or get furious and tell her she was bloody crazy again.

'It's a sad business,' said Harlan.

'Yeah.' Charlie straightened and scrubbed a hand over his wet, reddened face. 'It is.'

'But look,' said Harlan, putting his hands together and looking intently at Charlie's face. 'We'll give him a real East End send-off, yeah? Do it good and proper. He didn't have family left, did he? So we'll be his family. We'll do this for him.'

A pale ghost of a smile passed over Charlie's face.

'Yeah. That's what we'll do,' said Charlie.

Nula said nothing.

She just watched Harlan.

79

'Milly!'

Milly was walking down the drive at home one day when Nipper's car pulled up alongside her, the powerful engine idling. Milly kept walking, her face set. The engine stopped. She heard him get out of the car. She kept walking.

'Milly! Come on, stop, will you? I want to talk to you.'

Milly stopped walking. She turned on her heel and glared at him. It hurt to even *look* at him these days, after what she'd heard being said between him and Belle. They'd been *laughing* at her. Well, he had anyway. To be fair, Belle *had* been defending her. And Belle had warned her about Nipper. Maybe she'd been wrong to lash out at her friend. She was going to make up with Belle, soonest. She missed her.

'What do you want?' she snapped.

'What do you *think*?' he said, standing right there in front of her with his thick blond hair riffling in the breeze, his face twisted in contrition, his eyes pleading. 'Oh come on, Mills . . .'

'Don't you *dare* come here with that pathetic look in your eyes, thinking, "oh yes, poor old Milly, she'll forgive me because she's so grateful." Don't you fucking *dare.*'

'Look.' He ran a hand through his hair and stared at her. 'I didn't want Belle to know how I feel about you. That's all. So I told her it was only a laugh. I knew she'd tell her parents the whole thing and that they'd laugh about it, but then it might get back to Charlie and he'd bite my balls off. I didn't mean it, not a word of it.'

Milly was frowning. 'I don't believe you.'

'It's the truth. I couldn't risk Charlie finding out that we're in love.'

'You're lying.'

'No.' He was shaking his head, smiling. 'No, I'm not lying. My silly sweetheart, I'm not lying at all. I was lying to Belle, yes – but not to you. Your dad's a very dangerous man when he loses that temper of his. You know and I know, he wants you to get cosy with Javier. So I had to cover our tracks. To pretend there was nothing between us, even to Belle. You were never meant to hear any of that and I'm so *bloody* sorry if it hurt you.'

Milly was staring at his face. After turning Javier down the first time he'd asked, she'd just accepted a dinner date with him. 'I didn't . . .' she started. 'I thought . . .'

'I know what you thought. That I was a cruel bastard, laughing at you. That's not true. None of it's true.'

Milly stared at him. Well, dinner dates could be cancelled.

Nipper didn't know how he was keeping a straight face. It was fun, pulling her strings. And it was fun, shagging her. Poor desperate bitch.

He saw Milly starting to smile. 'I didn't realize . . .' she said.

'I know you didn't. I'm head over heels crazy about you.'

'Really?'

'Really. One hundred per cent. But we got to be careful.'

'Yes. OK. I get that.'

'Good.'

'Chrissakes come here and kiss me,' said Nipper.

80

Belle usually liked her trips into the Smoke. One of her dad's people – it used to be Beezer – always drove her in a nice big shiny Merc, dropped her right outside Harrods and in she went for a spree. Money no object. Anything Belle wanted, she could have.

In fact . . . well, there wasn't much she *did* want. Not today. She already had a walk-in wardrobe stuffed with designer gear, rack upon rack stacked with shoes, a cupboard full of Gucci and Chanel handbags worth a bloody fortune. But her mood was low. God, it was so sad about Beezer. He'd been a fixture in all their lives for so long, and to know that he'd done that, killed himself, it was just tragic.

Belle walked all around the store, stopped for a coffee, then did the rounds again. Nothing took her eye. Nothing appealed. A deep sadness seemed to be sapping her of strength, of purpose. She went back for another coffee, went into the ladies' loo and repaired her make-up, adding a slick of sugar-pink lippy and a squirt of perfume.

She paused then, staring at her reflection. Yes, she looked good. And men liked her. She'd had a few boyfriends, nothing serious; Nige Pope – or Einstein as all her group called him – she'd dated him for a while, but they hadn't really *clicked*. She'd never been actually *in love*, not even close to it.

She put her make-up back in her handbag and pulled a face at herself in the mirror. One day, Dad always told her, she would marry a wealthy man and she would be treasured, because she deserved to be. All the time, Belle knew she attracted attention from men. Even walking down the street, she drew stares. She was used to it. Used to Harlan trying it on too, the bastard. She frowned as she thought of him. He frightened her. They'd practically grown up together but she had never once felt comfortable around him and she hated the gang of young chancers he was gathering around himself. They were different to Charlie Stone's old workforce. She didn't like any of them.

Belle heaved a sigh. Christ, poor Beezer. That was so shocking. She couldn't seem to get over it. Her dad had been devastated about it, had actually shed a tear, and she had never seen that happen before.

In the mirror, she could see the toilet attendant getting up from her seat by the entrance to sweep around the floor, check the basins were clean, set out two fresh boxes of tissues, give this lone customer a brief smile as she went about her work. The woman had a job, a purpose.

And what do I have? wondered Belle.

I ride horses, I go to beauty salons, I get my nails and hair done. Beyond that, there was only the prospect of marriage to someone wealthy. That was it. She had no job. She'd had little real schooling. Her dad worked for Charlie Stone, was *tied* to Charlie Stone in the furnishings business, while her mum seemed – inexplicably – to hate him. But Charlie Stone put bread on their table, housed them in the gatehouse, they owed everything to Charlie Stone and his business.

She was sick of shopping. Recently, when she'd bought stuff, she'd just chucked the bags into her wardrobe and left them there. Forgotten all about them.

It would be nice to have something to fill her time. Maybe even a job. She thought of the furniture business – but then, Mum and

Dad had always been so determined to keep her out of that. She couldn't understand why, but it was a fact. Maybe . . . maybe somewhere in Charlie's company there might be room for her if she snuck in a side door and didn't let her parents know what she was up to.

She could spell and she could add up. She wasn't *illiterate,* she was quite intelligent. Not in Einstein's league, of course; Einstein who was now up at Cambridge doing clever things with physics and bacteria. But there might be something, if it was only pushing papers around a desk. She'd have to keep well out of Harlan's way, obviously, but if he was being groomed to take over from Charlie he'd most likely be working out of head office. So she'd try one of the smaller local offices. That way, at least she'd be achieving something, feeling better about herself. Because right now, she was so bored she could barely function.

Poor little rich girl, right?

That was exactly what she was. Nobody was going to pity her because she was loaded. A pampered silly princess. But she felt restless. Unsatisfied. She knew, deep down, that she could be so much more than this, given half a chance.

She picked up her bag. The toilet attendant had resumed her seat by the entrance. She smiled at Belle. Belle fished in her pocket and pulled out a twenty and dropped it into the attendant's tray.

'Thanks,' said the woman in surprise.

'You're welcome,' said Belle.

81

She was walking back down Regent Street when someone called out: 'Hey! Belle!'

It was Harlan. She could feel her smile of welcome freezing into a scowl of dislike at the sight of him. She hadn't been having a fabulous time before, but now her day took a distinct turn for the worse. Harlan fucking Stone. And he had his two attack dogs on either side of him, that musclebound fool who was mucking Milly about, Nipper, and his usual sidekick, Ludo.

They peeled off and crossed the road, weaving through traffic to reach the other side, leaving Harlan alone with her. 'You got a lift home?' he asked her.

Belle hadn't. She'd been planning to grab a taxi when she'd had enough. Right now, she knew she'd had enough already. Her misery over Beezer's death, her dread of his upcoming funeral, had ruined any enjoyment she might have felt today. The shopping trip had been a mistake. She shook her head.

'Come on, car's over here.'

She didn't even have the strength left to argue. He took her arm and guided her over the road. His Porsche was parked there. He opened the passenger door for her and she got in. Then he slid behind the wheel and started the engine.

'So what's up?' he asked, swerving out into the traffic. Someone honked their horn and he flipped the finger at them. 'You look shattered.'

'Nothing,' said Belle. 'Well. Beezer. I can't seem to get it out of my mind.'

'Ah yeah.' He drove with one hand on the wheel, relaxed, casual. 'Sad, that.'

'You were there when he did it. Weren't you.'

'Yeah. It was damned tragic.'

Harlan had twisted his face into a semblance of grief, but Belle wasn't convinced. She knew there'd always been aggro between Harlan and Beezer. They'd never got on. And she couldn't forget what Milly had told her, about Beezer spotting Harlan as a small boy going into poor doomed baby Jake's nursery in the middle of the night. But then – Harlan didn't *know* that Beezer had seen him, did he? Because if he had known, then if you were of a suspicious nature you might start thinking that Harlan could have given Beezer a little shove in the right direction, right over that balustrade and down onto the pavement, bashing his brains out – and silencing him in the process.

'Couldn't you have stopped him? Talked him out of it?' she asked, watching his face.

Harlan shrugged.

'How the hell could I? He did it before I even suspected he was about to. One minute he was there, saying how everything in his life was rubbish, then he was gone.' Harlan cast a grey-eyed glance at Belle. 'He wanted to do it, and nobody was going to stop him. As I said to Dad, all we can do is give him a good send-off and leave it at that.'

'That's pretty cold,' said Belle.

'It's a fact of life. Beezer wanted out. So he did it.'

Belle didn't know what else to say. She kept silent all through the drive home and Harlan didn't seem inclined to make conversation either. When he pulled up in the lane outside the gatehouse, she unsnapped her seat belt and reached for the door handle, lifting it. But she couldn't open the door.

'Handy that, isn't it. Central locking,' said Harlan.

Belle glared at him. *Shit.* This was why he'd stopped in the lane and not pulled onto the drive. There was a large privet hedge shielding them from the gatehouse. Very few cars passed by in the lane. No one could see them.

'Open the damned door, Harlan,' said Belle tiredly.

He was smiling.

'You're such an arsehole,' she said, crossing her arms in fury.

'Just trying to comfort you, Belle,' he said smoothly, leaning in. 'I know how fond you were of Beezer. It's a terrible shock, losing him like we did.'

'Don't you dare,' said Belle, turning her head away. Harlan's hand landed on her thigh and she was so glad to have thick tights on. If he'd actually touched her skin, she might have screamed.

'Oh come on, Belle,' he was saying. 'Now kiss me. You know you want to.'

'I *don't* want to,' said Belle, wishing she'd never got into the car with him. She was sick of him, always trying to feel her up. Sick of the way his eyes were always crawling over her.

Harlan's face loomed in close to hers. It was tragic that he was such a total turn-off, because he had regular grey eyes, a straight nose, thick light brown hair. He dressed well. But . . . Harlan Stone exuded some sort of toxic poison from his pores, it always seemed to her. She always felt that he had to work hard at projecting the right emotion at the right time, because in reality he felt nothing. Well, maybe not *totally* nothing. Now, she was pretty sure he felt genuine lust. She'd had a lot of years putting up with this, him always trying to corner her, trying to paw at her, when it was the last thing she wanted.

Angry, she drew back her hand and slapped his face, hard.

'I *said,* open the fucking *door,* you *creep!*' she burst out.

Harlan drew back. His cheek, where she had slapped him, was turning pink. His eyes, still staring into hers, were icy cold. His hand raised slowly and he rubbed his cheek.

'You'll be sorry you did that,' he said. 'That's a promise.'

Then he reached back and there was a loud *click.*

'*Fuck you,*' said Belle. She opened the door, stumbled out, and nearly ran into the gatehouse, her heart beating hard.

82

Beezer was buried in the family plot beside his mum and dad and his little brother Colin. It was the send-off Harlan had promised it would be. There were flowers and cars and lots of hymns, everything that Beezer could have wished for. Charlie made absolutely sure that the thing was done *right*.

Then when the ceremony was over and Beezer was laid to rest, they all went back to Charlie's place.

Nula managed – at last – to get Terry alone.

'Terry!' She grabbed his arm as he passed by. Couldn't deny, silly old mare that she was, that just touching him still had the power to excite her. He looked at her hand on his arm and his expression made her let go, quickly. 'I need to talk to you. In private.'

Nula could see Jill, with a right face on her, watching them from across the room.

'About what?' he asked.

'Not here.'

'Oh for fuck's—'

'*Look*,' said Nula sharply. 'I'm not arsing around here, Terry. This is serious.'

He let out a sharp sigh. 'All right then. Where?'

'Meet me out by the buggy in ten minutes.'

'This had better not be—'

'It isn't,' said Nula, walking away.

★

Ten minutes later, they were there by the buggy that ferried Charlie down and back beyond the orchard, to the reptile house or the helipad.

'Christ, I hate that bloody thing,' said Nula, letting out a jittery gust of cigarette smoke and nodding to where the rotor blades of Charlie's latest toy sat still and silent. 'He keeps saying, come up with me, you'll enjoy it. Like fuck I would.'

'What's this about, Nula?' asked Terry, sounding irritable and tired. His old friend had died; he was gutted and now Nula could see him thinking that here she was again, this pathetic *crazy* old bitch, giving him the glad eye.

Nula took another deep drag of nicotine. She'd taken up smoking about a year ago, when the worry of her life had felt like too much. She drank a bit, too. Much more stress and she'd be sampling Charlie's product, and then it would be non-stop down the highway to hell.

'I know what you think of me, the lot of you,' she said. 'Mad old Nula, always back and forth to the nuthouse. But I'm not a fool. I can see trouble when it's right under my nose.'

'What trouble?' asked Terry.

'Harlan.'

'What about him?'

'He's going to nudge Charlie out of the way, someday soon. I can see it. Can't you?'

Terry was silent for a long while. 'What have you heard?' he said at last.

'Nothing. I've seen plenty though. The people he's surrounding himself with. Things that have happened. Things like Beezer deciding to top himself and Harlan there as the only witness.'

Terry frowned at her.

'Charlie won't listen to anything I say about Harlan. But nothing's ever added up about him, *nothing*. Not from the very first moment he came into our home. And that's not me, being crazy. That's a fact.' Nula threw the stub of her cigarette to the ground and shakily crushed it with her shoe. 'Look,' she said.

Over by the house wall, Nipper was lounging in the sunlight, smoking. He'd been watching them. As Terry's head swung round toward him, he looked away.

'Him and the other one, Ludo, they're always hanging about, watching everyone. They're Harlan's men, one hundred per cent. Not Charlie's. Pretty soon, the manor and everything in it is going to belong to Harlan. You can count on it. And when that day comes, where does that leave me? In the crap, that's where. He hates me, he always has. Tried to fucking kill me once, I know he did, but he didn't succeed. And you, as Charlie's friend, as his right hand? You're surplus to requirements, mate, that's what *you* are.'

'Go on,' said Terry.

Nula shrugged. 'Nothing else to say. Only, if I were you, I'd be getting Belle right out of his way. Abroad somewhere maybe. Because once Harlan's in charge, her arse is fried. He's always had a thing for her, and once the brakes are off, he'll do whatever the fuck he likes with her.'

A muscle was working in Terry's jaw. 'He wouldn't fucking dare,' he said.

'You don't think so?' Nula gave a thin smile. 'You're kidding yourself,' she said, and walked unsteadily away. Then she turned and strode back to him. 'It's our twentieth wedding anniversary in a month.'

'So?' It was his and Jill's twentieth too, just gone; they hadn't made a fuss over it. He'd bought her some flowers, that was all. Charlie of course would be different. There had been talk for a long while about a big celebration for the event. But now Beezer had upped and died, maybe no one would be in the mood.

265

Nula shrugged. 'I'm going ahead with it. Right here. A big party.'

'You sure?'

'I'm thinking that it's what everyone needs after this. And it's a month away. That's time enough for it to look decent. I asked Charlie about it before the funeral.'

Terry stuck his hands in his jacket pockets and looked at the ground, then at her. 'Maybe you're right. Maybe we could all do with cheering up.'

'That's what I thought,' said Nula. She paused, staring at his face. 'I meant it, Terry. Every word.' Then she grinned. 'Wise words from mad old Nula!' Then her grin vanished and her eyes skewered him. 'I got something to ask you. And Terry – I want the truth.'

'Go on,' he said cautiously.

'Where did the pair of you really get him from?'

Terry was staring at her face. 'What?'

'Harlan. Once I tried to contact the woman who brought him here from the adoption agency all those years ago. I couldn't. It all stank, you know? No one in the office knew of her. People who'd been there, like *forever*. Nobody had ever heard of a Mrs Bushell.'

'Nula . . .' Terry half-turned away, eyes downcast.

Nula grabbed hold of his arm. '*Look*,' she said fiercely, her eyes blazing into his. 'All this has nearly driven me bollock-mad crazy. You *know* it has. Don't you think I deserve the truth now? After all I've been through?'

Terry was visibly wavering. 'Look . . .' he started, then stopped.

'What?' Nula's heart was pounding in her chest. Was she finally – at last – going to hear the truth from someone about that cuckoo that Charlie had thrust into their nest?

Terry's eyes met hers. 'I do think you've had a raw deal. I agree

266

with you on that. But if any of this ever gets back to Charlie, I'll deny it and *I'll* say you're mad too.'

Nula was nodding. 'All right. OK. Whatever you tell me, it'll stay between us. I promise you that.'

'She was a junkie,' said Terry.

'*What?*'

'Harlan's mum. We were in town, Charlie and me, and we went into this squat, and there she was, dead on the kitchen floor.'

He paused, hands in pockets, frowning heavily.

'Go on, for God's sake,' said Nula breathlessly. She couldn't believe it and yet she *did*. All these years, and here it was, confirmed. Charlie had lied to her. And Terry had colluded with him over it.

'We found the kid in a cupboard under the stairs, hiding away. God knows what he'd had to live with, what he'd seen and been through, with that skank for a mother.'

'Oh Christ.' Nula had to lean against the buggy; she felt dizzy all of a sudden. Shocked to her core.

'But Charlie straight away saw it as an opportunity. Well, you know Charlie.'

Nula was silent. Apparently, she didn't know Charlie at all. Her husband of nearly twenty years had deceived her in more ways than one. He'd not only fucked Terry's missus behind her back – *raped* her, for God's sake – he'd also foisted some dirty tramp's bastard onto her. When she had thought she was getting a normal child.

Terry went on: 'Charlie knew how much you wanted another kid. That you were gutted by the fact that you couldn't do it. And Charlie?' Terry gave a smile that was almost sad. 'Charlie's an empire builder at heart. He wanted a son. Someone to pass it all on to. And there was Harlan. Charlie saw the kid as a gift, a solution to a big problem. But he knew you wouldn't go for the true story. That you'd hate the very idea of it. So he . . .'

'So he lied,' finished Nula, her mouth dry, her mind in a spin. She'd been *right*. All this time, all the times Charlie had said to her, *You're crazy, what's the matter with you?* All the time, she'd been *right*.

'He was shielding you from the truth,' corrected Terry. 'He got one of our girls to pretend to be from the adoption agency. That's why when you contacted them they'd never heard of her. She'd never *been* there. It was all a lie.' Terry turned and looked her straight in the eye. 'So now you know.'

Nula's face was twisted in anguish. To think that Charlie had brought that *thing* into their home. Harlan had tormented her, tried to kill her. Nearly caused her to lose her mind. And Jake. Oh Christ – Jake!

'The woman. The mother. What was her name?'

'I've no idea. I never felt comfortable with any of this, Nula. I'm fucking sorry.'

Nula didn't say another word. She turned and walked away, back up to the house.

83

Milly was restless out in the sticks. She'd made up with Belle over that Nipper business, but Belle was off somewhere at the moment so she went into London, alone. She had spare keys to a flat Dad kept there, the lush place on the river with views up to Tower Bridge, so she moved in. She'd given Nula no explanation for the move other than: 'I'm so fucking bored out here. I'm going into town. Staying on there for a while.'

Dad had blown his top spectacularly over her giving Javier the cold shoulder again.

'Why not have dinner with the man?' he'd raged. 'Would it bother you so much to at least be polite?'

Milly had no answer. She upped and fled to the city, to get away from the whole rotten lot of them. Mum didn't even seem interested that she'd left. Nula was in one of her downtimes again, barely speaking, not engaging with anyone, just scribbling in her notebooks. Well, fuck it.

So Milly took herself off to the Smoke. She spent too much in Harvey Nicks, wandered around Tiffany's, offloaded a fortune of the very generous allowance Charlie paid her because no daughter of his, he always said, was ever going to have to work for a living. She blew hundreds in Harrods, raided Bond Street, then went back to the flat loaded with bags and flopped out on the couch, feeling a bit happier – until she thought of Nipper again, and wondered if she was being a fool, wondered if she was so desperate for affection that she'd just settled for sex instead.

Deep down she knew all too well that Nipper was a worthless bastard, Harlan's glove puppet. But at least her and Belle were together again, best mates. No way was a man ever going to come between them.

Suddenly she choked back a tear and looked at all the purchases surrounding her. Her pleasure in them faded instantly. Then there was the noise of male voices, and the key turned in the lock. She straightened with a guilty jolt. If it was Dad, he'd moan like fuck about all the shopping bags. It was one of Charlie's 'things' – he chucked money about like confetti on stuff for his own amusement, but he always complained if Milly or Nula or Harlan spent a penny.

But it wasn't Charlie. It was Harlan, with a few hard-looking young men coming in behind him. He paused when he saw her sitting there.

'What the fuck you doing here?' he asked.

'Right back at you,' said Milly, annoyed. She hadn't realized Harlan was staying here. She didn't want to share the place with him and his mates. She saw that Nipper had trailed in among them. He looked at her blankly. And there was Ludo, decked out in more chains than the *Queen Mary*, nudging Nipper, grinning when he saw that she was there.

Harlan came and slouched down on the couch opposite her while his mates wandered around the big room, picking up vases and artworks that were probably priceless – Charlie liked his art – and slapping them back down, disinterested, then stopping by the floor-to-ceiling windows to admire the view.

She felt uncomfortable, red-faced, seeing Nipper here. And he was ignoring her. It was clear that Ludo knew about their relationship, but Nipper didn't want Charlie finding out. And he didn't want to acknowledge her in front of Harlan, either. That must be why he was blanking her.

'I had the key for this place, so I thought I'd come on over here for a while and stay. What, the country getting too boring for you, was it?' asked Harlan.

Milly shrugged. She wasn't about to chat about family matters in front of all these tossers.

'You can go now,' said Harlan to the others, his eyes still fixed on Milly.

One by one they headed for the door. Meek as lambs, she thought. She'd seen her dad's people react exactly the same to an order from Charlie. Nipper didn't even glance at her as he left.

'I miss Beezer,' she said when the door closed behind the last of them. She'd always liked 'Uncle' Beezer. He'd been around all her life, a fixture. And he always made her laugh, however bleak her mood.

Harlan smiled. 'That stupid old fart? Old school, wasn't he. Old ideas, old ways. I don't think he liked me much.'

Milly didn't know what to say to that. Beezer had always been viewed with tolerant affection by the family. But not by Harlan. Again she thought of what she'd found in Harlan's room, and she thought of Beezer, and what he'd seen on the morning of baby Jake's death.

'Maybe he had reason not to like you,' she said.

'Meaning what?' Harlan's pale grey eyes were sharp as lasers on her face.

Milly shrugged.

'I said, meaning what?'

'You remember the party on the day of baby Jake's christening? Beezer saw you coming out of the nursery in the small hours the next morning. The morning Jake was found dead.'

Harlan's eyes narrowed. 'Beezer did?'

'Yeah, he did. And you never liked the baby, did you. I can

remember you watching Mum and Dad with Jake, I can remember how you used to look at him.'

'And how was that?'

'Like you hated him.'

'Christ, it must be a family thing,' said Harlan. His mouth was smiling but his eyes were very cold.

'What?' Milly was bewildered.

Harlan lifted a hand and twirled his fingers against his temple. 'The insanity. Like mother, like daughter, yeah?'

'I'm not mad, Harlan. Not in the least. And if Mum ever was, it's thanks to you.'

'What?'

'I found things in your room. Remember that day you were spying on Nipper and me in the pool house? I went indoors and into your room and I found . . .'

Her voice tailed away. Harlan had jumped to his feet and was across the carpet and grabbing her by the arm and hauling her up, so quickly that she didn't have time to react. She found herself staring into those icy grey eyes from inches away and she thought, *Oh Christ he's going to kill me.*

'Tell me what you found,' he said, shaking her. His grip on her arm was intensely painful.

'Just . . . ow! . . . I found the tape recorder. And the tape. The baby crying. You played it to frighten Mum, didn't you. To make her think she was going mad.'

He was silent for a moment, staring into her eyes. Then he said: 'I don't know what the fuck you're talking about.'

'Yes you do.' Her voice shook.

'No I don't. You're crazy, just like she is.'

'No. That's not true.'

He held her there, fixing her with that stare while he weighed up what she'd just told him. She could almost hear the cogs whirring in his brain. Then he said: 'Beezer thought he saw me, you say? Going into the nursery?'

Milly nodded dumbly. As a boy, he'd been weedy; thin. Now as a man he was very strong, while she was flabby and weak.

'He must have been off his head on something,' said Harlan. Suddenly he let her go. 'And Mills – bear this in mind. I wasn't there. Beezer imagined it.'

Her arm where he'd gripped it was throbbing with hot pain. Her mind was racing, any minute now he was going to warn her not to tell anyone. But she'd already told people. She'd told Belle. She'd told Mum. And Mum had told Dad.

'Who've you told, Milly?' he demanded.

Milly licked her dry lips. She could lie. But he'd get the truth out of her; she knew he would.

'I told Mum. She told Dad, but I don't suppose he believed her anyway, and . . .' Her voice tailed away.

'And?' He gripped her arm again and she let out a cry. 'And, Milly?'

'I told Belle.'

84

Belle asked Milly where the Stone manufacturing bases were. No one had ever told her anything about them.

'Why d'you want to know that?' asked Milly.

'Because I want to do something. *Work* at something.'

Milly looked at her old pal in amazement. 'But you don't have to.'

'I know I don't *have* to. I *want* to. I'm bored with hanging about doing nothing. I want to do something with my life, OK?'

'Well yeah. Sure. If that's what you want.'

'So . . . ?' Belle looked at Milly expectantly.

'I don't know where they are. How would I? You know the parents don't like us even asking about the business. And anyway it's dull as fuck. Sofas and armchairs? Beechwood frames and fabrics? Not exactly exciting, is it?'

'You really don't know where the business addresses are?'

'I really don't. Harlan does, but he never talks about any of it. And me? Kept in the dark and fed bollocks, that's me.' Milly pouted. It was one more example of her being treated like the useless one, while Harlan was the favoured son, granted all the inside knowledge. All right, she didn't *want* to know about the bloody business that kept them all in such style, but still – it did sting.

'So how are we going to find out where they are?' asked Belle.

'We're not,' said Milly, disinterested. Belle was off her head, wanting to schlepp to some damned factory or office to spend her days there grafting. The way Milly saw it, they were fortunate. They didn't have to lift a finger. OK, sometimes that was a bore. But then – so was working for a living.

'Oh come on. There must be a way.'

'Well – really? – all right then. I think you're mad, but maybe there's something in Mum's journals?'

'What?'

'I bet there'll be something about the furniture factories in there. But look, Belle, there's no point. If your dad or mine got wind of you working at one of their places, they'd blow a bloody gasket and you'd be straight out the door.'

Belle considered this. 'Yeah, I suppose.'

Milly was thinking too. 'They do visit the factories. They've got the manufacturing bases for the big retailers, but they've also got the accounts offices and admin departments and so on.'

'So?'

'Harlan said something about the staff at the admin and accounts offices never seeing your dad or mine at all these days.'

So they had to wait for Nula to go out, then creep into the sitting room and open the big pouffe where Nula stashed her current journals. There were a lot of them in there and they sweated for over an hour to find details of the family business.

'This is ridiculous. Can't we just ask your mum?' said Belle, getting impatient.

'Nope. She won't tell us anything. She never has, and never will. I've asked her before, and she always shuts me down.'

'This is so fucking silly,' said Belle, thumbing through. Then she stopped. 'Wait. What's this?'

There was an address in Clacton. She showed it to Milly.

'Do you know this address?' she asked.

'Nope,' said Milly.

'This could be it. One of the admin offices?'

'Yeah, but look, Belle. You won't get anything except a kick up the arse for your trouble.'

Belle ignored that. She made a quick note of the address and tucked it in her jeans pocket. Then she helped Milly load the journals back into the pouffe. Through the lounge window they could see the Bentley coming up the drive, Paul at the wheel this time. Nula was back.

'You're so fucking obstinate,' said Milly as she and Belle left the lounge.

'Quitters never win,' said Belle. 'And winners never quit.' It was something she'd heard Milly's dad say, more than once. And in that he was absolutely right.

As they were crossing the hall, Charlie came out of his study. Spotting Milly there, he hooked a finger at her. 'In here,' he said, and turned and went back in.

'Catch you later,' said Milly to Belle, and followed him into the study, closing the door behind her.

Charlie was pacing the floor, his face thunderous.

Feeling increasingly nervous, Milly waited.

'What the *fuck*,' he said at last, 'are you doing, mucking Javier about?'

'What?'

'You heard. He's a valuable business associate and would it hurt you to be nice to him? He's just been on the phone telling me you've cancelled a date with him. You've broken the poor bastard's heart.'

'What the . . .' Milly was gobsmacked. 'That's ridiculous! I don't like him, Dad. For God's sake, he's a horrible little—'

Charlie flew at her. He grabbed her arms and shook her, hard.

'You listen to me,' he snarled. 'You be civil to Javier. You hear me?'

Milly was staring straight into her father's face. She saw anger there, and in his eyes a hint of desperation. Suddenly, as if realizing he was going too far, Charlie let her go. He drew back, scraped a hand over his face.

'Go on,' he said. 'Off you go.'

Milly didn't need telling twice. She bolted out the door and was gone.

85

Belle drove over to the Clacton address next day. She checked the maps when she got there and then sat in the car, frowning and staring at what appeared to be a house set in a row of identical Victorian houses. She had expected a proper office on an industrial estate, but this was just a *house*.

She got out of the car and walked over. There was a small chequered black-and-white path leading up to a battered-looking front door with . . . what the hell? There was a mirror hanging on the outside of it.

Very odd.

She opened the little metal gate and walked up the path. There was a bell beside the door but it looked as if someone had wrenched it out of the wall. Undeterred, Belle knocked at the flaking wood.

Nothing.

She must have the wrong address.

But she knew she didn't. She knew she had the *right* one.

She leaned in to knock again. As she did so, a tiny black-haired woman opened the door a crack and let loose a torrent of some foreign language at her.

'I'm Belle Barton,' said Belle loudly. 'Is the manager here? Can I speak to the manager?'

What she *should* have done, she could see it now, was ask Dad if there was any work going in any of Charlie's factories. But then, she was nervous of doing that: she knew Dad would only put her off. He'd tell her not to be silly. To enjoy herself. Didn't she have a big enough allowance? And then she would have felt guilty, and awkward, and she would still be fed up and unsatisfied.

The woman stopped talking. She stood there, her eyes wide with alarm. A rabbit in the headlights. Getting annoyed at all this, Belle pushed forward. The woman was very slight, very small. She looked *malnourished,* really. It was easy to shove past her and go inside.

Now the woman started gabbling at her again, following behind her, touching nervously at the sleeve of Belle's coat.

Belle walked along a shabby hallway. To her left there was an open doorway. Empty desks in there. Like a normal office. But no one about. She walked on and then pushed open another door. Once it had probably been a kitchen. But as she entered she saw no cosy domestic scene. There were men in here – they looked Chinese or Vietnamese, like the woman – and they were wearing facemasks and protective coveralls. Pots of bubbling liquid were all around. Steam and smoke was rising. There was an acrid scent in the air. Belle almost choked the minute she walked in. She stood there and stared. They stared right back at her. Then they erupted into movement and started shouting at her.

Alarmed, Belle backtracked. Suddenly they were all clustering around her, clutching at her, trying to either force her out or to stop her leaving, she didn't know which. She ran along the hall, pushing past the woman and the men in their weird outfits, choking on something horrible, and she didn't stop running until she was back at the car. Then quickly she put the key in the lock with a shaking hand. She got in and locked the door behind her. They were gathering out by the gate of the house, pointing and yelling. She wondered if they were actually going to come after her.

Gasping, panicking, she started the engine and quickly steered the car out into the traffic.

What the fuck?

86

Belle thought about it for days afterwards.

'How'd it go then? Did you talk to the personnel people? Any luck? I think you must be demented to bother, but . . .' Milly shrugged.

'No,' lied Belle. She didn't want to discuss it with anyone, not yet. She was still trying to process what had happened. So far, it wasn't adding up; not at all. 'Actually, I didn't bother. You're right. What's the point? Dad and Charlie would only kick off if they found out I was working there. It was a stupid idea.'

Finally Belle came to a decision, made a quick call and drove up to Cambridge. It took just over an hour on a trouble-free M11. She parked up – the traffic in the centre was hell, but she managed to find a space. She walked over to the college and there he was, waiting for her by the porter's lodge.

'Einstein! Hello,' she said, thinking that he hadn't changed a fraction since their schooldays. He still had that long, solemn face, that carroty shock of hair. He was taller, but still gangly. His jeans were saggy but his white T-shirt was clean, with RED DEVILS emblazoned across the front. 'Thanks for seeing me at such short notice.'

'No problem. Nobody calls me Einstein any more, by the way. It's Nige. Hi, Belle.' He gave her a timid peck on the cheek. 'Although, I'm a bit pushed for time, as I told you on the phone. You want to sit, or shall we walk . . . ?'

'Let's walk.'

The place was so beautiful. Belle couldn't stop staring at the fabulous soaring towers of honey-coloured stone, the immaculate lawns sweeping down to the River Cam. The sun sparkled on the water and people steered punts with long poles.

'So how's chemistry?' asked Belle.

'Demanding,' he said. 'I'm working on biophysical and spectroscopic studies of macromolecule structure, dynamics and function.'

'Of course you are,' said Belle, laughing. He'd always been the brainiest of all her friends, stunningly intelligent. 'It don't seem like five minutes since you were scaring us all to death in the science lab at school, setting fire to things with a Bunsen burner.'

Einstein laughed too. 'I still do that.'

'I bet you do,' she said.

'You see any of the old crowd much? Davey or Phil? What about Milly? Didn't your dads work together?'

Belle's smile faded. 'I don't see Davey or Phil. But Milly? Yeah, we live side by side, we're big pals.'

'I liked her,' said Einstein. 'Nice quiet girl.'

'Yeah. She hasn't changed.'

'So what's the emergency?' he asked as they paused by the riverside. Two swans glided past, snow-white and elegant against the dark waters. 'On the phone you seemed anxious.'

Belle looked at him. 'I want to describe something to you. And for you to tell me what you make of it.'

'OK. Go ahead.'

Belle gave him the details of what she had seen at the 'accounts' office. She told him about the boiling liquids, the protective suiting the people wore. Everything she could think of, she told him.

Finally, she stopped. 'That's it,' she said. 'I wondered – do you think they were making glue? Glue for the furniture?'

'A bit improbable, don't you think? Why do that in an office?

Why not in the main production unit? Was there a smell?' he asked, frowning.

'Yeah. It nearly choked me.'

'Describe it.'

Belle thought it over. 'Like burning rubber,' she said.

He looked at her, his face very serious all of a sudden. 'You're sure about that?'

'Absolutely.'

'Positive?'

'Yes. Why? What is it? Do you know?'

'That isn't glue.'

'Then what the hell is it?'

'Belle – this could be serious.'

'What do you mean?'

'Look. You dissolve cocaine in ammonia, add water and bicarbonate of soda, then heat it until the liquid boils off. You'll get a harsh chemical smell, quite toxic. *Exactly* like burning rubber.'

'Whoa. Stop. You said *cocaine*,' said Belle.

He shrugged. 'When you're making crack cocaine, that's the vital ingredient. Crack gives a quicker hit than pure coke and a more rapid comedown. Dealers love it. Bumps up the sales. Belle, for God's sake, be careful. You say you walked into this place? You were bloody lucky to get out. Didn't they try to stop you?'

Belle nodded. 'Yes. They did.' If she hadn't run for it, who knew what might have happened?

'You ought to report this to the police. Like, *now*. Although I suspect they'll have cleared out already, thinking you've probably done that.'

Belle felt chilled with the shock of this, despite the bright sunshine and the beautiful setting all around them. She *couldn't* report it to the police. Charlie Stone and her dad were involved. And – *oh good Christ* – if this sort of thing was going on there, did they know about it? And what about the other sites? Was this a one-off, or were there more?

No. They couldn't know. This must be going on without their knowledge.

'Einstein – *Nige* – you've been a great help. Thanks,' she told him.

'Seriously, Belle. Please be careful,' he said.

87

Nula was in the vast gold-and-purple master cabin of *Lady of the Manor*, which was moored up near the Beaulieu River. They'd been sailing around the Med for a week or so, calling in at St Tropez, then Palma, then back to England. The crew had pampered them, and Nipper and Sammy had been there too, to oversee security. Nipper had travelled back to Essex overland the day before yesterday, leaving Sammy here on the yacht, in charge of things.

Nula was trying on the dress for tonight's party, clipping on her diamond drop earrings and worrying about ear sag. She'd been wearing drop earrings since she was twenty, and all these years of yanking down the flesh of her ear lobes had stretched them. She decided that once their 'big occasion' was over, she'd talk to her chap in Harley Street – he did all her work and he was very good, even if he did charge a bloody fortune – and get her ears prettied up.

She stared at her reflection in the floor-to-ceiling mirrors. Long ago, her horrible nose had been replaced by a neat turned-up retroussé and she'd got a set of bigger tits. More recently, she'd had her neck tightened up. Maybe a bit too tight? No, it was OK.

Nula turned back and forth in front of the mirrors, chewing on a hangnail. Then she stopped. Forced her hands to her sides. The full-length dusky pink Chanel gown she wore with its square shoulder pads and big puff sleeves was fabulous. Her hair was dark blonde these days – 'mouse' was long gone, a thing of the far distant past. She usually wore it loose, but for tonight it had already been dressed, sculpted up on top of her head in a retro 'victory roll' look.

Then the nerves kicked in. A big party. Her as the hostess . . . she raised her hand back to her mouth, then dropped it again. She took a deep, deep breath.

They'd made it, she told herself. They were rich. Successful. Loaded. Twenty years married and today they were going to celebrate their anniversary with a knock-'em-dead party back at the Essex place. But along the way there had been so many troubles. The business. The manor. All the shit that went with it. And . . . well, she'd had her troubles too. Mental troubles. Visits to hospital. Lots of them. Rotten, horrible times. Oh God, losing Jake. And Charlie himself. Her husband, the rapist. He'd attacked Jill, forced her to have sex with him. That disgusted her. *Repulsed* her. How could she celebrate their marriage when she knew the truth about him, knew *exactly* what he was?

And there were other things too. Harlan. All her suspicions about him, which had to remain unvoiced or Charlie would fly into one of his famous rages and pack her back off to the funny farm for further treatment. She was frightened of Harlan. The very thought of him made her pause, made a deep shudder run through her.

'You ready then, doll?'

It was Charlie, bustling in, filling the cabin with his high-energy presence. The bastard. She knew he'd loved this past week, soaking up the sun, lying up on deck sporting a tanned beer belly, big Gucci shades and a red pair of budgie smugglers. Elegant was never going to be Charlie's middle name.

'Unzip me, will you?' she said, and Charlie did. Nula slipped off the dress, putting it back into its protective coverall. She quickly dressed in her travel clothes: dark fitted trousers, white silk top and cream jacket. Then she picked up her bag, grabbed the dress for tonight's 'do'.

'Ready,' she said.

They were flying up to Essex in Charlie's pride and joy, which was at this moment parked up on the upper deck – his blue Jet Ranger helicopter. Charlie would be at the controls. They would land to cheers and catcalls from all their friends, and Charlie would preen and look so pleased with himself, while Nula would just be glad to be back on solid ground.

There are no old bold pilots, she thought, remembering something Terry had told her once.

Well, Charlie was bold. Reckless. That headlong, crazy drive of his had got them where they were today. But the truth was, she hated flying, full stop. It terrified her. So she had to brace herself, put a smile on her face. This should have been a happy day. But it wasn't, because of all the shit she'd been through with Charlie Stone. The day she'd met him, her life had started running down a long and unhappy path and Christ knew where she would end up.

But today she had to act the happy wife and mother. For this one day, she would force a smile and cut a cake and toast her husband in champagne; she would act out the lie that was her life.

88

Jill was in the gatehouse kitchen when Terry came in.

'All ready?' he asked her.

'Yeah. Think so.'

'You look great,' he said, coming over, giving her a kiss on the cheek and a hug.

Jill wasn't looking forward to this damned party, not at all. But she'd made an effort; she was wearing a red Carolina Herrera cocktail dress, a cream jacket, heels and matching bag. Terry would want her to put on a good show today and she'd do anything for him.

Jill stood in her husband's arms, feeling his heat, his strength. She adored him. Loved the bones of him. Then she thought of Charlie and Nula – they were like a curse, those two. And the Bartons were tied to them, they'd never be free. Charlie had never come near after that one time, and thank God for that, but he'd scarred her. Ruined her, so that every time Terry made love to her, it was always Charlie's face she saw. She'd stiffen and Terry would say, what's wrong? And of course she couldn't tell him.

'It's all going to be fine,' he said against her hair. 'I know you don't go for parties much, but . . .'

'Ah, it's OK,' she sighed. 'I've never liked Charlie, you know that. And that wife of his, what a bitch she is.'

'Nula? She's not so bad.'

'She's a nutter,' said Jill flatly. 'Always in and out of hospital, getting her brains fried. Ever since she lost baby Jake, she's been off her head. And the way she sneers down her nose at me. Snobby cow. And have you seen her nails?'

'What?'

'Her fingernails. Chewed down to the quick. And the skin all around them, chewed to fuck. I tell you, she's not right. She's a head case. And *he* ain't any better.'

'Well, just for today, you got to be nice to them, OK? And polite.'

'I wish you didn't work for him,' said Jill for about the thousandth time. Charlie was a beast. He was so flashy, so *false*. Everything was about creating a big impression – the *wrong* one. Because he was a bastard rapist really, and nobody knew. He was always flaunting his wealth. Laughing at the coppers. Pedalling his fucking drugs. Keeping his dirty secrets well hidden.

'Well, I do work for him. And it pays. We live like princes, don't we. So why complain?'

'I'm not complaining.'

'Sounds like it.'

Jill heard the warning in Terry's voice. No one criticized Charlie in his hearing. She shrugged and straightened. 'Nah, take no notice of me. It's gonna be great.'

'He's flying in from the yacht, they're down on the Beaulieu River. Making a grand entrance for the big occasion. You know Charlie.'

'I'm surprised he didn't want you with him.' Yeah, she knew Charlie all right. More than she *wanted* to.

'Listen, I don't question what Charlie wants. I told him I'd be happier if I was with him this trip, but he said to chill out and that he'd see us at the party.'

Belle came hurrying down the stairs. She was wearing a midnight-blue silk gown and full make-up. She'd bouffed up her tangled blonde tiger-striped hair and made up her dark brown eyes smokily with grey shadow.

Jill looked at her and could hardly believe it. Belle was turning into a beautiful woman and she felt such pride in her gorgeous daughter, such love for her.

'Don't you look great,' said Jill. 'Don't she, Terry?'

'She does,' said Terry, giving Belle and then Jill a hug. 'You both do. My two glamorous girls.'

He was smiling at them both, feeling the need to shield them, keep them safe.

Then into Terry's mind, uncomfortably, came Harlan on that day when he'd caught him terrorizing Belle in the garage, sneering at him, calling him the *help* when he gave him a slap and told him to stay away from his daughter. That little cunt was starting to really worry him, and it wasn't only to do with Belle, although that was a big part of it. He thought of Nula's warning that Harlan was a danger to Charlie and himself. How he'd dismissed it, thinking it was just crazy Nula spouting off again. But then there was Beezer's death, with only Harlan there as a witness. And Harlan poking his nose into every aspect of the business, taking a strong grip on things in town, things that had always been Charlie's pre-serve and were now – most definitely – Harlan's.

Belle was doing her best to get in the party mood, if only to please her parents, but the truth was she had been deeply troubled since the whole Clacton thing and her visit to Nige. She'd walked into something strange, that much was certain. Maybe she'd find out the locations of the Stone manufacturing sites and start checking those out too. Then she looked at her much-loved dad. He *couldn't* know about this – could he?

Then they all paused. Overhead, they could hear the clatter of a helicopter. A big one, twin-engined. Only one person in this area had a bird as distinctive as that.

'Christ, here we go,' said Jill with a sigh. 'Charlie's arriving. Making the big entrance, as usual.'

Terry went out into the hall and presently they heard the noise of him pissing loudly in the cloakroom. He never, ever shut the cloakroom door. It drove Mum mad. Jill rolled her eyes at Belle and almost smiled. *Men!* It was a brief moment of female solidarity, and Belle decided now was her moment.

'Mum? I went into one of the offices in Clacton,' she said quickly.

The half-smile vanished. 'What the hell for?'

'I thought maybe I could do something there. You know? A job?'

'What the fuck . . .' Jill looked outraged.

'And the people there – I know you don't approve, and maybe I shouldn't have bothered, but *listen*. This might be serious, really bad. I think . . . I think they were making drugs.'

In the cloakroom, Terry was pulling the chain.

'What the hell were you thinking of, going there?' hissed Jill, grabbing Belle's arm. 'You are *never* to go there again, do you understand me?'

Terry was running water in the basin, and whistling.

'But Dad has to be told. And Charlie. If they knew what was happening right there in their own place of business, then—'

'*Shut up!*' said Jill urgently. 'Listen. You don't mention this, you never say a *word* about this, not to anyone, you got me?'

Terry was coming back along the hall. Belle stared into her mother's frantic eyes and suddenly it all clicked into place. Jill *knew*. Dad and Charlie were in on this. They knew all about it. And so did Mum.

'OK folks, let's hit the road,' said Terry, coming back into the kitchen.

'I'll see you up there,' said Belle. Suddenly she had to get away, she had to think. With shaking hands she took her car keys from her bag. 'Going for a drive.'

'Make sure you're not late at the house!' shouted Jill after her departing daughter.

But Belle was already gone.

89

Nipper met up with Milly in a quiet lane not far from Charlie's mansion. She drove up and parked behind Nipper's Mercedes. Nipper got out of the car, stubbing out his cigarette beneath his heel.

'How long have we got?' she asked, and he had to stifle a laugh. She was wearing a tiny dress that was all chiffon and swirls of colour, and four-inch heels.

'Long enough,' said Nipper.

'Good,' said Milly as Nipper took her hand and led her down to the edge of the field. When they were out of sight of the road, Milly frowned. 'If Dad knew . . .' she started.

'He doesn't. And he's not going to,' said Nipper, pulling her in for a kiss.

'He's still keen on me and Javier,' she said gloomily. 'Just because he shoves a bit of business Dad's way, he thinks I'll fall into line? It's such *bollocks*.'

Nipper wasn't interested. He was working the flimsy dress off her shoulder. She looked ridiculous in the thing, like Dumbo in a tutu. He wondered briefly if she realized – as he did – that the days of Charlie Stone ruling them all were done. Charlie just didn't know it yet. Harlan had been talking to Javier, making deals that Charlie knew nothing about. Harlan was the main man now. It was obvious to everyone except Charlie himself.

He kissed her silky skin and popped one boulder-like breast out into his hand. Boffing Charlie Stone's daughter always gave him a frisson of excitement. Charlie didn't want Milly mixing with the staff.

'Don't worry about all that,' said Nipper. He turned, pinning Milly up against the trunk of an oak tree. 'None of it matters,' he said, kissing her harder, more urgently.

'Oh,' she sighed, pushing the filmy garment down over her hips so that it pooled at her feet.

No knickers, either.

He lifted her up – Christ, she was heavy! – parting her thighs, then Nipper pushed his cock deep into her wet depths. She moaned and wrapped her arms and legs around him as he hammered her into the side of the tree, pushing and shoving at her until he came.

All too soon – just like always – he pulled out of her, tucked his cock back indoors, zipped up. Unfulfilled, feeling somehow *cheated*, Milly picked up her dress and slipped it over her head. Then they heard it. Both turned toward the sound coming from their left, high up in the sky. It was a pin-prick of darkness against the blue, and then it came closer, closer, and then they could see. It was a helicopter.

'Daddy's home,' said Nipper, watching as the big machine whirred away to the right, going lower as it crossed over the fields.

Milly was silent, her eyes fixed on the aircraft. Then she drew away from him. 'I'm late. Gotta go.'

90

While Nipper and Milly were meeting up, Belle Barton was speeding along the country lanes in her red open-topped BMW. She was thinking over everything, and coming up with nothing that helped, nothing to get her out of a state of extreme worry and bewilderment.

She couldn't forget what she had seen in that place in Clacton. Or Nige's words to her. And the mirror on the front door of the house. Was that weird, or what? She'd looked that up at the library, and found that it was a Vietnamese thing, to repel dragons. So the people in there were from Vietnam. She remembered the bubbling vats, the throat-closing rubbery stench, all of them wearing protective clothing, goggles, masks. Making crack cocaine, according to Nige.

And Dad knows.

She thought of Charlie's furniture manufacturing business, which she'd always believed to be legitimate. Now, she was thinking otherwise. Jill's shocked reaction had confirmed her worst fears. The furniture business was nothing but a front, a cover for drug dealing. And her family and Milly's, and even Harlan, she was sure, were in on it.

Belle was in shock. No wonder Dad seemed to be doing so well. No wonder Mum had never had to work. Jill barely had to lift a finger. She had the nice gatehouse and grounds with plenty of help from cleaners, gardeners, ironing services and the rest. Everything on the surface appeared fine, prosperous. The

Stones and the Bartons were – apparently – living the good life on the back of a successful, *legal* business.

Only . . . they weren't. Not really.

Nothing was as it seemed. Belle's own aimless life no longer made any sense to her. Up to this point, she'd had fuck-all to do. She'd been sent to a goodish school but had never bothered to study much. She'd been a popular girl, a gang of friends all around her, Julia, Molly, Davey and Phil, Nige and the others, and she'd always taken pains to include shy Milly whenever she could. She'd been a prefect, then head girl. But she hadn't troubled herself with exams and she certainly didn't want the faff of uni, like ultra-bright Nige.

But what was she going to do, now she *knew* what had been going on under her nose all these years?

She had her shades on and the roof was down. The wind was streaking through her hair and sending it billowing back in a tousled blonde wave, messing up her careful hairdo. She didn't care. Freddie Mercury was blasting out 'Killer Queen' on the sound system, the bass notes booming along the verges, scattering cows and startling sheep in the fields beyond.

Mulling it all over and finding no answer, she was jolted back to reality as she saw something in her rear-view mirror. A silver-grey Porsche was coming up fast behind her. Damn, she knew that car. She put her foot down harder on the accelerator. The last thing she wanted was to chat to Harlan Stone. She'd never liked the fact that her dad worked for *his* dad. And now she knew the trade they were in, she realized that Harlan had to be involved too. Harlan was on the manor a lot now, getting into it all. He wouldn't give a single shit that his high life was paid for in blood and misery.

He was inching closer in the rear-view, matching Belle's speed.

He was flashing his lights. She could see him grinning back there, edging up closer and closer.

Fucker, thought Belle.

The Porsche was right on the BMW's tail now, and then . . . no, he wouldn't do it. Would he?

He would.

The Porsche thumped, jarringly, into the back of her car.

'Hey!' shouted Belle, jolting forward at the impact, the wind whipping her words away in an instant. 'Harlan, you bastard!'

Belle accelerated harder. But Harlan was there, right there on her tail.

Crumpppp!!!!

Again the Porsche hit the back of the BMW.

'You, Harlan Stone, are an arsehole!' yelled Belle. Dad would throw a fit if there was any damage, she knew. He'd bought her the BMW for her last birthday. But Charlie Stone would say, ah, the boy was only playing, where was the harm? It was only money, it was only a car, it was easily fixed.

Yeah – with drugs money, right?

Belle put her foot down harder and the speed dial crept up past seventy. Then she rounded a sharp bend and her heart leapt into her mouth. A tractor was pulling out from a field. She stamped on the brake and the BMW skidded to a halt. The Porsche, following right behind, slewed sideways and came to a standstill mere inches away.

That silly bastard could have *pulverized* her.

'Jesus!' said Belle and slapped the wheel in fright and rage.

Harlan was grinning across at her as if it was all one great big joke. The bearded tractor driver gave them both a long cold look, then went, unconcerned, on his way.

'You fucking idiot,' she snapped, full volume.

Belle was unfastening her seat belt, throwing the door open

and storming round to the back of the car, peering at the BMW's rear end to check for damage. There was a deep scratch above the number plate, nothing else. But damn – he'd scared her half to death. When she'd come round that bend at full speed and seen the tractor blocking the road, she'd nearly pissed herself.

'What's the problem, Belle?' Harlan was saying, getting out of the Porsche and coming to stand nearby.

He was such a moron. Superior. Smug. Snidely laughing at everyone's discomfort. She loathed him.

'The problem?' Belle scowled at him. 'The problem is you, you dick.'

'Hey! You don't speak to me like that,' said Harlan, the grin dropping from his face. He reached out and grabbed her wrist, squeezing hard.

'Ow!' Belle winced. 'God, you are such a—'

'A dick. You said.' The grin was back. 'You, however, are fucking tasty. You know that? Very tasty indeed. That dark blue suits you.'

'Oh shut your face,' said Belle. He was really hurting her. 'Come on, stop fucking around, Harlan. Let go of me.'

'Kiss me first,' said Harlan.

Belle shook her head. He'd been on about this for years. *You're lovely, Belle, you're tasty, kiss me.* And the groping, the patting. He made her flesh crawl.

'Fuck off,' said Belle, yanking herself free of him and staggering back a pace.

'What you gonna do, tell your father? Well shall I tell you something, Belle?'

Belle was hurrying back around the car, getting into the driver's seat. 'Whatever you got to say, I don't want to hear it,' she said, starting the car.

'Yeah? Well hear this,' he shouted over the sudden lion's roar of the engine. 'Your father would bring you to me tied up and naked, if that's what he was told to do. He works for the Stones. He follows orders, like a good boy. Your arse belongs to us. Don't you ever forget that. One day soon, Belle. One day soon.'

91

Nula was a nervous flyer. If the conditions were bad, she often refused to go up in the Jet Ranger with Charlie. She didn't hate the helicopter *quite* so much if someone else, some nice steady pilot type, was flying it. But Charlie was crazy. He thought dipping the damned thing up and down and making her clutch at her seat was a great laugh.

Newsflash: it wasn't.

Every time the craft shuddered, she felt her heart leap into her mouth. But now – thank God! – they were nearly home. She could see the yellow, brown and green fields streaking along beneath them. And she could see their lake in the distance, the sun glittering on its surface, and there up ahead was the big square welcoming shape of their house.

A few more minutes and this will be over.

Christ, she hated flying.

Suddenly the engine stuttered. Nula felt herself flung forward against the restraining strap of her seat belt.

'What the fuck?' she gasped out.

Charlie was staring ahead, concentrating. 'Only a glitch, babe. It's nothing,' he said.

Nula clung to her seat. *Just get us back onto the ground safely,* she thought.

The engine stammered again; a bigger jolt this time. Nula let out a shriek. Her heart was hammering against her ribcage. She felt slick sweat start on her neck and arms.

They were coming in, getting closer and closer. She could see the big H on the helipad now, see the sun sending up bright dazzling shimmers from the lake, throwing up a blinding shield of light. Then the aircraft canted to one side, throwing her against the harness again. It *hurt*.

Then again.

Nula screamed.

She heard Charlie say: 'What the fucking hell?' as he wrestled with the controls.

The thing was spinning now. Over and over, side to side, end over end. Her screams and Charlie's shouts merged and blended with the roar of the faltering engine.

We're going to hit the lake, we're going to hit the lake, thought Nula.

Oh Christ, please help us . . .

There was an ear-shattering bang, flames in the cabin followed by terrible pain – and then the whole thing began to plummet.

92

After Milly got back from her meeting with Nipper, she was plunged straight into talks with the events organizer over the food, the entertainment, everything. The place looked fabulous, there were TWENTY YEARS MARRIED banners strung up at the front of the house, CHARLIE AND NULA strung out across the back.

Hurrying upstairs, her stomach knotted with tension, she heard the roar of the helicopter's approach and then a stutter in the engine note – or had she imagined it? She went into the master bedroom and then over to the window. She could see the Jet Ranger, coming closer. As it passed over the orchard, it swooped to one side and started to spin. Feeling her guts clench, her eyes followed the craft as the spinning accelerated. Now it was whirling in dizzying circles, faster and faster, the nose dipping down, the whole thing shaking. The Jet Ranger was away from the orchard now, over the ornamental lake. Spinning like a top, out of control, and then . . .

Oh Christ!

Milly shrieked. There was a *bang* so loud that it shook the window frames and sent her staggering back a pace. Then the helicopter erupted into a ball of orange flame. It seemed to hang in the sky for a moment – and then Charlie Stone's pride and joy fell into the lake and hit the water, hard.

93

Afterwards, Milly had no recollection of leaving the bedroom or running down the stairs. Suddenly she was in the hall and her legs felt like jelly, her head like an overblown balloon about to burst. She was stumbling and shaking when she got down there, and Harlan was just coming in the front door and saying: 'What the hell was that? Did you *hear* that? What the fuck?'

'Get . . . phone . . .' Milly took a breath and tried to get the words out. She couldn't. Her heart was racketing in her chest and she kept seeing that fireball, the charred remains of the Jet Ranger dropping into the lake. She clutched a hand to her heart, tried to steady herself. 'Get an ambulance. And the fire brigade,' she managed to get out, her voice quivering. Her face was bleached of all colour. 'Dad's helicopter. It's crashed.'

There was only one electric buggy, and that was already down at the helipad. So after he'd called the ambulance and the police, Harlan ran, and so did Milly. They were joined by Terry Barton and Jill, then by Belle. Then Nipper showed up, and Ludo and Paul and Peter. They all went full-pelt over the lawns and down past the orchard and then to the lake.

In the centre of it, smoking, hissing, metal popping as it cooled in the brackish water, crackling as the electrics shorted out, was the wreckage of the Jet Ranger. Inside, there were two blackened, twisted things. Formless. Not human. Not recognizable as such, anyway. Charlie and Nula.

When Milly saw the things inside the ruined aircraft, she started to scream. Nipper and Ludo started forward, about to wade in, but Terry stopped them.

'It ain't safe,' he said. 'The thing might blow again.'

Ludo and Nipper stumbled to a halt. Everyone took a pace back, away from the water.

Harlan turned a furious face on his father's right-hand man. Milly was shrieking her head off. 'My parents are in there!' Harlan roared.

'There's nothing to be done,' said Terry. He looked pale, haggard. 'We got to wait for the fire brigade.'

'What the fuck *happened*?' demanded Harlan. 'Christ, Milly, will you *shut up*?'

Milly was wailing in anguish, her eyes locked on the downed craft. Belle stepped forward and enfolded Milly in a hug. 'Shush honey, shush,' she said unsteadily, and Milly's screams died to wrenching sobs.

Harlan looked over at Terry. 'You're supposed to *stop* things like this happening.'

It was Jill who spoke up in her husband's defence. 'How could he stop that?' she demanded. 'The damned thing crashed. How could Terry have stopped that?'

Away in the distance, there came the blare of a siren. It was coming closer.

'Help's nearly here,' said Belle to a shuddering Milly. But she looked again at the downed aircraft and thought that this situation was already *beyond* help.

Charlie and Nula Stone were, without a doubt, dead.

94

Only a couple of months since they'd buried Beezer, and here they were again. But not burying, not this time. *Cremating.* 'Poor fuckers were cremated *anyway*,' said Ludo loudly, and Harlan told him to shut the fuck up and show some respect, but he was smiling – *smiling* – as he did so.

At the local crem they all assembled and watched the red gold-braided curtains slowly draw apart, saw the coffins bearing the already burnt remains of Charlie and Nula Stone slide away into the waiting furnace. Then with horrible finality the curtains closing again. And that was it. Finished. They were *gone*.

Belle glanced across and there was Harlan in his black designer suit, his arm around Milly, who was shaking with sobs, her face drowning in tears.

Belle looked at her own father – Charlie's best friend since childhood – standing there like a rock, grim-faced but not crying because he was old school, he was tough; Terry Barton hardly ever cried. Then her mind went back and she saw it all again – the helicopter whirling out of control and plummeting into the lake at Charlie's house on what should have been such a great day for the Stones. It sent a chill right through her, every time she allowed her mind to replay it. She tried not to. But somehow she couldn't seem to make it stop.

Without Charlie Stone, without his huge appetite for life and all that it had to offer, there was a void in all their lives. The vicar had said how Terry had loved to sit with Charlie in Cooks' Pie and Eel shop in the Cut next door to the Young Vic, watching as Charlie devoured four portions of pie and mash and then finding room for a trip to the boozer. They'd all tried to laugh at that. With Charlie, everything had been excess. Eating, drinking – everything. His lust for life was monumental. And money. He wanted *stacks* of money – and he wasn't choosy, Belle now knew, about the way it was earned.

Without Charlie Stone, her dad seemed bereft and troubled. Terry spent hours on the phone, and then there were whispered conversations in the kitchen between him and Mum, conversations that abruptly ceased when Belle came into earshot. Everything seemed tense and unreal. Because now of course Harlan was in control. His new young bloods were ever-so-gently shoving Terry and the older men aside, forcing them out of the business, off the manor.

Since the crash and leading up to the double funeral, Belle had been watching Harlan. She thought that he seemed to have *grown*, somehow. Following the awful deaths of his adoptive parents, he seemed to blossom, to expand, to relax out into every corner of Charlie's manor and make it his.

Now she knew about the secret side of the business that the Stones and the Bartons were involved in, she wondered how she could have been so naive for so long. A furniture manufacturer's, paying for superyachts, million-pound cars and helicopters? If she really thought about it, it was a stretch. But add in a drugs enterprise with the high addiction rate that crack cocaine delivered, and the whole thing started to make sense.

Charlie had been a *drugs baron*.

And so – she didn't want to believe it, but she had to – her dad had been party to it all.

When the ceremony was over and they were back at the big house, everyone swilling back drinks and eating sandwiches, Belle went over to Milly, who was huddled on the sofa, staring into space.

'Can I get you anything, Mills?' she asked her, sitting down beside her.

Milly looked up as if surprised to find her there. She shook her head.

'This is the worst day,' said Belle. She squeezed Milly's hand. 'It's awful. I know it is. But after today, things will be easier.'

Milly nodded, saying nothing.

'Mills . . .' Belle hesitated. Milly was grief-stricken and she was going to add to it. Unless Milly already somehow guessed the truth . . . ?

'You know when I was talking to you about going into the Clacton accounts office and asking for a job?' began Belle.

Milly looked at Belle. 'Of course I do. You said you wouldn't ask Terry or Dad directly because they'd only say what the hell did you want a job for, didn't they already give you enough?' She sniffed and dredged up the ghost of a smile from somewhere. 'You were right, too.'

'Well, I went there.'

'You did?' Milly's attention sharpened. 'What was it, a complete disaster?'

'No, it was . . . it was bloody odd, Mills. It was a house in a row of houses, and there were people working in there, and . . .' She paused. She didn't *want* to say it. But she had to. 'I think – no, I'm sure – that they were manufacturing drugs.'

Now Milly was fully focused on Belle. 'Are you *mad*?'

'No. I saw it. And I checked it out. They were making crack cocaine.'

'Oh come on.'

'I talked with Einstein. He told me. After all, what have we ever known about the business our dads are in? Precisely *nothing*.

What have we ever seen from these factories? Nothing. What has anyone ever told us about all these wood and fabric "imports"? Nothing. We've been kept in ignorance. Fed bullshit.'

Milly's pallor was almost grey against her shapeless black funeral dress.

'I spoke to Mum about it. She went apeshit that I'd been there. She *knew* about it. So does my dad. And your parents did too. *And* Harlan. They've probably been running the whole thing for years, under the cover of the furnishings business. Mills – I didn't want to tell you this, but I *had* to,' said Belle.

'You really think my dad was dealing drugs?'

Belle shook her head. 'It's more than that, Mills. Dealing? No. That's the thin end of this. I think your dad was *way* above that sort of thing. What about Javier from Colombia, that bloke he's been trying to cosy you up with? There are families out there who make a fortune from drugs and Javier is probably from one of those. He wasn't doing anything with furnishings, that was all a blind. There are cartels, they're hugely wealthy people. I think your dad was in tight with them. And he wanted to get in even tighter, which is where *you* came in. Keep Javier firmly onside and Charlie could get a fortune beyond his wildest dreams.'

'I don't believe it,' said Milly, shocked.

'Neither did I, at first. But now? I do.'

'What are you going to do, Belle?'

'Talk to my mum again. And my dad. See what they have to say.'

Milly looked at her friend. 'More bullshit?'

'Probably.' Belle's eyes drifted over to Harlan, standing there chatting, laughing. Charlie and Nula were dead, and he looked like he was at a Christmas party, having fun. It was obscene.

'You know,' said Milly quietly, 'my mum was a little bit crazy, but I tell you Belle, this is where crazy really starts. When they let Harlan into their lives? They let a demon in. A fucking *monster*.'

Milly surged to her feet and was gone, out into the hall, shoving past the mourners, running off up the stairs.

'She OK?' asked Nipper, coming over to Belle.

Belle stared at him with dislike. Harlan's toy poodle. 'No. Not at all.'

He sat down on the couch. *Oh fuck off,* thought Belle. But he didn't.

'How do you think it happened? The accident?' she asked Nipper.

He shrugged. 'Helicopters are dangerous things,' he said. 'The servicing has to be top-notch. You hear of accidents. All the time.'

'Harlan told me it takes months for the Air Accident people to sift through it all. To find out what really happened.'

'Yeah. He's right. The AAIB are bloody thorough. But dead's dead, ain't that so? It won't bring either one of them back, no matter what they find.'

'I don't think I'll ever be able to forget that day,' said Belle.

It was so vivid in her mind, even now, over a month after the event. The panic, the shouting, the wail of the fire engines and the police cars, the ambulances to take the bodies away to the morgue – and then in the days after that, the Air Accident crew came in with heavy lifting gear, disassembling the wreckage that remained and taking it off to their headquarters in Farnborough.

Belle stared at Nipper, sitting there. He was watching Harlan, just like she was. 'You really think this was an accident?' she said.

Nipper's eyes swivelled to her face. 'What are you saying?'

Harlan's attitude was so relaxed, so *in charge*. He looked her way and half-smiled, and she felt a shiver go right through her.

'It suits him,' she said. 'Them being gone. Out of the way.'

'Don't let him hear you say that,' Nipper said, giving her a steely-eyed look.

'I'm not scared of him,' said Belle. She nodded toward Ludo, who was lounging against the wall beside the door. 'Or any of you pet apes he likes to hang around with.'

Then she thought of Harlan chasing her down the road in his Porsche, and his parting words to her, and suddenly she wasn't so sure.

'Well,' said Nipper, standing up, 'you fucking well ought to be.'

95

Milly sat on the bed up in her room, listening to the roar of conversation from the guests downstairs and glad to be up here, away from it. Away from the necessity to be polite, to play hostess. Because she guessed she *was* the hostess now.

Now that Mum was gone.

Milly gulped and blinked back tears. She felt scoured out, empty, finished. She sat there, slumped, and looked at the black bin bags stacked up high against the far wall of her bedroom.

Nula's things.

Her designer dresses. Her furs. Her jewellery. Her make-up. Harlan had sent that dead-eyed creep Ludo upstairs yesterday and the bastard had bagged all her mother's gear up and stuffed it in here.

'You'll want to go through all this, won't you,' Harlan had said to Milly. 'See if there's anything you want to keep? I might hold on to some of Dad's pieces, there's a few designer bits I like, but most of the stuff's too loud for my taste,' he said. 'I'm taking over the master suite, anyway. The boys'll move my stuff in there.'

Rotten bastard, she thought, but didn't dare say it.

Now she wearily got to her feet and went over to the pile of bags. Her mother's stuff. Crying, she opened the first. Such beautiful gowns. Sequinned and hand-stitched and worth a small fortune. And – oh God – here was the pastel blue shift Nula had been wearing the day before she'd left for the Med with Dad for

310

their pre-anniversary cruise. The last time Milly had seen her alive.

Milly clutched at the silky fabric, brought it to her nose, inhaled Je Reviens, Nula's signature scent. Sobbing, she dropped it back into the bag. Oh Christ. Oh *Mum*.

With shaking hands she moved on to the next bag, tearing it open. These were more personal, intimate things. Nula's Chinese tortoiseshell jewellery case. Her tablets. Dad had called them 'Nula's crazy pills'. That had been unkind. But she supposed the stress of living with someone as flaky as Mum must have told on him. Must have *frustrated* him, she guessed, because Charlie wasn't the kind that would ever succumb to a mental illness, and he had never understood Nula's pain.

Milly delved deeper. There was a big Louis Vuitton holdall in here, with notebooks inside. Nula had never been a reader. You either were or you weren't, and she knew that Nula had never picked up a book in her life.

'I'll read when I'm ninety,' she had always said.

But Nula hadn't lived that long. And these weren't books to read. Milly thumbed through a few pages and saw Nula's scrawled, shambolic handwriting. Ah! Nula's journals. These were the notebooks the psychiatrists and psychotherapists had encouraged Nula to write in when she was receiving treatment and in her day-to-day life; they had wanted her to pour out her troubles onto the page, to find some release maybe. Milly reached into the bag again. There was a whole stack of them, testament to Nula's long struggle with her mental health. There were more of them in the pouffe in the sitting room, the ones she'd shown Belle when she'd been asking questions about the business; she'd get those later, keep them all together in this bag. She couldn't just bin them. And she didn't want anybody else pawing through them. Maybe later, she would be able to look at them in more detail. Right now, she couldn't. It was too raw, all of it.

She thought of what Belle had told her about the Clacton place, the one they'd found reference to.

A crack factory, running alongside a legitimate furnishings business? Her father, a drugs baron? Her mother, going along with that? Belle's parents, in the know?

No. It couldn't be true. Could it? She wished she smoked or drank or something, because she was in a bad, bad place right now and she felt that it could only get worse.

96

The nightmare went on and on for Milly. She collected the two urns containing her parents' ashes from the undertakers, wondering – not wanting to, but unable to stop herself – how much of the dust inside the bronze-coloured urns was flesh, blood and bone, and how much was just scorched fragments of metal from the Jet Ranger.

Got to stop thinking about that, she thought.

And now came the reading of the will. In his office, Mr Gatiss the family solicitor read it out to Harlan and Milly. Milly was so dazed that for a long while none of the dry legal words he was spouting even registered. Then she saw Harlan sitting there with a big shit-eating grin on his face and said: 'What?'

Patiently, Mr Gatiss pushed his half-moon specs up his nose and read the will again.

This time, Milly paid closer attention. The gist of it was, Harlan got everything. *Everything.* Milly got an allowance, thirty grand a year, that was all. The rest went straight to Harlan. Charlie and Nula's entire fortune. The houses. The cash. The business. The nightclubs. The boats, the cars. The whole damned lot.

She sat there and thought *of course.*

She'd never been rated. She was just a girl. Harlan was the boy, the favoured one, heir to Charlie Stone's empire. She thought of coming downstairs to proudly display her first teenage party dress and Charlie saying, crushing her in an instant: '*Well no one's ever going to call her Twiggy, are they?*'

Subtlety had never been Charlie's strong suit. Mum had thumped his arm, shushing him, but Milly had got the message, loud and clear. She looked a mess. She *was* a mess. Fat and ugly. But Harlan? For Charlie, everything perfectly dressed and handsome Harlan did was OK. Nothing had ever changed that for Charlie, not even when Nula had started to hate Harlan and fear him.

For Charlie, Harlan could do no wrong. And here was proof of it.

Milly drove into town that night and went to one of the nightclubs Dad had owned. Now it was Harlan's. She ordered a Bloody Mary at the bar and then stood there, wondering what the fuck she was doing here amid the deafening noise of Diana Ross belting 'Chain Reaction' out of the sound system. She downed the drink and ordered another. Then she felt a bit sick. She wasn't much of a drinker. But she drank the alcohol because it numbed the pain.

Feeling hazy, she stumbled off toward the ladies and stood and stared at her face in the mirror, noting that her potato-shaped nose – *thanks, Mum!* – was shiny with grease, her lipstick gone. She dabbed powder on and added a slick of lipstick. Better. Well, a bit. Other girls were pushing in alongside her in the cramped loos, and a black-haired beauty with hard, knowing eyes came up beside her and met Milly's gaze in the mirror. She was exactly the sort of girl who'd always frightened Milly, reminding her of the snobby tomboy girls at school and at the stables, the ones who'd bullied her.

'Need a livener then?' the girl asked with a smile that didn't reach her eyes. She had a tiny square of cellophane in her hand, a couple of pills inside. 'Tenner?'

You never touched drugs. Not even cannabis, which everyone

said was harmless. That had been rammed into her brain, *nailed* into it, from an early age. Playing with drugs was Russian roulette. You could be fine on it – maybe – or it could induce psychosis. You could wind up a paranoid schizophrenic. Pull the trigger, her dad had always said, and see whether the bullet took your brain right out. Your choice!

Which was fucking ironic, given the fortune that Charlie Stone had apparently – according to Belle – made from selling the damned things. But looking at this girl, looking at the stuff in her hand, made Milly wonder.

Everything hurt. *Life* hurt, right now. Her parents were gone. She missed Mum already, much to her surprise, and she had once *adored* her dad, even if he did have faults, even if he was the world's worst crook, a fucking *drugs baron,* even if he'd never rated her at all. Now she was afraid of the future, under Harlan's thumb. He would be in charge, and she would be *nothing.* As per usual. She stared at the pills in the girl's hand. It made you feel better, they all said. Milly felt she would give *anything,* to feel better.

'You in or not?' said the girl, getting impatient.

Milly pulled a tenner out of her bag and handed it over. Then she tossed the pills onto her tongue, bent her head to sluice in water straight out of the tap.

For the first time ever, she let the good times roll.

97

Terry could feel a cold wind coming. Charlie had always laughed at Terry's sensitivity to atmosphere – because Charlie had been dead from the neck up, as far as any finer feelings were concerned. Terry was the one who sometimes sensed danger before it hit, and Charlie had been glad to have him around.

Now, with Charlie gone, it was like a part of Terry himself was missing. Guilt chewed at his guts day and night. He should have been with Charlie that day. What Harlan had said when that Jet Ranger crashed was absolutely right. It was his job in life to look after Charlie, to be his right hand, and he had failed. Feeling sick at heart, still he did the rounds as usual, checked out the dealers, visited the crack production lines and so far – *so* far – Harlan had left him alone to get on with it all, while making it perfectly clear that Terry answered to him now.

For the first time since he'd been a small boy forced to go to Sunday school by his mum, he went to the church on the manor, the one where he'd married Jill and where Charlie had married Nula, back in their old glory days. Somehow he needed to do this. He walked up the aisle, absorbing the peace of the vast place, his eyes fixed on the suffering Christ in the stained-glass windows behind the altar. Wondering why the hell he did it, he crossed himself and then slid into a pew and sat there, head bowed.

He thought of Charlie, dead, burned to ashes. His old friend. His mad, impulsive friend who'd been such a great laugh, such a ruddy fool, such a *mate*. As he remembered the helicopter crashing, his face screwed up in anguish. He should have stopped that happening somehow. *Somehow.* He'd lost his best friend in the whole world, but before that there had been other losses; too many. Little Col in that botched burglary. And Beezer, funny stupid Beezer in his poncy designer gear, who'd always made them laugh down the pub. Terry closed his eyes and tried to pray, but no words would come into his mind, nothing would come except his firm belief that this was an evil trade they were all involved in, and they were all damned to hell. God had punished Charlie and Nula for it and eventually God would punish him and his family for it, too.

God no. Please spare them. Spare Belle. Spare my wife. Take me. I know I've been bad. Just take me and be done with it.

'My son?'

He looked up. A priest he didn't know was standing there in a white dog collar and black cassock. Back in the day, the preacher here had been all hellfire and brimstone, but this one was new. Bulky and bald and with myopic blue eyes, there was a smile on his thin lips.

'Are you all right?' asked the priest.

'I'm fine. Thank you, Father.'

'If you need to talk . . .' he started.

Terry started to shake his head. Then he said: 'Would you hear my confession, Father?'

'Of course,' said the priest.

Then Terry thought of what he could say, what he *dared* say to this God-fearing man. 'No. Maybe I won't,' he said. 'I'm sorry.'

The priest stood there looking down at Terry with gentle eyes. 'It's never too late to find God,' he said.

Terry felt a tightness in his throat and for a moment he was afraid that he might actually start to cry.

'Maybe He wouldn't want to find me,' he managed to say.

The priest smiled. 'That's where you're wrong. God's love is for everyone,' he said, and walked on, up the aisle to the altar.

'Are you all right?' asked Jill over the phone later that same day.

She was at the gatehouse, and Terry was still up in town meeting a few of the lads, just checking things were running smooth. They weren't, of course. The trusted old guard were complaining about Harlan's up-and-coming young bucks, kids with bum fluff on their faces and big attitudes, trying to tell *them* how to behave. Terry smoothed things over as best he could, but truthfully he felt the same as any of them. Dispossessed. Shoved aside. He didn't tell Jill about his visit to the church. He couldn't.

'Where's Belle?' asked Terry.

'She's right here. Up at the big house in the outside pool, swimming. You OK?'

'I'm fine.' It was a lie, but still. He couldn't let Jill know that he felt shaky all of a sudden, unsure of the ground beneath his feet, fearful for the future. He was always the strong one, the one who looked after everyone else. He couldn't be seen to be weak, not ever.

'I'll call back later today. And tonight I'll be home, right?' he said.

'Right.'

'I love you.'

There was a surprised silence. He never said that. *Never.* It was understood between them; never spoken out loud. 'I love you too,' she said softly, but he didn't hear it.

He'd already hung up.

98

Terry had to meet up with Harlan at the apartment near Tower Bridge. He didn't like going there. Memories of poor bloody Beezer going over that balcony. Shit, if the poor old cunt felt so bad about his life, why hadn't he spoken to him or to Charlie? They were his mates. Close as ticks on a cat. If he'd confided in either one of them, they would have taken care of him.

If it really was suicide. But was it?

Terry remembered Charlie at Beezer Crowley's funeral, crying his fucking eyes out, the soft sentimental sod. But he'd been choked up too. Mates like Beezer passed through but once in anyone's life, and he was going to miss Beezer's stupid smutty jokes and his endless good cheer, which as it turned out had maybe been fake anyway, but what the hell. He would miss Beezer every day for the rest of his life. And now, Charlie too.

Christ, we're all going, one by one.

Maybe it was time to get out now. Just grab Jill, grab Belle, cut and run.

Shaking off his gloom, he went up in the lift and tapped on the door. Ludo opened it and Terry stepped into the grandly appointed apartment. It was flashy in the extreme, he'd always thought – typical Charlie and Nula. Huge Osborne & Little cream damask drapes at the floor-to-ceiling windows, massive white couches, vast tan-and-white cow skins on the floor, enormous cream and chocolate brown lamps all over the place. It shouted wealth and that was them, all right. Their money was always highly visible, like it comforted them after their poor childhoods to see it all out on display. Now, what had that all amounted to? Harlan would soon redecorate in the spare, minimalist style he favoured, which struck Terry as cold, just like him. Cold as ice.

The only person in the big open-plan room was Ludo, one of Harlan's chief boys, a blank-eyed dandy always togged up in designer suits, his dark skin gleaming, flashy gold chains draped around his neck. Ludo invariably smelled as perfumed as a tart's boudoir and he was neat as a new pin.

'Harlan here?' Terry asked. Maybe he was in one of the four bedrooms. Harlan liked to make people wait. Put in a late, grand appearance.

'On his way right now,' said Ludo.

'So what's the meet for?' asked Terry.

'You'll see. When Harlan gets here.'

There was something in Ludo's eyes. Something bad.

Terry felt his heartbeat pick up, felt light sweat break out on his brow.

'I need to make a call,' he said, finding that he needed to swallow hard to get his voice working.

'Sure,' said Ludo, indicating the phone by the couch.

'It's private.'

Ludo shrugged and displayed a rack of gleaming white teeth. 'We got no secrets from each other, bro. Anything you say, these ears can hear.'

Terry went and picked up the phone. Dialled the number. Waited. It was a damned long time, but finally, she picked up.

'Hi babe,' he said, keeping his voice even. There was a lot he wanted to say right now.

'Oh! Hi baby.'

There was strain in her voice. Irritation.

'What's the matter?' he said, anxious.

'Bloody Harlan's just pulled up on the drive,' she said. 'Stopped right outside. Oh, and there's another car too . . . yeah, that's Nipper's.'

But I'm meant to be meeting Harlan here.

Terry felt a moment's gut-churning panic, then he calmed himself. Breathed. If he could do nothing else, he could help his wife. Help Belle. By the sound of it, it was too late for the run code.

He watched Ludo moving around the room, picking up this, putting it down, moving along, moving around . . . now he was behind him, out of Terry's eyeline.

Christ.

There was very little time.

He said: 'The bag I left in the hall, is my pen in there?'

Jill was silent. She knew it was the *hide* code. That someone was with him, that he couldn't speak freely. And she knew the situation was dangerous. Then she said: 'What's happening?'

Terry gulped. He could hear Ludo, moving lightly behind him. He thought of Jill and Belle alone down there, undefended. This was it, what Nula had warned him about, the coup that Harlan had been plotting all along – and oh shit life had been so sweet . . .

'Just check the bag,' he said. *Hide, babe. Hide and for Christ's sake hide Belle too.*

'One thing Harlan asked me to tell you before he got here,' said Ludo from right behind him.

'What is it?' asked Terry, putting the phone back on the cradle, knowing it was the last time he would ever hear Jill's voice, knowing it was over now.

'Beezer? That fool weren't no suicide.'

He felt the garotte come over his brow, then down onto his neck.

Thinking time was over.

99

The concierge on duty at the Tower Bridge building was surprised when the lift opened late one night and two men, one black, one white, emerged towing four large suitcases behind them.

'Oh,' he said, and got to his feet.

He was instantly dazzled by the black man's brilliant smile as the two men made their way across the deluxe marble-encrusted lobby with its indoor cascade and luscious hothouse plants. They didn't pause; they kept heading for the revolving doors.

'Can I help you, gentlemen?' asked the concierge. It was his job to move any luggage down to the lobby for the residents, and he was a conscientious man, he took his duties very seriously. 'If you had phoned down, I could have done that for you.'

'No bother,' said Ludo.

Him and one of the other boys had spent a very messy four hours in the bathroom upstairs, both naked and busily chopping up the remains of Terry Barton in the bath before wrapping chunks of the guy in clingfilm to prevent any leakages. Then they had cleaned the place to within an inch of its life, showered, and got dressed. The night wasn't over yet. Next job? Dispose of the body parts.

But the concierge was already around the desk, taking one of the cases from Ludo's hand, assisting with a warm smile. He saw them out the door. Ludo turned and tipped him a twenty.

'*Thank* you, sir,' said the concierge, and returned to his post at the desk, pocketing the money and thinking, *What nice people.*

100

Belle was upstairs in her bedroom, wet-haired, having just done a few lengths up at the big house pool. Now she was stepping out of the shower, drying, slipping on a pale yellow cotton summer dress, scuffling into her sandals. Then she went to the dressing table and grabbed a comb and started pulling it through her hair. As she snatched up the dryer, something caught her eye through the window: Harlan's Porsche was parked up outside on the gravel drive. Behind it was Nipper's Mercedes.

Frowning, she switched on the dryer and swiped it back and forth across her hair. Then Mum nearly fell into her open doorway and stood there, her eyes meeting Belle's in the mirror. Belle felt a hot spasm of fear bolt right through her as she saw her mum's expression. She switched off the dryer.

'What is it?' she asked.

'I was shouting for you,' said Jill, sounding breathless.

'Sorry. Hairdryer.' Belle put it down on the dressing table. 'What is it? You're white as a sheet.'

'Your father . . .' Jill gulped, her words failing. Then she took a quick breath and managed: 'He's just been on the phone. He's told me . . . Belle, we've got to hide.'

Someone was ringing the doorbell.

Belle was looking bewildered. 'Hide? Hide from what?'

'There's no time to explain! We mustn't answer it,' said Jill. 'It's Harlan.'

That thin spasm of alarm deepened and gripped at Belle's

guts. She felt her heart thudding sickly in her chest, felt moisture start on her palms and under her arms. 'What's he going to do?' she asked, her voice barely a whisper.

Jill's eyes were suddenly full of tears. 'It's OK, it's OK,' she said quickly, and it was like when Belle was a little girl and her mother would try to reassure her, even though Belle always knew when there was something wrong. 'Don't worry honey. Your father . . .' Her voice died.

'Where is he? *Where's Dad?*'

The doorbell was ringing, again and again and again.

'He's in town. Somewhere on the manor. He phoned. He sounded . . . something was wrong.'

They stood staring at each other. Now someone was hammering on the door with their fist.

Jill's face was literally bleached with terror. 'We haven't got much time,' she said. 'Come on.'

Belle followed Jill out onto the landing and into the master suite, which was built into the eaves of the house so that at each side of the room there was a triangular crawl space hidden away behind the walls. There was a cupboard door set into the lowest wall, intended but never used for storage. The bats had spread out from the loft long ago, and there was all this bollocks about them being a protected species now – and anyway Terry kind of *liked* the bats, he always said good luck to the little bastards who shot out from under a gap in the tiles at night and whizzed around the garden. Sometimes, Terry liked to stand out there and watch them. Not Jill – the bats gave her the willies and she always thought they were going to get caught in her hair.

'They got sonar,' Terry would tell her. 'They ain't going anywhere near you, babes.'

'Go on, get in,' said Jill, nudging Belle toward the cupboard.

'But they'll know we're home – won't they?' asked Belle,

hesitating. She didn't like the thought of going in with the bats, not this close. Not at all.

Downstairs, someone was kicking the door. They could hear male voices.

'Our cars are locked up in the garage. They'll think we've walked down to the village.'

'Mum, I don't . . .'

'Get in!' Jill's eyes were frantic as she hissed the command. She was pushing Belle inside, hurrying her. 'Hurry the fuck up, Belle.'

Belle did as she was told and moved further along the crawl space so Jill could follow too. She pulled the door closed. Inside, the space was boarded so you weren't balancing on the beams. Feeling claustrophobic, Belle took a breath and tried to stay calm. Her breath was whistling in and out of her mouth and she could feel cobwebs brushing against her face as she went to the far end, tucked herself away in the corner under the roof beams, behind the chimney. Oh Jesus. Spiders. The big black ones that came out in October and scuttled across the floor, terrifying the bejesus out of you. She hated the bloody things.

Close by her head she heard the rustling of papery wings.

The bats.

There was a crack of daylight coming in under the tiles – the bats' exit hole. Dimly Belle could see them, moving restlessly, disturbed by her being in here, near to them. Their bright beady eyes and folded wings made her think of every vampire movie she had ever sat through, laughing her head off at the daftness of the idea. The undead! What a bloody joke. The smell in here was burning the end of her nose. Guano, didn't they call bat shit that? Or was that birds?

She turned her head a little and she could see her mother about six feet away, shooting the large bolt at the top of the door to secure it. Confined now with the bats and the spiders and whatever the hell else might be crawling around in here, Belle felt sweat break out. Oh Christ, she wanted, needed, to get out. But she had to stay quiet, stay still. Trembling, she pressed her hands to her mouth to stifle any small shriek that might escape if anything touched her. She tried to stay calm.

They were hidden. They would be safe. She told herself that, over and over.

But she didn't feel safe, not at all. Harlan and his cronies were at the door and that was reason enough to panic.

Then she heard it: *Whack! Whack! Whack!*

Down in the hall, someone was hitting the door with something heavy.

Dimly, she could see her mother's face, frozen in fear.

Then the front door caved in.

101

'Hey! Anybody home?'

It was Harlan's voice, loud, drifting up from the hallway of the gatehouse.

'Not much of a welcome, if you don't mind my saying,' he said, and there was a snicker of laughter.

Belle and Jill stared at each other in the half-light.

Quiet, mouthed Jill.

Belle nodded. She was bent double, sitting on her haunches. There was a fluttering murmur of leathery little wings above her head, like the dry rustling of autumn leaves or bees fanning a hive to keep it cool. She could hear the men making their way through the house, going into the sitting room, then the kitchen. Noises down there, like they were turning things over, breaking things.

Oh fuck.

But hadn't they all, deep down, been frightened of this, prepared for something like this, since Charlie's death? They had all been living on a knife-edge. Pretending all was well. Knowing it wasn't. And now, here it was at last. Harlan's reckoning.

Was Dad coming?

No. Belle had seen the answer to that in her mother's pale, terrified face. They were on their own here. And now she could hear a heavy tread on the stairs.

The men were coming up.

Belle shrank back further, into the shadows. Held her breath.

Felt sweat dripping into her eyes, smelled the odour of extreme stress oozing from her pores.

Got to hold on. Mustn't panic.

'They must have gone out,' said Nipper's harsh voice, so close by that Belle nearly shrieked.

There was a pause, then Harlan said: 'Or Terry warned them. Somehow.'

'Nah, Ludo dealt with him.'

It sounded like they were standing right by the bed, in the centre of the room. Two, maybe three of them.

Dealt with him? Oh Christ.

Belle flinched as a crash came, sounding as if it was right by her head. The bats stirred restlessly. The men were tipping over the bedside tables. She heard drawers opening. Then slamming shut. They were at the dressing table. There was a curse, then a huge crash as they overturned it. Peering around the chimney, Belle saw Jill in the faint light flinch back, away from the door. Someone rattled the door, pulling at the handle. The bolt held.

Then all at once the men were gone, out of the room, going along the landing to the other bedrooms and bathrooms. More crashes. She saw Jill's hand go to her mouth. Quiet, Belle. Hold on.

More crashes.

It was a nightmare and Belle prayed for it to be over. Wouldn't they go soon, be satisfied the place was empty?

They had to go.

She felt something skitter over the flesh of her forearm and jammed a fist in her mouth to stop a scream.

It felt like they had been in here for hours, but it was minutes. And now . . . oh Jesus, the men were coming back. They were back in the master bedroom . . . no! They weren't. They were passing the bedroom door, they were going down the stairs.

They were going.

It would be all right. Once they were gone, she and Mum would get in the car and drive, find Dad, all would be OK.

But Nipper said Ludo had dealt with Terry.

She couldn't allow herself to dwell on that now. If she did, she'd panic and give them away.

Then she stiffened. Shit! No!

They were coming back up the stairs.

Into the master bedroom.

There was the sound of movement near the cupboard door. Belle saw the door shudder and then something slid into the gap between the door and the jamb.

A crowbar.

There was a wrenching thud and the bolt pinged off like a pistol shot. The door shuddered open. Harsh light from the master bedroom flooded in on Jill. She let out a scream that pierced Belle's soul. Then they dragged Jill out of the hiding place.

102

Belle was cringing back behind the chimney breast, flattening herself into the corner by the rafters. She was gasping for air, sickened, terrified. The bats, right beside her head, fluttered their wings in unison. Their dark eyes gleamed like sequins.

'Where's Belle?' Harlan was asking Jill. Belle could hear every word.

'She went out to the village,' said Jill's voice. Unsteady. Panicky.

'He warn you?' asked Harlan.

Silence. There was a hard crack of flesh on flesh. Belle flinched and bit hard on her lip to stifle a yell of outrage.

'Answer me. Did he?'

Jill was sobbing quietly now. But she didn't answer.

'Check it,' said Harlan, and Belle saw shadows moving out in the bedroom. Nipper was checking inside the storage space, making sure Belle wasn't in there too.

They're going to find me, they're going to find me . . .

'Shit a brick!' said Nipper's voice.

'What?' asked Harlan.

'Fucking great spider in there. Hate those fuckers,' he said.

'She's not in there?' asked Harlan, sounding bored.

'No, boss,' said Nipper.

But he hadn't come beyond the jut of the chimney breast, hadn't come as far as the rafters in the far corner. That fucking spider had saved her . . .

'Get in there, have a look. The chimney goes up there, she could be hiding behind it.'

Belle felt an icy shudder of pure hysteria then. They had her mum. And now they were going to get her too. She could see shadows moving at the door and then movement as bulky blond Nipper wedged himself into the crawl space.

What to do, what to do?

Belle lifted a shaking hand and swiped at the bats.

Instantaneously they flew, chittering, not out of their usual exit hole because Belle was in front of it. In confusion and fear they bashed against her face in a leathery flurry, then they swarmed out through the crawl space door and into the master bedroom. Nipper fell back with a shout, swearing and stumbling as a hundred tiny projectiles flooded out over him and flittered around out in the main body of the room.

'It's only a few bats, what the fuck's wrong with you?' Harlan was saying, laughing at Nipper's alarm. 'Christ, you're such a bloody moron,' he said, and the crawl space door was kicked shut, bouncing against the ruined bolt to hang inches open.

More movement now, out in the master bedroom. Then footfall out on the landing, the heavy tread of the men and the lighter one of Jill, who was fighting them, trying to resist as they hustled her down the stairs. They were taking Mum out of here. To where? Belle heard car doors open and close. The roar of a motor. They were going. She heard car wheels crunching over the gravel driveway and out to the gate, then out into the lane and away.

103

The cupboard door was ajar and light was filtering in. She saw the spider that had spooked Nipper scuttle over the lip of the door and out into the bedroom. Tiny shadows moved out there. The bats, trapped inside the room, denied their exit route. She stayed still. Her hips ached where she was bent double, her arm was going numb, but she didn't dare move.

All was silent, but this could be a trap. He could be out there still, waiting. Knowing that if she was still hiding in the house, sooner or later she would have to show herself. Sweat was pouring out of her. She blinked, eyes stinging. Couldn't even move to wipe the moisture away.

Minutes passed. Then hours.

Slowly the light inside the crawl space changed, grew dimmer. Belle wasn't wearing a watch so she could only guess at the time. Maybe seven, eight o'clock in the evening? And still there was no movement in the gatehouse. Inch by inch, she began to relax. They really were gone. She moved a little, eased her aching joints. In anguish Belle thought of her mother. What would they do with her? She couldn't even think of it. She was powerless to help. But help had to come from somewhere, didn't it?

At last, it started to grow dark.

No movement anywhere.

When it had been full dark for over an hour, she braced herself and unfolded her limbs, stretching, feeling pins and needles stab at her arms and legs, feeling the trembling weakness in them from this enforced inactivity. She would get downstairs, phone the police or someone, and then help would come. Mum would be OK. She had to believe that or she would go stark staring mad.

Listening intently to every movement, the crackle of the beams as they cooled after the day's heat, she thought it's OK now. They've really gone.

Belle edged along the crawl space, past the chimney, and reached the cupboard door. Stealthily she emerged into the half-dark of the bedroom, bending double to get out of the low opening and then standing up, able at last to stretch, to get some life back into her stiff, frozen limbs. Dimly she could see the bats, still swooping confusedly around in their confinement.

She was crossing the room when suddenly she stopped moving. Wait. *Wait.*

She'd only heard one car going.

But there had been two cars pulling up. The Porsche and the Mercedes.

She was already moving back toward the cupboard when a large shape stirred by the bed. She turned, the breath catching in her throat, and stared at the man who'd been sitting there. Her heart was beating so hard she thought she would choke.

'Hiya, Belle,' said Harlan. 'I've been waiting for you.'

104

In the hours that followed, Belle learned the true meaning of terror. It brought cold sour sweat to your whole body and hot burning bile to your throat, bile you had to choke back because you couldn't, you didn't dare, show how frightened you were. Because he'd love that. He would *feed* on that. He'd taken her down to the reptile house. Now that they were in here, he was watching her, that mocking half-smile on his face. She wanted to lunge at him, to damage him, to make him pay, but she couldn't. Nipper and one of Harlan's other men were holding her still. They were Harlan Stone's boys, and they would do exactly what he said. She had no power here. None at all.

'I bet you're thinking, round about now, that you wish you'd been nicer to me,' said Harlan.

Belle stared at him with hatred in her eyes. Sweat trickled into them, making them sting. Outside, thunder rolled. Rain battered the roof. Inside, it was a jungle, wet ferns brushing her legs, humidifiers roaring, the heat crushing and damp, the trickle of small waterfalls a constant noise. And in the centre there was a large pond, black, brackish. Things moved in there, but she wasn't going to think about that.

Water torture.

Yes, that was what this was. Belle's legs were trembling. Her brain was in a panic, like a rat caught in a trap. There had to be a way out of this.

But there was no way.

I'm going to die.

The thought popped into her brain like gas rising out of a bog, bringing a fresh surge of terror with it. She was perched on the edge of the pond, standing on big ornamental rocks, the men holding her there. Water from the domed roof dripped, ran down her face. So wet and hot in here. Hot as hell. Stifling. She thought of her parents then, and pain roared up through her stomach, up into her throat. She was going to be sick.

'Pretty little Belle,' said Harlan, shaking his head. 'Bet you wish you'd played ball now, eh? Been nice?'

Belle glared at him, standing there so elegant; so handsome and calm and in control. While she was barefoot, wearing a tattered rag of a dress, soaked in sweat, her blonde hair plastered to her head. She was scratched and bloody from where they'd dragged her in here. If the men hadn't been holding her, she would have collapsed to her knees.

'So go on,' he said.

Belle gulped and stared at him.

'Beg me for your life.' He was smiling, but his pale eyes remained emotionless as ever.

Belle looked down at the water. There were things moving in there. Something long slipping in from the opposite side. Eyes, she could see eyes, reptilian and cold. The powerful swish of a tail. Her mother's words came back to her then: 'Keeping bloody snakes and lizards and caimans! Only weirdos do that.'

Caimans.

Charlie had fed them on live rats, whole chickens. But a caiman was like a crocodile, it would take a pig. They were plenty big enough to do that. They could also take a human being. No bother at all.

Oh Christ help me . . .

'Waiting,' said Harlan. 'What do you say, Belle?'

'I know what you did,' said Belle.

'Did?' He frowned. 'About what?'

'Beezer. Jake. And the business. The manor. I know what it is.'

The smile dropped from his face, leaving it cold and blank.

'Throw her in,' he said.

105

They grabbed hold of her and obeyed Harlan's command.

The black waters closed over her head. Belle went down deep, unable to breathe, unable to believe that anyone could do this to another human being. Gasping, trying to tread water, she came back to the surface and gulped down a wheezing breath. The water was warm, warm enough for the caimans . . .

The caimans! Her heart hammering, she blinked and saw Harlan standing there, with Nipper and the other one. They were watching her flailing around in the water. Enjoying the spectacle.

Bastards.

Her head whipped around. There were three big caimans in here, she knew that. Two of them she could see right now, out on the far bank. One of those was beginning to edge toward the water, ready to slip in and snap up this new and unexpected meal – *her.*

Panic overwhelming her, she looked around for the third one, the big one. Even Charlie and his helpers were scared of the damned thing, and she was in the fucking pond and she couldn't see it. Now one of the other two was sliding into the water, its soulless eyes fixed on her. In terror she started to splash to the edge of the pond, away from it.

Suddenly something gripped her left leg and she was yanked underneath the surface. She didn't have time to draw in air. Screaming, swallowing mouthfuls of foul water, she struggled, eyes opening, stinging, hurting, but she could *see* it. It was the big one. It had hold of her leg. She kicked out hard, catching it a solid blow to the head, but it held on. She couldn't breathe. Scrambling for the surface, she managed to get her mouth out of the water and gulped in air. Instantly she was dragged under again.

The bastard thing had her and now it was shaking her, turning, going into what Charlie Stone had always told her and his kids was the 'death roll'. It was horrible, like being churned in a washing machine. Belle felt herself spinning helplessly under the water, trying to fight for the surface but unable to get there.

Disorientated, her leg in agony, she felt blackness wash over her and thought, *This is it then. This is death.*

Then she thought of Mum and Dad. Maybe it was best to just let go. To let this happen. She was spinning, spinning, running out of air, and then something grabbed her head. Bright sparks lit her vision as her lungs were being starved of oxygen. She was suffocating, feeling hard hurtful nubs that were teeth digging into her scalp and her face with such force that she didn't know how she was bearing it. She would have shrieked if she had any air. Instead, she was trapped and one of these monsters had her leg, the other her head.

She kicked feebly, trying to get away and then suddenly – amazingly – she was free, or her leg was anyway. The water was boiling around her. Her chest was a wall of air-deprived agony, her head still crushed in the merciless grip of massive jaws. Then suddenly the big caiman let her head go and she was knocked sideways by thrashing tails and rolling bodies. Terrified, injured, she floated up and drew in a breath. As her head broke the surface and she gulped down the fetid wonderful air, she looked up.

Harlan and his cronies were gone.

In the pond beside her, the caimans were fighting. Over *her*, their unexpected meal. A movement drew her eyes over to the other side of the pond and she saw a third one slide into the water. Her heart seized up in her chest.

Got to get out of here.

Belle didn't so much swim as scramble to the edge of the pond. Panicking, gasping, she grabbed one of the rocks at the side and her hands slipped on algae. Crying with terror, she reached up further, certain one of the caimans was going to grab her in its jaws and finish her off with another death roll. Her shaking hands found a purchase at last and she dragged herself, hauled herself out and onto the stones.

Soaking, shuddering, she was unable to believe that she was still alive. Sucking in breath after breath, she looked down her body. There was blood everywhere. Her leg was bleeding heavily. Her face hurt. There was more blood on her dress, all down it, fresh blood coming from somewhere. But she was alive, and for now that would have to do. Shuddering, shaking, she levered herself to her feet. She was terrified that her leg was going to give out on her. That the bone might be broken. There were bleeding puncture wounds running all up her calf, as neat as if they had been stitched there. But she stood upright. Took a few staggering steps and thought *He'll be waiting outside. He'll catch me.*

She went out through the heavy polythene door, then – bracing herself – through the outer door. But there was nobody out here, not a soul. The buggy was gone. They were gone. She stood there breathing in the indescribable sweetness of fresh country air.

Harlan thought she was dead.

She *ought* to be dead.

Her head felt sore and strange. There was a warm trickle of blood coursing down over her neck. Her mouth felt weird, different; her ears buzzed like she was about to pass out; but she was alive. She would have to stay that way.

Mum, she thought in anguish. Dad . . .

Unsteadily, she started forward. If she could just reach the lane, she might have a chance. Someone would pass by, someone would help her.

They had to.

106

Nipper had dropped Harlan back at the house and, as instructed, gone back to the zoo to make sure the job was done. He was freaked out by the caimans, truth to tell. And the fucking snakes, he hated them. But orders were orders, so he took the buggy back down beyond the orchard, passing the lake where Charlie and Nula had carked it, and pulled up at the front of the zoo.

Bracing himself, he went in, passing through the heavy main door and through the thick plastic one. Christ, he hated it in here. So clammy. Everywhere was dripping wet and hot as a furnace. Sweat broke out on his skin the instant he was inside. Quickly, he flicked on the lights. You didn't know when one of those damned things could be lying up on this side of the pond and then you'd be toast before you could even look round. They could move fast.

He thought of Belle in there, thrashing around, getting eaten bit by bit. Poor cow. But then, she'd been bloody stupid, facing up to Harlan like that. Fucking suicide, that was. Gingerly, he stepped forward. The big one – George – was lying out on the far side bank, reptilian eyes blankly staring. Fucking thing. The other two were out of sight somewhere. In the water, probably hoovering up what was left of her.

Shit, what a way to go.

And all because she wouldn't play ball with Harlan fucking Stone? Because of what she knew about the drugs business, the dead baby and all that shit? Stupid cow. Fuck that. Nipper thought that he would have done the deed with Harlan himself, bent over and taken it straight up the arse if he had to, rather than risk being put in there with the caimans.

He heaved a sigh. Whatever. She was gone.

He turned away, thinking job done.

And then he stopped, staring down at bloody footprints.

Woman-sized.

Leading out, away from the pond.

Leading to the door.

'You what?' said Harlan.

He was in the sitting room of what had once been Charlie Stone's house and was now his. He was thinking, actually, that there would be a lot of changes made now that he was finally in charge. All this crappy decor would be going soon. And things would be run differently. Along smarter lines. Harder lines. There would be no room for sentiment, not any more. He was beginning to feel quite excited about it all – and Nipper's interruption was annoying. Nipper was standing there and telling him . . .

'You *what?*' he said, louder this time.

Nipper swallowed, feeling nervous. Harlan didn't like things being fucked up, and this was fucked up big style.

'She got out, boss. There were footprints, leading out. I looked around, took the buggy around the lake and everything, all around the grounds. Can't see her anywhere. But it's no problem. She's bleeding. Wounded. She won't get far.'

'You fucking moron.'

'Boss—' he protested. How was this his fault?

'Get the fucking car out. Check the lanes. Go find her. And this time finish the job, yeah? Do it right.'

107

Milly was bored. Belle wasn't about. She'd been down to the gatehouse and gone to the back door just like she always did and usually it was unlocked: this time it wasn't. She knocked but got no answer. The place was in total darkness. They were out. So, feeling restless, Milly went into town and back to the club and there was the black-haired girl again, in the bogs. She seemed to live in the bogs.

'Sorry, I didn't catch your name,' said Milly.

'That's 'cos I didn't tell you, bitch,' said the girl sharply.

'Sorry.'

Other girls were shuffling in and out, using the loos, chatting, styling their hair, applying lipstick.

'You liked the stuff then?' asked the girl.

Milly nodded. Anything she said seemed to offend the girl, and she didn't want to do that.

'Come over to my place, get some more,' she said, and turned away, going out of the door and back into the main body of the club. The heat and noise out here were overwhelming. Ahead of her, the girl led the way. They went up the stairs, and out, past Sammy – who ignored her – and his mate Gazzer, then onto the pavement. Then, not saying a word, the girl crossed the road. She ignored the traffic, Milly flinching in her wake as brakes shrieked and drivers cursed. They reached the other side alive, and the girl went to a shabby peeling door beside a newsagent's and unlocked it. She went inside, impatiently ushered Milly in after her, and relocked the door.

You never touch that crap. You got that?

It was Charlie's voice, ringing in her ears over and over as she was growing up. Drugs were for mugs.

But . . .

Truth was, she'd never felt that good, not ever. When she'd taken the drugs she'd felt invincible. Confident. Happy. All the things she never did, as a general rule.

'I'm Marsha,' the girl threw back over her shoulder as she took Milly up a steep flight of stairs.

'Milly,' said Milly, and the girl didn't even acknowledge that she'd heard.

Marsha pushed open a door at the top of the stairs and switched on a light. They stepped into a dank, depressing little room, full of all sorts of rubbish; unwashed plates and cups on every filthy surface, an unmade bed, a dirty dark grey carpet.

'Take a seat,' said Marsha, and Milly looked around. There was nowhere to sit, except the bed, so she sat on that, trying not to notice that it stank. The sheets were filthy.

'Right,' said Marsha, throwing her black biker jacket onto the floor. She slumped down on the bed beside Milly and reached into her bag and pulled out a water bottle with no screw cap on it; instead there was masking tape and tinfoil, and a glass pipe poking out of a hole in the side, the gap around it sealed with Blu-tack.

Milly started to feel apprehensive. She didn't know this girl. She had no clue what she was doing. Marsha pulled out a plastic-wrapped batch of several small cream-coloured rocks from her skirt pocket. She placed one of the rocks on the square of tinfoil and heated it underneath with the flame from a Bic lighter. After a moment the inside of the bottle started to fill with pale smoke. Marsha inhaled it through the pipe and started to smile.

'Now you,' she said, pushing it toward Milly.

'What is it?' asked Milly.

'Crack. Go on. It's good.'

Milly pulled the bottle toward her, put the pipe in her mouth, and inhaled.

108

Belle was in the lane, walking through the pouring rain. Lightning crashed overhead. She walked even though she could barely feel her legs. She was shuddering, and when she put her hand out in front of her in the strobing blue-white half-dark she could see it shaking, she could feel it, tremors zipping not only through her arms but throughout her whole body. She was going to pass out. She knew she was. She would fall down flat and someone would come hurtling through here in a car and then she really would be dead.

There were no streetlights out here. The rain was drenching. Thunder rolled in the distance, then more lightning split the sky, neon-bright. She had no idea what direction she was heading in or what she was going to do. She could hear owls hooting in the woods and far away in the distance a fox barked. Trembling, soaked through and shivery from the water and feeling more wetness, frightening wetness, drenching her, dripping down from her head and streaming from the punctures on her leg, she stepped up onto the grass verge, moaning with pain as she moved.

Then . . . Christ, a car! She half-turned, seeing the full beam of headlights, and thought oh thank God.

Then she felt a fresh bolt of terror.

What if it was them?

What if they somehow knew she'd got out of there and were coming to find her? Stumbling, groaning, Belle staggered over to the far side of the broad verge and there was a ditch. She sat down on her arse and let herself drop into it. It was deeper than she expected, and she felt her feet sink into muddy water up to a foot deep. Agony erupted in her leg and as she slipped down sideways her head was suddenly afire with pain. Trying not to shriek, she ducked down as the car rounded the lane. It was moving slowly, as if . . .

As if whoever was in there was looking for something.

The car glided slowly by, its headlights sweeping mere inches above her head. Then it was gone, up the lane. Teeth chattering, she crouched there and wondered if they'd come back. If she ought to just stay down here until daylight. But . . . she didn't think she'd make it through the night. Not here. It was cold, wet, and she was hurt. Hurt badly. She could feel blood still running down from her head, over her face. Her body was wet and her leg was in filthy muddy water; she'd die if she stopped here.

Sobbing with pain, Belle hauled herself hand over hand out of the ditch. For minutes she lay there on the grass verge, too weak to move. Thunder crashed overhead. She was losing blood. She had a horrible picture in her mind, of being found here in the morning, face down on the verge, dead.

No!

She was not going to die. Harlan was not going to win. No way could he have this final victory over her.

Belle pushed herself up, onto her hands and knees and from there to her feet. She staggered on. Somewhere there would be help. There had to be. And then she heard a car coming from the other direction. She wanted to walk out into the road, flag it down, beg for help – but it could be them, coming back.

Not the ditch. Not again.

But there was nothing else. No trees to hide behind. Only big hedges, either side of the lane. No safe shelter anywhere. The lightning would show her up. She'd be caught. Whimpering, she went back to the ditch and slipped down into it once again, feeling the horrible squelch and suck of the mud, shuddering at the icy chill of it.

The car was rounding the bend. Slow again. Were they checking, looking for her? The car cruised past, very slow. Belle held her breath. If they stopped, searched more closely, she'd be done for. They'd throw her back in with those monsters and that would be it.

The car slowed.

She couldn't breathe, didn't dare.

Then there was a roar from the engine and the car shot away, surging around a bend in the lane. The headlights faded. The noise of the engine faded too. Soon there was only the endless drenching patter of the rain and the hard, frightened thudding of her own heart.

Belle crouched there. She waited, shivering, agonized.

Then she clawed her way back up out of the ditch and lay there for long moments on the verge.

Got to move.

They could come back.

I can't. I can't do it, she thought.

She pushed up onto her elbows, forced herself to her knees and then to her feet. She walked on.

109

After seeing Marsha, Milly danced away the night and fell out onto the pavement at two with all the others who were leaving the club. One of the two bouncers on the club door, Sammy, stopped her with a hand on her arm.

'Miss Stone?' he asked, barely believing it. She looked shot away. He'd never seen her in the club before, mostly she was just at home, in the big Essex house, but now here she was and it was clear she was high as a kite.

'That's me,' she giggled, and started to stagger away. 'Hello, Sammy!'

'Hold on, hold on,' said Sammy.

There'd been big changes going on. But the king was dead and now Sammy supposed it was long live the new king – and that was Harlan. Harlan was a smooth despicable son of a bitch. Charlie would come straight out and bollock you if he had to, then it would be over, done, and you would be mates again. But Harlan was different. He was a fucking scorpion. He'd always strike with stealth. Sammy knew that if the Stone girl was in here getting wasted, and he let her stagger out into the night unattended, his arse, sooner or later, would get roasted.

'Where you off to?' he asked, watching her eyes pinballing around in her head. Wasted to shit, she was. No doubt about it.

'Home,' she shrugged. Then she smiled. 'Wanna come?'

Sammy gave his mate and fellow doorman Gazzer a glance that said: *All yours, mate.*

Gazzer nodded.

'Come on,' Sammy said to Milly, and took her arm again because she looked like she was about to wander off and he couldn't risk that. To Gazzer he said: 'I'm going to see Miss Stone home, OK?'

Gazzer nodded again. Sammy stepped out, holding on tight to Milly, and hailed a taxi.

Milly was staying at one of Dad's houses on the old manor. *Harlan's* house now, but still – he wasn't likely to come here. She thought of that swish penthouse with the lovely view of the river, so much nicer than this, but she wouldn't stay there any more, not since Harlan made it clear that territory was marked out as his, and *certainly* not since she'd learned that that was where poor Beezer had done a nosedive from its balcony and ended up ten storeys down on the concrete below.

She tried to open the door to the house with her key, but she couldn't *find* her key, and Sammy was there right behind her, a hulking presence, but she didn't feel embarrassed about this the way she usually would. Tonight it struck her as funny. Finally Sammy had to take her bag out of her hands and find the key himself. He got it in the lock and swung the door open, flicking on the lights.

'It's humble, but it's home,' trilled Milly, dancing up the hall to the kitchen. 'Coffee, tea or me?' she laughed.

So this was what it was like to be *high*. Milly had never felt anything like it. She felt . . . *beautiful*. She felt powerful. And so confident that she felt she could fly.

'No thanks,' said Sammy, looking around. It wasn't the Ritz, but it was OK. 'Anybody else here?' he asked.

'Why? You going to ravish me, are you?' she asked, coyly.

In fact, Sammy was concerned she might sick up and choke to

death. She was *right* out of it. And who'd get the blame then? The muggins who'd escorted her out of the club. *Him.* He had enough to worry about, without any more aggro on top. He shook his head.

'Someone ought to keep an eye on you. What did you take?'

'What makes you think I've taken anything?'

Sammy thought of the shy, mumbling girl that Milly usually was. She was like a shadow, and had always been overwhelmed by her flashy desperate-eyed mother and her loud as fuck father. She never exactly lit up the room.

'Because this ain't you,' he said.

'I'm bored with me,' she pouted. It was the truth.

'You're off your face. You don't want to go doing things like this, trust me. It's not safe.'

'I'm going to bed,' said Milly, shoving past him. 'You can stay if you like. Or go. I don't give a shit either way.'

He listened to her thundering up the stairs like a marauding baby elephant. Heard the slam of her bedroom door. Music started pounding through the floor. Frankie Goes to Hollywood, 'Two Tribes'. Then he heard heavy footfalls again. She was dancing.

Sighing, Sammy took off his jacket and made himself comfortable on the couch. He'd go up later, see she was OK. Before ten minutes was up, he was asleep.

110

On Beechwood Farm, Jack Tavender was closing up for the night. He'd eaten late after shutting the chickens away and bedding down Lady Marmalade and Goldie, fixing himself a meal from the stew he'd had simmering away on the hob for the last couple of days. Then Trix had started whining and scratching to be let out so he'd opened the kitchen door and let the black-and-white Border Collie shoot out into the night to do her business.

This had once been his parents' farm, but his dad had died years ago. Then only his mother had remained, so Jack had helped her out when she grew too old to cope with the manual work. Then she'd died too.

As their only child, he'd inherited this problematic, crumbling ruin. The farmhouse was old, sixteenth century in parts, and he was doing it up bit by bit, repairing the flat roof over the scullery, propping up the porch with a new oak support beam because one of these days that bastard was going to slip sideways and bring the whole front of the house crashing down with it. Parts of the walls were fixed with big iron stays, and a couple of the old post and truss barns were listed, which was a bugger because you could do sod-all to them without consulting some nob from up on high in the council. He had thought of trying to kit them out as holiday lets, if he decided to stay on. If the plans would ever be passed, which he doubted. But he hadn't decided anything, yet.

He was washing up the dishes, setting them on the wooden draining board to dry, years of training in tidiness and cleanliness still with him. Away in the distance, Trix was barking her stupid head off. Nutty bloody dog. His mum's dog, not his. Trix's favourite game was chasing cars or cyclists out in the lane, but this sounded closer, nearer to the farmyard itself. He yawned, stretching. He'd been working hard all day. Clearing out one of the haylofts in preparation for repairing the roof, which was leaking. He'd struggled up on the roof alone in the hail and thunder, fixed a tarp up there to hold it, for now. A hot bath, then he was turning in.

Drying his hands, irritated at the stupid mutt, he went over to the back door and opened it.

'Trix!' he shouted.

She was still barking.

'Fucking dog,' he muttered, pulling his boots back on. Trix had always been obedient when his mother'd been here to order her around. With Jack, Trix had got in the habit of playing up, wagging her tail, turning into a house dog when she was born to be working, meant for herding sheep. Well, they no longer had sheep here on the farm, they'd all been sold off, even his mum's prize South Downs ram, so Trix was redundant. Jack knew he ought to make her sleep outside, in the kennel, like the outdoors dog she really was, but somehow he'd got into the habit of having her in the house. She was dopey, a grinning loon of an animal, but she was company.

Grabbing the torch, he stepped out into the yard. The rain wasn't letting up and it was turning damned cold. Trix's barking was coming from near the biggest barn. She'd disturbed some rats, maybe. He'd had a big vet's bill last month when she'd tackled a nest and the rats had fought back, biting off half her left ear. He was going to have to get a cat, a good mouser, if he was going to stay.

If.

For now, he was treading water, making repairs, tending what little livestock was left – just the chickens and his mother's horses now, he'd already sold the sad remnants of the dairy herd which had once – so long ago – been his father's pride and joy. He was trying to decide what he was actually going to do with the rest of his life. And there was the dog, the damned dog. Maybe one of the other farmers around here would give her a home.

'Trix!' he hollered into the rainy night. 'Get out of there, you daft bastard!'

The torch's beam caught her, eyes glittering. She was standing at the big barn door, which was hanging open, and she was staring into the interior, her hackles raised.

'What you got now then, eh?' Jack asked her, but she paid no attention to him. 'You got more guts than sense, that's your bloody trouble.'

But he'd shut that barn door earlier.

Moving cautiously now, he edged forward. People did break in sometimes out here in the middle of nowhere, thieved equipment. One of the local farmers had even lost a tractor, for God's sake. He reached the dog and grabbed her collar. She let out a single bark of protest, then was still. Deep in her throat, she kept up a steady low growl.

Jack aimed the torch's beam into the depths of the barn. Hay bales were stacked up in there. Favourite playground for the rats. But this wasn't how Trix normally reacted to rats. Usually she'd be off in there, chasing them, getting her arse chewed – or her ears – and running up more sky-high bills for him to pay.

'Someone in here?' he called out.

He moved the torch's beam and yes – there was someone. Movement.

'What the fuck?' he said.

Lightning flared, and he saw what had moved.

There was a woman, lying beside the bales.

She was covered in blood.

When she heard his voice, she tried to get up. Tried to get to her knees. She looked at him blearily. Her face . . .

'Jesus bloody Christ,' said Jack.

'Help,' said Belle weakly. It came out as a wet croak. Then she fell back, unconscious.

111

Belle came to because someone was moving her. She was being carried. Everything hurt and she started to protest, but she didn't have the strength. A door was kicked open and then lights blared and she was being laid out on something hard as rock. Her eyes rolling in her head, she tried to focus. Oak beams above her. Wooden cupboards all around. A kitchen. Warmer in here.

Oh Jesus it hurt.

It all hurt so much.

Her hand fastened on the edge of what she was lying on. A big table. Something wet and hot touched her hand and she was catapulted back to that black-water pond and the caimans biting at her, tearing her to bits. She moaned, full consciousness coming back hard and terror with it. She swivelled her head to see what was happening, panicking all over again. *Agony.*

It was the dog. It was licking her hand.

And there was a bearded dark-haired man, moving toward a phone on an old oak dresser.

'No,' she tried to say. It came out weird. Her mouth felt odd. Nothing seemed to be coming out of it the way it should.

He didn't hear her or couldn't understand her. He was picking up the phone and starting to dial.

Nine . . .

'No!' she tried again but was ignored.

Nine . . .

'Don't,' said Belle, and with a lurch she threw herself off the table. She hit the floor and it hurt. She screamed, it hurt so much.

'Christ alive,' he said, and stopped dialling. He dropped the phone and rushed back across the kitchen to kneel beside her.

Belle grabbed his arm and tried to shake him. She couldn't. She was too weak.

'Don't phone for an ambulance,' she said, and it all came out wrong. She gasped, swallowed, tried to make her voice come out better. 'They're looking for me. They'll check the hospitals. Don't do it.'

'You're saying . . . ?' He was staring at her face, trying to make sense of her words.

'Don't phone ambulance. People . . . looking for me. Bad people. They'll check. They'll know.'

'Bad people?'

'Yethmph,' Belle heard her mouth say. Yes.

What the hell was wrong with her mouth? The left side of her face was on fire. It was agony.

'Someone's looking for you? Someone did this to you?' he asked. The dog crowded in, trying to lick Belle's face. The man pushed it back. 'Fuck off out of it, Trix,' he said, and then he turned back to Belle. 'OK. I'm going to get you back onto the table, all right?'

Belle nodded feebly.

He lifted her back up onto it. Got a towel from beside the sink, rolled it up, tucked it under her head. That hurt. She moaned, grinding her teeth together, swallowing blood. Then he fetched another from a cupboard and put it on her leg.

'This is bad, all this,' said the man, leaning over her. 'Your injuries. You need proper medical help.'

'First aid . . .' said Belle, wincing. It came out fast day.

He was dabbing the towel on her leg. 'These look like animal

357

bites. Puncture wounds,' he said. 'Not too bad. These'll heal OK. I'll clean them out, bandage them up.' Then he looked up at her face. 'The blood's good. Blood cleans wounds. You should have a tetanus shot . . .'

'No. Mumph.' Belle shook her head.

'What did . . . ?' He ran out of words. This was worse than bad. She'd been savaged by something.

'Caimans,' said Belle.

'Clean, yes,' he said, not understanding.

Then he moved up to her head, looked at her face. 'Bad news or good news?' he said.

'Wha . . . ?'

'Your face. It's very bad.'

Belle was staring at him. She was in pain and she was full of fear, all over again.

'There is no good news. Something's torn a lump out of your face. Your cheek's hanging down like a flap. I think that's why your speech is fucked. You need stitching up. You need a medic.'

Oh Christ. She'd gotten by since childhood on her good looks. She wasn't vain, but she was used to being the one everyone's eyes followed. It was just *her*. And he was saying . . .

'I'm not kidding around here. It's a mess,' he said.

Belle grabbed the edge of the table again, wanting something solid to hang onto when her world had descended into chaos. Out there, maybe they were looking for her, and if they found her she knew she was dead for sure. Out there, her father must be in danger. Maybe he was dead already. And her mother . . .

Again, the dog licked her fingers as if in sympathy.

'You'll have to stitch it,' she said to the bearded man, and she saw understanding right there in his eyes this time. 'Do it.'

112

'You've got to be fucking kidding me,' he said.

Belle stared at him mutely. *Not kidding,* her eyes said.

'These people—'

'Sew it up,' said Belle. 'You have to.'

'Who are they?'

'Bad. Very . . .' she gulped. Tasted blood again. She felt weak, so weak. And sick to her stomach. 'Very bad.'

He walked away.

No, he's going to the phone, they'll know I got away, Harlan will kill me, they'll finish it this time . . .

But he went instead to a cupboard, pulled out a blanket, brought it back and draped it over her. It was warm. She was still shivering, which was shock she guessed, or horror or some damned thing, but the blanket was good.

'Do it, yeah?' she said, closing her eyes, weary now.

'It will hurt,' he warned.

She knew that. 'Do it.'

He went to the cupboard again. Pulled out a first aid box. Brought it back to the table, opened it up beside her head. She didn't look. If she did, she knew she'd lose her nerve and let him use the phone and then she'd be fucked.

Then he was gone again. He came back and stood there, looking down at her, holding a dark green bottle in one hand. Then he seemed to come to a decision. He uncorked it and took a swig straight from the neck. Swallowed hard. Then he looked at her again.

'Want some? It's good brandy. Might take the edge off.'

Belle tried to shake her head.

'OK.' He started laying out the things he'd need. Antiseptic. Swabs. Cotton. A fine needle. When he had it all to hand and ready, he looked at her again. 'Sure?'

'No . . . choice,' she muttered.

He went to the sink and washed his hands; then he came back to her and started. The sensation of the needle piercing the flesh of her cheek, the cotton slithering through the bloodied, hyper-sensitive meat of it, was all too much when she had been through so much already. She screamed aloud, several times. The dog whimpered. Time stretched out and the ordeal seemed to last forever. When he was no more than halfway through, the pain was too bad and Belle passed out. Her last thought before she did so was of Harlan Stone's cruel smiling face. He would be in charge now, no one to stand in his way.

So she had to live.

She had to fight another day.

That thought stayed with her, following her down into blackness.

113

Sammy woke up next morning to the noise of someone being violently sick in the upstairs toilet. He padded in his socks through to the kitchen and stuck the kettle on, yawning. Well, she was alive. He brewed up, slopped in milk and took one mug through to the lounge. Hearing the toilet flush and sounds of movement, he took the other mug upstairs and found Milly sitting on the edge of the bed in yesterday's clothes, red-faced and looking like she'd been dragged through a hedge, her light brown hair hanging in her eyes, her clothes dishevelled. He put the tea down on the bedside table.

'Thanks,' she whispered.

'Feeling better?' he asked.

She shook her head.

'Take some aspirin. And lots of water. Flush it all through, yeah?'

She nodded.

'You staying on here?'

Another nod from behind her hair.

'Look,' he said. 'I know it's been bad. But it's going to get better now.'

Milly said nothing.

'Right. I'll leave you to it then. OK?'

'OK,' she said, then looked up at him. 'Thanks,' she said, but he had already turned away, gone out of the bedroom door and down the stairs.

Minutes later, she heard the front door close behind him.

114

Time passes fast sometimes, when you're having fun. When you're not, it drags its heels and you just want it to go, to be over. That was how Belle felt when she woke up. She was in a single bed, one of a pair. A threadbare towel was draped over the pillow beneath her head. She was still wearing her rag of a summer dress. It was dry now, stained all to hell, and stiff with her blood. Her head throbbed and her face was awash with pain all down the left side. Sooner or later, the pain would go; but for now, she was in the thick of it, gripped by it, consumed by it.

She thought of her mum and cried. The tears stung her face like a hot brand. She raised a hand to touch her left cheek, then dropped it again because she was too scared to go there. Sore-eyed, agonized, she lay there and watched the first faint threads of daylight penetrate the thin curtains at the bedroom window.

It will pass, she told herself.

But right now? She didn't believe it. She was wide awake and in pain again. Sleep was better, you couldn't think when you were asleep. You were out of it. She wanted so much to be out of it.

'Oh, you're awake.'

It was the bearded man, standing in the half-open door. As he stood there, the dog slid past him and came into the bedroom.

'Trix,' he said warningly.

The dog bounded up onto the bed, turned in a circle and lay down at Belle's feet, tail thumping the coverlet.

'Looks like you got a fan,' he said.

Belle didn't answer. She was watching the man warily. He could be anyone. He could be a fucking serial killer, how the hell would she know? Maybe he got off on stitching girls' faces up. Maybe he bloody enjoyed it.

'I'll get you some painkillers,' he said, and was gone again, leaving the door ajar.

He was back within minutes, carrying a glass of water and a strip of paracetamols. He came over to the bed, sat on the side of it. 'Here,' he said, and pushed out two tablets from the silver strip. As Belle struggled to sit up, he put a hand behind her head and helped her.

'Open,' he said, and Belle obeyed, putting out her tongue. He put the tablets on it and handed her the glass of water. Belle took it unsteadily, washed the pills down. Lay back down, exhausted by this simple act.

'You're going to be fine,' he said, and he stood up and left the room, closing the door quietly behind him.

Belle looked down at the dog. 'Hey Trix,' she said feebly.

Her voice sounded more like her own again. That was good. Half your face hanging off, you weren't going to sound good, now were you? Trix's tail thumped the cover once, hard. Then she put her head down on her paws, her dark liquid eyes on Belle's face, with one ear erect and the other, which looked half-chewed, flopping over. A dog was staring at Belle, and she didn't like it.

'How do I look?' said Belle. 'Good, yeah? Miss Universe, what do you think?'

With sore eyes she looked around the room. There was a padded nursing chair between the two beds, and what looked like a dressing table – but the two struts at the back of it that had drop-down hinges fitted were intended for three mirrors. There were no mirrors hanging there. There was an old-fashioned silver vanity set on top of the dressing table, two brushes – but no hand mirror. Wasn't there always a hand mirror with those things?

Had he taken them all away so that she couldn't see herself in them?

Oh holy Christ, how bad is it?

But she already knew the answer to that. She just wasn't allowing herself to take it in, not yet. She couldn't.

Once again she raised a shaking hand to her left cheek. It took every ounce of courage to do it. Her fingers touched painful swollen flesh, and the hard raised nubs of the stitches. Flinching, she quickly put her hand back down.

Belle thought of the wreckage of her life. She thought of her mum, dragged from the gatehouse and . . . and what?

And Dad! Where the hell was he?

Belle started crying again. She cried until she had no more tears left. Then she fell asleep.

115

'What do you mean, you can't find her? Fuck's sake, what's wrong with you morons?' asked Harlan, who was walking around Nula's sitting room in irritation, glaring at Nipper and Ludo.

Everything should have been neat and tidy, but this was a loose end and he didn't want any of those. All this hassle with Belle was holding him up. He was due back on the manor, he had business to conduct. The Air Accident people were phoning, asking to meet and discuss Charlie and Nula's crash. Another distraction. This was all such a fucking nuisance.

'It's like we say, boss,' said Ludo with a shrug. 'We've looked all over the grounds, everywhere. We been up the lane, both ways. We knocked on farm doors.'

'How many?'

'You what?'

'How many farm doors? There's at least twenty smallholdings around here and a lot of larger farms too.'

'Well not that many, I grant you, but . . .'

Harlan walked up to Ludo and he fell silent at the look in Harlan's eyes.

'You get out there and find that bitch, OK?'

'She couldn't have walked far. She was bleeding,' said Nipper.

'Yeah, that happens when you been in a tankful of caimans. As you useless fucking articles might find out if you're not very bloody careful. She should never have got out of there. You silly fucker, Nipper, I told you, you should have stayed there and made sure the job was done right.'

'We'll keep looking boss. Don't worry,' said Ludo.

Harlan's gaze held his. 'You better check the hospitals.'

'But, boss—'

'If she's managed to get some help, managed to get herself checked in somewhere, then she could start talking and it could be a problem. We don't want that, now do we? Check the hospitals.'

116

Days were passing, Belle supposed. She'd lost all track. Trix stayed on the bed except for when she went out into the kitchen to be fed, or outside to do her business. The bearded man fed Belle cool soup, mashing up bread in it so that it was soft and didn't pull at her stitched cheek. He made her tea and gave it to her cool, through a straw. Fed her more painkillers. She dozed and woke and dozed again, hearing sounds of someone working with tools nearby, maybe unscrewing something, but it didn't matter.

When she began to get stronger he helped her across the room to the loo with its built-in shower cubicle and waited outside the door to be sure she wasn't about to faint in there. While she was in there she saw what the noises had been. The bathroom cabinet door was missing.

Bet that had a mirror on it.

When nearly a week had gone since Harlan's boys had thrown her to the caimans, the man came in carrying some clothes, Trix following in high excitement, her tail going into overdrive as Belle reached out a hand to pet her.

'What's all this then?' asked Belle as Trix jumped up onto the bed, did her usual performance of treading around to get comfy, then lay down at Belle's feet, her face fixed in a grin.

'Clothes,' the man said, laying them out on the counterpane. 'They were my mum's, might as well get some use out of them. There's a couple of nightdresses, some dresses and a cardigan.

Some underwear. A pair of her old jeans and – yeah, a couple of my shirts. I dunno. Probably none of it will fit.'

Belle thought the shirts definitely wouldn't. Despite not being particularly tall, he was very broad across the shoulders, like he'd been doing weights.

'I thought that today if you feel well enough you could get in the shower, wash your hair, put on some clean clothes. It'll make you feel better.'

Belle stared at his face. He had very fierce eyes, dark blue. His expression could be scary, stone-hard, and the dark beard didn't help. When she watched him move around the room, she was struck by a lean physicality about him. At first, she'd thought he was older; now she knew he wasn't. He couldn't be more than late twenties, early thirties.

Belle was staring at his face.

'What?' he asked.

'I don't even know your name.'

'Jack,' he said. 'Jack Tavender.'

'I'm Belle Barton.'

'Good God,' he said, staring at her.

'What?' Belle turned her right cheek toward him, uncomfortable at being stared at.

'You're the girl in the red BMW. The racer.'

Belle did a double take. The dark beard, the eyes with that unnerving thousand-yard stare. The look of chilly contempt that tractor driver had given to her and Harlan on the day when he had chased her along the lane in his Porsche.

'The man on the tractor,' she realized in surprise. 'It was *you*.'

'You and that bloke were racing along the lane like bloody fools.'

'We weren't racing,' said Belle. 'He was chasing me. He's always been chasing me.' She raised a hand, indicating the ruined side of her face. 'And finally he caught me.' Her voice broke. She should have known that with Harlan it would either end in her domination or her death. But she'd ignored the danger signals and she'd ended up like *this*. 'His name's Harlan Stone.'

Jack nodded slowly then stuck out a hand. 'Hello, Belle.'

Belle took his hand: it felt warm and dry, and his grip was strong. 'Hello, Jack. And thanks. For everything.'

He shrugged that off as if it was nothing.

'Why are there no mirrors on that dressing table?' asked Belle.

'I didn't . . .' he started.

'And the bathroom cabinet door. There was a mirror on it, yes? And you took it off.'

This time, he didn't even attempt an answer. Their eyes locked. Belle lay back tiredly on the pillows. 'It's really bad. Isn't it.'

'Don't think about it. It will get better.'

'You're a rotten liar.'

'There'll be scarring. There's no doubt about that. But there's no infection. It's healing fine.'

'My leg feels OK,' said Belle.

'That's fine too. There might be some scars. Nothing too bad.'

Belle almost smiled. But she couldn't manage it. The stitches felt tight when she tried, pulling her face to one side. She must look like the Joker in *Batman*, she thought. Oh Christ.

'Must have given you a fright, a girl turning up ripped to shreds on your doorstep,' she said.

He shook his head. 'You're not ripped to shreds. You're here and you're alive. Everything from here on in is a bonus.' He paused, eyeing her face. 'Who's this Harlan Stone then? Any relation to that Charlie Stone character who moved into the big house? The one who died along with his missus in the helicopter crash? That damned thing was a bloody nuisance, zipping in and out, worrying the livestock.'

Belle nodded. 'Harlan's their adopted son. He's crazy and he's sadistic and he keeps a lot of pet apes around him, real nasty bastards.'

'Are you ready yet to tell me about what they did to you? And why?' he asked.

Belle gulped down a breath. Oh Christ in heaven. The black waters closing over her head. The pressure and the pain as the caimans struck. The terror.

'If you can't yet, don't worry,' he said.

Belle took in a calmer breath, then let it go. The panicky feeling abated. But she wanted to tell him, tell someone. 'I can do it,' she said.

'If you're ready.'

'I'm ready,' said Belle, and she started to speak, started to tell him all about Charlie Stone and her dad who worked with him, and Charlie's twisted viper of an adopted son, and how Harlan had pursued her all her life. When he'd finally seen her as a threat, he had thrown her in with the caimans, expecting them to finish her.

'But they didn't,' she said at last. 'I got away.'

His eyes had narrowed while she spoke. 'You think this fucker's going to keep looking for you? He didn't know you managed to get out, did he?'

'I don't think so. It's a miracle I did. I just kept going. But then I started to get weaker and weaker and I knew I couldn't go on and I saw the sign for Beechwood Farm, so I came through the gate and walked up toward the house, and then I felt like I was going to pass out for sure so I went into the big barn and that's where you found me. Or Trix did, anyway.'

He was silent for a moment, taking it all in.

'Go and have your shower,' he said. He stood up, Trix trailing after him, and left the room, leaving her alone.

117

They still weren't finding her after over a week of searching. They'd checked all the hospitals for miles around, and no Belle Barton had been admitted to any of them. So probably, Nipper said – and Harlan was tempted to agree – what had happened was this: she had fallen into a deep ditch or a culvert or some damned thing, it had been raining heavily at the time and she could have been swept away, downstream, into the river and out to bloody sea, who knew? And so she wouldn't ever be found.

'I don't like loose ends,' said Harlan for about the thousandth time. 'And I don't like fuck-ups. It makes me nervous, thinking that people I've put my trust in are not performing as they should.'

'She's dead,' said Ludo with a weary shrug, thinking that if Harlan had stuck around personally to see the thing finished, then they wouldn't be having all these damned problems in the first place. Which he would not say. He liked breathing. It was fun. 'Come on, she's gotta be dead.'

'Yeah, probably,' said Harlan.

Shit, he had other things to take up his time anyway. Deals to be done, changes to be made. But Belle was a thorn in his side. He'd lusted after her for so long and now all he wanted was a neat conclusion. Belle had decided she wasn't interested, and – worse – she'd dug up dirt on him and might blab about it. So she had to go. Sad but a fact. Fuck that bitch. Now he just wanted proof that she was gone for good.

'You keep looking,' he told them. 'I got business to conduct on the manor and that's what I'm going to carry on with right now.'

'Sure, boss,' said Nipper.

'Yeah, right,' agreed Ludo.

118

The shower did make Belle feel better, but it was odd, not seeing her reflection. She caught a faint misted glimmer of it in the showerhead but averted her eyes straight away. She wasn't ready for that yet.

It floated into her mind again, the horror of her situation. *Everything's gone. My family. Even my looks. Everything that ever mattered, all gone, all snatched away by Harlan fucking Stone.*

When she emerged from the bathroom wrapped in a big towel, there was a hairdryer on the dressing table and a pair of beige loafers on the floor beside the bed. From the pile of clothing she selected a too-big black bra and some practical unsexy Sloggi underpants, then sorted out a pale blue chambray shirt and a pair of Jack's mother's jeans to put on. They didn't really fit – his mum had been a tall lady, that much was clear – but they were OK around the waist, so it was fine. She turned them up at the ankles by a couple of inches, scuffed on the loafers. They didn't fit either, they were loose on the length and narrow through the instep. She went back to the bathroom and padded the toes out with toilet paper.

Better.

She picked up the ruins of her dress. It was thoroughly caked in blood, filthy with dirt. She remembered putting the thing on just weeks ago before everything had gone crazy. Remembered turning back and forth in front of her mirror in the gatehouse bedroom, admiring herself. She'd always done that, didn't every woman?

But now she was afraid. If she saw her reflection and some monster was staring back at her, what the fuck would she do?

Freak out. She knew she would.

She went out into the kitchen. Jack was making tea, slipping bread into the toaster.

'You want some?' he said, turning and seeing her there.

Trix, laid out in front of the roaring fire, grinned a greeting at her.

He paused, taking in this new Belle in jeans and shirt. Belle turned her head away, hiding her cheek. 'Yes,' she said. 'Thanks. What should I do with this?' She held up the ruined dress.

He put two more slices of bread in the toaster. 'We can wash it.'

Belle shook her head. She'd be reminded of what happened, every time she wore the thing. 'I don't want to keep it.'

'Then put it on the fire.' He indicated the grate, where the flames were leaping up from the crackling logs.

Belle walked forward, patted Trix and threw the dress into the fire. She watched the expensive fabric curl and burn. It was like destroying her past, watching that. Saying goodbye to the old life and maybe allowing for a new.

Allowing for what though?

For being scarred? For being ugly? She felt a shiver of apprehension, despite the fire's heat.

'Tea?' asked Jack.

Belle nodded and went to the table and sat down. Not too long ago, she'd been laid out on here with her life's blood streaming out of her. But what now?

'You can stay as long as you like,' said Jack. 'If there's any danger they're still after you, it's probably safest. You're not really fully recuperated yet, are you. Better to rest up. Get back to full strength.'

Belle felt relieved at his words. Truthfully, she was scared right now of the outside world. She'd been battered and bruised and abused by it. Here at least, with this unsmiling stranger, she did feel safe.

He was bringing the tea and toast over to the table, setting it all out with butter and jam and milk.

'Help yourself,' he said, pushing a plate toward her.

Belle buttered the toast, spread on jam. Then slowly, gingerly, she started to eat her first solid meal.

He was watching her face. Again, instinctively, she turned her damaged cheek away from him.

'Don't,' he said.

'What?'

'Don't turn your face away. I've seen it all before, anyway.'

Belle nodded, embarrassed. He was right. What was the point of hiding her ugliness from him? He'd stitched her up. He'd seen it all, at its very worst.

'I think I should see it too,' said Belle.

'You ready for that?'

'I have to see it, don't I. Sometime.'

'Maybe after we take out the stitches?'

'Will it look better then?'

'Probably not.'

Belle threw down her toast.

Jack looked at her intently. 'Look – you're still alive. You want me to fetch a mirror now? Right now?'

Belle stared at him mulishly. She wanted to say yes, if only to spite him for being so fucking casual about this. But she was afraid.

'No,' she said.

'OK. So eat your damned breakfast and stop feeling sorry for yourself.'

'You're a prickly bastard,' Belle observed.

'It's been said.'

'Your parents ran this farm?'

'They did.'

'You going to tell me about them?' challenged Belle.

'Nothing much to tell.'

'I don't hear any livestock about the place,' said Belle, gingerly eating the toast again, realizing that she was actually hungry for the first time in too long. 'No cows, no sheep.'

'My dad's prize dairy herd were sold off. The sheep too. All that's left are a few chickens, my mum's mare and a Shetland pony to keep her company.'

'Ah! She rode then.'

'She did. When she was a bit younger. More toast?'

'Yeah. Please.' She eyed him. 'And you. What about you?'

'What about me?'

'Have you got a job? What do you do?'

But his eyes were hard again, unreadable. 'Nothing to tell,' he said.

Then there was a knock on the door.

119

'Who the hell's that?' shot out of Belle's mouth. Her heart literally *leapt*. It was too late for the postman, and hardly anybody else ever called here.

Jack was already on his feet. He nodded to the bedroom and Belle scrambled up and quickly went over to it, slipping inside but leaving the door ajar so she could hear what was going on.

She heard Jack cross to the door, open it. And then all the hair on her arms and neck went upright in a spasm of fear when she heard Nipper's voice say: 'Hi, I don't know if you can help but I'm looking all round this area for my sister. She's run away from home and we think she was heading down here. The folks used to holiday here and she always liked it so we think she might have come back. Good-looking girl. Blonde. Brown eyes. Mum's going off her nut, she's so worried. You seen her?'

'What's her name?' asked Jack.

'Belle. I'm her brother, Neil.'

'Nah. Sorry, mate. Haven't seen her.'

'You're sure? She always liked this area, so we thought . . .'

'No. I haven't seen her. Sorry.'

Belle heard Jack shut the door.

Presently he came to where she was hiding and pushed the door open. 'You OK?' he said.

Belle was sweating, literally gasping for air.

'You can relax,' said Jack. 'He's gone. I take it you haven't got a brother called Neil?'

Belle shook her head and tried to start breathing again. 'That was Nipper. One of Harlan's cronies. I recognized his voice.'

'He's gone,' Jack repeated.

'What if he comes back?'

'Then we deal with it.'

120

They'd been checking the farms and smallholdings and all the hospitals around the area. They checked the lanes again, went miles out of their way and still she was nowhere to be found and frankly Ludo was now getting shit-scared. Harlan wasn't the type to tolerate failure, and he knew his threat of a trip to the caiman pool hadn't been an idle one. Ludo understood Harlan's concerns, he understood the wisdom of the scorched-earth policy, a total wipe-out of the old guard and their kin. You had to leave nothing. No single family member. Well, the others were gone. There was only Belle now.

'We got to find that bitch,' he told Nipper.

'Yeah, where?' Nipper demanded.

They were sitting in Ludo's flash motor staring morosely at the steady rain blurring the scenery beyond the windscreen. Ludo glanced in irritation at his colleague, who was lounging back, his feet up on the dash.

'Feet off the dashboard,' said Ludo, swiping at Nipper's expensive footwear. He sniffed. 'And what the fuck is that odour, man? You step in something?'

Nipper sat up. 'I fucking hate the country. Damned sure I've stepped in something, I've been traipsing around farmers' fields and yards – you seen those places? They got nothin' but mud and cow shit, and Christ knows what else. There ain't nowhere clean around a farmyard, I'm tellin' you.'

Ludo was incensed. 'Then you put the damned things up on my dashboard? I just had this beauty valeted, you do not do that.'

'All right, all right.' Nipper heaved a sigh. 'So what now?' Ludo with his flashy ways and tight-arsed clean habits sometimes seriously pissed him off.

'What now is we go on lookin'. We spread the net further, we knock on more doors, we go on. Because I'm not goin' back to Harlan Stone and tellin' him we can't finish this, OK?'

Nipper looked surly but what could he do but agree? He didn't want to face Harlan and tell him it was a no-go, either. 'Yeah. OK.'

Ludo started the engine.

121

The day came at last, as Belle knew it must.

'Right, let's get those stitches out, yeah?' said Jack after they'd had breakfast one morning.

Belle stared at him. 'What, so soon? Can't we wait a few more days?'

'For what? It's all healed up now, it's been weeks, it's best they come out.'

Sometimes, if she tried hard enough, Belle found that she could almost forget that she was scarred. While Jack went out most days about the farm doing jobs, she stayed in the house making herself useful. It was the least she could do. Mum had never liked too much intervention from anyone in her kitchen, but she'd shown Belle the basics so she could knock up a passable stew or a curry or even a risotto if she had to.

She did the washing, Hoovered the floors, wet-dusted the mantelpiece and cleaned out the fire. All things she'd never once done in her life. Above all, she tried not to think. If when she was preparing a meal she happened to glimpse her distorted reflection in a pan's surface, she was quick to look away. Mostly, she was left alone, and she was glad of that. Most days, late in the afternoon, Jack went outside with a towel over his shoulder and came back about an hour later. He didn't say where he went and she didn't ask, but his lack of communication did puzzle her and it did make her question her own relaxed attitude around him.

He could be anyone. A rapist. A killer. He could, in fact, be lulling her into a false sense of security, playing the nice guy, getting ready to pounce. But strangely enough, she trusted him, even though she had no reason to. Then she thought of her ruined face and thought: no. She was ugly. Somehow she kept forgetting that. No man would want her now.

She was hiding. Hiding from the world, hiding from her injuries, from herself. So far, she'd done a damned good job of it, too. But now Jack wanted to take out her stitches, and she had promised herself that, when he did that, she would be brave enough to look herself in the face once again, to accept that this was how it was going to be from here on in.

'Come on. I'll be careful. Let's get it done,' said Jack.

She couldn't keep avoiding it. She was terrified, but she had to do it. He wasn't going to let her put it off any longer.

'All right,' she said, and sat down at the kitchen table, Trix at her feet. Jack fetched antiseptic and scissors and got to work.

It didn't hurt much, really. He snipped and tugged . . .

'*Ow!*'

She felt a fresh rivulet of warm blood snake down to her jaw.

'Sorry,' he said, dabbing at it, and then he went on until all the stitches were out. Then he bathed her scars in watered-down Dettol, patted her face dry. She watched him. He had big hands, calloused and lightly furred with dark hair, but he worked delicately and carefully.

Soon, it was done.

Her face throbbed, but it was OK.

'Not too bad?' he asked, putting the first aid box aside and sitting down, his eyes on hers.

'Fine,' she said, swallowing hard, full of fear. 'Jack?'

'Hm?'

'A mirror,' said Belle. 'Please.'

'You're sure?'

Belle shrugged casually. She didn't feel casual. She felt terrified.

'Yeah. I'm sure.'

He went into the pantry and brought out a hand mirror. It was silver – obviously the one that was missing from the set on the dressing table in Belle's room. Then he sat back down at the kitchen table and placed it in front of her, face down, on the surface. 'Here,' he said.

Belle looked at it. The filigree work on it was very fine. Very pretty. She hadn't even touched it yet and already she hated the thing.

'If you don't want to do it yet, that's fine,' said Jack.

'No, I . . .' Belle gulped. 'This was your mum's, was it?' Belle found she was babbling with nerves. 'It's lovely. She had taste.'

'No she didn't,' he said.

End of conversation.

She stretched out a hand and picked up the mirror. Very slowly, she turned the mirror toward her – and then she looked.

There was a demon staring back at her. The left side of her face was puckered and purple and weeping fresh blood. To the right she was Belle – the same, unchanged. To the left . . . oh Jesus. The caiman had ripped her cheek right open in a V-shaped flap and the stitching had roughly repaired the damage. But she was altered forever. If she smiled, she would frighten children. Shit, she frightened herself.

'You OK?' asked Jack.

Trix licked Belle's hand and whined.

Shaking, unable to speak, Belle slammed the mirror onto the table, face down, and ran back to her room, closing the door behind her.

122

Milly hadn't intended to go back to the club, but after her first sweet taste of crack, she thought, why not? She was jittery, wanting more. Her low mood had returned all too quickly. She wanted that high free feeling again. Reality stank. Reality was her parents dead and realizing that hooking up with Nipper had always been a bad idea. It was Charlie's love she'd craved, she knew that now, but he'd been obsessed with the idea of a son, not a daughter, so she'd substituted sex for affection. Fallen for a crock of shit that Nipper had been only too happy to feed her. It was all so damned sad. And Belle was missing, she'd taken off somewhere, God knew where, without so much as a word. Milly had been down to the gatehouse again but there was nobody about, not even Jill. The place looked deserted and the front door was hanging off its hinges, which was weird, but she felt too wired to even think about what that might mean.

So here she was, alone as usual, back again in the club drinking voddy and Coke. She was looking around for the cool black-haired girl again. And there was Marsha, shimmying around on the dance floor with a bloke in a Stetson hat and a fringed tan suede jacket.

When she went to the loo, Milly followed.

There were other women in there, a crush of bodies, and Milly had to wait quite a long time, fiddling with her hair, reapplying lipstick, until Marsha came out of one of the cubicles and stood beside her and started adjusting her own hairdo in the mirror.

Milly swallowed hard. Suddenly she was nervous.

'Hi,' she said.

'All right?' said Marsha.

'Got any stuff?' asked Milly.

The girl started to smile. 'You liked it then?'

Milly nodded. Marsha rummaged in her handbag and pulled out a tiny packet. Three pills in there this time. 'Twenty,' she said.

It had been a tenner last time. But Milly didn't argue. And she didn't want the pills, they'd made her feel sick, she wanted the crack pipe, wanted that feeling back again, of being powerful and happy instead of the no-hoper she was. She was in the act of tipping the pills out into her palm when Marsha caught her arm.

'Too many people about this time, you twat,' she hissed, her eyes fierce.

'Sorry,' muttered Milly, blushing.

The girl turned away, pushed through the bodies to the door. Milly followed. She headed for the exit, her stash in her bag. She'd go home and take the pills. They would have to do, for now. She hurried out of the club and was in the act of hailing a taxi when her arm was grabbed.

'Hi,' said the man who'd grabbed it.

She turned, disinterested, impatient. She just wanted to get home and get high. The bloke was big, with a squashed nose and an immaculate suit. It was Sammy.

Milly twitched her arm free.

'You want to show me what's in your bag?' he said.

'What?' She couldn't believe it. She was Charlie Stone's daughter, and this bastard was *interrogating* her?

'You heard. You're in a rush to leave, the night's young. So, what's in the bag?'

'Mind your own bloody business,' said Milly.

'Miss Stone, your welfare *is* my business,' he said, and grabbed the bag.

Milly pulled it away from him.

Sammy grabbed it back. The bag shot open and its contents spilled out onto the pavement. In the light of the streetlamps and the club neons, there it was among the other detritus: the packet with the pills inside.

'Shit!' said Milly, and started gathering up her belongings. Sammy grabbed the packet.

'I'll keep this,' he said.

'Give it to me.'

'No.'

'I *said*, give it to me,' she hissed, teeth clenched with fury.

'You don't want to start on this junk,' said Sammy. 'Didn't last time teach you anything? Who sold it to you? That tart with the black hair? Was it her?'

'What if it was?' The pills were nothing, anyway. Just a sweetener. The crack was the stuff, the *real* stuff.

'Christ alive, what are you playing at? You can't do this.'

Milly drew herself up to her full height. 'I told you. It's *none of your business.*' Having said that, she stormed over the pavement and hailed a cab. She got into it, red-faced, humiliated, deprived of the only pleasure that she could have hoped for, and went home.

123

Every day, Jack would go out working around the yard, making small repairs and feeding the livestock. And every day, late in the afternoon, he would go out with a towel on his shoulder and come back an hour later. As summer was fading and the grass was getting thin, twice a day he fed fresh hay to the horses.

'Come out and see them,' he said to Belle. 'You won't see anybody around here for miles. And I'll be with you.'

'No,' she said, nervous, remembering Nipper at the door. 'That's OK.'

For days after the big reveal of her ruined face, she'd mostly kept to her room, hardly venturing out at all. Her leg was fine, the bandages off, but her face! Thoughts crawled through her head, the main one being that every time Jack had sat there talking to her, eating across the table from her, he had been forced to look at her ugliness. He'd never reacted in any way to it, which to her was astonishing. Used to turning heads, used to having men adore her, she could barely take it in. She was so changed. She was ugly, and that was it from here on in. She would have to get used to it, somehow.

When she finally came out into the kitchen again, started cooking meals again, petting the dog, mumbling a few words to Jack, she could see he was relieved.

'Come out later this afternoon and see the horses when I bed them down,' he said when she was washing up. 'Nobody's about.'

No one to see how disfigured she was. Was that what he meant?

'All right,' she said, because she was bored with indoors, going stir crazy.

In the afternoon he went out again, towel on shoulder, and came back an hour later.

'Where do you go?' Belle asked, curiosity getting the better of her.

'Nowhere,' he said.

'With a towel on your shoulder. Nowhere. Right. Did your mum have a pool here somewhere?'

Belle certainly hadn't seen one from any of the windows. She hadn't seen one when she'd been out in the yard, hanging out washing. Christ, she was so domestic all of a sudden! It startled her. She'd never lifted a well-manicured finger around the gate-house, never had to and never wanted to. Now her nails were snagged, her skin roughened by work. Before, she'd always been made up to the nines, but now she had no make-up and anyway, what was the point? Her face was ruined. Now, what the fuck was she? Some sort of hausfrau, cowering away from a world that had hurt her too much. She thought again of Mum, of Dad. Her heart sank and pain gnawed at her. Harlan had taken over Char-lie's evil empire and they were both probably dead. She herself was only breathing by luck alone.

Jack was staring at her face. 'What?' he said.

'Nothing.' She forced a smile and felt the scarring on her left cheek pull tight. Oh Christ. She turned her head aside, letting her hair fall over that side of her face.

'My mother didn't have a pool. Nothing so fancy,' he told her.

'So where do you go with the towel every day?' she asked.

'Nowhere special,' he said.

'You're a great conversationalist,' said Belle.

He grinned, his eyes not leaving hers. Dark blue. He had, she thought suddenly, beautiful eyes – black-lashed and crinkled from laughter at the corners.

Belle turned away. 'All right, fair enough. I'll stop asking. Waste of time, yeah?'

When dusk was setting in and the trees were black skeletons against the cool peach of the sunset, they went out and he loaded up the little trailer with hay.

The stables looked just about ready to fall down, but inside in a cosy clean loose box stood a big chestnut mare with a white blaze down her face. A tiny light-gold palomino pony was standing beside her, looking hopefully up at Jack as he came in and dumped the feed there for them. Immediately, they started to eat.

'What a beautiful horse,' said Belle, surprised. Jack's mum obviously had an eye for a fine animal. Belle herself had ridden at pony clubs and hacked out at the riding stables, but the chestnut was something else; a thoroughbred. She reached out a hand and stroked the mare's elegant neck.

'This is Lady Marmalade. Because of her colour. Or Lady, as she's called around here,' said Jack, watching the horses munching contentedly. 'She's twenty-three years old. But she looks bloody good on it. Needs riding, really, but I don't.'

Belle turned to him. 'So what do you do?'

'What do you mean?'

'For a job. For money.'

'This and that.'

'Evasive.'

'Private.'

'Same difference.'

Again he gave that sudden unexpected grin. Belle felt, to her absolute shock, a hard visceral tug of attraction. Christ! Why had she not noticed before? He was actually a handsome man. The realization of that made her feel even worse about her disfigurement. She turned her head away from him, concentrated on the sleek mare and the dumpy little Shetland.

'Come on,' he said. 'Let's go and eat.'

124

'We've always lived alongside Charlie Stone and his family,' Belle told him over their dinner of cottage pie. 'My dad worked in Charlie's business. Manufacturing furniture for the big retailers.'

'But it wasn't the real business?' prompted Jack.

Belle shook her head. 'I was kept in the dark about it all. So was Milly, Charlie's daughter. I'm sure now that the furniture making was only a blind. A cover for a drugs operation. A big one. Not dark corner small-time stuff, shady characters passing little packets to each other in the street. This was drugs on a massive scale, it was—'

'Hang on. If you were kept in ignorance, how come you know that?'

Belle wiped a hand over her face, forgetting the scar. Then she felt it under her fingers. *Horrible.* Quickly she dropped her hand back onto the table.

'I wanted a job. I didn't tell Dad or Charlie – I knew they'd put me off, tell me to go out and enjoy myself, whatever. But I was bored. I wanted something to do. So I found out where the company offices were and went to see if I could get a job. Only the office turned out to be more like a lab, with a bunch of Vietnamese chemists making crack. And then I realized what was happening. What was paying for the Stones' lavish lifestyle. The superyacht and the helicopter and the sports cars – things that are out of reach even for most millionaires. That's the life we've all been living, and sooner or later the whole thing had to come crashing down because into this mix came Harlan, Charlie's adopted son. But he didn't want to be just number one son. He wanted it *all*. He wanted to be in charge. And that meant that Charlie Stone and his missus had to go. And my dad too, and my mum and me, all of us – we were part of the old order, and all Harlan wants is the new, *his* order.'

'But he wanted you.'

'I wouldn't play ball. I knocked him back. He's weird and he's scary. I didn't want to be within ten miles of him.' Belle pushed her empty plate aside and looked at him. 'He did this to me. Scarred me. Harlan don't take rejection. And I flung stuff in his face. Stupid, yeah? I told him I knew what he'd done.'

'And what had he done?'

'Harlan murdered Charlie's legitimate son when he was a baby. Smothered him in the cradle. I'll never prove it, but I know he did. He sent Nula – his adopted mother – crazy, and then I think he had someone rig their helicopter so it would crash. Nula and Charlie were killed in it.' Belle gulped back a tear. 'Then my mum. And my dad . . .'

'Christ Almighty. But here you are.' Jack pushed his chair back, his eyes not leaving her face. 'You think they're still looking for you?'

Belle shook her head. 'I was in shock when I started walking away from the reptile house, seeing danger everywhere. I was half out of my mind. I thought I saw a car come past me a couple of times then slow down, as if someone was looking for me. But I dunno. Maybe I got all confused and imagined it. But then, Nipper did call in here, didn't he?'

She looked at him. 'So I guess I've got no reason to stay on any longer.'

'Where would you go?'

Belle couldn't answer that. She thought about Harlan. How much she hated him. *Detested* him.

'You'd need an army to fight Harlan Stone,' she said sadly. 'If you were crazy enough to do that in the first place.'

'Look,' said Jack. 'I meant what I said. You don't even have to think about fighting anyone. Stay on a while until you feel you're ready for the next move, whatever that might be. Don't rush. Things will get clearer and when you're ready, you'll know.'

'Right now I don't feel like I know a damned thing,' said Belle.

'Then stay. For now.'

'OK,' she said, and felt relieved. No decisions necessary. No need to examine the feeling she'd had when he'd grinned at her. No need to think about anything. Not even revenge.

125

Days passed. Ignoring Goldie's loud protests and Jack's warnings that she might be 'a bit fresh', Belle saddled up Lady Marmalade and took her out over the farm fields in the crisp bright sunshine.

I'm still alive, she thought, inhaling the fresh air, enjoying the power of Lady as she trotted and then cantered her briskly and then gave her her head and let her show her phenomenal speed in a full-out gallop over the rain-softened earth.

Later, she brushed the mare down, fed her and Goldie carrots and went to help Jack out by fetching a fresh hay bale. She couldn't even lift it.

'Want a hand?' he said, smiling.

'Yeah, funny,' she said, and he cut the string and she fed the horses.

She went back into the house just as Jack was going out again, the towel over his shoulder.

'See you in a bit,' he said, and walked off around the back of the garden.

'OK,' said Belle.

She waited a few minutes and then, curiosity overcoming her, she followed him, back around the outside of the old house, nearly slipping on the moss-covered flagstones. She paused. *There* he was – heading along the edge of the overgrown bottom field. She crossed the yard and then followed in his footsteps, keeping her distance. He walked head down, his steps light, springy. He could keep that up for miles, she reckoned. Tough bastard. At the far corner of the field, he vanished from view and Belle hurried on until she saw the slope he'd gone down.

She could hear the rush of the river here, could smell its cool dampness in the air. So *this* was where he went every day. And then she saw him.

He was down by the edge of the river, facing away from her. The towel was on the ground and he was stripping off his shirt.

I ought to look away, thought Belle.

But she didn't. Couldn't. She was mesmerized by the sight of him there, the sun trickling medallions of gold through the trees and onto his skin. The abs on the man! Then he turned and his tanned back was packed with muscle and to her shock she saw that it was also covered in scars, old ones she thought, that had long since turned to random puckered streaks of white. Was that why he was so unconcerned about her own disfigurement? She'd thought he was just being kind, trying not to show how appalled he was at the state of her face, but she could see that *this* might be the real explanation. He had scars of his own. He understood.

But where did he get them?

Now he was unbuckling his belt, unzipping . . .

I ought to look away . . .

Again, she found that she couldn't do it. Her eyes were drawn to his taut buttocks, his hard thighs. She'd seen naked men before, she'd had boyfriends, she wasn't a virgin, but the sight of *Jack* naked somehow sent her into a tailspin. She was intruding. Spying. It was wrong. But it was also amazingly erotic, watching him as he waded down into the water. She felt her nipples harden, felt heat and moisture between her legs.

He was in the water now, chest deep. Then he swam a couple of strokes, turned – and looked right at her, standing there on the upper bank. He was grinning.

Christl

'Going to join me then, Belle?' he shouted up to her.

Belle felt hot with embarrassment. He'd known she was here, all the time. Cringing, she turned away.

'Come on down. It's nice in here,' he said.

Nice? She couldn't think of anything worse than immersing herself in water. She turned back to face him and shook her head. 'No. Thanks.'

'You'd never make a detective,' he said over the roaring rush of the river. 'Trailing the suspect at a discreet distance? Not your forte.'

'You knew I was there all the time?'

''Fraid so.'

Belle sat down on the bank, clasping her hands around her knees. 'You rotten git,' she said.

'Yeah, that's me,' he said, and swam off across the river.

It looked so nice down there – cool and inviting. Up here on the bank, her back was in the sun and she was hot from hurrying to keep up with him, his mum's thick jeans heavy on her legs and his chambray shirt clinging to her sweaty skin. Maybe it *would* be nice to just dip her toes in. Maybe . . . but then she thought of black waters and terror. No. She couldn't do it. She couldn't even *think* of going in.

Instead, she watched Jack. He was a powerful swimmer, using the overarm stroke, crossing the water from bank to bank in six quick lunges. Then back again. He did that ten times, and then waded to the edge of the river and . . .

She *wouldn't* look this time. Belle scrambled to her feet and went back up into the sunshine and stared across the field, trying to get a grip on her racing pulse. Her heart was pounding in her chest; she felt breathless. She slumped down in the grass and sank her head into her hands. She sat there for minutes, unable to summon the strength to get up and go back to the farmhouse.

The water.

Him.

God, what was happening to her?

'Ready then?'

He'd dressed quickly and now he was standing right beside her, the damp towel over his shoulder, looking down at her. Belle got back to her feet, trying to compose herself.

'You know – there's nothing in that water except a few trout and maybe a newt or two. Granted, they don't get out to use the loo, but it's pretty clean really,' he told her.

'Don't laugh at me,' she spat out.

'You want my advice?'

'Go on then,' she snapped.

She was angry at him and embarrassed with herself. Failing to follow him unnoticed. Behaving like a Victorian virgin with the vapours at the sight of him in the nude. How fucking ridiculous. And being very noticeably terrified about getting back into any large body of water. Christ, she was a mess.

'When you remember it, the thing that scares you so much, kick it straight out of your brain. *Refuse* to think about it,' he said.

'Is that what you do? When you start to think about the thing that caused those scars on your back?' she threw at him.

'Yep.' He started to walk down the edge of the field, back toward the house.

'What caused them then?' asked Belle, trailing after him.

'Being in the wrong place at the wrong time,' he said, and walked on.

126

They'd been doing everything they could for *weeks*, and still Harlan was beefing on about it. The fucking *girl*.

'If you hadn't told him about the footprints, you fucking fool,' Ludo said to Nipper as they tramped through yet another muddy farmyard, 'we wouldn't be in this shit.'

'You say that one more time and I am going to knock you flat on your *arse* in this shit,' said Nipper.

'Yeah? You and who else, I'd like to know.'

'I'm back to town tomorrow, fuck this for a game. I had all this country crap growing up, I don't want it no more.'

'Ah yeah, you were a country boy, yeah? Well not me. Harlan'll skin your arse like a grape, anyway, you show up without that damned girl. He will eat you whole. Me, I'm different. I start a job, I fucking well finish it.'

'Yeah, that's fucking heroic, you carry right on.'

'I will.'

'Great.' Nipper looked up at this farmhouse. They were standing in front of this fucker and it looked just about ready to crumble into the soil. And hadn't he been here before with the missing sister sob story? He was pretty sure he had, and he'd drawn a blank. Nevertheless, he picked up the knocker on the door and let it fall. Inside, right behind it, came a scrabbling and pawing and then a dog started going apeshit, barking the ruddy place down. He shrugged. 'Dog's in, anyway.'

Nobody came to the door. They turned away, sauntering back

down the drive past old barns and crumbling outhouses and piles of rusty farm machinery.

'No bastard about,' said Ludo. He'd had the nous to pack wellies into the boot of the car this time, and he had them on right now, sparing his costly designer shoes. As usual, Nipper hadn't thought of that; his own once-elegant footwear was caked in mud.

They strolled back down to the gate by the lane where the sign read *Beechwood Farm*. They were big on tree names out here; they'd already been into *The Oaks*, *The Willows* and *The Spinney*. Nipper and Ludo had been told the same thing over and over again. No new girls around here, and who the fuck were they, asking? She's Nipper's, or *Neil's*, sister, they said, all sweet and innocent. She ran away from home and we're worried about her. Fuck off was mostly the reply to *that* sad old tale.

'Spinney's a group of trees,' Ludo told Nipper.

'How d'you know that shit?'

'I read, man. I looked it up. You know? Words on a page? You ought to try it. It was good enough for Shakespeare. It's a noble pastime.'

'Clubs and pussy, them's *my* pastimes.'

'How long before one of these yokels mentions us to the Bill?'

'Not long. But we'll be long gone by then, with any luck.'

Ludo phoned in to Harlan that night and told him the bad news. Still no sign of the girl anywhere.

'Maybe it's time we called this off, boss,' he suggested, flopping on one of a pair of uncomfortable single beds. They were in a country pub that offered rooms, set by the side of a fast A road; at rush hour, the noise of the traffic zipping through was deafening, and in the evening the noise from the bar below their feet was annoying. Neither of them, used to five-star establishments and the best of everything, was very happy with this arrangement.

Personally, Ludo thought that if he saw another field or another stretch of woodland then he was going to throw up or scream – or both.

'You keep looking,' said Harlan. 'Belle's smart. Smarter than you two tosspots. We call it off when I say so and not before.'

'Sure, sure.' Ludo rolled his eyes at Nipper, who was just emerging post-shower in a coarse white towelling robe. 'Only the natives are getting damned restless, you see what I'm sayin'.'

Nipper went over to his jacket, which was hanging over the back of a chair. Nipper always left doors open, drawers too. He left the minibar ajar – not that there *was* a minibar in this low-class set-up – so that everything inside it got warm and nasty. Nipper's clothes were always on the floor or draped over furniture. It infuriated Ludo, who was neat and shiny as a dollar, at all times. Usually, all he ever did was glimpse Nipper's domestic habits. But for now, with only the one room available and having to share with the bastard, he was confronted with it up close and personal. Which he didn't like. If Nipper snored, that would be the icing on the cake for Ludo. He would kill that fucker in his sleep.

'Fuck the natives and fuck you too, Ludo,' said Harlan. 'What I say goes. You stay there and you keep looking and you stick to the cover story. All right?'

'Yeah, boss,' said Ludo, watching Nipper get out his gun and check it over.

Nuthin' worth shootin' around here but pheasants, he thought. *And* peasants.

'You greased a few palms, like I told you?' asked Harlan.

'Yeah man, we done a thorough job. Local pubs, post offices, oil delivery men, shit wagons – you know they don't have mains drainage out here in the backside of nowhere, boss? I tell you, it's downright uncivilized – and we did the postmen. Anything and anyone we could think of, believe me, we've told 'em it'll be worth their while to reunite us with Nipper's long-lost sister. They got an incentive.'

'Good. Because I want her finished. We started this and we are going to bring it to the proper conclusion, you understand me? I want this tidy, and I know that tidiness is your middle name, you like things wrapped up neat, ain't that so, Ludo?'

It was. Ludo could sympathize, but he also thought that his boss would wrap *him* up neat, yeah, in a fucking *shroud*, if he ballsed this up. Nipper might be contented with near enough, that'll do, but Ludo never was. Not that he thought there was any chance they'd find Belle Barton, not now. Girl was dead in a ditch somewhere, she'd carked it, the poor cow. Pretty soon her body was going to honk and then someone was going to find it. No doubt about that. But he'd keep this up for as long as Harlan wanted him to.

'Yeah, that's the truth, boss. I like things wrapped up tight.'

'Then go to it.'

Harlan slapped the phone down and Ludo hung up. 'Shit,' he said.

'Won't stop?' guessed Nipper.

'Got it in one. Pass me the room service menu, man. I need *food*. Must be all this fresh air.'

'They don't do room service. We have to go down to the bar.'

Ludo rolled his eyes. 'Fuck *me*,' he said in annoyance. 'Man, one way or another we got to get this thing *done*. Find a dead body or find the girl still breathing. Either one, I don't give a shit. Or I am going to have to scout out some better accommodation as a matter of urgency.'

127

Next time Jack went swimming, he paused at the door, towel over his shoulder as usual.

'Coming?' he asked her as she sat at the kitchen table, Trix at her feet.

'No, I don't think so.'

'Well, the offer's there.'

'No. Thanks.'

When he'd gone, she mentally kicked herself. She was being a coward, and cowardice just wasn't in her nature. Or it *hadn't* been, before Harlan had thrown her into a tank full of caimans. She'd always been bold Belle, seizing every challenge. But now the thought of getting into water – *any* water – seriously scared her. Brought back too many awful memories. Made her think of the pain, the scars . . .

Oh Christ the scars.

She was stronger now. Fitter. Jack didn't have to mock her over the hay bales any more; she could lift them.

Her leg had more or less healed now, though there was a line of crusted tooth marks all up her calf to show for the experience. They reminded her of people who'd suffered shark attacks, who sported forever after a pale crescent moon of tooth marks. But worse, far worse, was her face. She spent long minutes every day staring at her reflection in the reinstated bathroom mirror, or at the dressing table mirrors that Jack had put back up.

She would never be the same again. Now even her name felt

like a mockery. Belle meant beautiful, didn't it. Which she wasn't. All her previous self-confidence was shot to hell.

She wasn't *Belle*, not any more.

Scarface.

Her right side was the same as it had always been. Her left . . . she would never get used to that damage. The puckered purple scarring, the distortion, the tightness whenever she tried to smile, an instant reminder of what was there, what would *always* be there.

He'd done this to her. Harlan Stone.

And more.

The anger and grief at the loss of her family ate at her, every day. And here she was, escaping from the world. Hiding.

Like a fucking coward.

Yeah, that was her. She was afraid. Scared witless of the water and of the world outside the safety of this place. And she was also . . . damn, she could barely acknowledge this, it was too fucking embarrassing . . . she was also scared by the way she was beginning to feel about Jack Tavender. Back in her past life, she had always been the cool girl, the one men turned to look at. Now, her scars had robbed her of that. Just once, she'd answered the door to the postman when Jack was off in the local market town, and the expression on the man's face had made her shrink into herself with shame. He'd been visibly shocked.

She was a mess, inside and out.

And there was something bad, something *worse*, it seemed to her, now. She could scarcely bear this, it was so painful to acknowledge, but it was the truth. She was hopelessly attracted to Jack, and getting closer to him day by day. And that was . . . Christ, it was just *sad*, because look at the state of her.

Next day and the next, he asked again. Did she want to come for a swim?

'No,' said Belle, but every day she felt worse about it.

Next day, the same. 'Coming?'

'No. Thanks.'

And again, the day after that.

The day after *that*, she was sitting there at the kitchen table with Trix and a towel.

'Coming then?' he asked.

'OK. All right. Did your mum have any bathers?'

He looked blank.

'A swimsuit?' Belle elaborated.

'Not that I know of. Sorry.'

Which was her perfect 'out' of this. Her heart was beating sickly in her chest with terror. But she was going to do it.

'Never mind,' she said, faking a breezy tone. 'I'll wing it, yeah? Go back to nature.'

Now she was committed. She couldn't say she was coming and then bottle it. They left Trix in the yard and walked down the edge of the field, and with every step Belle felt herself grow more and more afraid. Three quarters of the way down there, Jack stopped walking.

'You OK?' he asked, looking at her face. Instinctively, Belle turned her scarred side away from him.

'I'm fine.'

'You look a bit green around the gills.'

'I'm *fine.*'

He carried on walking, Belle following behind. When they reached the river, Belle sat down on the bank, feeling like she was going to hurl. Down in the dip, the water rushed on by, powerful and merciless.

Black water.

The monstrous things, old as the mouth of hell, ancient predators, slipping in, coming to get her . . .

'Don't think about it,' Jack reminded her, somehow reading her mind. He was shrugging off his shirt and dropping it onto the grass.

Belle drew in a shuddering breath and flicked up a glance at him. Instantly she was sorry she had. That was the other thing that flummoxed her, his so-casual attitude to his own body. She looked at his chest, furred lightly with black hair, and his arms, so muscular, so whipcord strong. Then he unbuckled his belt and unzipped, and she quickly looked away.

Her heart hammering in her chest now, sweaty from the heat of the day and so glad of the shady cool of the trees overhead, she heard him move away from her, down the bank. She heard him wade out into the water. She turned and looked.

He was swimming over to the opposite bank. Reaching it, he turned and ploughed back through the water and looked up at her.

'Coming in, then?' he said.

God, she was so sick of this. She didn't feel like *herself*, not any more. She'd had the shit kicked out of her. And that made her mad. She'd lost her nerve; she was broken. Broken by Harlan fucking Stone.

No. That won't happen. I can't let it.

She looked down at Jack, grinning a challenge at her. And *him*. So bloody confident. Strutting around in the altogether like it didn't matter a damn. She felt fury building in her. At Harlan, at Jack, at the whole damned world.

'All right,' she said. She stood up and quickly threw off the faded chambray shirt and his mother's old jeans. Then naked, defiant, she walked down to the water's edge and, steeling herself, she waded in.

128

The minute she was up to her chest in the water, it grabbed her: the terror.

'Oh Christ,' she said, shivering. The water was icy, and her mind was full of those monsters, tearing at her flesh, trying to eat her whole. She felt her breath catching in her throat, felt her lungs close, felt a scream building up.

Jack was suddenly right there, in front of her. Those fierce eyes were blazing into hers.

'Don't think about it,' he said, grabbing her shoulders, fixing her with his gaze. 'I've got you. You're fine. The most dangerous thing in here is us.'

Something slithered past Belle's ankle and she let out a shriek. 'What the fuck . . . ?' she yelled.

'What?' he asked.

'Something touched me.'

'Probably just weed or maybe a trout. I told you, there's fish in here. And newts and stuff.'

Trembling, Belle looked down into the water. It was gin-clear, not like the caiman tank. Weed was lapping silkily at her ankles.

Just weed.

Nothing bad. Jack was smiling.

'It's not funny,' she told him through chattering teeth.

Something darted down there. A trout. It brushed against her scarred calf. Belle let out another shriek and leapt forward, her arms going around Jack's neck.

'Sorry,' she said instantly, and started to pull away.

'Don't be,' he said, his eyes holding hers. His hands went to her forearms, keeping her there. 'You're bloody brave, Belle. You got in here even though you looked like you were going to shit yourself with fear. You did it.'

'Oh yeah. Brave as hell, that's me.' She was still shaking. But . . . it was nice, her arms around his neck. She felt safer, this close to him. Protected.

He was staring at her face. For one moment she thought he was going to kiss her, but he didn't.

No, of course not. All that's done with.

She turned her head aside, letting her hair drop forward to hide her scars. Her attention was caught by the droplets of water on his broad well-muscled shoulders. The texture of his skin was so different to hers. She was hotly aware now that they were both naked, that this could develop into something way beyond her control. She eased back, disengaging herself. Tried a couple of tentative strokes, not moving too far away from him. The stony chill of the water was better now that she was moving; it was sharply refreshing after the clammy heat of the day. Getting bolder, she struck out for the far bank and Jack swam alongside her.

God, this was . . . this was *nice*.

She'd always loved to swim, even as a tiny child. Now, the love of it came back to her. Gradually she stopped worrying about what else was in the water besides the two of them. She swam back and forth across the river, enjoying it, until she was too tired to swim any more. Then she waded out onto the bank and flopped there, exhausted, not even bothering to cover up with her towel because all that was done with, she was repulsive anyway, it didn't matter.

It was sort of liberating, somehow. She closed her eyes and relaxed.

All the fannying around she'd done in her past life, the hours spent in hairdressers and beauty salons being coloured, waxed, plucked, tanned, all that shit – she was never going to have to bother with that, ever again, because that life, that pampered, privileged, *false* life was over and done with. Here was reality. Day-to-day she wore an old relic of Jack's mother's – a pair of ill-fitting jeans – and a shirt of his that had a frayed collar and paint stains on it. No need to dress up and teeter around in high heels any more. No need for anything, because all that artifice, all that pretence, was over. She was ugly and all the preening in the world wasn't going to change that.

There was movement alongside her and she knew that he was right there. Drops of cool water splashed down on her skin. She heard him sit down on the bank. Then for a long while there was nothing but birdsong and the rush of the water. Her heart was beating hard. She could feel her nipples standing erect, could feel the ridiculous liquid heat between her legs, the longing for him, the readiness, her body opening like a flower. But he wouldn't want that. Of course he wouldn't.

'Belle?' he said.

She opened her eyes. Jack was lying beside her, leaning over her. To her shock she realized that he was laughing so hard she thought he was about to have a seizure. Actual tears were coming out of his eyes, he was laughing so much.

'*What?*' she demanded.

He gulped in a breath. 'The nerve on you! I thought you'd be wearing a bra and pants, and instead . . . Christ, you got more front than Blackpool. Walking around stark naked!'

He was off again. Laughing.

'*You're* naked,' Belle pointed out. She couldn't see why this was so damned funny.

'I'm a bloke. It's not the same.' Now he was staring down at her and suddenly nothing seemed very funny at all. He wasn't laughing, not any more.

Belle didn't know what to say to break the breathless silence between them. *It's OK, I'm ugly, you don't have to do a thing* sprang to her lips, but she couldn't seem to get the words out. She'd had men before – well, boys – but she had never, ever felt this raw unbridled intensity of lust until now. It was embarrassing, wanting him this much.

'Belle,' he said, and he was serious, his gaze intense as it swept down her body and then back up to her face. 'My crazy brave Belle, if you don't want this, then say so. Right now.'

She said nothing.

'Belle,' he whispered, and then he leaned down and kissed her.

His beard tickled her face. Scratched it a little, but she didn't mind that, she relished it. For one golden moment she forgot what she looked like and concentrated only on what she *felt*.

'You don't have to,' said Belle when he let her breathe.

'Yes I bloody do,' he said against her lips.

What the hell. If he was willing, then she certainly was. As his mouth took possession of hers all over again, Belle clung to his shoulders, smoothed her hands over those mysterious silky ridged scars on his back. His hands and then his mouth went to her breasts, drawing out her nipples until she thought she was going to simply go crazy – and then he moved lower, lower, until she cried out, spread herself for him, begged him to just do it, hurry, please hurry.

'No, I'm not hurrying this,' he said, trailing kisses back up her body. He breathed against her neck. His eyes met hers and he was half-laughing. 'I've waited too long, I'm going to make it last. I've been thinking about this for weeks, driving myself mad with it.'

He wanted her. Her – poor ugly Belle. Her hands slipped down between them and she felt how much she was desired as she fastened her fingers around that hard quivering column of flesh that jutted out between his legs. She smoothed her thumb across the tip of it and felt the moisture there, the readiness that equalled her own.

'Please,' she moaned, and Jack mounted her then, teasingly, slowly, slipping his cock into her inch by inch, withdrawing, then easing forward again, staring into her eyes all the time, taking leisurely pleasure in the sensations. Over and over again he teased her, teased them both, until he could take no more and pushed hard into her, convulsing.

Even then, when his pleasure was complete, he took care of hers, stroking her, caressing her, and finally bringing her to a wild pulsing orgasm that drew gasps of delighted surprise from her, blowing her mind with its intensity.

129

When the break came, it came so suddenly that it caught Ludo off-guard, but that was probably just as well. Exhausted after yet another long day traipsing around the countryside, Ludo and Nipper were in another country pub, in another set of sub-standard rooms with no minibar, a shower that spat at you, a mattress like to break your fucking *back*, in fact no *nothing*. Ludo was so pissed off with this situation now, so *done* with it, that his patience was just about at an end.

Then Nipper knocked at Ludo's door.

'Come the fuck in!' yelled Ludo, trying out the TV for the *Six O'Clock News*; the picture kept breaking up. He switched it off, threw the remote across the room.

'We got a break,' said Nipper, coming over to the bed Ludo was reclining on.

'Yeah, what?' Ludo rubbed his aching spine. '*I* got a break, I tell you. My *back* is broken from sleeping on this goddamned thing here that passes for a bed.'

'One of the postmen. A temp. Couldn't get shit out of the usual guys, they were tight as a drum, but this one didn't care. Says a new girl answered the door to him once at Beechwood Farm.'

'*That* place? Looks in shit order?'

'That's the one. He's never seen her there before and chatting in the sorting office he said no one else knew her either. Blonde. Brown eyes. Right age for our one. Says she's scarred up somethin' scary. And that fits too. She was bleedin' when she got out of the tank. Tough bitch, no doubt about it.'

Ludo swung his legs off the bed. 'Nothin' a bullet between the eyes won't sort out. Beechwood Farm, you say.'

'I do.'

'Tomorrow morning then.'

130

Belle and Jack slept together that night in the double bed in Jack's room, cuddled naked into each other like spoons in a drawer. When Belle woke, she was disappointed to see that it was morning already. Time to face reality. She was halfway out of the bed, thinking that yesterday had just been madness and that today would be an end of it, that he would regret everything, realize his mistake and snub her. His hand closed over her arm, stopping her movement.

'Where you going?' he murmured.

'Up. It's gone nine.'

He pulled her back down. 'Nah, stay a minute.'

Belle lay back down, turning so that she faced him, careful to let her blonde curtain of hair fall over the left side of her face.

'You're beautiful,' he whispered against her mouth.

Belle's mouth twisted. 'I *was*.'

'When I found you in the barn I thought I was having a nightmare. You were in a hell of a mess.'

'I know.'

'You're still beautiful.'

'Bollocks.'

'But I think it's changed you. Having this happen.'

'I'd better get up,' she said.

'Nah, you'd better kiss me,' he said against her mouth. Then gently, almost tenderly, he brushed her hair aside and kissed her scar. She thought of poor Milly, being used for sex by Nipper.

Was this what Jack was doing, right now? Was she just a convenient female, a hole to put it in? Was that it?

'I'm getting up,' she said, and this time he didn't argue.

Jack took the Jeep and went into the village that morning to get
in some food while Belle fed the horses then went down to the
coop to let the hens out. They were flapping and indignant at this
late start. She topped up their water and scattered feed for them,
then started gathering up the eggs, prior to going back up to the
stables to muck out and feed Lady and Goldie. Up in the yard at
the front of the house, Trix started barking.

'It's probably that old dog fox roaming about again,' she told
the chickens. Trix often barked when she sensed the fox moving
around the farm, looking for whatever he could find. 'You want
to watch out for him, you lot.'

Up near the house, Trix barked on and on.

131

Nipper was standing in the yard in front of the old farmhouse, eyeing up the dog. It was barking, hackles raised, staring up at him. A low growl rumbling in its throat. Couple of minutes it would be trying to bite. Not that it *had* a couple of minutes, the dumb fuck.

'Here, doggie doggie,' said Nipper with a smile.

He reached down and drew the knife from his expensive hand-made boot. He'd left Ludo spying out the land further down the drive, working his way up sideways, covering all the bases so that they didn't get any nasty surprises. Now he wished he'd taken Ludo's position instead of this one. Dog bites you, that's unfortunate to say the least. You got to get a rabies shot straight away. You don't want to die slathering and snarling like a dog yourself, and that's what rabies did to a person.

Sure enough, the dog leapt forward.

But Nipper was ready.

Down by the chicken coop, Belle heard Trix give one last coughing bark. Then the dog was silent. Belle stopped moving. Somehow, she hadn't liked that sound. She put the egg basket down on the ground and turned, listening hard. No more barking. Nothing. Her heart had picked up speed and the sun on her back suddenly forced sweat out of her pores.

'Trix?' she said out loud.

Over the clucking of the hens she could hear the wind, sighing through the beeches. No birdsong. The sun dipped behind a fast-moving cloud and as fast as she'd got hot, she shivered.

Something wrong.

She snatched up the egg basket, turned to go back to the house. She took all of two strides and then she was struck from behind, a hard blow that shoved at her shoulders and sent her reeling forward. She landed heavily on her knees in the dirt, dropping the basket, shattering the eggs inside. Yellow goo seeped out of them, pooling on the earth. Belle whirled around, started to get up, but a male voice said: 'No.'

Gasping to snatch in some air, she looked back to see who or what had hit her. There was a black man of medium height standing there, gold chains at his neck; he was wearing a designer suit that clashed with his muddy Wellington boots. She knew him straight away. *Ludo.* One of Harlan's crew. And . . .

oh shit

. . . he was pointing a small snub-nosed gun at her. He gave a grin with startlingly white teeth and shook his head.

'Well, ain't you led us a dance, little Belle.' Then his face scrunched up and he winced as he stared at the scarring on the left side of her face. 'Oooh, those damned things did tear at you, didn't they? Did a *right* job on you, girly.' Then he shrugged. 'Not that it's goin' to bother you much where *you're* goin'.'

'Ludo . . .' Belle started to get up again.

He shook his head. 'Nah, nah, nah. Stay right there, on your knees. Ugly bug like you, this is almost a kindness, wouldn't you say so? Now, hands behind your head and just keep looking away there, Belle, and soon all this will be over.'

'Ludo, don't. Whatever he's paying you . . .' said Belle, grasping at straws, at *anything,* because he was going to do it, he was going to kill her right now.

'What, you're offering better? Hard to see how. Nah, Belle.

Stay there and stay still. Let's not make this any harder than it has to be, yeah? I am doin' you a favour, sending you off to the angels – they won't care about the scars or anything like that. One minute, and you'll be out of it.'

'Wait!' Belle gasped in a breath. 'Ludo . . . my mum. What did he do with her?'

Ludo winced. 'You really want to know that? Well, it was quick. The same way *this* is going to be quick. I ain't no Harlan Stone. I'm a nice man. A good clean shot to the head, then it's done.'

Belle felt his words sink into her like knives. So Mum really was dead. She felt a wail of grief and rage building in her, threatening to escape.

'And my dad?' she managed to say.

'Finished that myself,' said Ludo.

'How?' demanded Belle, her voice cracking with strain.

'Garotte. It's quick and it's clean.' Ludo thought about that. Well, fairly. There'd been some bleeding from the neck, of course. Cheese wire cut deep. And there'd been a *lot* of blood when they'd cut the body up in the bath. But he was a nice guy; he would spare her *those* details. 'Merciful, see? That's me.'

The last vestige of hope left Belle then. It was no good. Nothing she could say or do was going to stop this. She knelt there in the dirt, the chickens pecking all around her, and felt a weird sense of peace come over her, nearly stifling the panic. Slowly, she put her hands behind her head. She closed her eyes.

Game over.

'That's it, Belle. Easy now and we'll soon be—'

But Ludo never finished his sentence.

132

There was an explosive *boom* that rocked Belle as she knelt there. She yelled out and her ears rang with the force of it. Half afraid to, she opened her eyes and looked around, craning wildly to see behind her, her hands dropping to her sides. All the chickens had scattered, shrieking.

Maybe that was it, she thought. *Maybe I'm dead and I just don't know it yet.*

What she saw was shocking. Slipping and sliding amid the slime from the broken eggs, she staggered to her feet, trembling, shattered, and properly *looked.*

Ludo was on the ground – or what was *left* of him. Above his designer shirt with its sharp two-toned collar, above the gold glint of chains at his throat, there was just a red, seeping hole. There was only blood and grey gore in a long slick where Ludo's head had been. And Jack was standing over him, holding the smoking twelve-bore that his mum kept for foxes.

As Belle stood there watching, starting to shake with reaction, Jack bent and snatched up the pistol from Ludo's hand. Then he straightened, looking all around.

'Any more of them?' he asked her.

Belle shook her head. *But Trix's bark, cut off.* She worked some spit into her mouth and said faintly: 'He usually works in a pair. Nipper. Tall blond—'

Then she was grabbed from behind. She felt cold steel bite against her throat and she was held up, feet barely touching the ground. Nipper. He was right there. His grip threatened to choke her.

His voice said, right by her ear: 'Drop those fucking guns or I'll cut her.'

Jack stared at him.

'I said, *do it*,' roared Nipper. Belle flinched and felt the steel press harder into her neck. He'd do it. She knew he would. They'd come here to kill her, to finish the job Harlan started.

Jack dropped the twelve-bore onto the ground with a thud. At the same time he lifted the snub-nosed automatic and calmly shot Nipper in the head.

Nipper collapsed to the earth, dragging Belle with him.

She wriggled free, horrified, and looked down at the dead man. There was a deep red rose blooming on his temple, a trickle of blood snaking out of it. His eyes were wide open with shock and he was still breathing. Shuddering, Belle stepped away. Jack came over and without a moment's hesitation made sure that Nipper was properly dead by firing another business-like shot into his right eye at point-blank range. Nipper flinched, once; then he stopped breathing.

'Will there be more?' he asked her, not looking at her; just coolly checking out their surroundings.

Belle coughed. She wondered if she was going to be sick. She tried to speak. She managed: 'No. I don't think so.'

Then she thought of Mum and Dad, and of Ludo standing there telling her how they'd died. The rage and grief pushed up and erupted in her chest. She strode forward and snatched the pistol out of Jack's hand and fired three quick shots into Ludo's corpse. Gasping, shaking, she then stood there staring down at the remains of the dead man. She felt Jack take the gun back off her. Dazedly she looked at him, feeling hot tears wet on her cheeks.

'Back in the house,' said Jack. It was an order, not a request.

133

Up in the yard in front of the house there was another horror waiting for them: Trix was laid out on the ground, her throat slit open.

'Oh no,' moaned Belle, staggering to a halt.

'More guts than sense, that dog. I always said it,' said Jack, but his tone was gentle. But when Belle went to kneel down beside Trix, he shook his head. 'No. Inside.'

Back in the kitchen, Belle slumped down into a chair. Jack locked the front door and went through and made sure the back was secure. Then he reloaded the shotgun and put it down beside the table. He went to the pantry and came back with brandy in a glass for her. 'Drink it up, it'll steady you,' he said.

Belle took a hefty swig of the brandy. It scorched all the way down, but then its warmth spread out and she started to feel a little better. If he hadn't come back when he did . . .

'You came back early,' she said. Her voice shook.

'Saw a car along the lane. It's been here before. Recognized the reg number.' Now he was at the back door. He turned and looked at her. 'Got to clean this mess up. Stay in here and don't answer the door to anyone. I'll be as quick as I can. The gun's there, loaded. Use it if you have to.'

Belle nodded. She felt woozy, which she guessed was part aftershock and part strong brandy. But she looked at him steadily. The way he'd reacted in that situation. The cold-blooded taking of two human lives. There was something *military* in the way he'd moved around out there. He didn't look shaken; in fact, he didn't look affected in any way.

'Jack?' she said.

He lifted his head. *What?*

'What the fuck *are* you? Really?'

But he didn't answer. He just left.

134

By the time the sun was sinking into the west, Belle was getting anxious. Jack had been gone a long time. Maybe Harlan *had* sent more people to search her out. Maybe Ludo and Nipper had reported where she was and there was backup coming right now. Maybe they were here already. Maybe they'd got hold of Jack, finished him, and maybe now they were creeping closer to the farmhouse, coming for her.

When the door finally opened, she leapt to her feet, reaching for the big heavy gun, not knowing *what* was going to come at her. But it was him. At last.

'Going for a shower,' he said, and walked straight past her into his bedroom, emerging moments later with some clean garments. Then he went into the bathroom and started throwing off the soiled ones he was wearing. 'Burn those, yeah?'

Belle gathered the clothes up, wincing as she smelled on them the iron scent of fresh blood, mingled with dirt and sweat. She took them over to the fire and tossed them on, one item at a time.

Hearing the shower start up, she went back to the table and sat there. She really ought to make them some food, but the thought of it made her want to puke. Her mind kept replaying those minutes before Jack had shown up. Ludo with the gun pointing at her head. She'd been *certain* she was about to die.

Finally Jack emerged from the bathroom, towelling his hair dry. He came and sat down at the kitchen table. Belle got up, made them both tea, then sat down again. He tossed the towel aside. Then he looked at her.

'All right?' he asked.

'All *right?*' She stared at his face. She didn't know him. She couldn't pair up the sensuous, almost tender lover with this *killer* who took life so brutally. He was a stranger to her. 'Yes I'm all right. I was nearly shot and then nearly knifed, but I'm fine. And now I would like to know what the *fuck* I'm dealing with here.'

Jack heaved a sigh.

'Answer my question. Tell me what the hell you are. Because you're *not* a farmer.'

Jack picked up his cup. Furious, Belle knocked it out of his hand and he grabbed her wrist, quick as a snake, hauling her half across the table and glaring into her eyes.

'Tell me,' she said through gritted teeth.

Jack let go of her wrist and Belle settled back into her chair. He righted the cup and poured in more tea. Added milk. Said *nothing.*

Belle scraped her chair back and stood there, fuming. 'Then there's nothing more to be said,' she said, and went off to the spare room, slamming the door behind her.

135

Belle awoke in the night, aware of sounds nearby. Not switching on the bedside lamp, she sat bolt upright, listening intently in the deep country darkness.

Had she heard something? Or was it a dream?

There!

Someone was moving about out in the kitchen. She wasn't imagining it and she wasn't dreaming either. Carefully, as quietly as she could, Belle pulled on Jack's mother's dressing gown and crossed in the faint moonlight that seeped through the thin curtains over to the door that led out into the kitchen.

Probably just Jack, she thought, trying to reassure herself.

But the sounds were stealthy, like someone moving and trying not to let their movements be heard.

She turned the handle and opened the bedroom door a crack. Instantly she was struck by a sudden chill and in the pale wash of moonlight she could see the bare table, the sink, the fridge and . . . the outside door was open. Cool breeze was wafting in. She couldn't see anyone in the kitchen. Not Jack, not anyone.

She opened the bedroom door wider and stepped out. Steadily, carefully, not making a sound, she crossed on tiptoe over to the back door and forced herself to look out there, into the yard. Nothing. No one. An owl hooted, so close that she jumped. If you believed in ghosts, she thought you might almost expect to see the pale shades of Nipper and Ludo coming, floating over the yard toward the house.

Then Belle's breath caught in her throat and she felt the hair on the nape of her neck stand on end. No. She couldn't be seeing this . . .

But she did see it.

There was someone coming up from the far end of the mist-shrouded yard, coming toward the house.

Shut the door. Shut it, lock it. Quickly!

She couldn't. Frozen with fear, she could only stand there and stare as the apparition drew closer, closer . . .

Oh Christ!

She stepped back, forced her frozen muscles to move.

Shut the door, shut the door, shut the door . . .

It was coming closer, moving soundlessly because ghosts didn't make a sound, did they?

'Belle?' it said, whispering.

'Jack?' She felt almost faint with relief.

He came up to the door, stepped inside, closed it behind him. Locked it. In the dim light of the moon, he looked at her. As her panic subsided, she started to feel boiling mad. He'd scared her half to death. 'What the fuck were you doing out there? The door was open, I thought . . .' Her voice tailed away. She didn't know what she'd thought. She only knew that he'd scared her, badly.

'I thought I heard noises down by the stables,' he said. 'Nobody there, though.'

Belle clutched her arms around herself, shivering. 'This is my fault.'

He said nothing. 'Come on. Let's try to get some sleep.' And he went off to his room and closed the door behind him.

Irritated, Belle stood there staring down the hall at his closed door. Thank you very much, she thought. And what did that say? It said fuck you, Belle Barton. Angrily, she went back to his mother's room and climbed back into bed and tried to sleep. She couldn't. She tossed and turned for over an hour, then she grabbed the dressing gown and went back out into the kitchen and then down the hall and into his room, closing the door behind her. In the faint moonlight, she could see that he was awake, too, arms behind his head, staring at the ceiling. She went over to the bed and tossed aside the dressing gown and climbed in naked beside him.

'Can't sleep?' he asked, slipping an arm around her.

'How the hell could I sleep? Now you're going to tell me not to think about it, but how can I not do that? They came here to kill me.'

'They didn't succeed.'

'I was lucky. Maybe next time, I won't be.'

He didn't give her any reassurance on that.

'You're an annoying man,' she murmured against his throat.

'You're a spoiled little princess,' he returned. 'And a bolshy cow.'

'Yeah, true enough.' She kissed his chest, feeling the reassuring heat of him.

Is this love? she wondered. This weird *connection* she felt to him, she'd never felt that before. The tingle when they touched, the leaping of her heart when he came into the room. Best not to question it too closely. He wasn't repulsed by her scars, and that would have to be enough. She trailed kisses lower, over his belly and downward.

Jack gasped and bunched his fist into her hair, but Belle pulled back and straddled him, feeling him hard and ready. Greedily she guided him inside her, letting out a long groan of satisfaction.

'Christ, Belle,' he moaned, trying to thrust upward while she rode him. But Belle was in charge now, she wouldn't allow it. She moved languidly on him, driving him demented with lust.

Finally he turned her, tossed her onto her back and entered her again, riding her in turn. At last he came, emptying himself into her. Then he saw to her pleasure until she was screaming, clinging to him, groaning his name.

136

In the morning Jack was up before Belle was even awake. She showered and went out into the kitchen. The door was open and the day was bright. A massive horsebox was backing into the yard in front of the stable block, Jack waving the driver back, back, back . . . there. He slapped the side of the truck. Enough.

Belle walked out into the yard and looked a question at him.

'Mate of mine runs a racing stable over in Berkshire,' he said. 'Lady and Goldie and the chickens are going there for the time being.'

Belle frowned at him. 'You really think there was someone out here last night? That they'd hurt the horses?'

'Why take the chance? They were going to cut you up, and they did for poor bloody Trix, so who knows what else they're capable of?'

Belle patted Lady's glossy neck and went into the barn, returning with two apples from the store, one for Lady, one for Goldie. Then she went back into the kitchen so she didn't have to watch the horses and the chickens being loaded up into the transporter. It was too sad. She'd actually been happy here, hidden away from the world, and seeing the livestock go was drawing a line under it all. Almost saying goodbye to it.

Rain set in within the hour and they passed the day indoors, watching TV and cooking a meal. Jack didn't go swimming, and Belle couldn't ride Lady out. In the afternoon they sat on the couch and dozed, both aware that this was somehow an ending.

That night, they made love in Jack's bed and then slept for a while. Belle awoke in the small hours and crept to the window. She tugged back the curtains and looked out at the silent, moonlit countryside. The rain had stopped and the concrete yard glistened like a mirror, tossing back the moonlight. Water plinked from the leaking guttering over the window.

It might be just about ready to fall down, but I've loved this place, she thought.

Then there was movement behind her and Jack's warm skin was against her back and buttocks, his hard-muscled arms snaking around her and holding her tight against the front of his body. He kissed her neck and looked out, just as she was looking.

'What is it? Can't sleep?' he murmured against her throat.

Belle shook her head. Suddenly she felt choked.

When she did manage it, her voice was low but steady.

'Jack?' she said.

'Hm?'

'I've got to go back.'

'Back . . . ?'

'Harlan started this . . . and I've got to finish it.'

She'd been thinking about this ever since Ludo and Nipper had burst into their private world and pulled it apart. The way she saw it, there was no choice. She had to somehow stop this – or she would be looking over her shoulder forever, because Harlan wouldn't let this go. You didn't say 'no' to Harlan Stone, so it was inevitable: one day someone would show up and kill her, maybe quickly if she was lucky or slowly if she was not, and she was afraid of that. Terrified. So she had to strike first.

Jack was silent for a moment.

Then he said: 'These people fight dirty.'

Belle turned her head and in the blue light of the moon Jack saw her scarred cheek pucker as she smiled.

'So do I,' she said.

137

Next day, she went out into the kitchen and there was Jack, sitting calmly at the breakfast table as if nothing was wrong, as if the whole damned world hadn't gone crazy in the space of one day. They'd been happy here, had fallen into a routine. She had half-way fallen in *love*, she thought, but maybe he wasn't capable of that, maybe all he saw in her was easy meat because she was scarred, desperate – and available.

She poured tea from the pot, slopped in milk, sat down opposite him. He watched her.

Then to her surprise he said: 'I was fifteen when I left home, left *here*, for the first time.'

Belle frowned at him. 'Why so early?'

'My father died when I was twelve. After that, my mother had a string of boyfriends. Some of them were OK. The last one wasn't. He didn't want a hairy-arsed resentful teenager mooching about the place and he made that very clear. He beat the crap out of me one day right in front of her, and she didn't say a word or lift a finger in my defence. Next day, I was gone.'

Belle said nothing. She was afraid that if she did speak, he'd stop. All too clearly she could picture him as a vulnerable boy, his dad dead, his mother mocking his father's memory with a succession of lovers. One of them beating him, hurting him. It was awful.

'Maybe she was scared of him?' suggested Belle.

'If someone was beating up a child of yours, what would you do?'

'I'd kill them,' said Belle without even having to think about it.

'At sixteen I joined up. Served in Northern Ireland. I was a sniper and then a section commander in the paras. Then I moved into special forces in the Falklands. I left the military and came back here because my mother was ill. Dying.'

Belle thought about that. His fitness. His *focus*. It explained so much. She was shocked, incredulous.

'Oh my Christ,' she said. 'Special forces? You're SAS, is that what you're telling me?'

'SBS, actually. Special Boat Services. I was the point man. First man in.'

'Good God.' She was silent a minute, taking that in. 'And the scars? The ones on your back?'

'My mate stepped on an IUD. It blew both his legs off. Killed him. I caught a bit of the blast. Got lucky.'

'So . . . your mother and you? You were reconciled before she died?'

'Nah. She was an old whore who more or less ignored me right up to the end,' said Jack with a rueful grin. 'But we made some sort of peace, I suppose. What did *you* do?'

'What?'

'For a living. For work.'

Belle let out a breath. 'Nothing. I told you. Nothing at all. Dad had plenty of cash and I was not encouraged to do anything except paint my nails, get my hair done, ride horses.'

'So you were – what? – a spoiled little princess?'

'Yep, that was me. Just waiting for a millionaire to stroll by and snap me up.' Belle's smile was ironic. That indulged and cosseted but somehow *unsatisfied* girl had been another life, another world. Now she was different, inside and out.

'What did you do with them?' she asked. 'With Ludo and Nipper?'

'Don't go there. You don't want to know.'

'And Trix?' Belle was really sad about Trix. The dog had been her companion, her friend, through the worst of her pain and misery. She was going to miss her. And it was *her* fault that Trix had met her end. If Harlan's goons hadn't been in pursuit of her, Trix would be alive right now.

'Same. Don't ask.' He stood up. 'You want some food?'

'I couldn't eat it.'

'So what now?'

'I don't know.' She still felt sick after the shocks she'd had, and disorientated. It was as if Harlan had reached out and touched her, and that made her shudder. Her mind was in turmoil. 'I've brought trouble to your door. I'm sorry.'

Jack shrugged. 'Today we just keep watch. Be careful. Give ourselves some time to think it all through.'

So they kept watch, and they were careful. The shotgun didn't go back in the cabinet. But no one came. After a thrown-together meal in the evening, Jack sat and watched TV for a while, and Belle went off to her lonely room – his mother's room – and tried to sleep.

138

All Harlan could think was, where the hell were they? They were supposed to keep in touch with him, tell him what was going on. Instead here he was, kicking his heels and getting lower on patience every day. When he was in one of the Stone nightclubs, he grabbed Sammy, who was loitering on the door, hauled him into the back office and said to him, had he heard anything?

'About what, Boss?' asked Sammy over the crashing volume of the sound system.

'Ludo. Nipper. They said anything to you? Been in touch?'

'No, Boss.'

There was taking the piss, and then there was *this*. Harlan was standing there in the middle of the floor tapping a baseball bat into his open palm. He was going to get some answers today, or else.

Sammy's face was wary as he watched Harlan with the bat.

'Boss?' he asked. 'Why would they talk to me? They'd talk to you, wouldn't they.'

'So you've heard nothing at all.' *Slap*, went the bat in Harlan's palm.

'No. Nothing.'

'Get some more boys down there, find out what the fuck's going on, OK?'

'Boss, they've probably got it under control.'

'Then they should be telling me that. Don't you think?' *Slap* went the bat again. Then Harlan pointed it at Sammy. 'You know anything, you better spit it out right now.'

'Nothing, Boss,' said Sammy, feeling his mouth go dry. These days, when you looked into the eyes of Harlan Stone you saw a funhouse party going on in his brain. He was losing it. He had this *obsession* about Belle Barton, finding her, getting *rid* of her, and it was taking over his entire life.

'I'm surrounded by fucking idiots,' snarled Harlan. *Whap.* The bat slapped into his palm again.

If he comes at me with that, I'm going to leg it, thought Sammy, bracing himself.

'Get some more people down there. Do it,' said Harlan.

Sammy fled.

139

Next morning, Jack was up early again. Belle heard him talking on the phone for a long time. Then they ate breakfast. With no horses to muck out and no hens to collect eggs from, Belle occupied herself by cleaning up the inside of the house while Jack prepared that night's dinner.

At just after one, a battered old Jeep rolled up at the front of the house and six men emerged from it. Through the kitchen window Belle saw them coming. There was something in the way they moved, the tense and watchful way they held themselves, that reminded her of Jack. He'd heard the Jeep pull up, and let them in to the house.

'Christ, here you are, Jackie boy. Talk about the arse end of nowhere,' one of them said.

Belle went to the door and looked out as the men greeted each other with hugs, back-slapping and a lot of swearing. The one who'd been driving flicked a look at her.

'See you've been busy,' he said to Jack with a grin.

He didn't seem to notice her scars. In fact, as they turned toward her, all six of them, *none* of them seemed fazed by the state of her.

Jack took her hand in his. 'This is Belle,' he told the men.

They nodded. Belle looked them over, staggered by a wall of solid testosterone. One – the driver – was ginger-haired, one was portly and clean-shaven, one had big black muttonchop whiskers, another had heartbreaking dark eyes, one was built like a bear and the last was slight, blond and twitchy, very fast-moving. Six men, and they all looked like trouble; like they could handle themselves. They all had that same cool assessing stare; just like Jack's.

'Belle?' Jack pulled her against him. 'Meet the boys.'

'Hi,' she said. These were the people he must have been on the phone to this morning.

'You said you needed an army,' said Jack, giving her a squeeze. 'You've got one. So what do you want to happen now?'

Belle looked at him. 'First I've got to find someone.'

'OK. We can do that.'

'I'll take first watch tonight, shall I?' asked the big one Jack had called Tank.

'Yeah. Good,' said Jack.

140

Harlan had been waiting a long time for this moment; he was ready for it. The Air Accident Investigations people called on him at the Essex house. They watched him gravely as they sat and discussed the helicopter crash.

'We are sorry to have to tell you, Mr Stone, that there was an explosive device on board your parents' aircraft, which caused catastrophic damage. There was no hope of the occupants surviving the crash.'

Harlan nodded.

'So tell me, Mr Stone, do you have knowledge of anyone with a grudge against either of your parents?' the older of the two asked. He was bespectacled. Jowly. Sporting an office pallor. He wore a tired tweed jacket and shiny beige trousers and a sympathetic but somehow *suspicious* expression.

'Well, no.'

'You're sure?'

Harlan could think of many, many people who would have wanted his adopted father dead. Rival drug lords; there were many of them and the market would only accommodate so many before the whole thing burst apart like a rotten carcass. That had been Charlie's worry for years. When you were in one of the top slots, there was always some bastard looking to knock you off it. Now the problem would be Harlan's, instead. Well, he could hack it. He had plenty of foot soldiers around him.

Then his thoughts turned to Nipper and Ludo. Where the hell

were those tossers? Give them a job to do and they fucked off out of it and left you in the dark. They should have come back to base with news long since. But there had been nothing. He promised himself that when the two of them finally showed up here, he was going to rip each of them a brand-new arsehole.

'My father was a respected businessman. Well liked. Popular,' said Harlan.

'We will be passing the matter over to the police now for further investigation,' said the younger AAI man, eyeing Harlan steadily.

'Yes, of course,' said Harlan, catching his breath and swiping a hand over his eyes. 'Sorry,' he said, and coughed. 'This has been so upsetting for us, as you can imagine.'

'Indeed,' said the older one.

'For my sister and myself,' elaborated Harlan.

'Is she at home today? Could we speak to her?' asked the older one.

Right now Harlan didn't have a clue where Milly was. He'd heard word she was hanging around the clubs and – silly cow – getting into the drugs scene. You never touched the product. That was for mugs. Still – so long as she was out of *his* way, everything was fine.

'No, I think she's in town. She's taken it very hard, all this. We have properties there, but I've no idea which one she's staying at. My father was rich, you know.'

'And now his wealth has passed to you and your sister.'

'Yeah.' Well – to *him,* anyway. Charlie had trusted him implicitly and had left the whole shebang to him. Milly had her thirty-grand allowance per annum, paid straight into her personal account. Small change, compared to what *he'd* got. 'But we'd happily give it all back if only we could have our parents returned to us.'

'Imports, wasn't it?' asked the younger one. 'Furnishings and such?'

'That's right.'

The younger AAI man snapped closed his briefcase. 'As we say, this is a police matter now.'

'Let's hope they catch whoever did it,' said Harlan.

'Yes,' said the older man, eyeing him beadily. 'Let's hope.'

141

The pills had been OK, but crack was better. Milly loved nothing better than getting spaced out, *properly* spaced out, on crack. When she inhaled from the pipe she was blissed out, removed from the world.

She was sucking on the pipe like an infant on its mother's tit, she was happy.

She was lying on her bed in one of Charlie's – no, *Harlan's* – London houses and feeling *soooo* mellow. And then, crashing noises. She didn't know how it happened but suddenly there were people all around her, scary-looking people, maybe she was having a bad trip? She'd heard that could happen. These were all big men, hard-looking men, and then someone was shoving through them, coming to the bed, and . . .

'*Shit* . . .' she murmured, thinking that this was indeed a bad trip, a *terrible* one, because she imagined she saw Belle standing right there by the bed looking down at her, but not beautiful Belle, not her friend who she'd missed these past few weeks, and fretted over when she wasn't off her face, wondering where the hell Belle could have got to. *This* Belle's face was scarred all down the left side, like something out of a bloody nightmare, so she had to be imagining this, it wasn't *real*.

Milly screwed her eyes tight shut. She didn't like this. Not at all.

When she opened them again, the monster Belle would be gone.

She opened her eyes – but Belle was still standing there. Still scarred.

'No, no . . .' Milly muttered, squirming on the bed, knocking the pipe and foil onto the floor. Knocking some of the precious rocks off, too. She lunged for it all, couldn't lose it, but it was gone, hitting the floor, gone, oh shit, *gone* . . .

'Milly?' said Belle.

'No, you're not there, you're not real.'

Now they'd found her, Belle couldn't believe what she was seeing. Her old friend Milly had always been plump. *This* Milly had dropped a shedload of weight and the effect was awful. She looked somehow *sunken.* Her face was gaunt and pale, peppered with acne. She stank of sweat, like she hadn't bathed in days.

Milly was muttering to herself, leaning off the side of the bed, scrabbling after what was left of that shit she'd been smoking. Belle was suddenly furious. Everything had gone tits-up in her life. Charlie and Nula dead. Her mum and dad, dead. Harlan after her. And now *this*.

'Milly?'

Milly's dirt-blackened fingernails were searching the floor like a beggar after crumbs. Belle saw that her fingers were burned from handling the pipe. Milly's eyes were bloodshot, her pupils dilated. She grabbed Milly's shoulder and hauled her back up. Then she slapped her hard, across the face.

'*Milly!*'

Milly clutched at her cheek in shock. Her eyes filled with tears of pain as they stared up at this creature who couldn't be Belle.

Belle slumped down on the filthy bed. The sheets were white fading to grey, and there was all sorts of stuff scattered about on it. Pencils and burned shards of foil. A make-up bag, the contents scattered, powder spilled, lipstick staining the sheets red. Ring-backed exercise books with dates on the front.

'You're not real,' said Milly, gulping back tears.

Belle looked at the ruins of her friend. 'Yeah. I am. Harlan did this to me, Milly. He did this.' Her heart felt like a stone in her chest. She didn't think she had a single tear left in her. Not one. Then her eyes fell to the notebooks. 'What are these? Milly?' Milly's gaze had wandered off and now she was staring at the wall, gone into some trance-like state. Slowly, Milly's focus returned to Belle. 'Mills? You been keeping a diary? I didn't know you did that.'

Milly's eyes fell to the notebooks. Slowly, she shook her head. 'Not mine. Mum's. You remember? Part of her treatment. S'posed to help her straighten her mind or something.' Milly's chapped lips lifted in a thin ghost of a smile. She nodded toward a brown monogrammed holdall open on the floor beside the bed. 'Did a load of the things. Don't think it worked, do you?'

With that, Milly lay back and closed her eyes.

'Milly?' said Belle loudly and got nothing back.

She turned to Jack. 'Someone is going to have to stay with her.'

Jack turned to his twitchy blond-haired pal. 'Stevie?'

'Yeah, sure.' Stevie gave a grin and cracked his knuckles.

Belle looked at Jack, worried at the relish with which Stevie had just spoken.

'Stevie had his troubles with stuff like this,' explained Jack.

'Spent two years after yomping across Goose Green stoned out of my brains,' said Stevie. 'Can't say I'm proud of it.'

'He'll know what to do. She'll be in good hands,' said Jack.

Belle stood up. She stared down at Milly, then cast a glance at Stevie. 'You'll look after her?'

'I will.'

Belle looked again at Milly, at the mess she was in, the chaos

surrounding her. The journals. She leaned down. Milly was starting to snore heavily. Belle picked up one. Date: 1983. Flipped
open the page. January. Nula's handwriting was neat as a school-
girl's, slanted backwards.

Christ I hate all this. Having him here. I think I'm actually in
danger but Charlie won't have it, he never believes a word I say . . .

Belle read that line, then flicked the pages on. Another one:
He's always down in that feed room by the zoo, he loves it in there,
he's weird and I keep telling Charlie but he won't listen . . .

There was information in here, maybe useful stuff about Nula
and Charlie and Harlan. Nula had poured her heart into these
notebooks, uncensored. Charlie had probably never seen them
and Harlan certainly hadn't – he would have burned them. One
by one, she gathered up the rest of the diaries and added them
to the ones in the bag by the bed. Nula had always puzzled Belle.
A woman married to an immensely wealthy man, supposedly
with everything in the world that she could want – and yet Nula
had always seemed a tormented soul.

I think I'm in danger . . .

Nula had been talking about Harlan. Now Belle thought of the
helicopter crash. The cartels? Or Harlan? Or *both* of them, working together to get Charlie out of the way?

Belle zipped the bag shut and picked it up.

'Right,' she said with a brisk smile. 'Time for some fireworks.'

142

The night after Belle's visit to Milly, Harlan was in bed in the apartment overlooking Tower Bridge. The city lights winked alluringly through the big floor-to-ceiling windows and the girl he had with him had been most impressed by this whole set-up. All in all, things were fine. All was quiet and productive at the factories, all the street people were behaving themselves, product trade was brisk, fresh imports were due in the day after tomorrow and the day after that. Nothing too bad to demand his attention, and he was getting some very nice head from the petite blonde who – in the dark with the light behind her – could easily pass for Belle Barton.

Ah, Belle.

Such a fucking shame about Belle. But he'd had to put an end to her. That business about her knowing about Beezer, and Jake, well, what the Christ else could she have known? *Anything.* And that was a danger to him; he couldn't risk letting her live.

There was still nothing but silence from Ludo and Nipper. He'd sent others to find them, but they'd found *nothing.*

He straightened, dislodging the girl lapping at his cock.

'What's up, hon?' she asked, but the mood was gone. He felt himself deflating. She noticed and started working him with her hand. He slapped her away.

'Ow! Babes!' she complained.

'Look, piss off, will you,' he snapped. Actually her hair wasn't the precise shade of blonde that Belle's was. *And* her eyes were the wrong colour. This one's were green like gooseberries, and round. Not dark and slanted, lush with promise, not like Belle's.

Fuck that girl.

She wouldn't cooperate. Wouldn't play ball. She'd walked into one of the Stone offices uninvited and started making trouble. One of his people had told him all about it, they were *sure* it was her. That bitch. Then defying him like she did. So of course she'd had to go. But was she *really* gone? Until he heard back from that pair of useless bastards – or from one of the others he'd sent off down there – could he be one hundred per cent sure? No. He could not. She'd tormented him all his life. And even now, not knowing whether she was alive or dead, *still* she tormented him.

He couldn't forget the way she'd stood there, right on the edge of the caimans' pool, and defied him, actually having the *nerve* to speak about Jake, saying she'd known what he'd done when it was all in the past, all forgotten, wasn't it?

It had been so easy. A pillow pressed over the little kid's face, and it was soon over. And it had been entirely justifiable. He couldn't ever be number two; he had to be number one, or nothing. But fucking Beezer, creeping about in the night! Harlan thought he'd managed to close the whole thing down, but Beezer must have talked before he shut him up for good.

'Get the fuck out of it,' he said coldly to the girl.

'All right, I'm going, I'm *going*.' She was grabbing her underwear and scrabbling around for her dress and shoes. 'Christ Almighty, what a charmer *you* turned out to be!'

'Go on, get *out!*' yelled Harlan, chucking his boot at her head. It missed and went sailing on and knocked a priceless Jackson Pollock from the wall. The painting crashed to the floor, breaking the frame. The phone started to ring as the girl ran out of the flat door.

Harlan snatched it up. '*Yes? What the fuck is it?*' he snarled.

'Boss, you better get over here,' said the voice of one of his lieutenants. 'You are not going to *believe* this.'

143

The Clacton office had been the first dedicated crack cocaine production unit in Charlie Stone's empire. Now it was Harlan's, *everything* was Harlan's, and he had taken a great deal of pleasure in seeing the day-to-day functioning of the place as the workers – mostly dirt-poor illegals that were *kept* poor and housed in filthy sheds round the back – did the complicated chemical business that produced the crack.

Harlan could remember the very first time Charlie had taken him on a guided tour of the manor. Charlie had – to be fair – taught him a lot. Told him about how you could smoke cocaine in its powder form by mixing it with tobacco – these were called 'primos', but they weren't good for delivering a nice big hit of the drug.

'Or you could freebase,' Charlie had told him.

Freebase was using alkalide ether to free the cocaine from the hydrochloride powder form.

'Flammable,' Charlie had told him. 'Too fucking dangerous.'

Harlan had taken it all in, soaked it up like a sponge.

He drove up to the Clacton place and there was a bustle going on out front. People milling around on the pavement, shouting and screaming. And . . . he felt his heart literally *falter* in his chest.

The house was on fire.

His crack factory was on fire.

Harlan got out of his Porsche and stared at it, not believing a thing he was seeing with his own eyes. The people in front of the building hadn't seen him. And that was good. They didn't know him, he didn't know them. Alec, his boy, had phoned him, but Alec would never tell a soul Harlan's name or anything else about him. He had more sense.

Harlan got back in the car and drove away, back to the apartment.

By the time he got there, the phone was ringing again.

Another fire. Another crack production line at another fake office, up in smoke.

Then another.

Then half an hour later, another.

What the fuck was happening?

144

Harlan spent a ragged, sleepless night sitting on the couch, drinking coffee and intermittently picking up calls. His biggest fear was that one of the other gang bosses had cut a deal with the Colombians and planned to off him after they had destroyed his business. It wasn't unheard of. But why would they trash the crack production lines? *He* wouldn't, in their position. He would keep them, and off the man in charge and all his backers. That made better sense, didn't it?

The night went on and the calls kept coming. One, then another, then another, until dawn broke.

Then the outcome was clear: all six of the bases where his imported cocaine was transformed into high-quality crack were gone. He phoned Javier, his contact with the cartel. Javier was in and out of England all the time, liaising between his Colombian associates and the Stone crew.

'What the fuck's going on?' was Javier's first comment, his accent as thick as maple syrup.

'You heard then?' Instantly Harlan was on his guard, thinking that maybe Javier knew all about the fires. That maybe he'd *lit* the bastards – or had them lit, anyway. Unlikely he'd get involved in any direct action. The only reason that slick pussy Javier ever used his hands was to get his dick out.

'You're in disarray, my friend,' said Javier, sounding almost pleased about it.

Yeah, did you do this? If you did, you are dead, *my Colombian friend, I promise you that.*

'Nothing that can't be put right. We'll set up again. It's bad, but it's solvable,' he said, very bullish. He didn't *feel* bullish, not in the least.

Someone was taking the manor, *his* manor, apart, piece by piece.

There was a pause at the other end of the phone. 'And what about this week's shipments? No problems there, I trust?'

'All fine,' said Harlan, thinking of his trips out to Bogota to press the flesh and do deals with Javier's lot. This latest load of cocaine was going to be concealed in scrap metal ingots on board a freighter sailing out of Santamaria in Venezuela. It would journey to Rotterdam and from there to Southampton. He hoped to God it would be OK. And what the fuck to do with it once it got here, with crack production out? He'd have to market the pure coke instead. Profit would be way down, but there was no other choice. Meanwhile, there was a Spanish cannabis subsidiary causing him problems, because the Spanish government was getting stick over lack of control on drugs. The Spaniards had tightened up on it, making many more vehicle searches and increasing patrols.

Maybe the whole damned thing's getting too *big,* thought Harlan.

The production lines going hit him hard. He sat in the apartment that night and literally shook with apprehension, convinced that his manor was falling. He'd been expanding hard since Charlie's death, feeling invincible. He'd got rid of the old guard, all the old pals Charlie had gathered around him, Terry Barton, Beezer, the lot of them. But maybe he wasn't as bomb-proof as he'd thought. Now he was transporting heroin, crack, cocaine, cannabis and a whole lot of recreational drugs besides, and he trusted no one – how could he? – so it was hard to stay on top of things sometimes. He'd spent a lot of these past few months motoring around Europe, even visiting Jamaica's Burke Road – and missing a hail of bullets by inches that had killed five other men. He'd got used to attending meetings in other very dangerous places too, places where you fully expected not to get out alive.

But he had. He was tough – a survivor. He'd escaped a rotten childhood, lived through having a disgusting junkie for a mother, adapted to the pressures of living in Charlie and Nula's world, blending in like a chameleon. But somehow he knew he'd got it wrong. He didn't *connect* as other people did. Charlie and Nula had obviously thought so, because they had preferred that fucking baby to him, had overlooked him after Jake's birth, seen him as an interloper, unwanted.

Well, he'd sorted that out. And he would sort this. He'd come through hell in his life. His mother had preferred heroin to him, his step-parents had preferred the new baby, and Belle? She'd preferred to meet a grisly end rather than be his girl. He was *used* to crap. So he would rebuild. And the Spanish muddle, he'd already laid plans to overcome that, getting guys with backpacks carrying the gear over the Pyrenees, staying in hostels and mountain huts then loading up in France when they reached the other side.

Problems? They were for solving. And he was the man to do it.

Then he got another call.

145

'You know Belle Barton went into one of the crack places? Well since the fires started they say she's been back. One of the Vietnamese said they saw a dragon woman,' said Alec, one of Harlan's boys. 'You know that funny thing they have, hanging mirrors on the outside of doors? One of them reckons he saw a woman reflected there and she was going to burn the place down. He said it was *her*, the same woman, but marked up bad. Scarred.'

Harlan held the phone away from his ear. He stared at it. Then he brought it back. 'What you bothering me with this stupid shit for?' he asked.

'She lit the fire. She had men with her, horrible big bastards, helping her. But it was her who set the fire. She was smiling, he said, and it was the most terrifying thing he had ever seen. Then the whole place went up and he was lucky to get out alive.'

Harlan thought of Ludo's last call to him. A trickle of something cold touched his spine, making him give a shiver. '*She's scarred up something awful . . .*'

'Call me when you've got some actual facts,' he said, and slammed the phone down.

He sat there, thinking.

Nah.

Belle was . . . well, where was she, exactly?

He took a shower, still thinking.

Was Belle somehow doing this? Was this her revenge?

Nah. He shook himself, dried off and got dressed.

Superstitious bullshit.

146

'My advice? Don't,' said Jack when Belle told him at the breakfast table that morning what she intended to do.

It had been a busy night for the team. Six crack production lines razed to the ground. Jack's pals were still in bed, so Jack and Belle sat there alone, drinking tea and talking in low tones. Belle had another one of Nula's diaries open in front of her. She was learning a lot.

'I've got to,' said Belle.

'It won't be pretty.'

'Even so.'

'Stevie's on it. He'll take good care of her.'

'Which involves what?'

'Keeping her hydrated. Keeping her confined. It's rough. And not pretty, like I said.'

'Jack,' said Belle. 'I have to. She's got no one. Only Harlan, and what fucking use has he ever been to her? Apart from him, all she has is me.'

'You want me to phone ahead?'

'No.' Belle stood up. 'Let's just go, shall we?'

Jack had been right. It wasn't pretty at all, what Milly was going through. When they entered the Deptford house where Stevie was keeping her, the first thing they heard was Milly sobbing and begging him to let her out of the upstairs bedroom.

They stood in the hallway with Stevie and he smiled.

'She's done a lot of that. And banging on the door. I boarded the window up or she'd have taken a run at it and broken her fucking neck more than likely.'

'Christ,' said Belle, rattled. Milly sounded completely insane, ranting that she would kill Stevie, and to *let her out* or by God there'd be trouble.

'I've left water in there, big plastic demijohns of it. Wouldn't trust her with glass. And there's the bathroom right there if she needs it.'

They stood there, all three of them, and listened to Milly making threats, sobbing, screaming.

'How long will she be like this?' asked Belle, horrified.

'Maybe another couple of days. Then she should be in the clear. She'll feel like shit, but she'll be OK. She'll always want it, though. That's the real danger. Once you've had a hit of that stuff . . . it's fucking evil.'

'What about the neighbours? Can't they hear all this going on?'

'We cleared out the properties on both sides,' said Jack.

'Can I see her?'

'Best not.'

'I want to.'

Stevie exchanged a look with Jack, who nodded.

'Righto,' said Stevie and led the way upstairs. At the top, he turned left and unlocked a door. Inside, everything went quiet. Stevie pushed open the door and stepped aside.

Belle stepped into the doorway. The first thing that hit her was the smell. Unwashed bodies; vomit; shit. And there was Milly, sitting on the bed. Eyes so big in her white face. All her previous chubbiness had vanished. She looked like death warmed over and served up as fresh.

'Milly?' said Belle, scarcely believing it could be her.

Milly lurched to her feet, her eyes fixed on Belle's face. 'You,' she said.

Then she came roaring across the room, arms up, hands hooked into claws, ready to rake her nails down Belle's face. Stevie caught her and held her away from Belle.

'Shh, shh,' he said, almost gently.

'You did this, you made them lock me in here, didn't you.' Milly's eyes were wild. Spittle flew from her mouth. She *stank*. 'Harlan told me about you. He warned me. You're not my friend. You wouldn't do this to me if you were my friend. I'm *glad* you're scarred now, you bitch. *Loved* yourself, didn't you. Well not any more. Now you're ugly like me. Now we're the same.'

'She don't mean it,' said Stevie.

'Yes I do!' shouted Milly, glaring at Belle with bloodshot eyes, trying to reach her with dirty clawed hands.

'You're going to get better, Mills,' said Belle. 'It's going to be all right.'

'Is it? Who says?' Now Milly was sagging against Stevie's grip. She began to sob helplessly.

'I do,' said Belle firmly. 'And it's the truth. Hey!' Belle reached out, grabbed Milly's shoulders. She shook her, hard. 'We're the can-do girls, right? *Right?*'

But Milly only cried.

147

Belle was quiet all the way back to the farm. When they were in the house, she said to Jack: 'I never realized it got that bad.'

Jack filled the kettle and switched it on. 'I've heard of these hookers called chickenheads. They're so desperate for crack that they don't take cash for services, only a single rock. Most of them start out saying that's stupid, they'll never sink that low, but they do, because crack's so addictive.'

Belle was watching him. She shook her head. 'Charlie and Nula Stone lived like royalty. So does Harlan. It destroys lives, what they do. And all the time, they live like princes.'

'Yeah, but somebody stopped Charlie Stone and his wife dead in their tracks,' said Jack.

'Harlan. It had to be.'

Jack squinted at her. 'His parents? That's harsh.'

'Not his real parents.'

'Still.'

Belle shrugged. 'Anyway. I'm going to stop him,' she said.

The kettle was starting to boil. Jack got out mugs, tea bags and milk. 'So what's next?' he asked her.

'Have you picked up anything on the phone taps in the Essex house or the Tower Bridge apartment?'

The one with the black muttonchop whiskers, Jason, had bugged the landlines at both properties.

'Yep. Stuff coming out of Santamaria and into Southampton

this week. He spoke to a bloke called Javier on the house landline. He's getting careless.'

Belle thought of Nula's notes, what she had already read there. So much. So bloody *much,* and there was still more to come. 'That's one of the Colombian cartel's main men. Javier Matias. I'll make a call to Customs and Excise.'

'And then?'

Belle nodded to the notebooks stacked on the table. 'It's all in here. Nula's journals. Charlie would have gone apeshit if he'd known she was doing this. But it's telling us so much. It's a bloody gift.'

She picked up one of the notebooks from the pile, flicked open a page, and read.

148

This couldn't be happening. It was not possible. Harlan was stunned and Javier's people were furious. The week's shipment hadn't even left Santamaria for Rotterdam and then on to Southampton, before Customs swooped.

'We had them in our pocket, we had everything sewn up tight, and now *this?*' Javier bellowed down the phone at Harlan. 'Suddenly they come in – new people, not the ones in our pay – and they start breaking open the scrap metal ingots and there is the cocaine, and they take it, they seize it, *our* product.'

'Something must be going wrong at your end, there must be a weak link in the chain,' said Harlan.

'There is a weak link, and it is *you*, my friend. It is your people, your operation. We are hearing there was a call made to your Customs and Excise, and they passed it on to ours.'

A call? What the fuck?

'Hold on, Javier. We're tight at this end. Water-tight.'

'Bullshit,' said Javier. '*Hijueputa!*'

Harlan's back went up. 'What you calling me, you wop bastard?' But he knew. Lots of trips with Charlie to meet with the Colombian cartel had made it very clear that *hijueputa* was *son of a bitch.*

Javier lapsed completely into his mother tongue then. Tossing more swear words down the phone at Harlan.

Harlan counted to ten.

Finally, Javier fell silent.

'Look,' said Harlan. He was choking with rage but he couldn't afford to fall out with Javier. 'Let's meet, shall we? Discuss this. You in London?'

'I don't know, I . . .'

'You are, yeah? Then come out to the house. Let's sit down and talk. We can work this out.'

Javier said nothing.

'Come on, Javier. How long we been doing business? I can sort this, I promise you.'

'No. We'll meet somewhere neutral.'

'OK. The Savoy for lunch? One on Wednesday? I'll book it.'

'You are not the man your father was,' said Javier.

Harlan gritted his teeth at that. 'Next week, yeah? At the hotel. That'll give me time to straighten this.'

'All right! I will be there,' said Javier, and slapped the phone down.

149

All the furniture cover business premises were torched next. Then two of the clubs. Then one of the snooker halls. By the weekend, Harlan's manor was decimated and everyone around him was nervous, backing away because he was knocking heads together. He shrieked at anyone who came near. When the police turned up, asking questions about the helicopter crash – as the AAI men had said they would – and about the destruction of his businesses, he sat through it, answered convincingly, then the instant they were gone he roared around the place, throwing priceless vases into mirrors, swiping bone china off the dining table, trying somehow to work off the murderous rage that was building up in him at the sheer *injustice* of it all.

His crew, one by one, faded away. With his loss of control of the manor came a loss of control of *himself*, making him dangerous. Fucker would as soon shoot you as look at you right now. His men weren't stupid: after one of them answered back and found himself battered to a pulp, they made themselves scarce.

Harlan left the Tower Bridge apartment and drove the Porsche out to the Essex place, passing the empty gatehouse where once *she* had lived, but like everyone else in his life she hadn't seen fit to be nice to him. He thundered up the drive, screeching to a halt outside the main house. He'd half expected to find it all gone up in flames, just like everything else, but there it was – solid, enduring. His house. Not Charlie's. *His*. Deep breaths, deep breaths. It was all going to iron out, he knew it. Javier would come to meet him, they would talk, it would all be OK.

Yeah.

It would.

Harlan got out of the car and looked around at his kingdom. *His*. Not Charlie's.

You're not the man your father was . . .

Those words had tapped straight into all his insecurities. Because he wasn't Charlie's son, it was true; he was the son of some random idiot who had screwed his drugged-up mother for a couple of quid – and he had been the result.

He stared around at the grounds. Empty now, the grass getting a bit long. Nobody about. No gardeners, nobody on the gate. Nobody on the door of the house. Everyone had scarpered. Bad news travelled fast, and the bad news was, Harlan was ready to kill the next bastard who said a word to him about anything. He wondered about Nipper, about Ludo. They'd been his closest, his best. Now where the fuck were they? Nobody knew. Others had searched for any sign of them; they hadn't been found.

They'd let him down. Just like *everyone* did.

He went into the house and closed the door behind him.

Inside, it was dead silent.

No Charlie.

No Nula.

No Milly.

Only him. He liked it like that. And when he met Javier at the hotel, he would put everything right. Start to rebuild. Yes. He could do it. He was confident that all would be well.

150

Jack was out on the farm with his ex-army mates, working on the barn roof. Tank was on the farmhouse door, keeping watch over Belle while she sat at the kitchen table, the Louis Vuitton bag on the floor beside her, steadily going through Nula's journals.

As she opened one of the seventies editions, she was surprised to see a picture of her and Milly as girls, tucked inside it. They were grinning up at the camera. Belle could see that the picture was taken behind the main house, beside the swimming pool. *The can-do girls.* They'd been happy once, cocooned from the world. Now reality had bitten hard, and tragedy had worn them down.

She started reading and suddenly she was sitting up, eyes widening as Nula's writing told of something awful, something Belle could scarcely take in.

Nula wrote: *Innocent visits? My arse. Once she told me, it was obvious. You'd have to be a fucking fool not to see it, not when you knew what was really going on. Jill was shit-scared of him. He fucking raped* her, *the dirty bastard. Didn't he ever get enough, with those bloody parties, with* me? *Of all the low tricks, to do that to his own best friend . . .*

Shaking suddenly, feeling a stony gut-deep rage take hold of her, Belle stared at the words for a long, long time. Then she snatched up the journal and went out the door, Tank dogging her heels.

Jack was up the ladder hammering copper nails into the barn roof's tiles, one of the others footing the ladder for him.

'Jack?' she called out.

He finished hammering and came down, staring at her face. 'You look like you seen a ghost,' he said.

She handed him the journal. Her hands were trembling.

'What?' Jack's eyes were fixed on her face.

'Charlie Stone raped my mum,' said Belle, and started to cry.

Jack pulled her into his arms and held her.

151

When Belle went to see how Milly was doing, she found that Milly wasn't upstairs in the bedroom any more. She was sitting downstairs in the tiny lounge of the London house, and to Belle's intense relief she looked better. Still skinny and listless, but her colour was improved and she wasn't shaking or swearing or demanding a hit. She was sitting beside an electric fire, the bars glowing red, holding her hands out to its warmth. When she saw Belle come in with Stevie, she didn't stand up. Belle went to the armchair opposite Milly's own and sat down. Stevie stood at the door.

'How are you?' she asked cautiously.

'I feel like shit,' said Milly, with a thin smile.

'You will do. For a while.' For a *long* while, Belle thought; maybe always. Crack was vicious and wouldn't loosen its grip once it had you.

'Stevie said you wanted to talk.'

'Yeah.' Milly's eyes went to Stevie. 'If we can have a moment alone . . . ?'

Stevie looked at Belle. She nodded. He stepped outside the door, closed it behind him.

'So?' said Belle.

Milly was silent, staring at the glowing fake coal of the fire.

'Mills?' she prompted.

Milly stared at Belle's face. 'You know what? I thought I was having a bad trip last time I saw you. God, Belle, what happened to your face?'

Belle gave a thin smile, feeling the scar tissue on her left side pull as she did so. 'Had a run-in with Harlan. And some caimans.'

'Jesus!' Milly's eyes were wide and horrified. 'Where is he? Do you know?'

Belle knew all right. Jack's mates were watching Harlan every second now, recording his phone messages, overseeing every move he made.

'He's at the house.' She thought that Milly was too fragile to take too much in right now. Later, maybe she would share the horror of all that she'd discovered in Nula's journals. But not yet.

Milly's eyes dropped to her hands, now clasped together in her lap. Belle saw a tear slip down her cheek.

'Mills, it's going to be OK. I promise you.'

Milly was shaking her head. 'No. It's not.' Her wet red-rimmed eyes met Belle's. 'It's all such a fucking mess. You know, I always felt pushed aside. First when they adopted Harlan. And then little Jake.'

'Mills . . .'

'And then they left everything to Harlan. Nothing for me except a yearly allowance. *He* was included in the business, *he* inherited the manor. I was like you, kept out of everything, too fucking useless to be involved. I was just the *girl*.'

Belle stared at the rage on Milly's face, taken aback. Milly was such a quiet person, usually; inoffensive. But all this had been boiling away inside her, and now it was overflowing.

'Mills,' she said quietly. 'You have to let this go. Forget Harlan. Forget the past. Make your own life now. Start again.'

'I don't know that I can,' wailed Milly.

'You? Damned sure. We're the can-do girls, remember?' Belle smiled.

Milly's smile was thin and trembling. But it was there.

'Yeah,' she said. 'You're right.'

152

'What's happening with Harlan?' Belle asked Jack when she got back to Beechwood Farm.

'Nothing much. He's been talking to Javier Matias from the cartel. Matias will be at the Savoy at one o'clock on Wednesday for a meet.'

Belle sat back, thinking. 'I want to go to the gatehouse. Get some things. It's safe now, I suppose?'

Jack nodded. 'I've been nosing around over there. He's just gone. Probably back to town. Place is deserted. You OK to go back there, after what happened?'

Belle shrugged. 'I'm fine.' *Don't think about it.* Jack's words to her. Wise words, too. She wouldn't think about *any* of it.

'Tomorrow morning then. OK?'

'OK.'

He yawned and held out a hand. 'Time for bed.'

They had closed the bedroom door on the rest of his mates. Most nights the others were up late, chatting, laughing. Maybe they feared sleep. Belle wondered if maybe in dreams all their past battles came back to haunt them. She didn't know. Now as she sat down on the edge of the bed, her hand slipped under his pillow and brushed unexpectedly against cold metal.

'What's this?' she asked, lifting the pillow, showing him what she'd found.

'Insurance,' said Jack, peeling off his shirt in the half-light.

Belle nodded slowly. She picked up the gun, weighed it in her hand. Remembered emptying three rounds into Ludo's dead body. *Don't think about it.*

Jack was watching her. 'Careful. It's loaded.'

'I'd be surprised if it wasn't.'

'Gives me the horn, you holding that,' he said with a grin.

'Yeah?' Belle stood up and came over to him, running the barrel of the pistol lightly over the skin of his chest.

Jack kissed her and took the gun out of her hand. Then he kissed her again; deeper, harder. When he drew back, his eyes were dark with hunger.

'Get on that bed,' he murmured against her mouth.

Belle was smiling. 'Is that an order?'

'You bet your arse it is,' he said, and picked her up and tossed her, laughing, onto it.

153

Next day Belle went back. It was the weirdest of sensations when Jack parked the Jeep in one of the pulling-in points a long way along the lane. They walked the rest of the way, looking all around; then they passed through the unattended and unlocked gates to the house and up the gravel walkway to the gatehouse. It was the same and yet somehow completely different. She'd played in the hallway as a kid, with Milly. They'd been so young, so innocent. Now the gatehouse seemed full of shadows, weird empty echoes of the past.

Oh Christ, poor Mum.

'OK?' Jack pushed the front door closed behind them.

Belle nodded and he moved ahead of her, down the hall to the kitchen. There could be cameras set up, booby traps, anything. Jack had warned her about all this before they'd left the farm. Told her to follow where he stepped and to be watchful, careful.

But as they moved through the gatehouse it became clear there was nothing. Just an empty, echoing building, a remnant of a past life that had stopped the day Harlan came marauding through it. Upstairs, the cupboard door Belle and Jill had hidden behind still hung ajar. There was a tiny dead bat on the windowsill – probably it had battered itself to death on the windowpane. There was no other sign of what had happened. Nothing at all.

'OK, pack up what you need then and let's get out,' said Jack.

Belle grabbed a holdall from the top of her wardrobe and stuffed garments in. Underwear, dresses, jeans, T-shirts, her one formal black skirt suit. She scooped up brushes, her hairdryer, some jewellery, then paused at her dressing table to look at the silver-framed pictures there. Her and Dad. Mum and Dad smiling, together. Then all three of them. Blinking back tears, Belle picked those up, put them in the holdall and zipped it.

'That the lot?' Jack asked as she grabbed some heels.

'Yeah.' There was nothing else left here. Not any more.

154

Harlan was wondering what he could do next. Disaster upon disaster had piled in on him, but he could rise again. After his meet with Javier, he would start to regroup. Smooth things over there, reassure the cartel that he was still their man. Get some new boys together, people he could trust – not like that bastard Ludo and that waste of space Nipper, who'd both let him down so badly.

He thought – briefly – that maybe something *off* had happened to them. But no. No way. Two hard cunts, searching the safe English countryside for one helpless girl? Nah. They'd given up, cleared off out of it; moved on to pastures new. Later, when all this was settled down, he'd find them. He'd track them down. And then they'd be sorry.

Yeah, it would all be OK. He'd talk to his associates in Manchester and Liverpool, make sure everything was fine with them and that they hadn't lost faith in his ability to pull this all back together. Of course they would have heard about all the misfortunes that had befallen him. They knew his manor just as surely as he knew theirs. There were people in place all around him, he knew that, reporting any dirt they found on him back to their masters. So they knew damned well – just as Javier knew – that he was in a hole.

But he could dig himself out.

He was *certain* of it.

From the city he drove the Porsche back to the Essex house. The grass was even longer now, no security on the gate. He let himself into the house. Empty. No cleaners. Nothing. The whole place looked tired. Dead flowers drooped in a stinking vase in the hall. In Nula's sitting room, on the mantelpiece, stood the two urns containing Charlie's and Nula's ashes. Turning away from them, he went back out into the hall, running his hand up the bannister as he went up to the master bedroom. His fingers came away coated with dust.

Things were going to have to change. He admitted to himself that he had lost grip lately. Let things slide. But not any more. After he'd settled things down with the cartel, he'd be back in the driving seat. Javier was meeting him at the Savoy. And he was looking forward to it. He'd grease up that little wop bastard with oily promises and grand reassurances, and Javier would soak up every word and go back to Bogota to tell the cartel that Harlan was back in control.

Soon, he would be. He promised himself that.

He'd wobbled a bit. But that was in the past.

Now he was here, cooling his heels, mentally preparing himself. He took a long luxurious shower and then towelled dry. He dressed in fresh jeans and a crisp white linen shirt. Then he stood looking out of the vast master bedroom window down the garden and over the grounds to the orchard and the zoo. No helicopter on the helipad, not any more. He thought of Charlie then, and that crazy old cow Nula.

Dead and gone.

Sorting *them* out should have solved every problem. But it hadn't been plain sailing since the crash. Far from it. Someone, somewhere, was making his life hell, tearing chunks out of his backside, kicking the shit out of his manor.

He thought of Belle. Still missing. Dead, or alive? He hadn't a clue. He thought of the scarred woman the Vietnamese had talked about. The dragon lady.

Belle?

Nah. Surely not. He went back downstairs. He'd have some lunch if he could find anything in the kitchens and then he'd go down to the zoo; he liked it down there, although that place, like the rest of his manor, had been sadly neglected of late. They used to keep a girl on to care for the reptiles, but she'd left, months ago. The caimans and the big boa had scared her. So he had no idea when they or any of the other animals had last been fed. None whatsoever. It was time he got a grip on things.

And he would.

He promised himself that.

Leaving the master suite, he paused at his old room and pushed the door open. It was empty now, all his stuff had been moved out. The master suite was *much* more comfortable even though it was bigger and he'd always had a liking for small, enclosed spaces. Still, he was getting used to the suite. It was fitting that the master of the house should be in there – and *he* was the master.

He kept telling himself that.

155

'He's back at the house,' said Tank, coming in the door at Beech-wood Farm. 'He's just taken the buggy out down the grounds. Past the orchard.'

The rest of them were sitting around the kitchen table, drinking tea. Belle drained her cup and stood up. 'That's my cue, then.'

'Ours,' said Jack, rising and going into the bedroom. He came back, tucking the gun inside his jacket. 'Come on then. Let's go.'

Belle and Jack went out to the Jeep. Jack drove along the lane until they reached the Stone residence, then turned in and sped up the drive, veering to the right and sending the Jeep bulldozing through the pampas grass, over the formal gardens, and into the orchard. They could see the white buggy now, parked up beside the seat outside the zoo. Twenty yards away from it, Jack stopped the Jeep, switching off the engine. He started to get out.

'Jack.' Belle caught his arm. 'This is my job. Not yours.'

He looked at her. 'You're fucking joking.'

'I'm not.'

'Belle. He's already had one crack at finishing you. You want to give him a second?'

'Give me the gun,' said Belle. 'And give me fifteen minutes. Then you can come in.'

Jack gave her the stare that made grown men crumble. Belle didn't.

'You won't change my mind,' said Belle. She'd been frightened

476

of Harlan Stone long enough. Now it was time to be the bold, brave girl she'd once been – the old Belle – and to set this straight.

He took the gun out and handed it to her. 'You're crazy.'

'Fifteen minutes,' she said, and began to make her way towards the zoo.

156

Harlan sat in the feed store for a while, then he pushed through the heavy-duty doors and through the thick plastic one, emerging into the central atrium where the caiman pool was. It felt like a semi-dark underground cave in here, with its ferns and waterfalls and humid, oppressive air. He'd always liked its feeling of enclosure.

But things weren't too good in here. He'd seen that straight from the off. Some of the poisonous frogs were dead in their tanks, the lizards looked seriously out of condition and the boa's big heated glass enclosure was empty. He went around the edge of the pool now, looking for the biggest caiman, George; but him and the other two must be in the water. Last time he'd looked down here, there had been a few tiny babies – but the others had probably eaten them; he couldn't see them now.

He strolled around to the far side, careful not to slip on the ornamental rocks. Then he looked across and . . .

'Belle?'

He gasped out the word as he saw her standing there, across the pond. His foot slipped and for a second his leg was in the water. He scrambled back. You had to be careful around the caimans. You couldn't *see* them, but they were there, and they were aware of you.

And right now? They must be hungry.

Harlan stepped back, further up the bank. He gave a nervous half-laugh as he stared across at her.

'Shit, I thought you were dead,' he said.

'Nearly was,' said Belle, and turned her face so that he could see.

Harlan winced. 'The caimans do that?' he asked.

'Yeah they did. After you told your boys to throw me in.'

'Well dammit, Belle, you shouldn't have been so fucking *awkward* about the whole thing,' he snapped.

Belle's stare was steady. 'What? About the fact that you killed baby Jake? Sorry Harlan, but some things do stick in my throat. Killing babies? That's not nice.'

'All right! I hold my hands up, I did that. And that fool Beezer, I did him too. Things were getting old. Getting tired. Charlie's reign was done, you know that. It was time for me to take over and Beezer was just one of the casualties of war, I guess.'

Belle pulled out the gun and pointed it at him.

'You sent Ludo and Nipper to find me and kill me,' she said.

'You're not going to use that. Look – you made me angry, Belle. You know you shouldn't make me angry. You were *mine*. You know that.'

Belle shook her head. 'You killed my parents.'

'I told you. They were the old guard. And if you hadn't been so fucking *obstinate* I wouldn't have harmed a hair on your head. You know I wanted you. You know what a good team we'd make.'

She stared at him, her eyes cold. 'Don't kid yourself. And anyway – I've been busy, Harlan. Pulling your manor apart. *Me*. You think you're a dangerous man to upset? You don't know a damned thing. Watch and learn, you arsehole.'

Harlan's eyes were fixed on the gun in her hand. 'So that's it? You're going to shoot me?' He shook his head and laughed. 'Nah. You won't do it. You and Milly, you're just *girls*. No danger to anybody except yourselves.'

'You think so? You're wrong. You killed them too, didn't you. Charlie and Nula.'

'I told you. They were getting in the way. I had plans for the manor. *Big* plans.'

And then Belle saw something move.

Something *big*.

157

'Harlan . . .' Belle's words caught in her throat. Her eyes were fixed on what was stirring right there behind him.

Shit, that thing's massive . . .

He must have heard something. Maybe a twitch of ancient muscle in the instant before the biggest caiman moved. Harlan's head whipped down, and back. He staggered forward a step, his foot slipping on algae-slimed rocks. A cry escaped him and then the caiman lunged, very fast, its jaws opening wide.

Harlan was knocked backward into the water and as fast as an express train the caiman was in there too, grabbing him with ferocious teeth, yanking him under. The waters of the big pool thrashed and boiled and Belle stood there frozen.

Suddenly, Harlan's head broke the surface.

'Christ, help me, Belle!' His eyes were wild with fear.

The thing was rolling, dragging him back under. Over the din of the waterfall and the roaring of the water as man and beast fought, she thought she could hear something else. Then she realized what it was; it was Harlan's bones, snapping like pistol shots as the caiman shook him in its jaws like a dog worrying a rat.

Shivering with horror, she got her legs to move. Treading warily, she rounded the pond with its inky black waters. He might be a monster but she bloody wasn't. If she could save him, she would. For a long while the waters were still. No movement. Belle looked around but could see nothing. No movement at all.

And then Harlan's head came to the surface, eyes open. There was a small smear of blood on his chin. His breath was wheezing in and out of his throat in tortured little gasps.

'Shoot it . . .' he said faintly.

The big caiman's head broke the still surface of the pool right beside his, its reptilian eyes without expression, without feeling. Then its jaws opened, wider and wider.

Belle aimed the gun. Then into her brain trickled the memories. Her mum. Her dad. Baby Jake. Charlie and Nula. And all that Harlan had made her, personally, suffer with his cruelty. All the misery he must be causing day by day, to thousands of people.

Her hand moved, realigning the gun.

Now she wasn't pointing it at the caiman.

She was aiming at Harlan.

He saw her movement and a weird grimace twisted his brick-red face as the caiman inched closer, ready to force the life out of him.

'You . . . ain't got the fucking *balls* . . . for that . . .' Harlan groaned.

Belle stared him straight in the eye. Then she let the gun fall to her side.

'You're right,' she said. 'But not having balls at least means I don't have to *think* with them.'

His eyes were still open, and horribly *aware*, as the caiman's huge jaws clamped down, covering his head.

Slowly, the massive beast sank down, into the depths, dragging Harlan Stone with him. The water closed over the pair of them with barely a ripple.

Belle stood there for a little while and then, carefully, she walked back around the pond. Then she stepped through the heavy plastic door and out through the main door where the warning notices were posted, and into the sunshine and fresh air, where Jack was waiting for the fifteen minutes to be up. To her, it felt like she'd been in the zoo for hours.

'You OK?' he asked.

'Yeah. Much better now,' said Belle. She thought of the phone lines straight into the feed room at the zoo. No, that wouldn't do at all.

'Where is he?' asked Jack. He took the gun she handed him, checked it; it hadn't been fired.

'In there. Something ate him but we don't know a thing about that. Jack? You can take all the taps off his phone lines now. We don't need them any more.'

158

Days later, Javier Matias was sitting at a side table in the Savoy Grill and getting pretty *fucking* annoyed. He flicked back his silk shirt cuff and glanced at his Piaget Emperador Cushion watch – it was his proud boast that it had cost him nearly half a million dollars – and scowled.

That son of a bitch Harlan Stone! Who the fuck did he think he was, to keep him waiting like this? One o'clock Wednesday, he'd said. Now it was nearly two. Javier was severely pissed off with Stone already, and now *this*. In all his business dealings Javier placed a great emphasis on manners, on punctuality. He looked around him at the other diners and his mood was not improved by their happy chatter.

'Would you like to order now, sir?' asked the waiter, coming over for the second time.

'You know what?' Javier got to his feet, slapping his napkin down onto the pristine table. 'I fucking wouldn't. And if that ass-hole Harlan Stone ever shows up, tell him he's finished. It's over. OK?'

Not waiting for a reply, Javier stormed out of the restaurant and was gone.

159

Tank and the others departed, leaving Beechwood Farm feeling weirdly empty. Slowly, things got back to normality. Belle rode out on Lady Marmalade, helped Jack around the farm, and late in the afternoons they swam in the river, until the weather turned and it got too cold.

The police had been in touch, leaving a phone message at the house about Harlan. When Belle returned the call and explained that Milly – Harlan's next of kin – was unwell, they told her that he had been found, dead and partially digested in the central pool of the zoo when someone in the nearby village had raised concerns about the animals kept there by the – clearly absent – owners of the house.

'My God. That's awful,' she said.

She sometimes thought of him, spitting bile at her in his last moments while the caiman ate him. Sometimes, dreams about that day woke her, sweating, in the night. She didn't know if there would be a funeral or a memorial for Harlan, and she didn't *want* to know either. He was dead; that was enough for her.

As the days were shortening and the leaves starting to fall, Stevie brought Milly to the farm and then he too departed.

Milly was so changed. Thinner, more serious.

Belle hugged her when she arrived. 'Mills! I'm so glad you're here,' she said.

Milly looked like she'd been through hell. When they spoke later, she told Belle that she still wanted the drugs, and that Stevie had told her she would want crack every day for the rest of her life but that she must never, ever take it, because that would be the end of her.

'The parents kept us two out of it,' Belle remarked. 'The manor. The trade. That's the one good thing they did for us.'

'Yeah,' Milly agreed. 'Just that.'

160

One bright morning, Belle put on her black Chanel skirt suit over her best underwear, then she slipped on matching heels and swept her hair back off her face in a tight chignon. Looked at herself in the mirror. Left side bad, right side good. She smeared on mascara and lipstick. Stared at her reflection. She wasn't beautiful young Belle any more. But the scar had given her a sober, pain-filled dignity. She looked a force to be reckoned with, no longer the exuberant girl. Now, she was a woman at the very height of her powers.

She went to the wardrobe, opened it, and there it was: the Louis Vuitton holdall containing Nula's journals and all Charlie's secrets. Nothing had been left out. Nula had listed his contacts, his movements and those of his associates. His regular shipment details. It was all in there. The *truth*.

Nula had known it all, and it had destroyed her.

Now, that knowledge was Belle's – and Milly's too.

She closed the wardrobe door and walked out of the bedroom into the kitchen.

Jack nearly choked on his cereal.

'Jesus,' he said, astonished.

'Is that good?' asked Belle.

'It's fucking terrific. I've got used to seeing you slopping around the place in my old shirts and Mum's threadbare jeans.' He shook his head and gave her that heart-stopping grin of his.

Handsome bastard, she thought, feeling her stomach turn over with sudden longing. There were lots of things she hadn't expected to happen in her life, and this was one of the big ones. She hadn't expected – not in a million years – to meet Jack Tavender, or to feel the way she did about him.

'Damn, you do scrub up well,' he said. 'Got time to go back to bed?'

'No,' said Belle, but she was smiling. 'Jack, can you get in touch with Tank?'

She told him why.

'OK,' he said, and went on eating his cereal. 'I'll have a surprise for you when you both get back.'

'A surprise? Like what?'

He tapped the side of his nose. 'Secret,' he said.

Milly came out of her bedroom and looked at them both. 'Ready?' she asked.

'Yep. Let's go,' said Belle.

161

At Mr Gatiss's office, the receptionist ushered them in and he looked up at them from behind his desk, peering at them over his half-moon specs. Belle saw him stare at her scar, almost wince; then his eyes went to Milly.

'Miss Stone, I believe? And you'd like your friend Miss Barton to stay and hear the reading? Please sit down. Can we get you both a coffee? Or tea?'

Belle shook her head. Milly too.

He was shuffling papers. 'Such awfully sad news. A catalogue of disasters, yes? First the parents. Then Mr Harlan Stone dying so horribly. Just tragic.'

'It is,' agreed Milly.

'So. Now let's see.' He unfolded a sheaf of papers, gazed at the top one and said. 'Well this is perfectly straightforward. As Mr Harlan Stone's only kin, you inherit everything.'

Milly squinted at him.

'The house. The gatehouse. The zoo . . . oh dear, such a tragedy . . . and the business, Stone Furnishings Ltd., in its entirety, and all the business premises, factories, clubs, all the monies in various accounts, the cars, the boats . . .'

Milly tuned out.

She had a loud buzzing in her ears, like a swarm of angry bees.

Mr Gatiss kept speaking, but she didn't hear another word. She walked out of the office with Belle, and Belle drove them back to the farm. She was a millionaire. Possibly a billionaire. If the authorities had ever seen behind the facade and got wind of the true nature of Charlie Stone's business empire, she wouldn't have got a bean. You couldn't profit from the proceeds of crime. But Charlie had been clever. He'd cheated them all.

So – unexpectedly, *miraculously*, Milly was rich.

Now, what the hell was she going to *do* with it all?

Later, she sat Belle down in her bedroom and said: 'I have to talk to you.'

'Go on.'

'Belle – I don't want it. I'm frightened of it, with the drugs. To have so much! I could do anything.'

'You're worried you'll start using again,' said Belle.

'Of course I bloody will! With all that?' Milly was shaking her head. 'Belle, I've thought it through. You could run it all for me, couldn't you. You could see to things. I don't want to get involved.'

'Oh come on, Mills . . .' Belle protested.

'No, I mean it, Belle. I'm serious. I want you to handle it all. I *can't.*'

Belle was quiet, taking it in. 'Well . . . I suppose the clubs could be usable still. Maybe the furniture business if we could make it "properly" legit.'

'You could do it,' said Milly eagerly. 'We're the can-do girls, yes? And you could do it? You always wanted to break out, get a job, *do* something. This is your chance. This is *it.*'

Belle didn't know what to say.

She had a lot of thinking to do, that was for sure.

162

Javier Matias sat comfortably in the back of a black A-Class Mercedes as it zipped along the motorway through almost horizontal sheets of rain. Javier was on his way to Gatwick, and home. *This fucking country,* he thought. People you couldn't rely on, weather that drenched you, no sun, only grey clouds. He was getting too *old* for this shit. Next time he would send one of the sons from his first disastrous marriage, or Elena, his daughter from his second. He couldn't wait to get home to Bogota, where there was civilization and blissful hot sunshine.

Of course he was going to have to make new deals now. Harlan was off the scene, and one of Javier's people had told him it had been in the papers: Harlan Stone had been eaten by his own pet caimans. A terrible accident. Truly tragic. But did Javier give a fuck? He did not. Someone would take over, and he would know as soon as there was a new boss in charge. Then, they would talk. For the moment, the shipments were paused. The other families wouldn't like that, but it was prudent. Things would settle, and then it would be business as usual.

He lounged back, luxuriating in his heated leather seat. He'd read the paper and now he was idly looking around, watching the cars and trucks on the inside while his driver smoothly guided the Mercedes along the outside lane. Then they hit a quieter stretch of road and a big Harley motorbike hovered alongside, two black-helmeted men on board, and he watched it with interest. Maybe he would have a motorbike like that. He could have anything he wanted, anything in the world, after all.

The helmeted head of the man on the back turned toward Javier as the bike roared along, keeping pace with the Mercedes. Then he leaned over and . . .

Clunk!

Javier straightened in alarm.

That *guevon* had attached something to the side of the car!

'Paolo!' shouted Javier as the Harley shot forward and was gone, out of sight in an instant.

Paolo's head turned.

Then the world exploded in Javier Matias's face.

EPILOGUE

Jack was cutting open hay bales when Belle came to find him after their visit to the solicitor's office. Around his feet was dancing a tiny black-and-white pup, tail wagging like crazy.

'God, he's so pretty,' said Belle, instantly cheered. 'Is this the surprise then?'

'Yeah. And he's a she.' Jack scooped the pup up and handed her to Belle. 'A little mini-Trix. How'd you two get on?'

Belle shrugged. 'Turns out Milly's mega-wealthy. Hello, gorgeous.' She kissed the puppy's head.

Jack stood still, staring at her. 'You're serious?'

'Deadly,' said Belle. She looked at him. 'It's done then? The Tank thing?'

'It's done.' Tank had been an ammunition technician in his army years, specializing in deployment, disposal and setting of IEDs; he'd seen to Javier Matias.

'Need a hand here?'

'Always.' He leaned in and kissed her.

Belle leaned in too, twining her arms around his neck. The pup, caught between them, wriggled and let out a yelp. Carefully, Belle set her back on the ground.

'Jack?' she said, frowning.

'Hm?' He was pulling her in again, but she resisted. 'What?' he asked, his dark blue eyes holding hers.

'What will you do now? Will you stay here, on the farm?'

'Dunno,' he said. Then he grinned. 'Mind you – there's always a war going on somewhere, with my name on it.'

Belle nodded. She had a handle on Jack Tavender now; he was an adventurer, always looking to new horizons. She'd drifted into his life and it was good luck alone that he'd been here, on the farm, just when she needed him. Six months earlier or six months later, that might not have been the case. Maybe he'd sell this old place. Move on. Maybe he'd go soldiering again, to a new future that didn't include her. Or maybe to one that did. Her feeling was that whether they stayed together or were apart – even at the far corners of the world – they would probably come back together again, drawn by the powerful magnetism they shared. Maybe this was love. Belle wasn't sure about that. But it was certainly something very like it.

Belle sighed. 'Milly's freaked out by it all, you know. Her inheritance. She wants me to take over. Handle things. The business. The manor. Which is scary. And sort of exciting.'

'What do you know about business?'

'Nothing.'

He shrugged. 'You could do it.'

'Maybe. You know – we ought to take a holiday. Your mate over in Berkshire could look after the horses and this little one here for a couple of weeks and we could all go down to the Med. You, me – Milly too.'

'On what?'

'On Charlie Stone's yacht. *Lady of the Manor*. Actually – it's *Milly's* yacht, now.'

He tilted his head. 'So,' he said. 'She's the lady of the manor and you're the boss of it.'

'The clubs could be salvageable,' she said. She knew that Milly was going to have a mountain to climb, but she was determined to help her do that. They were the can-do girls, after all. Strong together, weaker apart.

'They could.'

'Don't fancy the furniture business too much though.'

'It's all out there, Belle,' he said. 'It's all waiting for you.'

'Yeah. It is.'

She would have a new life now. She was free of the toxin of Harlan at last. Free of the suffocating shelter that had been imposed on her because of Charlie Stone's drugs empire.

One thing was certain: she knew that this new life of hers was never, ever going to be dull. She could grab it, embrace it – *enjoy* it, at last. And she would.

NAMELESS
JESSIE KEANE

**They took her children away, and she will
fight to the end to get them back . . .**

In 1923, mixed-race Ruby Darke is born into a family
that seems to hate her, but why?

While her two brothers dive into a life of gangland
violence, Ruby has to work in their family store. As
she blossoms into a beautiful young woman, she
crosses paths with aristocrat Cornelius Bray, a chance
meeting that will change her life forever. When she
finds herself pregnant, and then has twins, she is
forced to give her children away. At that point she
vows never to trust another man again.

As the years pass, Ruby never forgets her babies,
and as the family store turns into a retail empire, she
wants her children back. But secrets were whispered
and bargains made, and if Ruby wants to stay alive
she needs to forget the past, or it will come back and
kill her.

Nameless is a gripping underworld
thriller by bestselling author Jessie Keane.

LAWLESS
JESSIE KEANE

Only the lawless will survive . . .

It is 1975 and Ruby Darke is struggling to deal with the brutal murder of her lover, Michael Ward.

As her children, Daisy and Kit, battle their own demons, her retail empire starts to crumble.

Meanwhile, after the revenge killing of Tito Danieri, Kit is the lowest he's ever been. But soon doubt is thrown over whether Kit killed the right person, and now the Danieris are out for his blood and the blood of the entire Darke family.

As the bodies pile up, the chase is on – can the Darkes resolve their own family conflicts and find Michael Ward's true killer before the vengeful Danieris kill them? Or will they take the law into their own hands?

Lawless is the heart-racing sequel to *Nameless*, from bestselling author Jessie Keane.

RUTHLESS
JESSIE KEANE

**She thought she'd seen the back of
the Delaneys. How wrong could she be . . .**

Annie Carter should have demanded to see their
bodies lying on a slab in the morgue, but she really
believed the Delaney twins were gone from her life
for good.

Now, sinister things are happening around her
and Annie is led to one terrifying conclusion: the
Delaneys, her bitter enemies, didn't die all those years
ago. They're back and they want her, and her family,
dead.

This isn't the first time someone has made an
attempt on her life, yet she's determined to make it
the last. Nobody threatens Annie Carter and lives to
tell the tale . . .

Ruthless is the fifth book in the
compelling Annie Carter series by
hit crime writer Jessie Keane.

STAY DEAD
JESSIE KEANE

When you bury your secrets, bury them deep

Annie Carter finally believes that life is good.

She and Max are back together and she has a new and uncomplicated life sunning herself in Barbados. It's what she's always dreamed of.

Then she gets the news that her old friend Dolly Farrell is dead, and suddenly she finds herself back in London and hunting down a murderer with only one thing on her mind: revenge.

But the hunter can so quickly become the hunted, and Annie has been keeping too many secrets. She's crossed and bettered a lot of people over the years, but this time the enemy is a lot closer to home and she may just have met her match . . .

Stay Dead is the heart-stopping sixth
book in Jessie Keane's bestselling
Annie Carter series.

DANGEROUS
JESSIE KEANE

Whatever the cost, she would pay it . . .

Fifteen-year-old Clara Dolan's world is blown apart following the death of her mother. Battling to keep what remains of her family together, Clara vows to protect her younger siblings, Bernadette and Henry, from danger, whatever the cost.

With the arrival of the Swinging Sixties, Clara finds herself swept up in London's dark underworld where the glamour of Soho's dazzling nightclubs sits in stark contrast to the terrifying gangland violence that threatens the new life she has worked so hard to build.

Sinking further into an existence defined by murder and betrayal, Clara soon realizes that success often comes at a very high price . . .

FEARLESS
JESSIE KEANE

Two women. One man. Let the fight begin . . .

Josh Flynn is the king of the bare-knuckle gypsy fighters. His reputation is unblemished; his fist a deadly weapon. Claire Milo has always loved Josh – they were destined to be together from the day they met. Two gypsy lovers with their whole lives ahead of them, if only Josh can find a different way of earning a living instead of knocking the living daylights out of another man in the boxing ring. One day, she knows something really bad is going to happen. She can feel it . . .

Shauna Everett always wants what she can't have, and nobody, especially Claire Milo, is going to stand in her way. She's had her eye on Josh Flynn for years, and she knows just how to get him. If it means playing dirty, then so be it. What has she got to lose?

In a world ruled by violence, crime and backstreet brawls, only one woman will win. But how low is she prepared to go to achieve that goal?

THE EDGE
JESSIE KEANE

If you live on the edge, you may just die on it . . .

With a mind sharper than a razor blade, it was only a matter of time before Ruby Darke fought her way to the top. From humble beginnings she became the queen of London's retail, but she didn't get there by obeying the law.

Now, with her son Kit and daughter Daisy finally by her side, she's ready to start a new chapter in her life but, unknown to all of them, enemies are circling.

There aren't many who threaten Ruby Darke and live to tell the tale. But this time, she may just have met her match.

THE KNOCK
JESSIE KEANE

**For some, being on the wrong side of the law
is the safest place to be . . .**

Dora O'Brien had a good start in life, but things went bad when she began to mix with the wrong company. Pregnant by her gangster lover, she found herself on the streets and then in the grips of a bent copper called Donny Maguire.

When her daughter Angel is born, Dora is already under the influence of drink and drugs, and handed around to Donny's mates. Growing up in the shadow of her mother's abusive relationship, Angel is nothing like her, but when matters turn murderous Angel is forced to grow up fast, and survival becomes the name of the game.